STAND UP, BARRY GOLDMAN

By

David J Cohen

© David J Cohen 2021

Published by TTTTTT Publications 2021

The right of David J Cohen to be identified as the Author
of the Work has been asserted by him in accordance with the Copyright, Designs
and Patents Act 1988

https://davidjcohencoms.com/

First paperback edition June 2021

Cover design: Rafael Andres

ISBN 978-1-9993138-2-1

*This book is dedicated
to Vivienne and Malcolm*

CHAPTER 1

I had seen Harriet Fink at the youth club and she had intrigued me. She was tall, serious and Jewish. Like me, she was not part of the crowd but, unlike me, this didn't bother her. I'd never spoken to her and thought she hadn't noticed me. She hadn't, until now.

"That was quite funny, Barry," she said. "I didn't know you were a poet."

"Yeah, well, it's, y'know, stuff I think of," I said, painfully aware how clearer the words were on the page than those that came out of my mouth.

She laughed, the faintest tinkle - with me or at me? I wasn't sure, and for a moment wondered if This might be It. I'd long convinced myself that no one from her stratosphere was ever likely to enter my dreary orbit. Until now.

Harriet didn't look like the glamorous waifs who glided round Theodor Herzl Juniors in their jazzy tops and lightly flared loon pants. She dressed like my mum – sensible pleated skirts and plain white blouses. But she was talking to me.

All I'd wanted for as long as I could remember was a woman to love, someone who would look past my crippling shyness, accept me for who I was and love me back, a soulmate to live with in contentment for the rest of my days: friend, lover, companion, mother to our children. Time was running out: I was getting old. Next year I would be eighteen.

How would I find this creature? Here was a starting place: poetry reading.

I hadn't planned to perform at Chapeltown Community Centre that afternoon but had been encouraged by Mum and Dad. They'd guessed correctly that the only way they might inveigle me into Leeds Jewish Life would be through arts and culture.

I studied Harriet. Her proximity demanded further investigation; what were teenage hormones for if not to reduce the complexity of all human relationships to first impressions of physical appearance? When I'd said Harriet was tall, had I meant elegant? For serious, thoughtful? And by Jewish, did I mean "life partner that my parents would accept"?

"What are you looking at?" She laughed again, this time enough to produce a gentle smile. I'd never seen her smile.

"Uh, oh, nothing, sorry." Sorry for what I had no idea. "Saw the time, I have to go, bye."

"See you," she said, and stepped away.

I didn't have to go but picked up my windcheater from the cloakroom and left, wondering if my interminable life of singledom was coming to an end.

Waiting in the gloomy spring drizzle for the number thirty-six to take me back to Moortown, I attempted an objective summary of those five glorious minutes when Barry Goldman, embodiment of nonentity, became Barry Goldman, Poet.

I liked jokes and making them rhyme. Teachers gave me bad marks for putting them in my English essays, so one day I thought I'd collect a few and read them out loud:

I was a bouncing baby, eighteen pounds to be precise
When mother first saw me she thought that she'd been
pregnant twice
As they held me up to slap me and caress me upside down
Imagine their surprise and fear for I was right way
round.

I'd said those lines to the bathroom mirror on several
occasions. Enjoyed writing them and thought some might be
amusing, but had no idea what to expect. I was a harsh critic
of my physical appearance and assumed every girl who ever
encountered me thought the same. I'd glared at those big,
watery brown eyes staring back at me and narrowed them
sternly, judging, and realised I looked quite funny. I turned
one way, then another, noticing if I gazed to the left my sharp,
angular nose appeared outstandingly graceless.

The event, for me, was... unusual. No. How about extraordinary? That still didn't come close to explaining the sensations I felt through my whole body - unlike anything I'd ever
come across.

Reading my poems in front of people involved a new discovery. When a room full of people laughed, I had to wait until
they stopped before I carried on. My teenage peers had found
them funny. Harriet Fink had laughed.

The sound of eighty of my contemporaries laughing at
something I created was nice – was that too genteel a word?
Like being validated, bathed in human warmth and kindness,
and belonging. Many of these were feelings I was experiencing
for the first time, and at the same time.

None of these people had ever been nice to me. Maybe they
could tell I thought they were all a bunch of idiots.

I hated the youth club and disliked almost everyone who
attended. The boys were slobs and the girls I dismissed as

incapable of independent thought. I bet myself not one of them would have read Women, Resistance and Revolution, or been aware that the author of that great book, Sheila Rowbotham, was also from Leeds.

If I hadn't been fearful of social interaction, I might have got to know them better and discovered things about them that would have challenged my set views. They could have got to know me, too, and learned that the main reason I read Women, Resistance and Revolution was because I'd seen a pretty student reading it, and wondered if she'd fancy me if she saw me reading it, too.

It spoke to me in other ways, made me understand why Dad went to work at the factory and Mum stayed at home. Older sister Judith had long since fashioned her own escape to London, the glamorous alien capital city I could only dream of visiting. Dad was the boss of the factory, like his dad before him. My future was already mapped out.

The bus arrived to return me to the dull, suburban life and habitual safety of normality. Only then did I see a bulky, wheezing teenager steaming towards me. I leapt on board, hoping the driver would head off before Maurice Harvey's lumbering body reached the bus, but this rare display of athleticism was enough to propel him in.

I took a seat at the back, hoping he hadn't seen me, but the boorish lump was on a mission: to fill my personal space with Maurice Harvey. Unusually, there was urgency and purpose in his every move. He plonked his ample behind on the seat beside me, taking up more than half, as he considered his right.

"Goldman," he said, still panting from the exertion. "You. Me. We need to talk. Now."

CHAPTER 2

I'd never seen Maurice so agitated.

He opened his mouth to speak. Nothing came out. Grabbed the bar of the seat in front, like a drunk holding a wall as if his life depended on it.

In some ways, Maurice was my closest friend. We shared a love of comedy and Leeds United, spent many hours together watching Steptoe, Porridge, Reggie Perrin, and Leeds United. We conversed at length in comedy catchphrases and sporting metaphors, which was enough to engage us. We never discussed our feelings. We were teenage boys.

"What did she say? What did she say?"

"Who, Maurice? What are you talking about?"

He breathed out heavily, "Ha, ha, ha," as though he was being sarcastic. It took a moment to understand he was trying to say another word.

"Harriet?"

"No, Barry, the Queen." He smiled, his breath and sarcasm back. "Shlemiel, who do you think? Course I bloody mean Harriet." Maurice was the first of our gang to understand the power of swearing in Yiddish, the language of our grandparents. "She came to talk to you!"

I shrugged, still confused. Maurice had no difficulty talking to girls. He was so in love with himself that he imagined all womankind felt the same way. If one girl didn't buy it, he moved on to the next. There was no universe I knew of in which Maurice Harvey could be jealous because a girl spoke to me.

"You're weird."

He was not wrong about this. As far as I knew, none of the other boys in my class wrote silly poems about themselves. Or claimed to be in favour of women's lib, apart from the bra-burning aspect. I enjoyed the moral superiority of my pioneering attitude towards women for a 1970s Leeds teenager, silently weeping myself to sleep each night at my inability to ask out the ones I fancied.

Having regained the power of speech, he regained the power he had over me.

"What did she say? Why did she come to you?" The words spilled out in a torrent, relieved that Maurice's breath had re-turned to deliver the logjam of vitriol at the back of his throat. "Harriet Fink. The ice maiden. No boy has ever spoken to her, even Andrew Duffy says she's out of his league. But you! Look at you in your grey-patterned tank top and your beige flares, dressed like a schlock"

Skipping past the pain of his wounding judgment of what I thought my coolest performing outfit, I started to see the Harriet Fink he described. Of course she was beautiful, attractive and unattainable, I could see it now. But in my world, all girls were like that. It hadn't occurred to me that Maurice Harvey and even Andrew Duffy had ever experienced fear of rejection. Even if she wasn't It, or the pre-It, there was a sudden excitement in the possibility that she might be Another, a proto-Muse.

I'd thought the momentary pause in the conversation was Maurice building energy for part two, but that was it.

"Answer me, you big shmock," he said, narrowing his already tiny eyes with an accusing look. "What did she say?"

"I dunno, something about the poems..."

"What do you mean, you dunno? Did you ask her out?"

"What?"

"Harriet Fink came up to you. To *you*," he added, helpfully emphasising his incredulity. "And you didn't ask her out? You're a bigger shmegegge than I thought," and he was back in control, that mocking laugh a relief I hadn't got one better than him by asking her out.

Maurice and I were an odd couple, everyone agreed. We hadn't sought each other out; our connection was forged through the sturdy bonds of compatibility between our mums, Sybil Goldman and Irene Harvey. They had been teenage friends during the War and assumed their sons would continue the attachment.

They shared a lively sense of humour but whatever differences attracted the two of them had extended over time. Irene was brash and extrovert – a perfect match for Gerald Harvey, a man as loud as his jewellery. Mum had fallen for the more strong, silent "my-dad" type.

However well two mothers get on, there's no guarantee the kids will hit it off. But we both supported Leeds United and the only way our parents would allow us to watch the team every fortnight was if we went to the game together.

The trouble with people like Maurice was they thought everyone was like them, happy to trample on people's feelings to get what they wanted. The trouble with people like me was I thought everyone was like me. Maurice may have acted in a boorish, unpleasant way towards his fellow humans, I told myself, but deep down even he was capable of decent behaviour.

"We spoke for two seconds. Why should I ask her out?"

"Because she's a bird. And you're a bloke." He'd switched seamlessly from mockery to anger.

"We're both people," I said, wondering if that was some-thing I'd picked up from Sheila Rowbotham.

"You twat!"

"What if it was her decision? If she fancied me, why wouldn't she ask me?"

"Because she's a bird. And you're a bloke," he smiled, savouring the repetition. "Bloody hell, Barry, you're a bit thick sometimes."

However harshly I judged his Neanderthal attitude, I was jealous of Maurice's approach to women. I should and could have asked her out. I could live with Maurice's anger and mockery, but not his gentler pity.

"What are you waiting for?"

I stared out the window, disappointed to see we were still in Chapel Allerton, four stops before Maurice's departure.

"You're not a puftah, are you?"

"Course not," I said, "but what if I was?"

He made an exaggerated move away from me.

"Oh my God. The poetry. Not fancying Harriet. You're a puftah." Oh, no, not the voice. Please don't do the Monty Python gay man voice. "It's not me you fancy, is it, ducky?" he asked, doing the Monty Python gay man voice.

I formulated a concise reply about the changing attitudes to gender prompted by the sexual revolution of the previous decade. Questioned Maurice's own sexuality, speculating wryly on whether his arcane attitude to gay men was borne out of the successful suppression of his own homoerotic desires.

What came out instead was:

"Bowie's a puftah."

"I'm not sitting next to him on a bus."

Maurice shuffled the mass of his behind away from me exaggeratedly, his discovery of my alleged homosexuality combining with his limited medical knowledge to suggest my affliction might be contagious.

"And he's got a gorgeous bird. How long have I known you, Barry? Ten years? Is this why you're so crap at getting off with women? Is it because you don't fancy them? Were you thinking about getting off with me all that time? Have you always been queer?"

"I don't know. Have you always been fat?"

Maurice stared, shocked. Our comedy insults were usually borrowed from our favourite TV shows. "Your majesty is like a stream of bat's piss," as the Python chaps said. I'd observed Maurice rude, angry, loud, mean, sarcastic; this was the first time I'd seen him wounded.

"Sorry," I said, feebly. Which made things worse.

An angry silence hung over the rest of the journey. Maurice usually got the better of me, and I usually allowed this to happen. It occurred to me that my life could be different; maybe I had some power over its journey, an ability to ask girls out. I quickly dismissed the thought as I headed back to the bosom of my parents, where a life of suburban contentment and factory bossing stretched ahead.

When I got home, Mum was busy as usual doing everything while listening to Radio 2; washing up, preparing supper, smoking a fag. Mum was not tall, and the pile of dirty pans on the side of the board almost reached her neck. She was loving, kind and unpretentious, face stern (to me, anyway), her bright blue eyes making me feel like she could tell what I was really thinking. She had this amazing skill of being able to smoke and talk at the same time, hands free. I tried to emulate this whenever I sneaked off to the bathroom for a quick puff, but the smoke always whacked the back of my lungs and the front of my eyes simultaneously, and the cigarette would fall out of my mouth into the sink, damp and unsmokeable.

"How was the club?"

"Okay, thanks," I replied, working hard to conceal my excitement at having been approached by Harriet.

"Was Maurice there?" she asked, over the faint ka-tank of washing saucepans in the kitchen sink.

"Yes, we got the bus home together."

"Oh, that's nice. Glad you're still getting on with Maurice."

"Mhm."

I looked in towards the kitchen, drawn by the familiar smell of Sunday-night supper: fish fingers and chips. As if from nowhere, a steaming bowl of peas seemed to fly in front of me.

"Perfect timing!" Dad said with the exaggerated eye-brow-raising he liked to use when attempting to entertain, while holding a steaming bowl of overcooked tinned vegetables.

Dad was tall and handsome with a thick head of hair, but the bushy eyebrows and over-sized nose made him look less like the dashing film-star lead and more that he was wearing a Groucho Marx mask.

He worked hard to keep our evening meals lively. Judith was in her final year at university and rarely home for more than a few days each year. None of us had quite managed to fill the Judith-sized gap that had entered our lives, but Mum and I appreciated his brave attempts.

"Fish hands for supper!" he exclaimed as though for the first and not the hundredth time.

"I'll have the thumbs, please," I said on cue as I followed him to the table and poured out three even tumblers of Robinson's diluted orange squash.

"Sorry, we've only got fingers," he said convincingly, as though he'd only that moment checked with Mum.

"Everything okay?" Mum asked, plonking our fish fingers and chips on the table, attuned as always to the slightest difference in my mood.

"Yeah, sure," I lied breezily, although I'd felt a pang of sadness that Judith was no longer here, which we all felt from time to time. But this time there was a melancholic imagining of what Sunday nights would be like for them alone when I, too, would be gone come September, to the exciting new world of student life. We were the first generation of Goldmans to go to university – even Dad accepted that I shouldn't join the family firm straight away – and that a graduate with fancy gown and mortar board might confer some extra credibility on H Goldman and Son Quality Outfitters.

"All set for another exciting week at school?" Dad asked, smiling ironically.

"Ooh, yes, double statistics tomorrow."

"Benjamin Disraeli," he boomed in his gentle Yorkshire accent; he loved to roll the "Israel" part around his tongue and remind me that this country had once elected a Jewish prime minister, even though he'd been a practising Anglican. "There are three kinds of lies-"

"Lies," I joined in, "Damned lies and statistics-"

"Have I quoted Disraeli before?" he asked.

"The probability is one hundred per cent," I said.

"Don't forget next Saturday," Mum said, coming in with her plate.

"What about it?" I asked.

"What do you mean?!" Mum said, mock wounded.

"The Eurovision Song Contest!" said Dad.

We followed many ancient traditions in the Goldman household, kept alive for thousands of years by Jews across the world: lighting the candles on Friday night to welcome Shabbat, eight days of Passover that marked our escape from slavery in ancient Egypt, and now, watching Eurovision with Grandma Rebecca.

This new ritual began in 1973, when Israel made its debut. While others wondered on which map it had been decided that Israel was a part of Europe, I'd been bickering with Dad about the Yom Kippur War of that year. We got on for the most part, but this was a problematic subject. He was Israel, I was Palestine; there was no chance of a peace breakthrough on this subject.

No self-respecting teenager had time for Eurovision. Even Maurice, whose eclectic tastes had marked him out as the only Jew I'd ever met who adored rock and roll. The rest of us had long been led away from the plinky-plop nonsense that passed for music in the eyes of parents and toddlers by Radio 1's maverick DJ John Peel, who had introduced us to messy, angry rock stars like Bowie, Roxy Music, Bob Marley, Led Zeppelin, Slade and many more. There was no room for you in my gang if you were seventeen and still liked Abba.

Assuming my Eurovision watching days were over, I'd arranged to perform at a student folk club, depending on the outcome of today's performance.

"Oh, I was planning on going out next Saturday."

"Really?" said Mum, anxiously. "Where to?"

"Well it's partly school related," I partly lied. "You know I'm writing poetry for my English exam. I want to try it out at a proper poetry night, to er, check."

"What do you need to check?"

I could say anything and they would have no idea what I was on about. "The scanning."

Monty looked at Sybil.

"Whereabouts?"

"Headingley."

Sybil looked at Monty.

In Moortown, where we lived, the word Headingley meant "students", which also meant "long-haired hippies", "drugs", "girls who didn't wear bras", "left-wing politics", "loud, thumping music" and "people who have absolutely nothing in common with us." Lazy prejudices and stereotypes, each one categorically correct. Why else would I want to go there?

"It won't be late. Be back in time for the final scoring."

"I suppose he could go if Maurice goes too Sybil."

"Ah, not sure I'll be able to go with Maurice."

Mum, hardened by years of negotiating with teenagers, held my gaze firmly.

"Either you go with Maurice or you don't go at all."

That was it, then. I was going with Maurice.

I ran to my room, although it felt more like flying. I couldn't wait to discuss the Harriet meeting with my two closest confidantes.

"I think I'm in love," I told Joni and Yoko as we lay in bed together.

"Hoo boy," said Joni. "Someone's got it bad today."

"Is that so?" asked Yoko, not quite believing me.

"She liked my poetry," I said, slightly defensively. Joni smirked.

"Sorry," she said. "Do go on."

"I could have asked her out and I blew it. And now I think she'll be seeing Maurice Harvey."

"Always the bystander, hey Barry?"

"He's seventeen, Joni! Let him make his own mistakes and learn from them."

"Do you think I'm making a mistake, Yoko?"

While it was true I lacked whatever missing magical component teenage boys required to ask girls out, in my fertile imagination I was able to converse easily with beautiful women. It didn't matter that I'd never met Joni Mitchell or Yoko Ono; I knew them well through the lyrics they wrote, printed inside the album covers strewn across my single bed. Who better to make sense of my awkward teenage feelings and guide me on the painful voyage towards sensual fulfilment?

I loved Pete Townshend's raw anger, Ray Davies's barbed whimsy, and David Bowie's haunting apocalyptic musical paintings of Five Years and Life On Mars. But Joni especially understood there was no darker, scarier place on earth than your own tortured soul. She and Yoko told me what I needed to know if I wanted a girl to be attracted to me.

Problem was, they rarely agreed on anything.

"I don't think you're making a mistake, Barry. Not yet."

Joni snorted.

"You never know," Yoko continued. "Sometimes you don't realise you have erred until a long time after. The water flows to the source but the river still runs by your feet."

"That's a bit cryptic for me, Yoko."

"Reading poetry, eh? That's one way to 'impress the ladies'," Joni said, unimpressed.

"How did the gig go?" Yoko asked.

"Yeah, the gig, it was good. Actually, it was great."

"Really?" said Joni. "What was the best thing about it? Apart from falling in lo-o-o-ove," she added, caustically.

I thought for a moment. "Do you know what? Can't remember a single thing about it. People were laughing, and they applauded at the end. It felt good."

"Oh, man, one gig in and you're hooked," said Joni, seriously.

"Isn't that a good thing?"

"Sure. Yesterday you were a poet. Today you're a poet and a performer. Which do you want to be? Whatever you decide, one will suffer."

Joni was in a mood again. Blue. From the moment I'd set eyes on her I'd been in love. I'd heard her songs but it was only when I saw a clip on TV that I tumbled. She had long blonde hair and wore a fancy pink dress, which makes her sound girly, but the song, the voice – it was like they were from outer space. Poor Joni. She'd only ever wanted love to bring out the best in her and her lover, but in every song it sounded like he had failed to live up to this simple task. Many of her songs told of her failure at love, which she usually put down to her own weaknesses. Maybe I could be the one to end to her disappointment; sure, I was only twelve at the time, but one day we would meet and she'd hear my poetry and fall in love with me.

Was Joni no longer It for me? Was she jealous of Harriet?

I turned to Yoko for assurance. If Maurice had ever discovered my secret liaisons he would have mocked me mercilessly, but at least he would have seen the attraction of Joni. Using his personal scoresheet method for rating women he "wouldn't have kicked her out of bed for farting". But Yoko? "The woman who broke up The Beatles? Weird."

I adored her proud, composed profile, staring ahead on the dog-eared cover of Approximately Infinite Universe, concentrating on something. Not looking at the camera like every other pop star. Yoko never needed our approval.

"You discovered a new America tonight. Be careful not to abandon your first home." Enigmatic, but clear – something she might have said to her husband. Joni was even blunter.

"The worship from the crowds may soothe the pain of life's rejection for a passing moment," she said, "but as soon as you walk off stage, real life comes back to whack you on the ass."

Yoko and I were used to Joni's mood swings. You always knew when she'd met a new man, and when he had, yet again, failed to live up to her exacting standards. Someone's not getting their end away tonight, as Maurice would have said.

Not for the first time, I sensed that Joni's conversations about me were really about Joni.

Sometimes even the approximately infinite patience of Yoko was tested to its limit, and she couldn't help jabbing Joni's pain with a stick.

"Joni, should we come back later? When you've forgiven whichever bastard just inspired your next song?"

"A ha ha ha ha ha," she laughed, like at the end of Big Yellow Taxi. "Says the woman married to the biggest bastard across the universe."

And Yoko was reminded why, on days like these, it was best to steer clear of Joni.

CHAPTER 3

"Poetry," Maurice sneered, investing so much contempt for the word it was almost poetic.

He had agreed to accompany me to the reading on condition that I set him up for a conversation with Harriet Fink at the youth club next Sunday, but still maintained a sulk the size of Wales all the way to the Pack Horse.

I understood what he meant. At school, the rambling rambles of Wordsworth and innumerable sonnets of Shakespeare had sparked no interest in the form – ooh, look, every poem is exactly fourteen lines, whaddya want: a medal? Then I heard Brian Patten on the radio reading his poem about a seven-year-old boy machine-gunning the classmates he didn't like and finally understood what the fuss was about.

I'd been to the Rambling Dalesman's Folk Night a couple of times with Judith. We had endured the lurid sea shanties delivered tonelessly by bearded civil servants on their night off in Aran sweaters. Had been rewarded with Peel favourites Martin Carthy and the Oldham Tinkers.

Waiting to perform after a bloke delivering an awful tale of the hideous slaughter of a beautiful princess in gory detail, I could feel Maurice next to me fidgeting loudly and sighing.

This was my second time in front of an audience, but the first where I encountered stage lighting. Initially taken aback by the brightness, I averted my gaze, ignoring the blotches of ultrabright colour jumping in front of my eyes as I took out my little black diary. For a second I was Mr Brownlow, the one teacher who commanded respect across the school – not because he had a loud voice or was particularly large, but for his air of quiet authority that no one questioned.

Five minutes, three poems, a couple of introductions in between. I'd been thinking about Harriet all week, nothing but Harriet, and imagined she was there and I was performing directly to her.

During the second poem I started to feel confident enough to glance away from the book and look below the blinding light at the audience: an earnest, bespectacled student, a sweet couple holding hands, Maurice staring at the stage, mouth wide open. He'd never seen this side of me but, to be fair, neither had I.

After my set was over, the interval began. All the lights came on and I noticed another change in Maurice.

"Bloody hell," he whispered. "Wall-to-wall totty." Maurice's love affair with live performance began the moment he discovered that many members of the audience were attractive young women.

* * * * *

"Boys! Come in!"

Dad beamed as he steered us towards the living room where the TV was louder than normal so Grandma could hear better, "You've made it for the scoring. Beers, lads?" He raised his eyebrows and without waiting for an answer went to the kitchen. Mum and Grandma were transfixed by the Eurovision Song Contest, hands poised either side of a bowl of salted peanuts.

"Hello, Maurice. Did you enjoy the poetry?"

"The poetry? Oh, yes, thanks, Mrs Goldman," he replied, remembering why he had agreed to come.

"Oh, 'ello," said Grandma in her sweetest grandma voice as we joined the family hunkered round the telly. "Who might you be?" Grandma had worked hard to lose her Yorkshire accent, but it always returned after a glass of stout.

"Maurice," said Mum. "Irene Harvey's boy."

"Oh, that Maurice. I like your father. Very successful businessman," she said pointedly, the moment Dad returned with two frothy glasses of beer.

"And where would we be without successful businessmen, Rebecca?" Dad asked with a hint of edge.

I could tell from his breath he'd been drinking, but not enough to rise to Grandma's bait. When Dad and I watched male comedians on the telly doing jokes about sour, miserable mothers-in-law, there was a part of me that felt uncomfortable with the stereotype but another that thought blimey, that miserable battleaxe you're mocking sounds exactly like my grandma.

"Is he the one that's good at maths?" Grandma asked Mum, like Maurice wasn't in the room.

"That's his cousin, Clive," Mum answered before Maurice could. "Maurice plays rugby."

"Sport is good!" Grandma shouted at Maurice. "Tell that to him," she pointed at me. "It builds character. Sport is good!" Maurice laughed, pleased to have his disparaging views of me confirmed by my own family.

"Jews don't do sport," Dad laughed.

"Mark Spitz! The swimmer," Grandma exclaimed. "He's Jewish. The tennis player–"

"–Tom Okker," I said, exhausting the list of famous Jewish sportsmen from the previous three decades.

"Exactly," said Grandma. "Whoever heard of famous poets?"

"Pam Ayres," said Mum helpfully. "She's on the telly."

"Maybe he could be on the telly," said Grandma, referring to me, I thought. "Look!" she said, pointing to Pete Murray, who was hosting the show. "He's Jewish! He's on the telly."

I recognised him as one of the old hosts of Top of the Pops; he'd been replaced by the younger DJs like Noel Edmonds and Dave Lee Travis and even, occasionally, the mighty Peel himself.

"Pete Murray isn't Jewish," said Dad.

"He is!"

"How do you know?" laughed Mum.

"Remember the Mannings from Manchester? Changed their name to Murray."

"Was that the Zimmerman Mannings or the Zermansky Mannings?" Mum asked.

"They changed the name, Becky," said Dad, "to make them sound less Jewish! Murray is not a Jewish surname!"

Grandma turned to Maurice. "Never forget you're a Jew," she said, darkly, changing the tone of the conversation. "The goyim won't."

We'd left the folk club for this? I thought. I'd promised Mum I'd be back early, but after the success of my gig, Maurice was outraged at the idea of leaving before the interval was fully played out.

"This room is humming!" he'd shouted, practically leaping from his chair. "All the birds fancy you."

"What are you talking about?"

He grabbed my arm. "Those two at the bar: the blonde one was laughing all the way through your set." He dragged me to where two students were ordering drinks, introduced me to what he perceived to be the less attractive one, and tried to ingratiate himself with the blonde who, seconds earlier, I'd been assured was only interested in me. They made their excuses and left me with Maurice.

"Turns out she liked your poems but she doesn't fancy you."

"Thanks for chatting her up on my behalf, Maurice."

"You're welcome," he beamed, disappearing in search of further female gain.

Several people looked at me in an odd way but appeared too shy to approach. This is what being me is like, I thought.

Ever since I'd understood the difference between being a virgin and not, I'd always assumed Maurice was not, but it was one of those things you could never know. If you had to ask a boy if he'd done it with a girl, something about that question proved you obviously hadn't done it yourself. He was so confident in the way he talked about whether a woman was a goer in bed (suggesting an element of personal experience, which he never denied) and was the only person I knew to brazenly admit to owning a secret stash of porn mags. These two factors alone had been the clearest evidence that Maurice was not a virgin. Now I was less sure.

Maurice had returned, swaggering comically, holding a green pound note covered with a telephone number drawn in orange-red lipstick. He snapped it triumphantly in my face.

"Hubba hubba," he'd said, turning the note to reveal the name Yvonne, scrawled over the Queen. "Now we can go."

It was recap time on Eurovision when every country played a short extract from the songs they'd already performed in full. Each tune was greeted by a generalised national platitude from Grandma or Mum. Ireland were first. "They've suffered," said Grandma, the highest compliment she could give, although I never knew if the select group of victims they had joined referred to the wandering Jews of history, or people with an ever-increasing list of ailments.

More copycat, bland, unmemorable European pop songs slipped by, one chorus at a time. No doubt at all, Britain did music better than any other country; it was hard not to sit through these pale imitations and wonder if European music could ever come close to ours.

I knew the British entry, the DJs had been playing it on Radio 1 for weeks, Rock Bottom by Lynsey de Paul and Mike Moran.

"This is the best," Dad said. It wasn't bad. Lynsey de Paul was one of those pretty pop singers the mums liked and boys like Maurice fancied. For those of us already educated in the nuance of attraction by Joni and Yoko, Lynsey was an English lightweight. Her workaday singing voice had me yearning for the last generation of belter-outers, Cilla, Dusty and Sandie Shaw. Rock bottom indeed.

"Nonsense," said Grandma. "Israel was the best by miles."

"I like the French one," said Mum.

"Anti-Semites," said Grandma, "they won't let Israel win: watch the scoring."

"You can't judge a whole nation on how they score in the Eurovision Song Contest," said Dad.

"Don't tell me the scoring isn't fixed," Grandma sneered with hostility. Even Maurice was surprised, looking at me in mock disbelief.

"You have no evidence," Dad said, knowing he could never win an argument against Grandma.

"What about when Cliff Richards won?" she asked.

"Richard," I muttered pointlessly.

"He's Christian. They had to let him win."

"What?" even Mum was incredulous at this suggestion.

"The Christians run everything," said Grandma.

"Even the Eurovision Song Contest," said Dad.

"Shut up, Monty, it's Israel now," said Grandma, as the next replica pop monstrosity came up. "See," she said triumphantly. "The best. And she's prettier than Lynsey de whatnot, wouldn't you say, Maurice?"

He smiled and prodded my side.

"Have you been to Israel, Maurice?" Grandma asked politely.

"Yes, we've got family in Netanya," he said.

"Tell him," she said, pointing at me.

"Mum, stop talking, I'm trying to listen," said Mum.

"He hates Israel."

"No, I don't–"

"Let's not argue," said Mum.

"Nobody's arguing," said Grandma, "I'm just saying this one is what we call a self-hating Jew. He wasn't properly brought up to support Israel," she added, inferring with characteristic unsubtlety that her useless son-in-law was complicit.

It was true that I was full of self-loathing: I lacked confidence, hated school, how I looked, my inability to get a girlfriend, how the world was awful – and that I was already destined for a deathly future in trouser manufacture. But that was a whole list of self-hating reasons before I even got to Jew.

Dad crossed his arms and looked sternly ahead, saying nothing.

"Israel's great, Barry," said Maurice. "You should go."

"I keep telling him that," said Dad, no longer my ally in this conversation.

Maurice leaned in and whispered "Female soldiers. Phwoarr."

"Grandma, I'm not anti-Israel. They need to work out how to live side by side with the Arabs."

"Tell that to the Arabs," said Maurice, slapping his knee and looking away. Thanks, Maurice: one dad is plenty for me already.

We watched for a few minutes in surly silence when the phone rang. Mum went to answer. It was usually for her, although her friends knew not to ring when Eurovision was on.

"Why aren't Yugoslavia on?"

"I told you, Becky, they haven't entered this year."

"I bet the Russkies put a stop to that. Like they stop Jews emigrating to Israel."

Mum called from the kitchen.

"Barry, it's for you."

"Barry wants to live in Russia. He's a communist."

"Socialist grandma," I countered irrelevantly.

"It's Harriet."

Maurice's eyebrows rose involuntarily. I stood up and felt my stomach jump to join me, went to the kitchen and took the receiver from Mum.

"Hi, Harriet."

"Oh, hi, Barry, hope you don't mind me ringing."

"Course not." My love.

"I got your number from my dad, he knows your dad."

"Right." Business-like. Don't think she's asking me out.

"Have you heard of Allen Ginsberg?"

"Vaguely. Someone to do with Bob Dylan? Poet?"

She's definitely not asking me out.

"Jewish poet. I have to read him before I go up to Oxford."

"What do you mean 'up'? Oxford is south."

"It's what you say when you're going to Oxford or Cambridge University."

"What do I say, then? I'm going diagonally to Bristol?"

"Ginsberg is amazing. I thought you might like to read him; some of it's very funny." I'd never had such a long conversation with Harriet. She spoke fast and lucid, jumping with ease across a range of subjects. "I can lend you my copy. You coming to the youth club tomorrow?"

I hadn't thought about that until she suggested it. Was she asking me out? Technically, yes – even if it was somewhere we were both planning to be, anyway.

"Sure."

"I'm surprised you're still going," she said, killing even the slightest notion that this might in any way be construed as a date. "I thought you might have abandoned us for the performing life."

"I did a gig tonight," I said.

"Really? Why didn't you tell me? I'd love to have come." The excitement this generated sent a surge of exhilaration through my body, pushing out of my penis. Maurice was right: I should have asked her out. If only to avoid spending the night with Maurice. "Have you got any plans for August?"

"August? Haven't thought that far ahead."

"I'm planning to go to the Edinburgh Fringe."

"What's that?"

"It's an arts festival."

"Ah. Okay. Is that the Edinburgh Festival?"

"No. Well, yes. It's on at the same time."

"I've heard of that."

"Yes, lots of famous companies like the Wooster Group."

"Aha." Not famous to me, then.

"The Fringe is more our kind of thing. Student theatre. Funny poetry."

"Don't say 'Like Pam Ayres'."

"No, more like Brian Patten. He'll probably be performing there, too." There it was, the jumping stomach again. Poetry. Patten. Love. Harriet.

"Sounds great."

31

"My brother's at university there. I'll be staying in his flat."

"You like my poetry, then?"

"Yes, I told you last week. Original."

"Thanks." Does that mean you'd like to go out with me? I still couldn't read the signs.

"Okay, see you tomorrow."

"Sure. See you there."

"Byee."

I placed the phone back on its cradle.

Edinburgh with Harriet. And Brian. My two loves together, partners in rhyme.

I wasn't in a rush to discover who had won the Eurovision Song Contest and knew Maurice would be desperate to find out what Harriet wanted. I gave myself a moment to savour the pleasure. Harriet had rung and asked me out. Sort of.

I came back in as France were being hailed as the winners of the 1977 contest.

"Did you ask her out?" Maurice asked urgently.

"Uh, not really."

"See that?" yelled Grandma, "anti-Semitic voting."

He laughed and punched me on the arm.

"Puftah," he muttered silently.

CHAPTER 4

It was a typical August day in Leeds: gloomy clouds promising the kind of persistent, dreary rain that was such a common feature of the summer holidays. At least we were travelling away from it but where we were heading, the clouds looked ominously darker.

Convinced I could persuade Harriet to go out with me if she could see me perform, I had decided to stay with her at her brother's flat in Edinburgh. The problem was it was Maurice who had convinced me; now he'd be staying, too.

That Headingley show had opened his eyes to a new world, not just one that offered an endless supply of attractive female students. Maurice was staying in Leeds to study business at the polytechnic and had decided, he told me one evening after a typically brilliant Perrin repeat, to be my manager.

I laughed almost as much as I had during the Reggie episode. "Who do you think I am?" I asked. "Elton John?" He didn't need to know I was only performing poetry to get a girlfriend. I suspected he only wanted to be my manager for the same reason.

"Obviously, there's nothing happening now. This is a long-term plan. I get to learn about business through practical experience. It'll be led by you as much as me."

"I don't know what you're talking about, Maurice. I go to a gig and read poems. I don't get paid."

"Well, you should!"

"If I'm lucky, the promoter buys me a drink."

"I've already told Harriet I'm your manager."

"What?"

"She thinks it's a great idea."

"What are you talking about? Why are you talking to Harriet about my poetry?"

"Because you told me that she was going to the Edinburgh Festival! There are idiots out there prepared to pay money to see people like you read poetry, you shmock. Why can't I be a part of that?"

"What on earth has it got to do with you?"

I resisted at first but was intrigued at the idea of performing in a different town. I started to pick up snippets of information about the festival. Monty Python began there. Peter Cook. Must have something going for it.

It was going to be a long, dull journey on a long, dull coach. Maurice had prepared well, arriving at the station overladen with magazines: Goal, Football and Shoot! – not exactly the A to Z of Poetry Management. But the new football season was about to begin.

Leeds United – The Bar Mitzvah Years – were the greatest team in the land, feared and hated because we were so successful. We also had a reputation for playing dirty, which as every football fan knows is a shameful reputation to have, unless it's your team. I may have been a weedy, wimpy, cerebral, intellectual outsider, but when it came to Leeds, my loyalty and sense of belonging was as fierce as that of the most violent National Front supporter. We had a lot of them.

On Saturday mornings, Maurice and I worshipped at Moortown synagogue without enthusiasm, but by afternoon were devoting ourselves to the true Gods sent to deliver unto us an array of championships and cups. We watched that team grow old and grumpy together. They survived the bile of the media and breezed through forty-four days of being managed by Brian Clough, but that's another story.

"Got any gigs lined up for me?" I asked, as giant sluices of rainwater slapped angrily against the coach windows.

"No need," he said confidently. "We can sort them when we arrive."

"How do you know?"

He looked up from his magazine, momentarily, irritated. "I investigated at the... library. Nothing I could do beforehand." And he went back to reading about our prospects for next season.

Maurice's soul wasn't completely lacking in poetry. Deep down he knew, even as his own life had barely begun, that the great days of our football team were finished. The legends had moved on, their replacements mere humans. The glory days were over, and Maurice's Proustian sense of remembrance and loss, recollections of goals scored and opponents hacked, was as keen as that of the most angst-ridden author. Even so, I was a little disappointed not to see more evidence of his new-found interest.

We travelled beyond Harrogate, further north than I'd ever been, sensing the countryside might look quite beautiful if we could have seen it beyond the clouds. Maurice was tense – and not in a way I was used to seeing.

"Everything okay with you?" I asked, mostly to alleviate the boredom.

He answered with a shrug.

"I appreciate what you're doing," I said, "but you know if nothing comes of this management thing it doesn't matter."

He didn't answer, but that seemed to put his mind at rest. Rather fast for my liking.

"Maurice, can I ask you something?"

He turned to face me, article about Kenny Dalglish half completed.

"How serious are you about managing me?"

I could tell from the pause that he was constructing an answer, implying that he'd thought about this for the first time.

"Do you want to be my manager, or did you think it would be a good way to get off with Harriet to pretend to be interested in my poetry? Is that it?"

Maurice squirmed. I scoffed, triumphant.

"What made you decide to persuade me to go to Edinburgh?"

"As soon as it became obvious that you didn't want to go out with her–"

"What are you talking about!? That's not obvious at all!"

"It was to me."

"Great. Do you seriously think I'm going all the way to Scotland to read some bloody poems?"

"I think you're going all the way to Scotland to try and get off with Harriet and frankly I don't fancy your chances, mate."

Somewhere in the surly silence that followed, I sensed Maurice didn't want to fall out with me over a woman – at least, not yet.

"They have a place at the Edinburgh students' union called the Fringe Club. You turn up and ask to perform and they put you on stage. Sounds pretty easy."

"Thanks, Maurice."

Maurice gave one of his more familiar grunts and returned to speculation about Liverpool's chances in Europe this coming year.

Our rickety bus crept and crawled through Scottish border country, along roads that juddered up and down like camel humps, through miles of open countryside. The rain, less intense but settling into a monotonous rhythm, washed away any glimpse of colour into a dull, dark grey. I'd never seen so much open space, so few houses, until it felt like we were heading so deep into the unpopulated unknown I thought we might never see another person again.

The drizzle thinned out. We emerged like bleary-eyed strangers to the more populated towns and villages, but the colours didn't change. Grey was the national shade, each house hewn out of the rocks around us, terraces of stern fortress, designed perhaps to keep the foreigners away or, more likely, to trap the warmth indoors.

"Come on then, Barry. What do you know about Scotland? Ten things."

"It's cold. And wet. Is that two?"

"No. Men wear skirts."

"I knew you'd say that. Anything else?"

"Glaswegians are hard."

"Hard but funny. Billy Connolly."

"Andy Stewart."

"Who?"

"Scottish rock'n'roll singer. Sounds like Elvis."

"Billy Bremner."

"Eddie Gray."

"Peter Lorimer. Kenny Dalglish."

"Dave Mackay. George Graham."

"Come on, we must know more than just footballers."

"Bill Shankly?"

Turned out we knew a little more – porridge and tossing the caber, to be precise – but nothing could have prepared us for Edinburgh.

As the coach rolled west into the centre, rays of sunshine pierced the clouds and, like the curtain rising on a spectacular West End theatre show, introduced us to the afternoon's star performer. Ladies and gentlemen of grotty, grim Leeds, Motorway City of the '70s, prepare to be dazzled in a life-changing moment as we present to you – Edinburgh!

Dark, imposing terraces loomed over us, broody and magnificent. The streets were cobbled like in films set in Victorian times: wide, grand and beautiful. Gawp away, Leeds boy, we know we're outstanding, you're not the first to notice. No, these were not streets, they were broad avenues, intimations of what lay ahead. We were heading into the centre of town when what looked like a massive mountain range loomed astonishingly into view, larger than any of the grand buildings surrounding it. This isn't what British cities are supposed to be!

Edinburgh was unlike anywhere I'd been, and I'd been to Manchester, Sorrento, Blackpool and Filey. The nearest I'd seen to anything resembling Edinburgh was Harrogate, and there was no towering cliff face behind Betty's Tea Rooms. Was it possible to fall in love with... a place?

A dismal, concrete John Lewis briefly interrupted the grand old architecture, but at the top of the hill a military-straight road stretched into the distance, verdant park on its left plunging into the depths of Edinburgh and straight back up to a giant brooding castle that could have come out of a Dracula movie. Except we weren't in Transylvania: we were in the middle of the capital city of Scotland in 1977. All that was missing was a chorus of heavenly angels singing Hallelujah.

Edinburgh Terminus offered a prospect north from the city, to a wide body of water many miles away. The view was so wide and deep it was like looking at a map of the British Isles with its familiar Firth of Forth gap at the neck, where the head of northern Scotland leans towards its Celtic brother in

Ireland. In the foreground, another deep, plunging hill, gentler but longer, meandered towards the magnificent suburbs.

We stepped off the coach. The air stank of brewery. A man with a ginger beard and blue-and-white hat stumbled towards us, swearing incoherently, but the lone, familiar stereotype merely emphasised how nothing else was as imagined. Well-dressed couples in brightly coloured cardigans and fancy rucksacks on their backs wandered, maps in hand. It was the height of the tourist season, but as far as I was aware no one went on holiday to a town or city. Apart from Sorrento. Who in their right mind would choose as a metropolis of drizzle and occasional sunshine, just because it's got a castle and a mountain in its centre?

Americans, that's who. The heavily accented rantings of the drunk man faded and were replaced by the curious, drawling inflection I recognised from Hollywood films. They were all carrying the same brochure, all heading to the same place: a tall, terraced block, lighter than the black and dark greys around us but still pretty old. At first I thought it was flats, but a giant sign in the window read "Venue 64", and the tourists joined a small queue outside the building. Why would American tourists be queuing outside an anonymous tenement block at four o'clock in the afternoon? What was it for? A visa extension? The English tea experience? But then Maurice came back from the phone boxes and said:

"I've spoken to her brother. Harriet's gone to a play."

"At four o'clock in the afternoon?" It hadn't crossed my mind those tourists might be going to see a show; shows happened in theatres at 7.30 pm.

"This is the Fringe, putz. If you want an audience you're not going to compete with the poncy ballet, are you?"

"What are we going to do?"

"Her brother's at home, he's given me directions. Not far at all."

Walking past Venue 64, we saw a garish poster by the American queue, advertising Romeo and Juliet by William Shakespeare. The photo of the leads showed two punks: a white-faced girl with heavily pronounced cheekbones and jet-black hair pushed under a leather cap, like Siouxsie from Siouxsie and the Banshees, and a young man with spiked-up hair that looked like an anti-pigeon guard or an elderly relative's kitchen clock. The idea of a play performed in this manner made me part intrigued, part sneery. I heard a voice in my head saying "punk Shakespeare? Bloody nonsense" that sounded exactly like my dad.

Punk was enjoying its moment in the mainstream. Bands like The Jam, The Stranglers and Eddie and the Hot Rods were in the charts; the music had moved on from what I'd heard on John Peel, and even the saccharine DJs on daytime Radio 1, Gods of musical taste for the masses, were playing their songs.

I was still resistant to punk's charms. It had arrived in the late summer of 1976. Siouxsie had appeared in every newspaper as its beautiful, shocking face, a vision of PVC and fishnet and wearing a swastika armband, which had been enough to persuade me that this great new fad was to be avoided. One more commercial attempt to use teenagers to sell fascism as fashion, like the skinheads before them who for years had blighted my life at school and Leeds United.

"Punk Shakespeare? Bloody nonsense," Maurice said as we strode beyond Venue 64.

We walked past St Paul's and St George's Church, currently not a place of worship but home to the Oxford University Revue. Further inspection of their poster revealed four rather posh-looking chaps, staring at one slightly less posh-looking chap in a leather jacket with the now familiar circled anarchist

"A" painted on it. His slightly half-hearted two-fingered salute to the others made me think this must be some kind of comedy show. Even the posh, brainy kids had discovered punk.

"Leith Walk, this is what we want. Number 397: he said it'll be easy to spot."

On our right was Edinburgh Playhouse – at last, a building that was an actual theatre. From here it looked as though it was set to plunge down a steep hill towards the railway line.

Numbering became haphazard. We thought we had missed the house, then Maurice laughed and pointed at another charcoal-grey tenement, 397 daubed scrappily, three feet high, in bright white paint. The front door was wide open, and I wondered if Edinburgh was like how Grandma described how the rest of Britain used to be before the foreigners came, when you could leave your front door open and no one would steal anything – probably because you had nothing to steal, but there you go.

We trudged up the grey stone slabs of stair, past several thick, heavily bolted doors on each floor. The front may have been open but you'd have needed serious kit to break into any of these strongholds.

The stairs continued forever. Finally we reached the third floor, Maurice wheezing but with just enough breath to whisper "red door". Harriet's brother opened it. He was tall, serious, confident, like his sister but older, mature, no-nonsense.

"Laurence Fink," he said without a trace of a Leeds accent, offering us each a stern handshake. "Harriet should be back soon, bathroom," he said, pointing pointlessly at a room with a bath and a toilet, struggling with politeness to hide his irritation at the intrusion of unknown strangers. He indicated the impressive, tall-ceilinged living room and kitchen, and reached the end of the corridor, "here's your room, bit basic but you'll be fine here. I'll put the kettle on," and turned back to the kitchen.

Maurice and I looked inside our assigned broom cupboard. That wasn't a euphemism, it really was a cupboard that contained a wobbly Bex Bissell hoover, floppy mop and two narrow mattresses that literally took up the whole floor.

"I guess you and Harriet, you know…" I said, part mocking.

"Yeah, yeah," Maurice replied airily. "We'll sort that later."

In Laurence's living room I saw one of those brochures the tourists had been carrying, casually open on the floor. It was the Edinburgh Fringe programme. Dozens of shows, every day, every time of day. Some circled in biro, modern plays, poetry readings, Oxford and Cambridge student comedy shows. I felt embarrassed by the insignificance of my puny body of work when measured against the industrial level of energy and creativity on display here.

Harriet breezed in moments later, less formal than I remembered, clothes less prissy. I appreciated everything about her and cursed how I had apparently ceded my desires to Maurice Bloody Harvey.

"Hi guys. Sorry I wasn't here: been to see the most amazing show." This lively new Harriet was another revelation. "It was brilliant! Hilarious. All about an Irish village where everyone rides around on bikes and one man bumps along the road so much his body molecules mix with the bike and he becomes half man, half bicycle–"

"The Third Policeman?" I asked?

"Oh, my God! Have you seen it?"

"No, it's one of my favourite books."

"You've read it? That's amazing."

"Flann O'Brien. Any time the man-bike stops walking he falls over to one side."

"That's right. It's a bunch of Irish students; I hadn't planned to go but they were so funny, I saw them on the Royal Mile handing out leaflets."

We talked at animated length about the genius of Flann. We may as well have been speaking in Gaelic for all the sense it made to Maurice. He sat sulking in the corner, slumped in the comfiest chair in the room, holding his footie magazines for comfort. I wondered if there was still hope for me in this epic battle for the maiden's fair heart.

"There's this venue where anyone can try out new stuff. It's called the Fringe Club – hi, Maurice – and I checked–"

"–Yes, Brian Epstein here mentioned it to me."

Harriet laughed.

"The earlier you arrive, the quicker they book you in. Shall we go tonight?"

"Sure," I said, side-lined spectator turned active participant in a moment.

"Food first," Harriet said, finally putting her bag down but still energised. "There was this brilliant juggler on the Royal Mile, throwing three flaming sticks, made these tiny kids hold them–" and she walked out of the room, leaving us to wonder if there was a horrendous punchline to that story, but she had already conveyed enough of her excitement at the Fringe performers to encourage me to get out there right now and start slaying them with my ironic sonnets.

"I'll work out my set for tonight," I said, leaving Maurice to his footie mags, considerably more relaxed at the prospect of leaving them together if I could shine on stage.

CHAPTER 5

After a lively supper with Laurence, who relaxed and turned out to be as funny and quirky as his sister, Maurice, Harriet and I walked into town with our topographically challenged Fringe map to guide us. We'd enjoyed an animated discussion about Irish versus Jewish humour, although Maurice communicated his lack of interest through a selection of heavy sighs and irritated tuts, barely speaking all evening.

We walked back up towards the plunging park I'd seen earlier, home to what could only be described as a Victorian spaceship. Maurice pointed, I laughed.

"That," said Harriet, excited with her new role as tour guide, "is a monument to Sir Walter Scott. The writer of Ivanhoe," she added when it was clear we had no idea who she was talking about.

"Ah," we said together, aware of the TV version. Another famous Scot to add to our tiny list.

"Imagine a statue to a writer in Leeds!"

"Do we have writers?" Maurice asked.

"Jeff Christie?" I said, imagining a monument to the creator of Yellow River.

"Dunno about a statue," said Maurice, "but go into Leeds any Saturday night and you'll find a yellow river streaming down The Headrow."

Princes Street, the ramrod thoroughfare I'd seen when we arrived, bordered two different city centres. North lay a grand and perfect grid of squares defined on our map as "the New Town", although it looked pretty ancient and was only new in relation to "the Old Town", south of the border. The New Town was your snooty relative who ambled up and down hills at their own gentle pace, formal, rich and everything in its place as it should be. South was twisty, messy and dangerous, all castle and rock face, steep steps and constricted alleyways.

We were heading south.

Down and up we went, across narrow streets that spiralled and climbed, up dozens of steep steps – "Robert Louis Stevenson walked these streets seeking inspiration for Kidnapped," Harriet explained – and down again, through a Victorian arch and down, deeply down, a descent into hell, overpowered by the brewery fumes and dark mists that hung moodily over the Old Town.

The map wasn't completely accurate, but we sensed we were heading in the right direction. Every corner turned brought a new shock: a stunning view of the castle, a sudden reminder of the shocking poverty in those tenements that had been left to rot, away from the benevolent gaze of the international theatregoer.

And, everywhere we looked, people. It was eight o'clock, late summer light fading, temperature dropping to an uncomfortable chill, but the entire population was outdoors, either going to a show or being one.

A small gang of teenage punks walked sullenly downhill, passing a dozen fresh-faced students in full Roman costume, handing out leaflets. Two couples who looked the same age as

Mum and Dad were laughing and joking in tones I could barely translate. I knew what an isolated Scottish accent sounded
like – specifically Billy Connolly's, whose records I knew off by
heart – but the accent was different, even though Glasgow was
not much further from Edinburgh than Leeds from Sheffield.

The Glasgow voice was all over TV: cheery and sing-song
with a hint of menace, the character always a gangster you sym-
pathised with because you knew they'd grown up in grinding
poverty, and everyone was called Jimmy. This Edinburgh lilt
was less menacing and musical: was this an historical thing? I
had no idea and wasn't sure I'd learn more at a time when the
city was heaving with American tourists, English students and
Russian ballerinas.

We turned back on ourselves, up another hill, into a
housing estate so steep it was hard to tell where the flats ended
and the rock began. The punks followed. There were only four
of them and they couldn't have been more than fifteen years
old, but we were lost, tourists with a giveaway map, and they
knew where they were going.

They muttered among themselves, stopped and looked
towards us. A sallow-faced boy wearing the now obligatory
leather jacket called out – "Hey!" – and even though his voice
had barely broken my stomach leapt in fear. Under the jacket,
his tee shirt had been deliberately ripped across the chest and
midriff with a hint of violence, and carelessly put back together
with safety pins. No swastikas, at least.

"Looking for the Fringe Club?" We smiled silently, keen not
to antagonise the locals with our middle-class English accents.

He pointed to a small opening in an alleyway at the top of
the hill.

"Thanks," I said.

The entrance was tall, narrow and stern, like an angry giant
parent who'd been waiting up for you all night. Inside, the hall

had been transformed by a mass of brightly coloured posters, a dayglo defiance of Mum and Dad, an explosion of entertainment – by us, for us.

Maurice was right: there were plenty of places left on the bill, and I was scheduled to go on in less than half an hour. I'd been expecting something acoustic-folk-clubby but the room was more like a rock music venue, and the atmosphere was charged. The audience was standing and noisy like at the football. There was still time for me to pull out.

On stage, the Roman-costumed students we'd seen earlier had gone straight on and were acting their undergraduate hearts out for their friends and a few genuine fans at the front. I had no idea which play, but it included lines telling the audience the time and venue of where they'd be performing the full, three-hour production.

I left Harriet and Maurice at the back and stood close to the stage, watching the students struggle, unable to veer away from their script and forced to perform in badly stitched bedsheets.

They were replaced by two acrobats: a man on a unicycle dressed like a circus clown and yet another punk: no leather jacket but a bin liner, fashioned to look like a shirt, and drainpipe jeans with holes torn in random places. He may have been into anarchy but juggled with discipline and ferocious efficiency. Three, four, five, six, seven juggler's sticks, their meticulous orchestration of anarchic mayhem sending the crowd wild.

The men somersaulted and cartwheeled off to aggressive whoops and cheers. For a moment, the stage was empty. Would there be any shame in pulling out now?

A drunken, ranting local with no show to promote came on stage, a directionless missile of menace.

"Avan yi mara calamo," he shouted. We had no idea what he was saying but we got the tone.

"Bar's that way!" a loud Scottish voice called from the

crowd, provoking a wave of laughter from the front row.

"Yeeur a munna larabu, garama... students!" he yelled with ferocious hostility, and off he went to the loud ironic cheers of the crowd, replaced by two fresh-faced lads. The drunk stuck up two fingers to the backs of the new act, and the crowd roared.

I went behind to where the performers had been emerging and started at the sight of the teenage punks we'd seen on the way to the gig. Performing after me, I was relieved to note.

Hidden backstage, I could no longer tell what was happening out front, but it didn't sound great. The double act were performing to an expectant silence, I could smell a change in the mood.

I was on next. This was not like any of the gigs I'd done before. The crowd had been too polite to heckle the last act but were growing restless for entertainment. I'd experienced nervous energy but this was fear you could touch and smell: Leeds United fascist hooligan fear.

I was steered firmly forward and greeted by a loud and angry heckle from the drunken Scotsman who had been on stage earlier. I couldn't tell what he was saying but he seemed offended by the length of my hair and the fact that I looked like a student. Nothing from my gentle poetry readings in Leeds had prepared me for this.

A few students shouted at the drunk to shut up, but most eyes were on me. Come on, wimpy, middle-class hippy boy, the room was thinking: show us what you're made of.

I froze and for a moment the audience saw the look of fear on my face. But this wasn't stage fright. A few feet away, below the glare of the spotlight, I saw Maurice, watching me on stage, for sure, but with his right arm draped around Harriet's shoulders.

How would this show work out? I no longer gave a fuck.

I waited behind the microphone stand – not for protection,

but as a weapon. A weapon of amplification. A chorus of bullies from school flashed past my eyes, Michael Connor, Steven Burke, Simon Brazier, each louder than the next, always the boys with the loudest voices who intimidated the most. Here was my moment to join them.

I calmly took the microphone out of its stand, let the drunken ramblings continue for a moment then looked to the audience.

"Ladies and gentlemen," I said, "you will not believe that this man is a philosophy student at Cambridge University."

A few laughed but the ranting got louder and angrier.

"Listen to that accent! Such authenticity. You won't believe he went to Eton! His show must be brilliant." The ranting dropped to a mumble and the heckler disappeared, to huge cheers from the crowd.

In my life I'd been no stranger to humiliation. But until now I'd never inflicted it on another. The audience loved me for it.

"Good evening. My name is Barry Goldman and I'm a frustrated teenage cliché. This first poem is called I'm A Frustrated Teenage Cliché."

I'm a frustrated teenage cliché
In a dark frustrated teenage rut
In a dark frustrated teenage city
In a dark frustrated teenage hut.
I'm searching for piece of mind
And peace on earth
And ban the bomb
And an end to poverty, starvation and human greed
But above all this I want, I need
A girlfriend.

The audience roared their approval. I walked off six inches taller, warmed by the triumph in the gladiatorial arena. My teenage punk tormentor smiled, "Not bad, mate", which made me feel great, and gave me a sudden urge to discover more about punk.

I hung around backstage a little longer, savouring the admiration of my peers. I wasn't ready to re-join the others.

By the time I stepped out, the crowd had grown considerably. The room was filling urgently with punks. Spiky-topped, hair dyed pink, girls in torn fishnets and the kind of Dr Martens boot favoured by the more psychopathic United supporters, boys in black plastic bin liners, kids with daisy chains of safety pins clipped from earlobe to nose like a miniature Christmas card display.

And not all kids and students: grown men in their twenties, hair cropped to the skull like the fascists who liked to tear through Leeds city centre on Saturday afternoons when the team were otherwise occupied away from home.

I wanted to escape but the crowd pushed forward from the back, and I had to be part of it. The stage was empty, crowd bustling with anticipation. A tiny drum kit stood at the front, two small guitar amps behind. The lights dimmed and the crowd roared.

But the roar was premature. The next act was not a band.

A young, average-looking man, average height, shuffled nervously to the front. He was dressed in full Shakespearean costume: dazzling red breeches, lurid green waistcoat, and a pair of bright yellow fishnet stockings.

Didn't he realise what kind of audience this was? Was he aware of the danger? Some shouted angrily, others laughed, but Shakespeare Boy didn't flinch. He walked centre stage, ignoring the din below.

"Good evening, ladies and gentlemen,' he began, in a confident southern English baritone. "Shakespeare was the greatest English playwright–"

"–You're no' in England now, sonny," came a furious shout from the menacing dark.

"–and he gave us a gift. The gift of the English language," and his emphasis on the word English riled the audience further. I wanted to jump on stage and save this patronising, misguided prick from a kicking – if I hadn't been so scared myself.

"Ladies and gentlemen, my first extract, in homage to our current surroundings, is an excerpt from the Scottish play–"

"–Macbeth!" someone shouted.

The actor recoiled in affected horror and, for the first time, I wondered if this was some kind of wind-up.

He fixed his gaze in the direction of the heckle, momentarily commanding the crowd, and continued, sternly, "We never refer to the Scottish play by name."

This inevitably led to a rousing chorus of "Macbeths". A couple of guys up front spat at him, but he carried on as if the only problem was the famous actorly superstition that saying the name of "the Scottish play" was bad luck.

"Very well," he continued. "Be it upon your safety-pinned Celtic heads. I shall block the ears of the ghost of Mister Garrick." And now a few of the audience entered the spirit of the moment and yelled in mock English accents "the Scottish play".

He smiled indulgently, even as another well-targeted gob of phlegm whacked him on the cheek and rolled gently down his jaw.

I looked at his eyes in search of fear. There was none.

"Act one scene one," he bellowed. "A forest. Three witches are brewing a poisonous concoction, dancing in perfect time around a steaming cauldron. Worry not, my friends; this play is less than two hours long."

Some were laughing, smiling at each other in disbelief. Others were furious.

He cleared his throat.

"I," he began like Laurence Olivier, abruptly opening his eyes wide, "am an anti-christ." The audience whooped and cheered with relief.

"I don't know what I want," he continued, "but I know, ladies and gentlemen, that you do, so please welcome to the stage three fine young Scottish gentlemen performing under the soubriquet," his voice swelling with each word, "Hermann Goering's Hermits!" – and he raised his arms slowly and leapt into the astonished crowd.

For a moment, we stared in shock, wondering if he might have killed himself. But he jumped up and ran round the back to cheers.

The crowd pushed forward. I was propelled to the front, feet leaving the ground, hemmed and rammed by the punks. Only a few feet from the stage but I could barely make out the band through the faces and bodies in front. I recognised my new punk mate as the drummer and frontman, his two buddies a respectable distance behind as they plugged in guitar and bass.

"Alright," Wee Drummer Boy declared from behind his kit. "We started practising three days ago. This is our first gig. This song's called Kenneth McKellar Can Kiss My Cock".

He yelled "Onetwothreefour" and the band exploded into their first number, a racing, raging blast. The crowd went wild, literally, jumping up and down, bouncing and crashing into each other, and me. Were they dancing or fighting? It was hard to tell. I'd often seen Leeds fans kicking off at the Kop end, and from a distance it looked choreographed. In the middle of it, the smell of violence was real. I felt a shot of pain as the hot end of a cigarette brushed my cheek.

Wee Drummer Boy sang, his voice powerful and gruff for one so young. The song was over almost before it had begun. The crowd roared. "Thanks. We only know the one song, so we're gonna play it again. Onetwothreefour," and before the crowd had a chance to protest they were off again, playing the same song faster and better. Plus we now had an idea what the chorus sounded like and we all joined in, like when I'd seen The Beach Boys live at a field in Lancashire in 1974.

They ran off as quickly as they'd entered, the crowd streamed to the bar, and within a few moments a couple of toffs called Stephen and Hugh began performing amusing comedy skits to a crowd that barely outnumbered them. I walked away, aware my clothes were covered in beer and sweat, some of it my own, elated.

I retired to a quieter corner, lit a Players Number 6 and tried to make sense of what I'd witnessed. Mad Shakespeare Guy had thrown himself into the crowd, crossing the line between performer and spectator. Perhaps tonight, I thought, I had thrown myself in the opposite direction.

A young man walked towards me, slightly familiar, beaming.

"Barry?"

"Yeah..."

"Loved your set. I'm Kris. With a K. You were great."

It took me a moment to recognise him in his normal clothes. It was Mad Shakespeare Guy.

I tried to say something sensible but was lost for words. "You... that was astonishing. Have you done that before?"

"With the punks? No. Met them yesterday. They were practising in the church hall next to where we're performing."

Kris with a K didn't look like a punk but he had short hair and wore the kind of Ben Sherman shirt favoured by skinheads and the Left.

"But that was their first gig. How come they got such a big crowd?"

"I know, it's amazing," he said in a middle-class accent I couldn't place. "As soon as there's a gig, word gets out. You not a punk fan?"

"I am now. Don't think I ever want to see Genesis live again."

Kris laughed. "Let me get you a drink."

We found a quiet corner near the bar. Kris ordered two pints of Heavy like an Edinburgh regular. I had no idea what Heavy was; it looked a bit like Guinness and had a malty taste, and the high alcohol content went straight to my head. I could hear myself talking too much, as if Kris was a girl I was trying to impress. It surprised him that this had been my first ever gig in Edinburgh, and I talked him through my previous shows as he smiled patiently.

Finally, I remembered to ask about his performing background.

"Haven't done much," he said modestly. "I'm at drama school. We're at the Chaplaincy Centre, doing Twelfth Night."

"Ah, hence the costume."

"Yep."

"You done much comedy?" I asked like a polite parent.

He looked at me for a moment, nodding, searching for an answer that suggested more. "I guess you could call it that. I like to surprise people."

"I noticed."

"Challenge people's perceptions. I know it sounds a bit wanky. But... Friend and I staged a fight in our hall of residence, then played it out as a gay love scene. Done a few shows at Birmingham Rep, nothing too fancy: Shakespeare and Pinter. One-man show for the college earlier this year."

At this point, my three gigs felt like a grain of sand on comedy's beach. Despite his modesty, Kris with a K was the full deal.

We talked about our comedy heroes – Tommy Cooper, Steptoe and Son – but his knowledge was full of insight. He hadn't just sat laughing in front of the telly like Maurice and I; he'd studied their techniques, read books, devoured their secrets to inform his own stage persona.

We swapped addresses. He gave me his parents', in Exeter, though he was studying in Birmingham, and I gave him the Bristol hall of residence I was about to move to.

"What time's your show?" I asked.

"Three o'clock in the afternoon. Don't come. It's awful."

"Is that what it says on the leaflet?"

He grinned, the conspiratorial smirk of a comedy soulmate, a massive smile that made me feel loved and think "I will do anything to be the friend of this incredible man."

I meandered home, Walter Scott's spaceship my guide, laughing drunkenly to myself, head filled with this new friend from a new world, one I'd be joining in a few weeks.

At the flat, Harriet was distressed but relieved to see me. "Thank God, we lost you and suddenly there were punks everywhere. We searched all over."

I looked in the living room and saw Maurice, slumped in an armchair, crying big, fat tears. Had my gorgeous Harriet dumped the lump? Was this my moment to strike?

He looked up at me, eyes red and blurry. "Elvis Presley's dead."

CHAPTER 6

Wardrobe doors are flimsy
Desktop weighs a ton
Bed is small and narrow
Sex only space for one
No room to swing a kitten
Not much use for my needs
So why am I so happy?
Cos it's no longer Leeds

Whittock Hall was a lively and delightful modern campus of student accommodation two miles from Bristol city centre, a complex of contemporary apartments set in beautiful gardens with everything you needed on campus. Judging by the dissimilarity between this brochure description and the reality of the dump, it also had an outstanding marketing department. The impressive drawings and professional photographs managed to avoid showing the one thing to spoil the vision: namely, the presence of students.

A new city where I knew nobody. No sister, no parents, no old friends; for the first time in my life, I was truly alone. Yeeha!

I had escaped without having to tunnel underground or stage a riot. Done my time. What would I achieve with this new-found liberty? Comedy? Punk? Poetry? Comedy punk poetry? Love? A future of endless possibilities beckoned.

A busy day lay ahead of registration and acclimatisation. Important homework undertaken in Leeds had established the whereabouts of my department, the students' union and the nearest record shop, amusingly named Rocksy Music. Enrolment would probably take an hour or so, the union another hour, leaving the rest of the day to immerse myself in Rocksy Music's unknown pleasures.

My parents had driven all the way from Leeds, and registered that Bristol was far enough that I wouldn't be expected to come home much other than during the holidays. I'd been expecting Mum to be emotional, but it was Dad who took my flight from the North personally. Expressing feelings was not in his compendium of behaviours, but his grumpometer, which had been steadily rising over the last year or so, was set to maximum as he found fault in every aspect of my new life.

"What if there's a fire?" Dad asked. "Who'll wake you up?"

"The smoke and fumes?"

"How many people are you sharing that bathroom with?"

"Six."

"Six! What if you're desperate?"

"I'll pee in the kitchen sink."

"Barry, don't be disgusting. And stop complaining, Monty. You haven't stopped moaning since we left the house."

I'd had the presence of mind, when applying for student accommodation, to obtain a room of my own. Under "additional information" I'd written 'smoker' (true), and 'often stay up late practising reading my poems aloud' – not untrue, but an exaggeration designed to ensure not having to spend my first three months at Bristol University in the company of some weedy scientist or macho rugby player.

After the exhilaration of Edinburgh, the last few weeks in Leeds had dragged, hours and days taken up in feverish antici-pation of what could possibly lie ahead, all the time confined to the dull routines of family life.

Harriet had already gone down to Oxford even though she continued to call it up. I knew Maurice wasn't sleeping with her in Edinburgh because his snoring kept me awake every night. If there had been a moment for me and Harriet, it had passed, and we bonded platonically over quirky Fringe comedy and poetry. I couldn't stop thinking about Kris, describing his amazing performance which sounded less amazing to anyone who hadn't seen it. I hoped to bump into him again – where or how I had no idea – introduce him to my friends and watch them fall in love with him, too.

"I don't understand why he couldn't have stayed in Leeds," Dad said like I wasn't standing next to him as he and Mum prepared to go back.

"Kids don't stay in their hometown anymore," Mum said, like a round-spectacled sociologist in a tank top on a Panorama documentary about the rise of social and geographical mobility in 1970s Britain.

"Sharing with six people," Dad muttered, and so on, even as we hugged goodbye with assurances I'd be back for Chanukkah.

"And you'll call every Friday night?"

"Every Friday night."

"We'll call straight back."

"Every Friday night, sure." A small price to pay for my freedom.

Sleep was fitful that first night, uncomfortable in the tiny, unfamiliar bed whose mattress had long since had any shape or spring pummelled out of it by years of twisting, turning and frequent masturbation.

I woke to the pleasures of being a grown up, no longer having to hide cigarettes and lighter like at the parents'. What delight to start the morning with the addict's routine: fag taken from pack, smell of tobacco and touch-taste of paper on lip, a flickering flame, deep inhalation and the first of many hits of instant nicotine rush that would see me through the day. I watched the smoke mingle with the room and thought about "my parents' house", defining Leeds no longer as centre of the universe but a place I used to live. This merited a self-indulgent moment of melancholia, imagining Mum and Dad waking to the realisation that their little babies, who had long ago left in spirit, would never be returning.

I saw them as most remembered in recent years: Dad, half-dozing in the armchair as the flickering images of the TV screen passed across his eyes; Mum next door, ironing in the kitchen, phone cradled to ear and talking out the side of her mouth without allowing the cigarette to fall out. A skill I was still working to perfect. I imagined Dad and the armchair as a single entity, Mum and the ironing board as one item, wrote this down on a scrap of paper and immediately felt better. A new poem was emerging.

These moments of solitary freedom disappeared as I came into contact with the crowds queuing for breakfast in the canteen, acres of fresh-faced young women and men the same age as me, in various states of homesickness and excitement about the months and years ahead. Sooner or later, I would have to examine my own excitement and bravado when measured against the hundreds of new recruits in this artificially created city of teens, and admit to being as terrified as the rest of them.

Queueing for breakfast, overwhelmed by the sounds of over-keen conversations and forced laughter, the alert young faces, casual but smart clothes and above all the finely tended hair, male and female, it became apparent I was once again an outsider. The rare Jew at school, the only poet at the football, I was about to experience life as a new, exotic foreigner in the midst of the crowd. Exhibit A: The scruffy Northerner.

Baffled by the volume of cut-glass accents and conversations about specific A level results achieved, which Oxford colleges had rejected them and where home was in relation to Guildford, I felt like someone who had been placed in this environment for a bet, or a scientific experiment, then remembered it was my choice not to go to Liverpool or Newcastle or London, or anywhere I might expect to find people like me.

I had gate-crashed an early-morning toffs' breakfast party and headed to its version of the kitchen, a seat on the far corner of the farthest table from the food bar, next to an empty seat so I wouldn't have to engage with anyone and infect the air with my flat vowels, unfashionable corduroy trousers and long, dank hair.

Hoping to get away before facing the terrors of Revealing My Northern Accent, too late, someone came and sat with me. He was tall and handsome with thick, wavy blond hair, delicate features, indistinguishable from so many of the boys around us. But instead of the standard male uniform of rugby shirt and casual slacks, he wore jeans and a light denim jacket, the small "No Fun" badge on its collar a secret signal of a fellow punk.

He saw me looking at the badge approvingly.

"Before you ask," he drawled comfortably in the accent du jour, "I genuinely don't give a shit what A levels you got." He smiled.

"That's lucky: still waiting to hear mine. They're being flown back to me by racing pigeon."

He held out his hand "Charlie."

"Barry. From Leeds."

"Ooh, Jackie Charlton."

His knowledge of my Leeds was an intrusion. Leeds was where nothing happened, the past. It hadn't crossed my mind that the infamy of our despised football team might have registered with the soft southern rugger chaps.

"Where's Guildford?" I asked. "And why has everyone who lives there come here?"

"Do you honestly care?"

"Nope. What are you studying? He asked, also not caring."

"Politics and sociology."

"Snap!"

"Are you a virgin? That's the only question people are working towards isn't it? Well? Are you?"

I smiled, wondering what to say. "Well…"

"I'm a virgin."

"Yeah, me too."

"Why else would we be here?"

"To study, of course. To prepare us for the outside world."

"By losing our virginity," he said.

"Now you mention it, that answer to my politics professor at the interview was probably what got me a place here."

"Politics? We'll be studying in the same building. I'm doing economics and sociology."

"You want to be a pop star too, then?"

He smiled.

"You like punk?" I asked, nodding to the badge.

"Love it."

"I'm off to pick up New Boots And Panties!! today."

"There's a shop near where we're registering."

"Yeah – Rocksy Music."

"No 'x'. Great name."

Half an hour later, we caught the same shuttle bus into town. Charlie was from Guildford, funnily enough, had attended a public school near Brighton, and was studying at Bristol because he'd failed to get into Oxford. I would never have spoken to him if he hadn't come up to me, but punk had brought us together.

We exchanged stories about our Moment It Happened. I told him about Hermann Goering's Hermits – "Perfect!" he laughed. Charlie's brother had taken him a year ago to the 100 Club in the West End of London, a tiny room where, in a single night, he witnessed The Clash, The Jam, The Stranglers and, he said with particular excitement, The Cortinas.

"Haven't heard of them. What's so great about The Cortinas?" I asked.

"They're so young. Still at school. And from Bristol. They'll be on somewhere round here soon."

We bonded further over politics, and I was surprised to discover Charlie knew as much as me about the Israel-Palestine conflict, and that our views were in rough accord. After we'd registered to study and spent hours and pounds at Rocksy Music, we headed to the students' union.

Bristol was a beautiful city, its lavish university buildings dotted around a triangle of bustling streets, helpfully named the Triangle, dominated by the Wills Memorial Building, a grand, gothic-looking tower that had actually only been built at the start of the century.

"You know this place was built on tobacco and slavery," Charlie said. I didn't, but had already felt uncomfortable and slightly curious, catching the bus from our hall down Blackboy Hill to Whiteladies Road.

"In the eighteenth century, Bristol was the leading slave port in the whole of Britain. That's why Bristol is so wealthy. And probably why Africa isn't."

"Is that Wills Building as in Wills Whiffs?"

"What?" Charlie looked at me as a public schoolboy looks at a northern oik.

"You're not a smoker, I guess. Maybe your butler is?"

It was my turn to talk knowledgeably. Wills Whiffs were cheap cigars manufactured in Bristol for the working classes.

Not their most successful product. Wills made the kind of cigarettes that showed you were serious about smoking – Capstan Full Strength, Woodbine and Castella cigars. They smelt to me of the terraced stands at Leeds United.

"If you see a bloke in a pub with yellow-stained fingertips, you're probably looking at a Wills smoker. Do they have pubs in Guildford?"

"I think so. We got them a few years ago, same time you got electricity."

The students' union was a hideous reminder of the insensitivity of 1960s town planning to architectural heritage. Even the most brutal fan of brutalism may have questioned the construction of a concrete slab in the middle of a lattice of leafy squares and tidy townhouses, and wondered if it had been designed for a bet.

Inside, the noise of shouty students drowned our conversation. It was a culturally wider demographic than my hall of residence but still white, middle class, fashionably liberal, men in polyester shirts and women wearing brightly coloured sweaters whose necklines varied from demure to boldly plunging. A couple of blokes like me, no dress sense. Enough long-haired guys to remind me of Dad watching Top of the Pops, thinking he was the first man to sneer "Look at that hair, you can't tell if it's a girl or a boy", but he carried on watching because he could tell quite clearly that Suzi Quatro was a girl.

Hundreds more organisations competed for our interest: canoeing, beekeeping, caving, football card collecting. I scurried past the Jewish Society, wondering if they might spot me because maybe you can just tell these things. They didn't, but I furtively pinched one of their leaflets, if only to give me something to talk to Mum and Dad about. Those ties to Leeds were not going to disappear simply because I had moved 230 miles away.

I was excited to join any performing group that might have me, but the poetry society seemed very po-faced and the drama stall was buzzing with impossibly glamorous-looking people from Guildford. I put my name down instead for a small, unpromising comedy revue company tucked behind the drama society like its dirty secret.

They were called Bristol University Theatre and Comedy Horde (which produced the hilarious acronym BUTCH), but even they expected you to audition first and I put my name down to be contacted for the Christmas production of Molière's Le Misanthrope.

Charlie persuaded me to join Socialist International and mock the idiots who would join the Communist Revolutionary Order because they liked to think of themselves as communists and revolutionaries when they were neither. Unlike us.

He was already deep in conversation with a lively blonde-haired blonde woman with an authoritative understanding of the Argentine Dirty War. She spoke with a pronounced European accent and was publicising a meeting about the South American dictatorship. Charlie would be going to that meeting. I wasn't the only teenager whose passion for left-wing politics was aroused partly by the beautiful women attracted to it.

"Hey, Barry, come on over. This is Ingrid."

"Hi, Barry. You joining us today?"

"Sure," I said, filling in the form.

"Ingrid knows Rupert. My brother in London."

"Punk man?" I asked.

"Yeah," she said. "He's a cool guy, he gets it. What about you, Barry? What brings you here?"

"International socialism? I guess."

We talked about Western corruption, how America and Russia colluded in the Cold War, the struggles for democracy in Chile, Rhodesia, Iran and Palestine, and how we all fancied

David Bowie. We talked about a world gone wrong, laughed, too, and at the end of the day continued our conversation at the Nelson Mandela Bar, although not one of us knew who Nelson Mandela was or why the bar was named after him. We talked about the shocking conditions in our own communities, and the changes punk could bring to the world. Emboldened by alcohol, our statements became stronger and more passionate, opinions spouted as facts, so that, by the end of the evening there was no world issue so thorny, no dilemma too insurmountable that our little group of three couldn't solve.

I didn't remember leaving the bar, vaguely recalled laughing hysterically but not why, saying something on the bus about how weird that in 1977 there could still be a road in modern Britain called Black Boy Hill, being aware of the stars in the sky and declaring something very profound about how tiny I was in relation to the universe, and vomiting on a tree.

For the second morning running I woke in a strange room - but not the one from the day before. The furniture was the same but bigger, I was lying on a few cushions, and there appeared to be two people asleep under the bed sheets. Between puking in the woods and this moment I had absolutely no idea what happened, aware only that Charlie was no longer a virgin.

CHAPTER 7

Upstairs at 830pm, the Jewish Society was running a talk with slides about the joys of working on a communal farm, or 'kibbutz', near Jerusalem. One floor down, Socialist International was holding a discussion, "Israel and Palestine: The Cold War by Proxy". Which would I go to? I may have left home but I could hear the argument with Mum and Dad as though they were standing next to me.

"How can you even think that's a choice?" I imagined him sighing.

He was right, there was no contest: Socialist International was meeting next door to the Nelson Mandela Bar, and Monday was Pints-At-Half-Pint-Prices Night.

"Thanks for joining us, comrades; my name's Gordon," said a man called Gordon. "Welcome to today's meeting, and hello to all the new faces," he beamed, waving regally around the room.

We were few, a dozen or so earnest middle-class, left-wing soulmates. Ingrid and Charlie's relationship still seemed in good shape, although after that first night I was determined to no longer be present to witness its nightly consummation. However equal Charlie and I may have been as virgins at the start of university, as far as I could tell he had now surged forward in the League of Understanding What Girls Want.

Gordon was, by a distance, the oldest. He looked at least 22. The few features visible behind his thick beard and glasses suggested a studious postgraduate. I guessed he was a scientist because I was young and ignorant about science and assumed, having watched the Open University on BBC Two, that every postgraduate with a thick beard and glasses was a scientist. I didn't yet know that attacking the bourgeois state and its agents, the police, could be an academic pursuit. My ignorance on this, and many other issues about Gordon, would be corrected by the end of the meeting.

"This summer's victory of the right-wing Likud party in Israel marks a dramatic turning point in the Israel-Palestine conflict," he said, while rolling a cigarette. It was odd to hear someone saying this who wasn't me, and with no middle-aged parent tutting in the background. "The new prime minister, Menachem Begin, was a renowned Irgun terrorist who attacked the British Mandate in Palestine and orchestrated the Naqba–"

"–Hang on, Gordon: can you slow down, please?"

"I'm sorry, Matt: what's the problem?"

"There's a few new faces here. Perhaps they could use some background to the conflict?" There was general enthusiasm for this approach. "Can you start with explaining how the state of Israel came about?"

Matt was a proper punk: short and slim, skinny black trousers, chunky black sweater, cropped black hair fashioned by gel into the now familiar spiky clock. Unusually for a man, he wore a small earring in his left lobe.

Gordon began by explaining how Israel was formed in 1948, three years after the end of the War, when the horrors of the Holocaust had become known. He talked about the Six-Day War of 1967, which I'd remembered as a small child: exciting pictures on TV of tanks rampaging through a desert, Mum and Dad snatching moments for low, murmured conversations, anxiety gripping the Goldman household. Then, as quick as the panic began, it was over. "We" won.

I was a kid, it was great, Mum and Dad were never happier.

There were no Arabs in Leeds as far as I knew, which made them all the scarier. Gordon told us part of the story I'd never heard, how the state was created in the aftermath of the horrors of the Second World War, which involved forcing thousands of Arabs out of their homes in the British-run colony of Palestine and into neighbouring countries.

"Even so," he added, "we should never forget the six million Jews that the fascists killed."

"You could start by not using the word Palestine," I imagined Dad muttering.

Two characters emerged who captured the imagination of the world: Yasser Arafat, leader of the Palestinian Liberation Organization, whose persuasively elegant analysis of the US bankrolling of Israel's military might and cool shades earned him a place on the cover of Time magazine, and Leila Khaled, the hijacker whose daring deeds and exquisite cheekbones launched a thousand teenage male fantasies.

"Always had an eye for the pretty ones," I heard Dad mutter from hundreds of miles away.

"Shut up, Monty," said Mum. "I haven't heard this bit before."

Gordon made no attempt to gloss over the horrors of the Second World War, and how the decision of the newly formed United Nations to provide a homeland for the Jews was the proper, humanitarian response, relighting his rolled-up cigarettes between drags. Unusually, he used brown papers that smelled of liquorice, and the air in the room grew thick with an aroma two parts tobacconist to one part sweet shop.

"The Six-Day War was swift and precise but created more problems than it solved," he said. "For the first time, Israel took complete control of Jerusalem. Israel's victory led to a massive migration of Americans to the country, and thousands of Soviet Jews demanded to be allowed to go."

"Is this why you moved away from Leeds? So you could forget you're a Jew?"

"Mum. Dad. Go to bed. No supper! I'm eighteen. I don't have to have these imaginary conversations with you. Carry on, Gordon."

"Jerusalem has for centuries been the spiritual home of Jews, Christians and Muslims."

"One day they'll all live happily together," said Ingrid, raising a few eyebrows, "when they realise God doesn't actually exist." A relieved laugh rippled across the room.

"Now you have a country where the most obstinately religious Jews and Arabs live side by side," said Gordon. "You get an increase in anti-Semitism in communist countries, and more Palestinians either forced to leave or stay in places like Gaza under Israeli rule."

"And isn't that when the American Jews started to finance the huge agricultural revolution?" a young man asked. This was the kind of thing I said to Dad all the time, but there was something in the way he said "Jews" that pulled me up, like when Reverend Stevens at school used to say "Jesus was killed by the Jews," spitting out the last two words while looking directly at me. Like Charlie, he was assured, well-bred, handsome; I guessed that he had received the letter telling him he had failed his Oxbridge exams at his parents' house in Guildford.

"That's true, Sebastian," Ingrid replied, "but you have an arms race developing between the United States and the Soviet Union. It's much bigger than a few people in America investing in the new democracy."

Gordon continued, bringing us up to the present day, but Sebastian's intervention took me back to Leeds, and those arguments with Dad and Gran. "You'll always have to fight the thick racists on the street," Dad had said. "That's the easy part. It's the posh ones who went to public school you have to watch out for."

CHAPTER 8

The first Friday-night conversation had gone well enough. there were plenty of exciting, superficial topics to fill the space – nothing too controversial. I'd begun by studying quite hard, enthused by my first encounters with Plato and Socrates, who sounded like a laugh. I wanted to understand and love Marxist economics but my failure to understand a word in lectures gave a whole new meaning to the phrase "class struggle".

Mr Muckle, my sociology lecturer, turned out to be none other than Gordon Muckle of Socialist International renown. His authoritative, booming voice, genuine breadth of knowledge and even-handed approach made him ideally suited to the job of explaining everything that was wrong with society. He was equally uncompromising in his refusal to be bound by the norms of hygiene and dress sense, but the sweet smell of his roll-ups suppressed any body-odour issues and attracted enough hungover students and their nostrils to ensure a full house each Monday morning.

Next phone call was harder. The novelty had worn off and there was little more to observe other than I'd grown another week older away from their lives.

It wasn't too bad with Mum; she'd always enjoyed sharing local gossip and wasn't going to change now. If the subject became too sensitive I could always deflect her with a quick question back.

"How's your studying?"

Bor-ring.

"Er, fine. How's Grandma?"

"Hmm," she said, and through the phone wire I could hear her eyes rolling. "She fell yesterday, went to check and she was moaning and writhing. When I suggested she might need to move into a home she suddenly got better and jumped up faster than Olga Korbut."

"Sounds like she wanted the attention."

"You know her well. Anyway, here's Dad."

"Hi, Dad..."

"Hn."

"How's things?"

"Mm."

"I heard a funny one in the shop today, I asked if they were getting my record magazine in and the shopkeeper said 'I've no ideal'."

"Mhm."

"Took me a moment to work out he was saying 'I've no idea.'"

"Ah. Right, yes. Well, nice to have had a chat. Here's your mum again."

"Hi, forgot to remind you, it's Judith's birthday next week: remember to send a card."

"Everything okay with Dad?"

"Sure. Why?"

"He sounded distracted."

"Oh, you know him: always moaning about the business."

"Okay, speak to you next week. Bye."

Charlie was excited to discover I wrote and performed poetry.

"We should start a punk band," he said. "Can't be that hard."

The Sex Pistols had finally released their album Never Mind The Bollocks, which we listened to on Charlie's Dansette record player. But the Pistols were already passé and there was so much else to choose from: The Clash and Buzzcocks (not The Jam because they were Tories) and XTC, who were only down the road in Swindon.

"I've always wanted to be a singer," Charlie said.

"Okay. Can you sing?"

"Who cares?"

I told him I'd give it some thought, but I wanted to find out first if my performing skills would be called upon for a part in the BUTCH production of Molière.

On the night of the audition there were about thirty of us. Instead of being seen individually, we gave our little presentations in front of the whole group.

Amid this ragtag collection of wannabe Spike Milligans and Ronnie Corbetts, one performer stood out. Joan Biased, as she called herself, bounced on stage wearing a tuxedo, bow tie, waistcoat, top hat, tails, cummerbund – like a star of silent movies. Her hair was cropped short, in a bob, as if to emphasise the masculinity of the outfit, face painted white so it was hard to read her features. Everything about her was mesmerising. All eyes looked to the stage, she looked like she had arrived from another planet.

Then she started singing.

The words were familiar: how many roads must a man walk down had been asked a thousand times in a thousand folk clubs. The power of Dylan's existential clarion call to a better world had diluted over time, reduced to the kind of fortune-cookie philosophy on the posters of student bedroom walls, usually accompanied by a picture of a babbling country stream or a swimming hippopotamus. But I'd never heard it sung like this.

Was it a genuine artistic interpretation, a hideous disharmony of warbling designed to emphasise the despair of man's inevitable propensity to make war? Or was it a joke? Was this another performer, like Kris, challenging the perceptions of her audience? Nobody was sure.

Then she started moving.

She swung her arms away from the body, gesturing to the audience. It was a familiar move, the kind of open-palmed pleading I'd seen singers like Cilla Black and Shirley Bassey perform on Top of the Pops. But she carried on moving her arms further behind, forcing her chest forward but otherwise staying absolutely still.

I had heard dozens of versions of Blowin' in the Wind, but none came close to this rendering.

Somewhere in the caterwauling it was possible to make out another "How many" question, and when she said "deaths" her hands came in a single, violent swift movement from behind her back and rested across her front, folded across her chest like a body in a coffin.

"The answer, my friends, is..." she crooned in notes so low they buzzed through the microphone and vibrated across the room, "a fart."

For an instant there was a silence like death itself, a heart-stopping second of incomprehension before the moment of realisation, followed by a unified guffaw that almost blew the roof off.

It was downhill from there. Joan occupied the stage for a few more minutes, giving Donovan's Universal Soldier and Barry McGuire's Eve of Destruction similar treatment, only without the jokes – or, rather, joke.

She left the stage to a smattering of polite applause. I was on next.

"Good evening," I began, aware that the last few moments could not go unremarked. "I'd like to continue with my own interpretation of the remaining eight verses of Eve of Destruction."

The crowd laughed, relieved. After that first Edinburgh gig I'd performed a few more shows, and each time picked up new skills. I'd learned to acknowledge the mood of the room, and would never have mocked that stranger to her face but understood the advantage of playing to the crowd. I'd spent so much of my teenage life measuring the chasm between popular kids and me in miles not yards. Now I could make a roomful of strangers like me in a moment.

It did make for a slightly awkward exchange when I nipped backstage after to see Joan perched cross-legged by a table in the corner, taking off the white face make up.

"Hello, Barry!" she said cheerily.

She'd removed most of her costume and was wearing only a singlet and pants. I'd never been so close to an attractive woman in such a state of near nakedness, all previous experience of this confined to the pictures I'd seen in Maurice's magazines. Embarrassed by this thought, I turned away, cheeks burning.

She leapt off the table and came towards me, offering her hand, a firm shake and I felt an electric shock of touch that aroused me instantly. I blushed more and shifted my legs in the hope of disguising that, unlike her, I had no control over my body movements.

"Celia," she smiled.

"Barry," I offered jokily. "You know that though, already, of course," I continued, filling the silence awkwardly.

For someone who appeared to have tanked so horribly on stage, she seemed remarkably unflustered. I wondered if she had the slightest inkling of how bad things had gone for her.

She leapt back on to the table and carried on removing her make-up, calm as before. With banalities already used up I had no option but to mention her performance.

"That move you did with the hands was... amazing," I said, groping for a positive.

"So many performers don't even think about their physical presence in the room," she said, animated now, without a "thanks" or an admission that there may have been any part of her gig that wasn't amazing.

"Have you heard of Lecoq?" she asked, and once more I felt an involuntary movement in my trousers. I shifted again, raising my eyebrows in question.

"French meem teacher," she said. Then, registering my bafflement, "Some people pronounce it 'mime'."

Everyone pronounces it with an 'i', I thought.

"I studied under him in Paris. Not *under* him, you get my drift," and she cackled heartily, a big, man's, Sid James laugh that was endearing and inclusive.

I learned that Lecoq was a French sports coach who had become friends with actors in the 1960s, and realised the importance of physical movement in performance. He ran a 'meem' school for actors in Paris, where Celia had studied for two years.

The course was physically demanding, empowering and exciting, she told me, and honestly, if you're even thinking about spending any time on stage, Barry, you need to pay attention to every aspect.

"You've obviously never thought about that," she said, as though tonight's gig had been a triumph for her and a disaster for me.

"Yes" I said, no longer able to hide my irritation, "but I have thought about what the audience for comedy might be expecting."

"Of course. Nothing pleases me more – or them – than fulfilling their expectations. But Barry," she said, moving close, exciting me in a way I'd never felt before, "your body."

"Mhm?

"Do you use it?"

"Suppose not. I have ideas of what I want to say, write them down. Once the words are on the page, I might play around with them a bit. But for me, that's the hard work done."

"Well, it is," she said, leaping back to the table and grabbing a pair of light denim jeans, "if all you care about is writing poetry," and in a single swift movement the trousers were on. "But that's not true with you, is it?"

"What?"

"Why do you perform?" she asked, in a voice muffled by the bright-yellow jumper slipping over her mouth.

"Go on, tell her!" Maurice screamed in my head. "To cop off with beautiful women like you!"

She looked at me, curiously, and I wondered in the stillness of the cold, dank room if she was considering whether she fancied me.

"It's okay," she said, finally. "Some of us take a lifetime to find out. Others just wanna show off."

"What about you?"

She smiled and walked over to me, close, my personal space.

"I am on a journey of artistic exploration. Sometimes the audience choose to come along for the ride. I don't care whether they like it or not."

"You can say that again!" I let out, finally relieved that she was aware that her show had bombed.

"Fancy a drink?" she asked.

"Sure."

We took a table in the corner of the bar and carried on talking over pints of Thatchers cider. Celia was impressive in so many ways – engaging, graceful, articulate, beautiful, the first woman I'd ever met who drank pints of West Country scrumpy – disappointing in others. I didn't want to talk to her anymore about her performance, wanted to find out more about her. She wasn't interested in personal small talk like where we lived and what A levels we got, but spoke entertainingly and at length about different tribes from around the world and their rituals, physical theatre and absurdist comedy.

She nattered with intense excitement about the Situationists, French anarchist actors she knew who challenged all our preconceptions of theatre, unaware that I had none beyond some lazy prejudice that theatre was for toffs.

Ingrid and Charlie came over from a meeting to say hi, but almost as quickly as I introduced her she jumped up and said she had to go. She looked for a moment right into my eyes, smiled in a way no woman had ever smiled at me before, pecked me on the cheek and bounded out.

I walked back to Whittock Hall with Charlie and Ingrid, brain addled by scrumpy and that smile, virginity still intact.

CHAPTER 9

"The Clash! X-Ray Spex! Generation X!"

I'd been half-dozing while writing about Thomas Malthus and his population theory when Charlie rushed in with his scrunched up copy of New Musical Express, listing the bands coming to perform in one massive gig at the Exhibition Centre, Bristol's biggest venue.

The steady trickle of punk records through the summer was turning into a deluge. Proper grown-up musicians swept along by the revolution released albums that harnessed the raw energy and anger of the time to their own popular music-writing skills: Elvis Costello, The Stranglers, Blondie, The Boomtown Rats, The Adverts, and Eddie and The Hot Rods, whose anthem Do Anything You Wanna Do defined working-class aspirations and the do-it-yourself nature of punk.

Rocksy Music sold amateur singles from all over the country, records from Norwich and Cardiff and Bridgwater – Bridgwater! Backwater, as the locals called it, was a farming town in Somerset as far removed from the London scene as it was possible to be. The seven-inch singles were sold in paper bags with badly scrawled labels, but we knew the songs because Peel had played them on national radio.

Charlie and Ingrid were fashionable punk. It wasn't such a leap for him to go from denim to leather, and Ingrid could carry any style with confidence. She hadn't yet elected for the thick fishnet tight and mascara look, but her shirts were now tastefully ripped in strategically safe places and she too opted for the leather jacket. When they walked down the street together, everyone stared and wondered what the hell such a cool couple were doing hanging out with the greasy-haired hippy with less dress sense than their parents. I hadn't yet found the courage to get with the uniform, but my straggly long hair, flared corduroy trousers and tank-top chic was sufficiently unfashionable to be approved of by the punks.

We'd been to a few gigs – tiny rooms in pubs packed with sweaty, leather-jacketed blokes and women with starkly painted faces watching their mates make the kind of music their parents would hate. It was exciting and fun, matching the energy and electricity of that first gig in Edinburgh.

"It's next Friday; me and Ingrid are going and I'm picking up the tickets from Rocksy Music today. Do you want one?"

"Yes, please. How much?"

He scrunched his face. "One pound fifty." I let out an involuntary whistle.

"Well, it's worth it. Bloody hell, The Clash. Hang on, isn't next Friday's meeting Argentina's Missing Activists? Isn't Ingrid…"

"…a massive Clash fan? Yes."

"Good to know she's got her priorities right."

"Yeah, and going to The Clash will be a bit like going to a normal political meeting," he said.

"Only with dancing."

The following Friday I was hanging around in my room getting in the mood for the show, listening to Hanging Around by The Stranglers on my stereo hi-fi, when I was surprised by a knock at the door. I went to open it and almost jumped in shock.

"Hey, Barry."

"Kris!"

"Good to see you mate."

"You too. What's happening?"

"I'm doing a gig here tonight. A pub in Redland. Wanna come?"

"Ahh, sorry mate, got tickets for The Clash tonight."

"Oh, okay. More a Pistols man myself."

"We're going to the pub first. Come and have a drink."

"Sure."

We took a bus into town and caught up on each other's performing news since Edinburgh. Kris knew all about the Situationists, of course, and it was fun making him laugh with my tales of Lecoq. He was full of comedy talk – theatre, too – and he made me laugh when he said he was performing Krapp's Last Tape. He looked at me in mock surprise.

"It's a play by Samuel Beckett," he said.

"Okay," I said, not sure whether to believe him.

Walking through the centre of Bristol, past the Hippodrome (where bands like Genesis played) and the hideous post-war department stores that had emerged from the rubble of the bombed city centre, we noticed a steady flow of young punks weaving in and out of the roads, playing chicken with the traffic and joshing each other to see who could best shock the locals.

Nearly all the punks I'd met at gigs had been sweet, calm and unfailingly polite. Most were still at school; the ones who came to the record shop were invariably shy. Punk was the first tribe they had belonged to. We struck up conversations, swapping stories and recommendations based on Peel tunes heard the night before. I bonded with these strangers, who were exactly like I'd been a couple of years ago.

Not tonight, though. My Leeds United nose had sniffed the potential for trouble.

Charlie and Ingrid were already drinking outside when we arrived at the pub. The Naval Volunteer had a history as graphic as its name suggested, where excited boys the same age as us were plied with booze and signed up to a life of travelling round the world, only to wake from a drunken night to discover they'd been enlisted to fight some hideous imperial war on an ocean in the middle of nowhere.

Kris said hi to Ingrid and Charlie-and my nerves calmed – no awkward silence or embarrassment. Kris went inside, and squeezed into the queue for pints.

"Who's running the meeting tonight?" I asked Ingrid.

"Meeting's cancelled." She smiled. "I was hoping Matt would but he's gonna be here tonight."

"Thought he looked like a bit of a punk fan," I said.

"A fan?" she said. "He's playing bass with The Wasters. Local band. They're first on the bill."

"Oh, my God! Someone I know is in a band!"

A group of punks started singing in the street, the kind of good-natured-bordering-on-hostility chant of the increasingly sozzled football fan. It was one of the better chants; the existence of rival football teams in the same city had caused both sets of fans to up their game. This was a group of Bristol Rovers supporters, singing their anthem "Follow The Rovers" to the tune of Waltzing Matilda.

Kris returned with our drinks; we tried talking but the noise drowned us out. The football fans had walked past but we could see more punks heading towards the venue, jumping into each other and chanting a newer, vaguely familiar song – "White riot! White riot!" A Clash song written earnestly, no doubt, to show solidarity with the brick-throwing black kids who had rioted a few years earlier in immigrant city communities like

Chapeltown, birthplace of my parents and home of my own performing debut. "White riot, white riot!" Hearing it from what sounded like a bunch of drunken football fans, the lyrics took on a different meaning.

Kris and I took a moment away from the others and finished our pints.

"You going back to Birmingham tonight?"

"Yeah. Be finished in time for the last coach."

"Shame you can't stick around longer."

"Hey, listen, I'm running a monthly club for comedy," he said. "Come up to Birmingham some time and do a show for us."

"Sure. Bit of a way to come, though, for a five-minute set."

He smiled, raised his eyebrows, forced me to laugh out loud. You're a performer now, Barry, he must have thought. You go where the gigs are.

"I'll call you sometime," he called as I walked off. "Be in touch."

Whoever chose the Exhibition Centre for this concert had allowed their ambition to overtake cold-headed reality. We were hundreds, impressively, but the main hall was designed to hold two thousand people. Pink Floyd would have struggled to fill this giant, soulless cavern, tall and long, empty for three-quarters of the space.

That didn't mean there was no sense of excitement. Because of the relatively small crowd, you could choose to spectate from a reasonably safe distance, or push to the front and join the shouting, swaying mob, bouncing against each other in what appeared to be a spirit of good-natured anger, if it was possible for there to be such a thing.

Charlie and I were excited about The Wasters, and went close to support Matt. The band got a massive cheer when they came on; a lot of the crowd knew them and had seen them before. A scraggy singer in white t-shirt looked thoroughly pleased with himself, enjoying spotting his mates over performing to the rest of us.

"Wow! Rock-star Matt!" I shouted over the pulsating blast of the PA system.

"What?"

"I said rock-star Matt! Next stop, Madison Square Gardens!"

Charlie smiled and nodded; hadn't heard a word.

Matt was barely visible, dwarfed by the combo of giant speakers to his left. Two songs, three minutes later, they were gone.

We moved back as the crowd nearer the front began to swell. The sound system was blasting out a ton of great numbers – Red Shoes by Elvis Costello, Psycho Killer by Talking Heads, God Save The Queen by The Pistols, of course, the great crowd-pleaser – but the incessant chanting of White Riot was building over it. I lit a cigarette nervously. The nicotine hit cleared my head and for a moment everything was fine. Most of the chanting was good natured but there were a couple of guys whose eyeline I was working hard to avoid. Skinheads, low foreheads, angry faces, combat trousers and expertly shined Dr Martens boots with steel-tipped toe caps, guaranteed to cause maximum damage to heads and groins.

Generation X ran on stage, with purpose. Great name, great looking; here was a bunch of kids born to play in rock bands, who happened to come of age when the bands were punk. The lead singer was drop-dead gorgeous, cheek bones visible from Mars. Some of the women in the audience started screaming like they were at a Bay City Rollers concert – ironically, I was hoping, but couldn't be sure.

As soon as they finished, the familiar and now tedious White Riot chant recommenced. I wanted to go closer to see X-Ray Spex; they weren't as overtly political as The Clash but their mixed-race lead singer Poly Styrene was already one of the more eloquent orators in this growing anti-movement. I moved forward, avoiding the small but increasingly vociferous chorus of White Rioters. The band came on but instead of stopping, this time the chorus grew louder, and angrier, and threatened to drown out the band.

"Who d'you wanna hear?" Poly yelled from the stage. "X-Ray Spex or the fascist twats?"

The crowd cheered and a chant of "X-Ray Spex" started up, an atonal counterpoint to the White Riot mob. A scuffle broke out a few feet to my right. A tall, crop-haired geezer, bigger than the thugs I'd seen earlier and wearing a leather jacket with a swastika painted on the back – not ironic, for sure – leapt on stage and looked to be heading for Poly. The guitarist stuck his foot out, made him trip, carried on playing as if nothing had happened. The band must have been used to this kind of attention. Poly dodged, matter of fact, to one side as a pair of breezeblock bouncers grabbed the thug and threw him back into the crowd. Brutal but effective. His fall was cushioned by friends and enemies alike, but mostly enemies, and he was swiftly raised by two security-guard-shaped tree trunks and escorted out of the building.

The White Riot singing stopped for long enough in the next break to make it possible to talk.

"Unbelievable," said Charlie, who looked traumatised.

"I've never seen anything like it," Ingrid added.

"Reminded me of every Saturday afternoon watching Leeds United."

"You've seen stuff like this before?" she asked.

"I'm Jewish. They're Nazis. We've got history."

The raw excitement of the skinhead movement had turned many teenage boys from weekend hooligans into more serious practitioners of the fighting arts. Gangs co-ordinated calendars to arrive for specified scraps, bike chains replacing fists as the preferred weapon of havoc. In Leeds, Jewish youth clubs were staked out for random acts of violence. Our city, with its infamous football team, rising unemployment and proximity to Bradford's growing Pakistani community, became the central breeding ground for neo-Nazis.

The Clash restored order. Joe Strummer's heartfelt insistence that the anthem of the night was a call for unity with our black brothers and sisters was met with cheers of relief but that didn't make me feel any better. Punk's anti-fashion chic of swastikas and leather caps may have been more of a wind-up than a serious philosophical embrace of Third Reich philosophy, but tonight White Riot had sounded less like an earnest call to multiculturalism and more like a football chant.

CHAPTER 10

The first thing I noticed as the train pulled into Leeds, apart from the teeming sheets of winter sleet smacking persistently against the window; the heart-stopping moment of excitement as we passed Elland Road; row after row of the anonymous 1970s tower blocks, built to replace the row upon row of back-to-back houses; the bleak black Victorian workhouse of a fortress that was Armley Jail; the giant TV mast miles across the dreary fields of Emley Moor... okay, there were so many things to take in on my return to Leeds for the first time in three months, the longest I had ever been away. But for all its fuelling of childhood memories and the fact that so little had changed, it was unfamiliar. I was a tourist in my home town.

A forlorn, balding Christmas tree stood by the Bake'n'Take at Leeds City station. Dog-eared posters of Santa advertising the Christmas and New Year Radio Times festooned the windows of WH Smith, while the now familiar traditional sound of Slade's Merry Xmas Everybody trickled through the tinny tannoy in Boots.

Christmas spirit never found its way into our Jewish household. The Queen's Speech, Morecambe and Wise and a turkey supper on The Big Day were the small concessions to the traditions of our adopted homeland. My parents were easy to spot among the throng of worried mums and dads waiting for their loved ones to return from college: they were the only ones not overwhelmed with bags of useless presents salvaged from an afternoon of elbowing hell among the department stores of The Headrow.

I studied them closely before they'd had a chance to see me, familiarising myself with the physical figures whose lives I'd shared every day for nearly two decades before ceasing contact, like a death. Dad – still tall and handsome for his age, beginning to be worn down by years of grim work and our fractious teenage rebelliousness, I thought. Mum, well into her forties, kind face showing early signs of age. Both solid eastern European stock, a look I'd barely come across in my three months away – how I must have looked to my new friends and acquaintances.

It took a second to adjust my face and pretend I hadn't seen them before they spotted me. Another childhood throwback – never hurt their feelings, always lie. There was an awkward moment with Mum – we both wanted to embrace, but she didn't want to impose and I didn't want to look like a needy child. She offered a cheek, I kissed and put my arm on her waist, offering the faintest of hugs, mixed message, unsatisfying for both of us. I loved Mum, she loved me, but we didn't always know how to show it.

"Look at that shirt," she laughed, suppressing an urge to unfold the creases from three months' neglect of ironing.

I unloaded my scruffy belongings into the boot of dad's Volvo and climbed in the back, the whiff of plastic upholstery reminding me I hadn't been inside a car for three months. Mum and Dad made small talk as I watched the city, housing estates and finally the suburbs fly by.

"You need the car tomorrow, Sybil?"

"Wouldn't mind, Monty, if you can get a lift–"
"–Hnnh, okay–"
"–I've got to pick up Mum's cardy from Marks."
...Clay Pit Lane, Meanwood Road, Buslingthorpe Lane, back in Leeds alright...
"Remember, I'm hosting the Ladies' Zionist Fellowship tomorrow, so you can't watch telly from seven thirty to nine."
...Scott Hall Road, Potternewton Lane, fancy a spliff...
"Judith coming home?" I asked.
"Not this year, love. She's spending Christmas Day at her new boyfriend's in Hendon."
I tried to hide my disappointment but Mum saw through me.
"She'll be here for a couple of days before New Year, though."
"Can you manage without Corrie, Barry?"
"What's that, Dad?"
"You won't be able to watch Coronation Street tomorrow night. Your mother's
got a charity meeting."
"Ah," I said, not really taking in how hard my dad was trying to be nice.
"You're obviously learning a lot down there," he said. "Especially how to speak
in a southern accent."
"Monty," Mum snapped. On the way down she'd probably ordered him not to wind me up.
"I'm surrounded by southerners," I said.
"Aye, northern university not good enough for you."
Mumble grumble. Bloody Leeds.
Bloody home. Here were the dark-red carpets, the beige sofa with frilly cushions, bookcase of Encyclopaedia Britannicas and half a dozen volumes of Jewish prayer books, the wooden

antique tables and Capodimonte lamps. I worried nostalgia might overwhelm me; instead, I felt a longing for Bristol. We had a nice house, I thought, the kind that Pete Seeger might make fun of in an anti-bourgeois folk song. But the more I had learned about Guildford, the more I realised we were several rungs down the middle-class ladder.

I picked up a pile of letters on the kitchen table that Mum hadn't bothered to forward. They were from friends, the bank, school. Few people had my change of address – another link to the past still un-severed.

My bedroom had become another spare room, like the one Judith had long since vacated, an ageing teddy missing one beady eye the only reminder of her life spent there. There were no signs of punk or poetry. I missed having my own stuff, missed Charlie, Kris, the buzz of being around people my age. Charlie was my best friend; we had discovered more common ground beyond music and politics – sense of humour, passion for football, aversion to hard work. He played bass while I strummed guitar. We drank in pubs at night, spent odd after-noons discussing the rising geo-political tension in Iran while watching Kojak re-runs on TV, placing small bets on such questions as "Would Telly Savalas next appear on screen with or without his hat?"

Most of the mail was rubbish, but the letter from the bank was unwelcome.

"Dear Mr Goldman," it began, politely enough. "According to our records, your account has become overdrawn, and stands currently at minus £46.32p. Please rectify this immediately." – all civility abandoned – "In the meantime, we have charged you £10 for going overdrawn." Thanks, so that's minus £56.32p.

This would look bad. Dad would gloat after I'd snapped that I was perfectly capable of handling my own finances. I took the only possible course of action: hide the letter and hope he wouldn't find out before the next grant cheque arrived.

"Staying in tonight, Barry," Mum asked – or said – over supper.

"Sure," I said, to her relief. "Haven't made any plans." No money. Can't go out.

"There's a film about Entebbe on the telly."

"Mhm?"

"It's got Liz Taylor in it, Burt Lancaster," said Mum, as if this might sway me.

"Sure."

She returned to the kitchen, satisfied for now.

Earlier that year, a plane of Israeli passengers had been hijacked by Palestinians and flown to Entebbe Airport in Uganda. Israeli soldiers had stormed the plane, killing the hijackers and freeing the hostages.

The hijacking was carried out with the help of Uganda's dictatorial president, Idi Amin, and could have provoked another Middle East war. By any definition, it was completely unjustified. Yet, in my default teenage position, suspicious of every move made by Israel, I'd felt uneasy about the 'victory', and the gung-ho celebrations afterwards. I didn't want to spoil today's Return of the Prodigal with a row about bloody Palestine.

I switched off my mind and tried thinking happy thoughts: autumn sunshine across the Bristol Downs, golden leaves falling across the paths of Brandon Hill, with its glorious, uninterrupted view of the rolling Mendip Hills. England's green and pleasant non-Jewish land.

"Imagine if they'd got away with it," said Dad, spoiling for a fight. I said nothing.

"Given in to that bastard Amin. Then what?"

I wondered what Kris was doing right now.

"Might as well hand Israel over to Arafat."

"Mhm," I said, neutrally.

For years, our row about Israel had gone round in circles because we were trapped, neither of us going anywhere. Now I had left.

"Dad, it's the holidays. Let's not argue."

I felt sad, wanted to hug the man whose every waking moment was consumed with business worries.

"What is there to argue about? A bunch of Arabs hijacked a plane and threatened to kill dozens of innocent civilians."

I was an adult now, free to talk to him about adult things. I wondered if he'd ever talk to me about how he felt towards his parents.

"Can we agree to differ?"

"No. Because you're wrong, and it's time you started supporting Israel properly."

"I can't support a state that illegally occupies Palestinian territory–" Aarrggh, he'd done it: he'd wound me up! I took the bait!

"–In 1948 they offered everyone the chance to leave in peace. It was only the Arabs who stayed to fight who got killed."

"Fine, fine, if you say so," I tried, which was worse.

"Israel is a legal country, recognised by the whole world–"

"–Yes, yes, it is–" This isn't about Israel, Dad, is it? It's about your work worries.

"–a good, democratic country that treats its citizens well–"

"–absolutely–"

"–admired by everyone apart from a few Arabs who want to wipe us off the map."

He ran out of steam, coincidentally as Mum returned with a bowl of steaming hot custard.

"Dad, I'm a student, in Bristol. Got my life there. Let's not talk about Israel."

Dad thought about this for a moment and smiled apologetically.

"Okay, Barry. Sorry. Tell me all about your life in Bristol."

Right. I'm broke. Went to a talk about Israel being a racist state. Smoked pot for the first time. Saw actual proper Nazis, in England, at a punk gig. Yes, I'm a punk rocker now, Dad; try putting that in charge of your family business.

"I quite like the course. And I've met some nice people." Still a virgin.

"How are the finances?"

"Ah – actually now you mention it... I was wondering... just to tide me over... if I could borrow a hundred quid or so?"

He laughed and smiled, not like the Dad I knew and loved; my question had taken him to another place I hadn't seen before. He looked at Mum, she looked back, shook her head sternly – a kind of "Don't tell Barry" look, which was ridiculous, seeing as I was literally two feet away from her.

"Sure," Dad said. "A hundred pounds might be possible. Got a bit of a Christmas rush on. Could use an extra pair of hands over the holidays."

"You want me to work at the factory?"

"Why not? Might as well familiarise yourself with the place. You need a hundred pounds, that's how most people get a hundred pounds; they take a job and work for it."

"But... what about my course work?" and I must have gone bright red because Mum laughed and I chuckled slightly, found out in that moment as having lied every Friday night about how hard I was working.

"Cutting patterns. Take you five minutes to learn."

"Okay."

"Start tomorrow. Leaving the house at eight o'clock."

Offered the perfect moment to discuss my changing views about joining the family business, so soon after our Israel row felt like a bad time. I wondered if there'd ever be a good time, or even then if I'd be brave enough to take the chance.

CHAPTER 11

The unremittingly dark, grey factory of H Goldman and Son Quality Outfitters hummed like a drone. The relentless rhythm of automated sewing machines, a bright strip light above my head, Mohammed singing some kind of tuneless dirge three feet away. It was new when Queen Victoria was alive but had barely been modernised since. In busier times, there would have been a hundred people working here; today, there were maybe half that.

The work was, as Dad had said, straightforward. Cut the cardboard around the pattern, find the colour material as written on the pattern, place the cardboard on the material, cut around it, gather together the finished samples and take them to Ron on the first floor.

Trips to the first floor were always exciting. The partially glass roof was less filthy and natural light flowed in. Ron was a laugh; he was big and fat and made jokes all the time, and was surprised when I joked back. He was wary, as well he might be: how was he supposed to communicate with the boss's son? Dad had warned me not to get too friendly with the workers; there were sensitive negotiations going on, and it wouldn't help to be joking among the agitators against the filthy capitalist who had fed and clothed him, educated him enough to conclude that the world's biggest problem was filthy capitalists.

Ron couldn't stop me joking about Leeds United, or last night's TV, or being entertained by his banter with Julie the secretary – "Morning, luv, two sugars, please." "Two sugars?" she replied, looking at his stomach. "You on a diet, Ron?", and Ron would turn his big fat face away from her in shock like a prim aunt who had accidentally overheard the word "knickers".

Mohammed, not much older than me, was always smiling, the butt of jokes among the workers but he took it all with politeness and good grace. They were also wary of him. We children of immigrants developed an unspoken bond through this, although he was quite religious and while I was there he spent a lot of the time preparing for a fast and the approach of Islamic New Year. Fasting was what religious people did, that was as much knowledge as I thought I required on the subject.

The others had learned over time not to invite Mohammed to the pub at lunchtime, but felt sufficiently comfortable to ask me to join them for a pre-Christmas drink. Dad, head buried in ledgers strewn across his desk and preoccupied with the information they had to impart, nodded unthinkingly as I asked if it was okay for me to go for a swift one with the workers.

Decades ago, the streets around the Bricklayers Arms would have bustled with builders and weavers, painters and stitchers, and presumably enough bricklayers to have a pub to themselves. Now it stood alone, yet hardly triumphant, in what must once have been a row of shops – a solitary, seedy, run-down joint, broken bricks sprawled on either side like the punchline to a bad joke, remnants of a forgotten manufacturing hub transformed into a National Car Park.

Westgate Olympic swimming pool, on the other side of the car park, told two stories of Leeds, past and present: the one about the city shaking off its grimy, industrial past, redefining itself with a bold, modern structure to bring pride and business to this neglected back-end of town; the other about a discredited council still paying off the way-over-budget white elephant, with its incorrect Olympic pool specifications and architect John Poulson who had been jailed for bribery and corruption.

The pub was as dark and dank as the factory, but at least they sold beer. A few old men sat still and silent, together but drinking alone, a smattering of flat caps, false teeth and fingers gnarled and yellow from years of tobacco and drudgery.

"Pint of mild, Jim. What you having, Barry?"

"Oh, it's okay. Don't worry, Ron—"

"—Bloody Nora, can't even buy the boss's son a drink. Against union rules?"

"Okay, buy me a drink and I'll put in a good word for you. Half a bitter, please, Ron."

"Hear that Jim? Pint of bitter for the boss's son. Arrows please, pal. You a sporting man, Barry?" Ron asked, as Jim handed three golden darts to the portly stitcher.

"Do I look like one?" I asked. "Then again, do you?"

"Ron's sharp," said Julie. "One of the best."

"Come and have a game of arrows. Jim!" The barman unsmilingly handed me three vastly inferior-looking darts. Jim had three strands of hair brushed across the top of his head in an attempt to hide his baldness but serving only to highlight it.

"Wasn't sure you'd be a drinking chap," said Ron, emphasising the last word in a mannered voice to acknowledge the social and cultural chasm between us.

"I'm a student," I said, emphasising the last word as he had, and Ron boomed his familiar laugh, as big as the belly it came from; you could hear it at work cut through the thrum of the machinery and rumble across the factory floor.

"We've got a right one here," laughed Julie, alive to the novelty of the temporary removal of the barrier of professional

formality between her and the Goldman family. It was a satis-
fying moment: I was learning, through performance, how to
win over a roomful of strangers.

I knew my place, and they knew theirs, but laughter cut
across class boundaries, and a sudden involuntary stiffness
below entertained for a fleeting moment the thought of a quick
snog behind the stationery cupboard, like two characters in a
sitcom: the boss's son and the pretty secretary.

"Watch what you say, though," said Ron, pushing the
boundaries. "He might be handing us our pay packets in a
couple of years."

"I don't think so," I smiled.

"But it's a family business," Julie said, looking concerned,
wondering if I knew something they didn't. I did. They saw a
greedy management refusing to pay them more; I knew money
was tight. My internationalist approach to employment and
solidarity with clothing workers across the globe was not going
to effect an immediate wage rise for their Taiwanese brothers
and sisters, and it wasn't going to put any more food on their
tables. My knowledge was my power, and now was not the time
to share it.

"I write poetry. I could no more run a business than Ron
could run the marathon."

They laughed, equilibrium restored. Ron walked to the
dartboard, chalked our names and the number '501' under
each: the number of points required to win a round.

I'd played darts once or twice in the common room at
Whittock Hall – a novelty to the Guildford fellows, but I was
familiar with the game. Every pub in Leeds had a board. The
maths students were especially impressed at my ability to
count backwards from 501.

This was the first time I'd seen Ron take anything seriously.
He fixed his gaze ahead, at a slight angle to the board, still like

a statue, arms by his side, then slowly, dart in right hand, he drew his arm into the gunsights of his eyes. If he'd been a rugby player, his considerable bulk would have been used as a human battering ram; here, all seventeen stones of Ron was fixing his feet to the ground. In slow motion, his arm tensed back like the string and spring of a bow, hesitated for a moment, then snap! The dart shot out of his hand and pierced the lower black oblong of number twenty, barely a couple of millimetres shy of the much smaller section which would have scored him triple twenty, or sixty points.

If he was annoyed, he didn't show it. The same ritual began, only now, using that first dart as his place-maker, he exploited its proximity to guide the next one and it landed with a satis-fying thwack, comfortably inside the small red rectangle that scored him sixty – and again, with his final dart, another sixty. I may have fancied myself as a writer but Ron's performance was poetry. He strolled up to the board, in a simple movement extracted the darts, and chalked the number '361' under his 501, returning to the table and the welcoming dimples of his chunky glass of beer.

My go. I wasn't unused to performance pressure, but this was different. How should I approach this? I may have been out of my depth, about to take a hit for the toffs, yet in the game of life I held all the arrows.

"Stop overthinking it, you daft 'aporth," Ron called. "Throw the buggers."

I tried to remember Ron's stance, then, peering ahead, threw my first dart – thud – nineteen! Not bad. In truth, I'd been aiming, like Ron, for triple twenty, but my darts were much heavier than his and I could see mine drifting lower in flight. Next dart – damn! Just outside the top of the board, narrowly missing double twenty, or double top as we experts called it. I'd over-compensated for the previous dart and this was too high. Number three – whack – comfortably inside the twenty cheese wedge, a miserable thirty-nine total for my darts, I chalked up '462' and stepped away.

"Can I use your darts, Ron?"

He raised his arm as if to clock me one, comedy style.

"No, lad, but you can have a feel."

He handed over one of his precious babies, allowing me to admire the craftsmanship. Ron's missile was shiny where mine was drab, the shaft streamlined while mine was clunky and his feathers delicate and designed aeronautically, unlike the crude, plastic lumps at the top of my darts. I made all the right approving noises and handed it back carefully, proud to have been accepted enough to touch Ron's prized jewels.

Ron threw his next three arrows: another 140 and he was down to 221.

"Five more arrows could do it," he told me. "three triple twenties, nineteen and a double eleven."

I threw again, determined this time to develop a style that was more in keeping with my body shape. I shook my shoulders, that felt right, my buttocks were clenching and thud! Double top.

"Ay up," laughed Ron, "it's the ruptured duck."

I could only manage two more twenties down to 382 – still worse than Ron had managed after one throw.

He walked up to the oche in an exaggerated mime of how I had, stood like me, threw like me, and still managed to score triple twenty.

"Good stance, Barry," he said. "I might try that again some time." He threw another triple twenty, and then, with a flourish, nineteen.

"You're toying with me now," I said, and gamely threw my darts: two more twenties and one that thwacked promisingly into the triple nineteen wire, only to bounce annoyingly out and onto the floor.

Ron needed eighty-two to win. He took an extra moment, like he was nervous, then threw his first dart, almost randomly. Triple twenty: twenty-two required. Second dart landed as slap in the middle of double eleven as it was possible to do. Third dart not required. Applause rippled around the pub. Maybe that was what brought the old men here every lunchtime. Ron was an extraordinary darts player.

My work that afternoon was almost as wayward as my dart throwing. I'd never drunk a whole pint at lunchtime and suddenly the act of cutting cardboard with a large pair of scissors was an almost impossible task. The alcohol loosened my inhibitions and I found myself for the first time initiating conversations with Mohammed.

"Did you know Ron is a brilliant darts player?"

"I was unaware."

"Amazing. Played him down at the Brickies. You should join us one day."

"I'd love to, pal," he said in his thick Leeds accent, "but I don't drink alcohol."

"Me neither, not much anyway. In fact, I reckon my dad will go mad when he realises."

"I shouldn't think so. Mr Monty is a kind and decent man."

"Really?"

It always jolted me when my dad was referred to as Mr Monty, to differentiate from when his dad, Mr Ralph, had worked here. "Mr Goldman" would have been confusing. Whenever Mum phoned Dad at the factory she'd say: "Can I speak to Mr Monty, please? It's Mrs Monty."

"No, no, no, trust me: I've worked for some pretty rotten types over the years."

"How old are you, Mohammed?"

"I'll be twenty in April."

"How long have you been working?"

"Since I left school. Nearly five years. Been called all sorts since I started. Not your dad, though. He's the best."

That evening, I stayed late in the office. With the holidays approaching, there had been an air of strained celebration. Everybody knew the business was struggling but there was also a sense that Dad would pull through, because he always had.

I felt bad about arguing with him the day before, and offered to help more as he combed his way through the giant ledgers on his desk, face grimacing tightly in concentration and fear. I asked what I could do but he wasn't listening. His mind was somewhere else, brown eyes staring somewhere in the middle distance and – something I'd never seen before – they were moist.

"Let's get to it, champ," I said unthinkingly, although later I realised that, in borrowing his favourite phrase from my childhood, I was at that moment reversing the hierarchy – taking over the less-remarked-on family business of parenting, and he was the child.

CHAPTER 12

Two days into January, 1978 was more or less indistinguishable from 1977. It was still cold and misty and rainy, I was still single, still a virgin, still in Leeds. United were at home to Newcastle. Maurice had called a few days earlier to check if I was going.

"You look different," was the first thing he said when we met at the thirty-four bus stop. "Student life has changed you."

"You don't. Student life hasn't touched you."

"Yeah, there's becoming a student, and there's doing business studies at Leeds Polytechnic. Still living with my parents."

"You must have met loads of new people, though?"

"Nah. I'm with the rest of the Leeds Jews too thick to get away like you. How's Bristols?" he asked, weighing his imaginary breasts as he said the name. "Teeming with shicksas, I bet."

"I am a novelty," I said, as we stepped onto the bus. "You don't get many of us there. Northerners."

"So come on, you must have done it by now with a non-Yiddishe southern mama?"

"Why are you so obsessed with sex?"

"Why do you pretend not to be?"

"Whatever happened with you and Harriet?"

"Yeah, well," Maurice sighed, and I waited for elaboration. He looked out of the bus window, but there was nothing to see apart from drizzle and grey clouds. I waited for him to turn back, to hear some forlorn tale of unrequited love, but he carried on staring.

We kept clear of the subject for a while, making Leeds United small talk as we huddled along Lowfields Road with the rest of the blindly loyal football faithful.

He told me about his boring course, how his parents were planning to retire soon and expected him to go into business. He wasn't bothered that they saw him as an economic asset. It wasn't until we settled into our sardine-cramped seats at the back of the Elland Road stand that I tried again.

"Come on, Maurice, you and Harriet. Did you do it? What happened?"

"Nothing bloody happened."

"The way you were talking before Edinburgh, sounded like you were writing the wedding invitations."

"Nothing happened. Nothing was ever going to happen. Now watch the bloody football like all the normal people here."

Maurice and I had sat here for years and witnessed glorious victories and epic defeats. Today was the kind of pitiful display we had grown accustomed to more recently. The athletic Gods of our youth were now middle-aged mortals with paunches, and the only swiftness they displayed was to temper. Newcastle were toying with us.

"When did you know nothing was going to happen?"

"What?"

"At what point last summer, when Harriet and I were getting on so well at her brother's in Edinburgh, at what point did you realise she and you were not going to happen?"

"I'd have thought that was obvious."

He looked at me like I was a child.

"I realised it at the point it was obvious she was mad about you."

"Hey?"

"I mean, come on, Barry. Plays, poetry, jokes about Samuel Belfitt."

"Beckett. Rod Belfitt's our reserve striker."

"Whatever."

Newcastle scored.

The rain poured.

"Anyone could see she wasn't interested in me. It's not my fault you're such a wimp that you don't even try and make a move."

"Maurice!"

"Come on, admit it. You had a brilliant time there, didn't you?"

He had a point. Unlike Leeds, who lost two-nil, beginning 1978 as they had ended 1977.

It was a grim, unutterably awful journey back into town, wet and dark, bus heaving with angry, irritated Leeds supporters. There were enough dads and sons to keep the atmosphere reasonably civil, but a small gang of crop-haired, leather-jacketed teenagers swore defiantly and sang aggressively for the whole journey. One or two had the anarchist sign painted on their jackets, but most had "NF" daubed across the back. No Future, The Sex Pistols had sung, then later No Fun, a cover of a song by The Stooges: these had become two of punk's most popular catchphrases. But round here we all knew that that wasn't what the letters stood for. The National Front was in the ascendant, and racist hooligans who signed up for the party were everywhere – punk gigs, football matches, my local youth club and now this bus.

We'd laughed at them in our schooldays, when they were viewed as an eccentric minority, chased them off Soldiers' Field at Roundhay Park when they'd warned us they were coming for the Jews, but they were few then and we were many. Now, their numbers were growing and their time, they were sure, was coming.

On the way back from football, I made a dutiful visit to Grandma, who was "unwell", according to quotation marks added by Mum after she handed me the spare keys.

Becky lived in a compact, modern block of flats round the corner from us. Inside always smelled of chicken soup, boiled potatoes and Jewish grandmother. It was late afternoon, midwinter dark, but whatever the season it was always dark in Grandma's bedroom.

I felt slightly sorry for her, alone since Grandpa had died and with little by way of entertainment, apart from her weekly game of rummy with the widows from across the corridor. But whenever I came round it was like watching a melodrama set in a gloomy bedroom where the matriarch held court, pale and sickly and weak of voice, on her movie-scene death bed.

"Oh," she said, expressing surprise to see me, disappointment that I wasn't someone else, probably Mum bringing her tonight's meal. "Nice to see you," she said with unusual warmth, maybe sensitive to the let-down my arrival had symbolised.

"How are you feeling today?" I asked, arranging my features into a look of social workerly concern.

"Better, thanks," she said. "Sleep not so interrupted last night."

"Can I get you anything?"

"Oh, no, don't you worry." Who said I was worried, Grandma? I was being polite. Anyway, not sure you know the meaning of that word; let me get you a dictionary.

"Shouldn't you be at university?"

"Heading back next week."

"Bristol, isn't it?" Here we go...

"Yes, Grandma, that's right."

For a moment she sat in silence, and I wondered if she was seriously considering not mentioning It.

"Not many Jews in Bristol." Bingo! Grandma's statistical knowledge of the whereabouts of the entire Jewish population in Britain was peerless. "A lot of anti-Semites there."

"Thankfully I've not met any yet, Grandma."

"Judith's in London. Why didn't you go there?" Too many Jews, Grandma.

"Barry," she said, as though a new thought had entered her head. "Can I ask you a question?"

"Sure."

She adjusted the pillows behind her, and turned to look at me, like we were two adults having a proper conversation.

"Do you think Judith will get married?"

"I don't know, Grandma. I think she has a boyfriend."

I shuffled uneasily on the wicker chair by her bed. She'd never spoken like this to me before.

"That girl is so lucky."

"You think?"

"In your mother's day, a woman could go to university or get married. You couldn't do both. Such a clever girl, she was. Should have gone to university."

"Would you have been happy for that?"

"Of course!" she snapped in a more familiar tone. "Swept off her feet, she was. Your dad would be more than enough, she said." Ah, right, we're back on the more familiar territory: having a go at Dad.

"They're a good team," I said loyally.

"Yes," she almost conceded. "She's a good daughter."

"He's a good father."

She didn't answer for a while. Didn't disagree, which was progress, I thought.

"Well, I'd better be heading back, Grandma. Nice to see you."
"Come again before you go off."
"Sure."
"Barry," she said. "Don't go into the family business."
"Okay..."
"Find a steady job. Do something else. Take care," she said and turned back to signify that the scene was over, and I should leave.

As soon as I got home, I rang Harriet and arranged to meet for a drink at the Friesian Cow. She had settled straight away into university life, energised by the intellectual challenge of English literature at Oxford University, finally meeting people capable of stretching her brain power, unlike the dullards who had plodded in her shadow through Leeds Girls' High School.

"Honestly, Barry, it's so intense. We had to read the whole Jane Austen canon in two weeks, and all the criticisms, then they gave us less than a fortnight to write up our own essays: five thousand words!"

I nodded and smiled, turning my half pint of Tetley's Bitter round the sodden mat, too shy of my ignorance to ask what a Jane Austen cannon was.

"My tutor, you won't believe it, Marcus Riley, he's one of the greatest authorities on eighteenth-century literature, I'm so lucky."

"I've got a bloke who's written at least three pamphlets about the use of our police force as agents of state suppression."

"How's your course going? She finally remembered to ask."

"Ha, it's okay; not quite as excited by the subject matter."

"Why aren't you studying English literature?"

"I, ah –"

"For your poetry? Which I love."

"Really?" I blushed. "Didn't cross my mind. I quite like reading. Analysing not so much."

"It's so not like that. Reading literature every day, it gives you a feel for the language, the rhythm. You should change."

"Perhaps."

"I hope you don't mind, I quoted some of your lines to Marcus and he was blown away."

I raised my eyebrows, amazed.

"He said some of it reminded him of Belloc."

"You sure he didn't say it was Bellocs?"

She laughed again, like when we were all relaxed in Edinburgh. How could I have missed the signals?

"You'd like Marcus: he's funny, too. You should meet him. Come and stay with me one weekend."

"Sure," I said. "You and Marcus... are you..."

"What? Well, no, he's my tutor, he's eight years older than me. Now you mention it, though, I wonder if sometimes ... I don't know, I find relationships quite hard to understand. I don't read the signs."

"Me too."

"Really? Ever thought you fancied someone but that they didn't fancy you, then later you find out they were really keen on you after all? Has that ever happened to you?"

"Now you mention it... how about you? You're saying it's happened to you?" I paused, savouring the moment. "When was the last time?"

Harriet blushed.

"You really want me to tell you?"

At that moment I was more in love than I'd ever been.

"Go on."

She sighed. "Okay. I... I had, I don't know, I was really keen on Maurice Harvey."

"Mhm."

"You know the rest: he came to Edinburgh and spent the whole time in a rotten mood and I had no idea why, but I thought if he wanted to tell me he would. Then right at the end, before you left, he poured his heart out to me. But he'd been acting like such an idiot the whole time we were there I'd gone off him completely by then."

"Maurice, eh? Aren't you two a bit...? I mean, even chalk and cheese share two letters."

"Ha! I know it's unlikely, but you know what they say about opposites attracting."

Sure. I also know what they say about poets and poetry lovers, for all the bloody good it appears to be doing me.

"I shouldn't have said anything. I know he's your friend; don't tell him I told you."

"Of course not," I said. Don't worry, I won't say a word – not yet, anyway. Withholding that piece of information was the only pleasure I'd take from this miserable episode.

"What do you want, Barry?" Yoko asked later that night. Most of my records were in Bristol but a few reminders of my early lovers remained in Leeds.

"I don't know. Meet someone? Fall in love. Lose my virginity?"

"That wasn't my question," Yoko sighed.

"Sounded like it to me, pal," I said in my thickest Yorkshire accent.

"What are you looking for in a relationship?"

"How can he know until he's in it?" asked Joni. "Isn't that the magic of love?"

"It's the magic of fairy tales and the silver screen," said Yoko. "You've been sold the unattainable dream, Joni, of fulfilled desire."

"Each relationship teaches me something new. Even if it teaches me not to screw up again with that kind of guy."

Joni was less combative these days.

"Is that how you see love? As a process of elimination?"

"It's like art," said Joni. "Each affair brings you closer to the truth. Sometimes it can happen. Keeping it real, that's the hard part."

"Sorry to interrupt," I humphed. "Your love life is all guys lining up to ask you out. Mine is about listening to their records."

"That was the point of my first question," said Yoko. "You call yourself a feminist, but it's still all about you: the male needs."

"To meet someone, to fall in love," Joni mimicked me gently, attempting an English accent, "to lose my virginity."

"That was terrible!" laughed Yoko. "Believe me, no Englishman ever spoke like that."

It was nice to see the two of them bonding, at my expense. Both had come through difficult times and were happier now. Yoko was a mum. John, who had achieved so much in his youth, had stumbled drunkenly through the mid-life crisis of his early thirties and was still young enough to become a dad again, at thirty-five. Like everything else in his life he was a pioneer, modelling a novel character I'd only started to hear about: the stay-at-home house husband. John, incredible as it seemed when looking back on his previous life, his mean lyrics about girls, and women – in one song, when a woman refuses to go out with him he sets fire to her furniture, for crying out loud – had become a women's libber.

"You're trying too hard," Joni said, gently. "Love happens when you're looking elsewhere."

Joni had come through a period of introspection and despair and was more in love than I'd ever seen. This affair began slowly; her new lover hung out in small, smoky bars and shunned popularity. His name was jazz and, unlike her previous lovers, didn't come on to her: she found it, and began to get to know it. Slowly at first, in a couple of songs on The

Hissing of Summer Lawns, then more boldly, dancing in the dark moods of Hejira – and, now, with Don Juan's Reckless Daughter, she'd truly embraced the form.

"That," I said, "is not helpful."

"'Life is what happens to you while you're busy making other plans'," said Yoko.

"Ooh, I like that," said Joni. "I don't always understand your little sayings but that one works for me."

"Not one of mine," she sighed. "I read it on the back of an old Reader's Digest."

Joni hadn't surrendered herself to jazz. Like everything and everyone else in her life, jazz was taken, tinkered with and bent into shape so that by the time she did it, it wasn't jazz at all. Joni allowed people like me to enjoy it without having to profess a liking of the form. It was one more addition to the Joni rock-folk-soul experiment, a love that was not a process of elimination, as Yoko had mocked it, but an accumulation of passion and experience towards a life that would be complete only at its end.

The next day at the factory, Mohammed was no longer there. At lunchtime, I found Dad and asked why.

"It's not your business," he answered sharply, still capable of scaring me despite my age.

"Did he do anything wrong?"

"There's not enough work. We had to lay him off."

"Then how come I'm here?"

"You're cheaper."

He walked away before I could reply. That night at tea, I told Dad I wasn't going back and he should reinstate Mohammed.

"If you'd rather not have the money that's your loss."

"Mohammed's a hard worker."

"What's that got to do with you?"

"And he worships you."

Dad looked at me, surprised, then turned away. We carried on eating in sullen silence for a few moments. Mum looked over to her two blokes, silent, unable to take sides.

"Listen, Barry. You don't know anything. Anything. Until you come back and start working properly for me, not hanging round with the riff raff and coming back from lunch stinking of beer, you get no say in it."

"Don't worry, I won't be back. Ever!"

"Barry!" Mum cried.

"Get yourself a proper businessman to run your poxy factory."

Dad looked at me, wounded, as I stormed out and up to my room.

That told them. I could have used the extra cash but principles were more important. Ascending the moral high ground where the air was pure, I quit working for Mr Monty - a full day before my time was up.

CHAPTER 13

The incredible year of punk had ended with Mull of Kintyre spending Christmas and January at number one, closely followed by Floral Dance by the Brighouse and Rastrick Band featuring Terry Wogan.

According to Johnny Rotten, punk died at the start of 1978. "Ever get the feeling you've been cheated?" he sneered as he stepped off Winterland stage in San Francisco as Johnny Rotten for the final time, a fitting end to the short but spectacular career of the Sex Pistols, the band that had changed everything, forever.

But in the rest of the world, it had barely begun. Punk tore down the walls that existed, largely in our heads, between the Gods on high and worshippers below. Musicians would throw themselves off stage and into the audience as Kris had done the first time I'd seen him, utterly assured that the crowd would catch them and throw them back. Each time it happened, the line between performer and spectator blurred. That's me in the crowd, those are my friends on stage, tomorrow it could be the other way round.

Up and down the country, teenage punks were setting up bands on Monday, writing songs on Tuesday, rehearsing on

Wednesday, playing their first gigs on Friday and splitting up due to musical differences on Sunday. By the following Monday, they had become four new bands.

Charlie and I were determined to form our own and spent three hours on a wet Sunday afternoon working on the vitally important priority of thinking up a name. Having discussed and dismissed The Heartless Pigs, Stunted Union, Shittock Hall, Whittock's Bollocks, Whiteladies Riot, Ingrid's Toaster and Japanese Railway Systems, we settled on Student Grunt.

As if that wasn't hard enough, writing a recruitment notice for the band proved tougher. Negotiating into the night, we finally agreed on a wording that pleased neither of us but we finally became too exhausted to reframe, and posted it on the notice board of Whittock Hall Common Room:

Wanted: drummer, bass player for new punk band: STU-DENT GRUNT. Influences Pistols, Clash, XTC, Talking Heads, Costello, Stranglers, Saints, Generation X, Cortinas, Chelsea, Damned. Own gear essential, van an asset, no time wasters. Auditions Room B26 Sunday 23rd 2 pm.

The only bands in that list we agreed on were the Pistols and Cortinas. After last year's Exhibition Hall fiasco I'd gone off The Clash, and we argued for nearly an hour about their bourgeois tendencies. I didn't want to include them, but for Charlie their presence was non-negotiable.

"What are we if we're not trying to change the world?" he asked. "Joe is holding up the signpost," he said, like he and Strummer were best mates. I thought that was rubbish but was pacified by the inclusion of the much-mocked Damned, whose 1976 single New Rose was the first punk hit and, in my view, yet to be surpassed, and XTC, whose discordant guitar solos among their big pop tunes set Charlie's teeth on edge.

The only phrase we both agreed on was "no time wasters", although we had no idea what it meant, but it was on every advert we'd ever seen for bands.

After all this, learning to play instruments, write songs, rehearse and perform would be a doddle.

We were both working hard to conceal our surprise and disappointment when, half an hour after the specified time on the advert, we hadn't had a single enquiry.

"Do you think there aren't many punk fans in Whittock Hall?" Charlie asked me at 2.30 pm on Sunday 23rd in B26, otherwise known as my bedroom. He'd been sitting on my bed for half an hour, while I'd been slouched over my crappy acoustic guitar, working out chords to songs we'd like to learn. So far, we'd settled on Bodies by the Sex Pistols, and a punk version of the nursery rhyme Goosey, Goosey Gander. I'd thrown in a couple of my own half-formed ideas, but even I understood there was no place in the repertoire of Student Grunt for the Joni Mitchellness of their sentiment and melody.

"Maybe there aren't *any* punks in Whittock Hall," I said.

Me on guitar and Charlie on vocals sounded less like the Pistols and more like Simon and Garfunkel, if Garfunkel was rubbish at singing and Simon awful on guitar.

"I'm bored now," said Ingrid, who had agreed to join us for the afternoon, promising a different perspective on the cast of hopefuls we had expected, with diminishing optimism, to have been queuing down the corridor.

Ingrid shared my views about The Clash. Like me, she had grown up as an outsider, her Swedish family having moved around Europe with her father's job at NATO. Charlie had been relieved to learn he was not a military man but an administrator, although what little I'd discovered about his own background so far suggested a family with links to some of the former glory days of British imperialism. He'd surprised us both one drunken evening, revealing his birthplace had not been some anonymous maternity ward in Guildford but under the care of the British Hospital in Bombay, his father's final posting abroad before ending his career in one of the few remaining job locations of the Empire – Britain.

"Whatever turns people onto punk has bypassed Whittock Hall," I said.

We didn't belong in their world, which was already mapped out for them. Oh no, we were the fun group, the pioneers, the new leaders, except our idea of fun currently involved sitting in my bedroom auditioning for a punk band, only the band didn't exist yet and nobody wanted to be a part of it. Another hour passed and we'd given up before there was a knock on the door.

"Come in."

And if by now the idea that anyone would audition for us seemed like an absurd idea, it was even more of a shock when the door opened and Celia walked in.

I didn't realise quite how long and awkward my silence had been until Celia asked,

"Oh, I'm sorry, am I too late?"

"No, no," Charlie said. "Come in, come in. Please!"

"My shift didn't finish until a few minutes ago so I couldn't make it any sooner."

"No no, it's fine," I said, delighted but confused by her presence.

She took off her long, slender grey coat and hung it next to my Marks and Spencer dressing gown, a perfectly mismatched couple. She was wearing a grey tabard over a dark sweater and a pair of worn out jeans and sensible trainers.

"Have you seen many people?" Celia asked. Ingrid instinctively laughed, rendering obsolete any prospect of lying.

"Not a soul," I said. "It's great to see you. Charlie, Ingrid, this is Celia. We met at a comedy thing last year."

"Thing is, we're kind of covered for singing," said Charlie.

"The advert said you were looking for a drummer."

"Oh great, you're a drummer," I said.

"Yes...?" she said, then, when a response didn't come, "Only, I don't see a drum kit."

"No," said Charlie, "We don't have one ourselves."

"Right," said Celia. "And you were expecting a drummer to bring their kit to the audition?"

Charlie and I looked at each other, embarrassed. I wondered if "no time wasters" referred to us.

"How did you find out about the band?" asked Ingrid, which was probably the first question we should have thought of.

"I work here," she said. Then, off the blank looks, "In the kitchens, preparing the food. You don't really see us."

A worker in our midst! A member of the downtrodden masses we were so keen to stand up for. Our servant.

"Saw your advert the other day in the common room. Had no idea it was you."

"Do you have a drum kit?" Charlie asked.

"Not a full one," she said. "Bass, snare, hi-hat."

"That's great," I said. "Remember Wreckless Eric at the Exhibition Centre the other week?"

"That's right," said Charlie, "Ian Dury on drums. That was his entire kit."

"I don't often bring it to my solo gigs unless I can get a lift."

"Are you in a band at the moment?" I asked.

"No. It's something I've been experimenting with as part of the live show. I'm pretty good, actually."

I looked at Charlie, he looked at me. I looked at Celia and smiled. She smiled back, and for the first time since she came in I remembered how attracted I had been to her.

"Guess you're in," he said.

The nervous energy that buzzed through that meeting had not diminished by the weekend, when Student Grunt gathered in a small room by Whittock Hall canteen for our first rehearsal.

The space doubled as a storage cupboard for the cleaning staff. Celia set up her kit with several vats of chemicals on one side, and on the other a cluster of mops and buckets, like a chorus of stick-thin, white-dreadlocked backing singers.

Charlie owned a bass guitar and a small, battered Vox amplifier. I still had my acoustic, which failed almost every punk credibility test; it was old and fashionably worn, while I still had long hair and could easily have been mistaken for being in a band like the Eagles or Smokie.

None of us knew what to expect when Celia manoeuvred gracefully behind the kit. She had dressed perfectly for the occasion in tight white tee shirt, black leather jacket, black trousers and bright yellow sneakers. We expected a few small flourishes, a little warm up before we played our first song; instead, she sat still, poised, ready to come in when the song started.

"Do you know Bodies by the Sex Pistols?" Charlie asked.

"Of course," she said, impressively. "Ready when you are."

Charlie counted the slow intro that came in for a few bars before the song speeded up. "One, two, three, four –"

The bass guitar plodded into action, like a pensioner walking to the chemist. My acoustic was immediately drowned out by the noise but then Celia brought the track to life.

She was a brilliant drummer.

The song speeded up, as did Celia, keeping perfect time. She wasn't just a great drummer: she was mesmerising to watch, like at the comedy audition. There was no "meeming" here, but a wall of noise. It was amazing, considering how small the kit was. Some of the time she barely seemed to be moving, all energy coming from her diaphragm; other times, she stretched her arms in a flourish of crazy shapes. Charlie might have been lead singer, but Celia was our star.

"That was amazing," said Charlie.

"How long have you been playing?" I asked.

"A few weeks," she said, turning away modestly. Celia came to life when performing but as soon as we stopped, her presence barely registered among the buckets and mops. "What's next?"

I dug out some scraps of paper from my guitar case.

"Song here that's a bit different. What are you like with reggae?"

"Reggae?" said Charlie, and Celia began playing instantly, I had no idea what she was doing but it sounded like reggae to me.

"This song's called Yorkshire Reggae Boy," I shouted over the drums. Charlie gestured for Celia to stop.

"Hang on, Barry. I love reggae, but look at us. We've barely picked up our instruments. Let's at least learn how to play punk."

"Okay," I said. "I can probably get away with changing the words to Yorkshire Punk Boy."

"How about we play it punk, but give it a reggae sound?" said Celia.

"Is that possible?"

"Let's see."

I began playing the song faster, punky. Charlie joined in, gingerly. I tried speeding up the words, Celia bashed away instinctively, then when we got to the chorus she changed effortlessly to a reggae beat.

Inspired by Celia's playing, our choice of songs became more ambitious. For fun, we tried Anarchy In The UK. She didn't know New Rose so I played it to her on an old cassette and she followed perfectly, even catching that heart-stopping, stomach-jolting moment in the intro when the drums interrupt a workaday, pub-rocking intro as if to announce "Rock. Is. Dead! This. Is. Punk!" Hearing it live, played by this amazing woman, caused my whole body to shake with excitement.

Comedy? Forget it. I was in a band. I wanted to be a punk star now.

I don't remember everything that happened next. We finished playing. Celia packed her gear, she asked if she could store it with me overnight so she wouldn't have to drag it home that evening and we took it to my room. Alone, mostly silent, placing the drums and my guitar against the far corner of my little cell, the silence felt significant and she thanked me. The next part I remember so well. She leaned in to kiss me on the cheek goodnight, but then her lips found mine and she kissed me on the mouth and I felt her tongue against mine. Is this some kind of sign, I wondered? Have there been signals all evening? Is she kissing me out of pity? I heard Maurice's voice telling me to shut up, you idiot, she wants a shag, responded, and before I knew it we were kissing, undressing, manoeuvring round my narrow college bed. Now I understood how little I knew about women, and sex, and what I was supposed to be doing, but somehow we found a physical, naked connection and my body did what it was supposed to do. And even though it was as baffling as it was exciting, I knew this was an act I could learn to love, and turned gently over in the bed, looking up at the ceiling of my room, no longer a virgin.

CHAPTER 14

Nine o'clock, Monday morning. Gordon Muckle was talking us through the Great Police Strike of 1919.

"The so-called Great War was over but in Britain there was a real fear that the Bolshevik revolution would take hold. Unions were forming, strikes broke out spontaneously, there were race riots against blacks in port cities like Liverpool and London, but the main point to remember, the crucial fact, is this: Barry Goldman is no longer a virgin."

On some higher level I had dreamed of a love so deep that transcended the vulgarity of doing it with a woman, but doing it with a woman had been presented as the most important rite of passage into manhood. The chapter of my life called "Virginity" came to an end, but I had no idea what to expect next.

I had imagined a thousand different versions of this moment. Sometimes they had involved what might be called intellectual foreplay with Harriet or Joni (not Yoko, her newly revived marriage too intrusive to the fantasy); others were baser and involved Raquel Welch, Diana Ross, Suzi Quatro or the dancing Swedish secretary from The Producers. I can't have been the only teenage male to find the phrase "Bialystock and Bloo-oom!" erotically charged.

I was attracted to Celia but wasn't yet aware of an emotional connection. Is that what comes next? I wondered. Is that how relationships are? We'd been told my parents' generation didn't lose their virginity until the wedding night. Having got this most important life event out of the way, was my next stage to get to know her?

At school, Tim Duffy told us that on his 16th birthday his dad took him to a prostitute, as though this was the correct etiquette for teaching a boy how to become a man: that he learn how to do sex from an experienced woman he would never meet again.

The word I can best use to describe the event was surprising. I hadn't been expecting it, and then when it happened I had no idea what was going on. A physical deed had taken place, one that for the first time hadn't involved my hand, but I wasn't certain I'd done it correctly.

"In Liverpool, more than half of the police force refused to work. In some areas public order broke down, and there was an orgy of looting and rioting."

An orgy, eh? That was the oddest thing about last night: looking around this room at the earnest young creatures, wondering which, if any, had yet experienced sex and who was still a virgin, I was torn between wanting to stand on the desk and beat my chest, proclaiming "I had sex last night, losers!", and lie on a psychiatrist's couch to discover why this supposedly magnificent rite of passage had felt so ironically unclimactic.

That combination of glowing pleasure and growing anxiety continued through the day. I'm not a virgin anymore. How did I perform? I did it. Might she never want to see me again? We had sex! Would I ever want to see her again? Of course. We might have sex again and I've got a better idea what to expect.

And how much was my urge to be in a band down to the anticipation of an exciting rock-and-roll lifestyle? Was it Celia

I wanted? Or the band? Surely the whole point of being in a band was to get off with lots of different women without having to ask them out?

The drum kit was still in my room; she'd have to come back for that, which felt like a flimsy notion on which to hang the most important relationship of my life so far. More questions: where did she live? How would I get hold of her? Charlie had her telephone number; I'd have to ask him for it. That could be a bit weird. But I got it from him, anyway, tried to call, no reply.

I dropped her a note at the kitchens, not wanting to see her working there, which worried me more, but certain she wouldn't want me to see her there either. I suggested we meet in town and go for a walk. I got back to my room the following day and found a note arranging to meet, which ended "see you then honey x", and spent the next sixteen hours pondering the "x" and the relative status of the word "honey" within the lexicon of amorous nicknames.

We met by the entrance to Brandon Hill park, halfway down Jacob's Wells Road. The sun was bright but failed to take the chill off the January air. I was wearing my thick grey coat and woolly scarf for protection, long hair scruffily refusing to form a shape. Celia had her workaday coat I remembered from the audition. Her hair hung perfectly down the sides of her face, immaculate, and I marvelled again, still baffled at the physical incongruity of our pairing.

We walked briefly in silence, past the old sign forbidding the beating of carpets after 4.30 pm, me filling the empty space with pointless words.

"What time are your shifts?"

"I start around six thirty, finish at ten. Then four until eight, unless I've got a gig."

"Mhm."

We carried on up the winding path to Cabot Tower, struggling with small talk.

"Where do you live?"

"A flat in Redland. Pretty poky."

"Are you a student?"

"Second year. Have to pay my way through."

"Right," I said, curious why this seemingly well-spoken English woman was not supported by her family. "What are you studying?" I asked in a silly voice and, to my relief, she enjoyed this humorous attempt to mock the opening conversation of every new student.

"American Literature."

"Aha..."

"Spent weeks looking through the courses and universities. This looked like the one involving the least amount of work."

I laughed.

"Seriously. Performing's all I want to do."

"Why aren't you studying drama?"

"Oh, I'm not interested in that stuff. I mean, you're not, are you?" she asked, suddenly concerned she may have hurt my feelings. I was touched.

"Nah, politics and sociology. A joint honours degree in not having a clue what I want to do."

"Drama courses in Britain are all about the past."

"You think?" I said, as we reached the top of the hill, and sat together on a bench overlooking the south east of the city. "I saw a poster for punk Shakespeare in Edinburgh last summer."

"You went to Edinburgh?" she asked, leaning forward, excited. "I want to go this year."

"With the comedy group?"

"Hopefully. They contact you if they're interested." Not surprisingly, neither of us had passed the Molière audition a few months earlier. "I'm determined to go regardless."

"Maybe we could take the band up," I said, unable to stop myself wondering if Harriet might be going again.

Imagine spending an entire month at the Fringe with Celia as my girlfriend, living together in a tiny space, me pining for Harriet. But what if Celia was It and I'd missed my chance there? I wished I was all grown up like Charlie and Ingrid and understood how this couple thing worked.

"Barry?"

"Yes?"

"Do you have a spare key for your room?"

"What?" What! We haven't even been on a date yet.

"I need to pick up the drum kit while you're out. I'm using it on Friday and have to practise."

"Ah, right. I'll look for it when I get back."

"You're kind," she smiled, and held my hand for a moment. If she'd spotted my momentary look of panic when she'd asked for the key she didn't show it, or maybe chose to ignore it.

And for the first time I got a sense of what was happening. She wasn't just physically attracted to me. She liked me as a person.

CHAPTER 15

The fascists were scheduled to march at 4 pm.

Two violent Bristol City fans had been allowed out of prison on parole. The National Front had planned to march in celebration through Knowle, a predominantly white working-class area in south Bristol. I didn't know a single person who had been to Knowle. Why should I? There was no student accommodation in Knowle, no gigs, no record shops, no grand municipal buildings. None of the wealth that built this city had found its way there.

Gordon had summoned us to his flat in Montpelier a few days earlier to organise our strategy. I'd expected a commune, all wooden floorboards and Save The Whale posters; instead, it was a cosy, two-bedroomed basement with nice carpets and modern lighting – the kind of place I could have brought my parents to. "See, Mum, not all socialists take drugs and live in hovels... well, they don't live in hovels."

"The only way to beat fascists is to let them know there are more of you than there are of them," Gordon said. "Way more. If they muster fifty marchers, we need a hundred. If they can make a hundred we need two hundred."

"How do we do that?" asked Sebastian.

"We mobilise. Make sure all the relevant societies are contacted. Posters everywhere. The students' union. Your halls of residence. Lamp posts. Gigs."

"We're playing on the demo," said Matt.

"Really?" I said, half-wondering if Student Grunt might be able to get a slot at the gig.

"Surely the police won't let us march," said Ingrid. "You know there'll be a line of them three bodies thick, blocking our way."

"Sure," said Gordon, smiling, the moment he'd been waiting for. He led us to the back of his living room, where a map of Bristol was spread across the dining table.

He paused, ensuring he had our full attention. "That's why we turn up in Knowle an hour before the fascists."

Two generations earlier, the Gordon Muckles of Britain were army officers, spoke in clipped accents about night-time manoeuvres, aerial strikes and tank formations, the maps of countries in the heart of central Europe. Gordon was from a working- class family in Swindon and had no military links, apart from a dad who'd seen action in southern Italy in World War Two, as part of the catering corps. A man who had literally served his countrymen. Gordon didn't have a double-barrelled surname or handlebar moustaches but he was involved in exactly the same activity as them, fighting and defeating fascists.

"The most important thing," said Gordon, "is the element of surprise."

Charlie and I instinctively glanced at each other and smiled, recalling the Monty Python "Spanish Inquisition" sketch.

"We don't want the police to be wise to our numbers until it's too late for them to do anything about it."

Gordon knew everything there was to know about demonstrations. In 1971, he marched through Bristol shopping precinct to protest the Vietnam war. What would the Viet Cong have made of that? In 1973, he joined the sisters in solidarity against a proposed new Abortion Act, and after the 1975 riots in St Paul's had walked arm in arm with his new friends from Bristol's West Indian community to protest against the cavalier use of stop-and-search by local police. He saw teaching us as part of the struggle and probably marched every morning to lectures.

We peered over the large ordnance survey map.

"There are six buses that go through Knowle from different parts of town, from three different stops: here, here and here."

He pointed to various locations, his finger serving as a perfectly decent substitute for the long, fancy sticks we'd seen in a dozen war movies on TV on wet Sunday afternoons.

Matt began humming the Dam Busters theme.

"The fascists are going to be marching here," he said, ignoring Matt and pointing to the high street.

"How do you know?" Ingrid asked.

Gordon smiled enigmatically. He didn't just know everything there was to know about policing methods; he had contacts in the local force, officers and detectives he'd chatted to about procedural work. Who doesn't want to moan about their job to sympathetic strangers? And how much more will they tell you off duty in the pub, with tongue-loosened tales of crowd control techniques and management incompetence?

"The phone boxes are here; we have designated marshals who'll monitor the march on the ground. The police will block off these roads from around two thirty. We'll already be lining the streets, loads of us, carrying placards, handing them to locals, phoning each other as soon as we see groups of fascists gathering."

"Do you think we should be carrying anything? For protection?" Ingrid asked.

"No!" said Gordon, thumping the table with his fist, making us jump back. "There's always the possibility we'll be arrested. Do you want to be taken down to the station with a jemmy down your trousers?"

"The fascists will be tooled up," said Matt.

"They won't attack if they're outnumbered."

We gathered nervously outside the Wills Memorial Building at lunchtime on march day, awaiting further instructions. We didn't stand out although, unlike the Guildford posse, none of us were wearing green wax mackintoshes or blowing air kisses. Soon we were twenty, thirty, forty. The Union of Hindu Students stood with Friends of Allah, the Jewish Society shared pavement space with Palestinian Action, and there was even room for members of the hated Socialist International (Permanent Revolution) Order. On other days, such a gathering might have required police protection of its own.

Gordon arrived and split us into three smaller groups.

"We don't want to bring police attention to ourselves yet. They'll be concentrating their numbers on Knowle, at 4 pm. Where their job will be to protect the NF."

"Fascists!" Sebastian called out.

"Yes, Sebastian, welcome to the British police state!" he grinned and walked off to inspire another band of foot soldiers.

Thanks to Gordon, we knew which bus to catch, at which stop, and before we left he'd introduced us to the marshals.

Since our meeting at Gordon's, tension had increased, thanks to a TV interview on World In Action with Margaret Thatcher, the leader of the Opposition, that had excited fascists up and down the country.

"People are really rather afraid that this country might be rather swamped by people with a different culture," she said, adding that "if there is any fear that it might be swamped, people are going to react and be rather hostile to those coming in."

All my life, racists had been easy to spot. Mostly male, short cropped hair and aggressive tattoos, they stood out, and when they weren't marching into our Jewish neighbourhood to shout abuse, as occasionally happened, were pretty easy to avoid. This was the first time I'd heard their beliefs articulated by a respectable and respected politician, on a hugely popular TV show.

Enoch Powell's speech ten years earlier had frightened all whose families had arrived recently in the UK, but he was seen as an extremist, no longer so powerful. Thatcher's interview was the first time someone in such a commanding position had used such inflammatory language. He'd spoken of rivers of blood, she talked of being swamped. The words were different but for all her terribly polite "rathers" and "reallys", the message of hate was the same, the language biblical and apocalyptic.

As we huddled together in the constant drizzle I wondered if we'd be heading to Knowle aboard Noah's Ark.

There was fidgeting and anxiety; Charlie was there but Ingrid, our appointed marshal, had disappeared. It was a relief to see her jogging towards us, Charlie concealing his fear from everyone except me.

"Change of plan," she said urgently, catching her breath. "Big Filth presence in town; best avoid them and walk round the side." She showed us a hastily drawn map, scrawled on the back of a photocopied statistical academic paper. Raindrops blurred the biro marks but it was clear enough: head west towards Temple Meads train station, the long way round, and pick up a bus from there.

The collective mood improved slightly as we walked off, armed with a new diagram.

"Maybe the fascists have been gathering in town," said Charlie.

"Do we know where we're going?" asked a cheery Hindu student with a gentle Welsh accent, dress more summer camping weekend than anti-fascist demo.

"Do any of us know where we are going?" I asked philosophically, my stock comedy reply whenever I heard that question.

"Where I come from, that question has been asked for centuries," she said earnestly.

"Oh," I said, embarrassed by my ignorance and keen not to appear racist, here of all times and places. "Where's that?"

"Swansea. Couldn't you tell?" she smiled.

We carried on down Park Street, past blue-overalled workmen and middle-class shoppers purchasing sandalwood-scented candles, oblivious to our forthcoming battle to the death with the malignant forces of modern Nazism. At College Green, Bristol's grand municipal corner of town hall, lake and cathedral that thought it was Versailles, we were joined by another group of anti-fascists from the nearby polytechnic.

Walking through the side streets of Bristol town centre, in near silence that combined grim determination with fear of panicking the rest of the group, we became aware of several more groups of around twenty students walking in the same direction. The local folk of Knowle were in for a shock, but so were we. This march may have been all about the racial divide but there was no gulf more pronounced in Britain than class. The people of Knowle would have known of our university – some probably cleaned its science labs and cooked in its kitchens – but we had never visited back, before today.

Arriving at Temple Meads station, our mood was sombre. It may have looked as though we were going to a funeral. Maybe we were.

With buses infrequent and Knowle barely half an hour's walk away, we decided to continue on foot. Charlie and Ingrid were keen to chat, and for once not about the geo-political fault lines in Argentina.

"Are you and Celia...?" Charlie asked, eyebrows raised in expectation.

"Funny you should ask," I said, stringing them along for laughs and playing for time while I worked out what I was prepared to tell them. I was still unsure how much I wanted people to know about us, but I couldn't be in a band with Charlie and Celia and keep it from them.

"Yes we have been seeing each other."

"Have you been seeing a lot of each other?" Ingrid asked, gurning and grinning like Kenneth Williams in a Carry On film.

"Cheeky."

"Are you guys going to be like the Velvet Underground?"

"Great knowledge Ingrid." I was deeply envious that Charlie had a girlfriend whose understanding of music extended to awareness of Moe Tucker, one of the few female drummers in the world of rock.

"Don't patronise me."

"I was thinking more like the Honeycombs," I said, although no-one else was aware of the only other known female drummer. No one possessed more useless rock music information than me.

"I'd better watch the band dynamic," said Charlie, "I'm outnumbered now."

"Ingrid maybe you could join us?" I said "We could be a punk Abba."

"I'm from the right country."

It was out there, then: Celia and I were now officially a thing. After that short exchange, something was different. When I'd been talking earlier to my Swansea Hindu marching comrade, I'd been wondering if she was single. Announcing the relationship with Celia made it real. I'd finally admitted it to myself.

What if I die today? What if a scary fascist with "love" and "hate" tattooed on his knuckles knocks me to the ground and my head cracks open on the pavement? "Who's that enigmatic woman standing a few yards back from the graveside like they do in films?" Mum and Dad will ask of Celia's presence at my funeral. I'll die never having resolved my relationship with Joni or Celia. If I return to Whittock Hall alive, I told myself, I will make that my priority. Well, Joni for now.

Walking was slow, funereal, as we passed the George pub, closed but displaying a large Union Jack that flapped menacingly in the blustery rain. The traffic was choking Wells Road: a few police cars and Special Patrol vans had driven past, each siren wail tightening the knot in my stomach another notch. Student pedestrian traffic was also increasing, the few locals heading towards Knowle centre eyeing us with curiosity. What a strange crowd of long-haired, scruffy, multicultural oddities we must have seemed.

A bizarre, incongruous sound rang through the wind above the constant purr of traffic, like a melodious ice-cream van – except no one sold ice cream in England in January. It took a moment to work out that among the dawdling traffic of police cars, work vans and buses, an open-backed lorry was transporting the St Paul's Baptist Church Steel Band towards the small group of citizens whose sole aim in life was to rid their city of people like the St Paul's Baptist Church Steel Band.

Locals watched, mouths open. Mums with small children pointed, their kids laughed and jumped around, dancing absurdly to the merry noise like the audience on Top of the Pops. Old ladies with shopping trolleys stopped, stared briefly and walked away, a couple of sallow, spotty boys looked up and sneered, but that was the limit of protest. Even the hardiest of racists were infected by the bright summer sound.

Ahead, we saw another group of students, and another. This was no longer a moving file of pedestrians: it was a large gathering. More familiar music drifted towards us from an open-backed lorry.

"Look!" I said to Charlie, pointing behind us. "Matt's band!" We laughed and cheered and confused the marchers around us by singing along with the lyrics to Neat Neat Neat by The Damned, as interpreted by Matt's group. The music was not to everyone's taste, and a small group yelled "Bring back the calypso!"

The police erected barriers along the road as fast as they could, under pressure from the size of the crowd, taken by surprise by our early arrival. Gordon's plan had worked.

With less than half an hour to go before the march officially started, the mood changed from tense to celebratory. My fear of shaven-headed fascists leaping from behind a wall had turned to mild curiosity as to whether any would show at all. Drivers in cars slithering slowly along hooted in support and were greeted with cheers, the stern-faced ones meeting with good-natured football chants.

Eventually, the barriers stopped us going further. The road cleared, traffic diverted around the corner or away from the centre. The steel band parked a few yards away, but we could still hear the music of sunny summer afternoons.

Our fellow students huddled noisily behind the barriers on the other side of the road. Having worked on his vocal technique since our first rehearsal, Charlie was practising projecting and leading a call and response. What he lacked in originality was made up for in volume.

"One, two, three, four, Smash the National Front!"

"Smash the National Front!"

"Smash the National Front!" this time, sung.

"Smash the National Front!"

Local shoppers were cheered as they squeezed through the crowd, shown deference and politeness. If I'd been one of them I might have hated us, but many were won over by our middle-class charm, while others thanked us for making the effort to show the fascists they weren't welcome.

A hush fell across the crowd as it became clear that the Nazis were coming through. Banter with the police, good-natured up to this point, turned to hostility. Coppers who'd been joking with us moments earlier went quiet, facial expressions hardened. Arms locked. Angry jeers began.

"Fascists out!"

"Pigs out!"

"Smash the National Front!"

Police in fluorescent yellow jackets emerged from the turning off the main road. There must have been a hundred or more. Tucked inside their group was a small band of people, twenty or thirty at the most, at least five police for every one of them. This was as much fascism as Bristol could muster – a small gang of men and boys, aged between sixteen and forty, avoiding eye contact. Frightened. Good, I thought. All beer and bravado with their mouthy mates, today needing half the entire Avon and Somerset Constabulary to avoid a kicking of their own.

I vaguely recognised some from a few punk gigs I'd been to – one tall, a little older than the rest, square-jawed, spider web tattoo half-emerging from the side of his neck.

They disappeared around the corner to massive cheers. Cars returned to the street, including the much-loved calypso truck. The police weren't letting us leave but what did we care? I popped out my packet of John Player Specials, lit up a cigarette and enjoyed the sweet moment of craving relief. Strangers hugged. Charlie and Ingrid held each other close and I longed for whatever it was that made them so comfortable in each other's intimate company. In this moment of triumph and joy, this celebration of a great battle fought and won, I wanted someone to love, too, and wondered if it might be Celia.

CHAPTER 16

Hello, darling, it's your dad here. I gather you've lost your virginity. Tell us all about it. Is she a looker? Is she a goer?

"Hi, Dad."

"Hnh."

I've lost my virginity.

"How's things?" I asked with strained jocularity.

"Mhm," he answered, maybe still in a sulk. We hadn't had a civil exchange since our Christmas row.

"Everything okay?"

"Handing over to Mum."

"Hello, Barry."

"Hi, Mum." I'm not a virgin anymore.

"How's the course work going?" Too busy shagging to keep up with that, hurr hurr.

"Okay, thanks."

"Everything else alright?" Also strained.

"Sure..." Could she tell, over 230 miles of crackling phone line, that I was enjoying carnal pleasures with a non-Jew?

"Did you get the letter I sent?"

"Oh, yes, thanks for the forty pounds; that'll come in really handy." Two mouths to feed now.

"The normal cheque might be a bit later than usual. That's a little New Year present to tide you over."

"Thanks, Mum. Everything okay with the factory?"

"Yes, of course! A few minor cash flow problems but otherwise all fine."

"Dad seems grumpy."

"Oh, you know him..."

"How's Grandma?"

"Same as ever. Yesterday she complained about having poorly blood."

"Poorly blood?"

"I know. Whatever cure the doctors find, she'll always discover a new illness."

"Ha ha. Yes... You know deep down she loves you."

"What do you mean? What are you talking about?"

"Oh, nothing. We were chatting about when you and Dad got together."

"What did she say?"

"Honestly, Mum, it was nothing."

"It must have been something."

"When I was up last time. Saw a new side to her. She was, dunno, quite warm."

"Yes, she's not always the old battleaxe you're used to."

"Okay. When, ah, do you think the cheque might be coming?"

"Not sure exactly. Don't spend too much this term, okay?" Bit late for that, Mum. Your forty quid is all that stands between me and an overdraft.

"Sure, no problem. Any other news?"

"Not really." No other news? Judith's new job? Aunty Eva's angry dog? What's up, Mum?

"Okay. Call you next week."

"Sure."

144

"Love to Dad."

"Byee."

That week, I was preoccupied with drama. Celia and I would hear soon whether we'd made the cut to go to Edinburgh with BUTCH. The University Revue Group wanted me to read my poems in their Easter showcase and had asked me to take part in writing and performing the sketches in between.

Our first rehearsal took place on a bright March Saturday afternoon in one of the dull, windowless meeting rooms at the union. I'd auditioned in the same room two weeks earlier, where I'd been greeted by two identikit students who I guessed had failed to get into Oxbridge and hailed from the vicinity of Guildford.

Hugo was tall, thin and fresh-faced, with light ginger hair and rosy-red cheeks. He wore the standard student uniform of smart but casual beige trousers, plain blue shirt, and a chunky white sweater hung over his shoulders, arms tied round his neck like those of a cricket-playing chum. But when he stood to announce his name and shake hands, his tall, gangly thinness marked him out as different, almost odd. I could see how he had been drawn to comedy.

Camilla was short and blessed with an infectious cackle. Black polo neck, sensible tweed skirt and black tights, she wore her hair in a military-precise bob as wide as it was long.

They'd given me a sheet of paper with a speech that seemed to be for someone with a northern accent, written by someone who had probably never heard a northern accent. Lots of funny words about things that got made in factories. I gave it my best Leeds brogue but, after a couple of tries, Hugo coughed and said "Can you try it without attempting the northern accent?"

"It's where I'm from."

"Really? You don't sound northern," he said, with a flash of irritation. "Maybe say it normally," he said, and I imagined young Hugo's face being flushed down a public school toilet, before adding the word "accents" to the list of performing skills beyond my capabilities.

"Thank you," he said at the end without looking up, and a kind of finality that suggested my brief invasion of his precious time and space had come to an end.

A fortnight later, I was astonished to see my name on the list of those chosen to go to Edinburgh. But no Celia.

If she was jealous of my success, she hid it well. She had discovered The Theatre of Infinity, a like-minded troupe of comical misfits and grotesques who challenged the bourgeois notions of what was meant by an enjoyable night out at the theatre. They were a semi-professional group and had their own plans to go to the festival.

That suited both of us – to be in Edinburgh at the same time but not working together.

The convenience of being on site for early work starts meant she was in my room a great deal. We had gone straight from sex to cohabitation in my tiny student hutch, without dating.

After that first momentous evening, where I hadn't a clue what was going on, I discovered what the fuss was about. Celia didn't ask if that was the first occasion, and I didn't let on, but next time she patiently led me through a number of stages on the way to The Act. I had heard of the word "foreplay" but it hadn't featured in many conversations with Maurice, or in the self-help, single-hand publications at the back of his wardrobe.

Edinburgh rehearsals dragged on through the spring. Bristol Fashion was a sketch show utilising the combined waggishness and enforced jollity of the cream of our student comedy elite. My place was secure in the show; I would appear in three short spots, a total of ten minutes that would help change the pace and allow costume changes for the rest of the cast. It was the sketches in between that were proving more of a challenge. As a member of the team, I was expected to pitch in with ideas and perform if Silent Shopkeeper or Policeman Number Two were required.

There were no windows in the rehearsal space, but it was the inability to connect with each other's sense of humour that sucked the air, life and joy from the atmosphere.

I loved sketches, my favourite comedians made them – Dave Allen, Les Dawson, Morecambe and Wise – but having seen Kris transform the mood of a room from dark hostility to hysterical laughter, this felt like comedy from another era. I'd seen the future but was trapped in an inferior student version of the past.

"Alright, darlin', fancy a shandy?" Hugo asked in what I thought he imagined would pass for a working-class cockney accent. Camilla was at his side, preening herself like working-class Hugo's bird, which was funny, and made us laugh.

"Hang on," Hugo said in his normal plummy accent so we knew he was no longer playing the oik. "What's so funny?"

"Not you!" shouted one good-natured heckler from the back of the room.

"Sorry, Hugo," said Fat Toby. "Camilla pulled a funny face." Fat Toby wasn't fat, but he was short and round with a round face and round spectacles, and for comedy purposes he insisted on being known as Fat Toby. Like Hugo, Toby had earned his place in the group as much on the basis of physical appearance as the possession of actual funny bones.

"Can we please continue with the sketch?" Richard boomed, imposing his directorial authority on the keen but undisciplined mob. "We have five more to read through today. Hugo, please concentrate on your performance."

"How am I supposed to do that when they're –"

"Laughing?" asked Richard, pointing at us. "Audience laughter is a requirement, whether at you, with you, or at someone sharing the stage who is not you."

147

Richard was a lecturer from the drama department. He was much older than us, in his early thirties, with piercing blue eyes and a sharp, pointed nose, immaculate dress sense and a delightful enthusiasm for Carry On films. He was out and proudly gay, an inspiration to many around him and a source of revulsion to others.

Hugo recovered from the gentle humiliation and stepped back into what he believed to be character.

"Alright, darlin', fancy a shandy?"

"You buyin'?" asked Camilla in a marginally less insulting version of the same accent as Hugo.

"Sure fing, doll."

"Yeah, I fancy a sha... a shandy," she said, cackling like Sid James.

"So that's a pint of bitter for me, and an 'arf a shandy for the lady."

Camilla cackled again, and we all laughed again. Hugo winced, but walked off without protest, as Debbie and Andrew, the other cast members, walked on stage.

"Alright, 'Shell!" Camilla said.

"You alright, Trace?" said Debbie, in a slightly better trained working-class accent. "This is Todd."

"Alright, Todd!" Camilla screeched, nudging Debbie in the ribs. Andrew, playing the part of Todd, smiled inanely. More laughs. Debbie, petite, blonde and pretty, was studying for a PhD in astrophysics but knew her job today, which was to play the dumb blonde.

"I like your new bloke," said Camilla. "Does he talk much?" Andrew was a handsome, serious-faced, leading-actor type capable of Cary Grant silliness.

"Naah," said Debbie. "He's from Wales." The technical crew, who had to stop and watch the first rehearsal of each sketch, chuckled again. Speculation was extensive and bets were already being taken not on if, but when, Andrew and Debbie would become an item.

"I'm from Wales," Andrew said, unusually for this show in a genuine accent. Andrew was not from Guildford but north of Cardiff, and his distinctively soft Welsh Valleys accent added another dimension to the otherwise limited range of voices on display.

"Really?" said Camilla, arching her eyebrow archly. "I had no idea." More laughs.

Hugo returned, miming the holding of two beer glasses almost as badly as he talked in a working-class accent.

"Oy!" he shouted, crashing the imaginary glasses down with such force that if they'd been real they would have shattered into a thousand pieces. He stared at Andrew. "You lookin' at my bird?"

This got the best laugh so far, and Hugo relaxed. I got the joke: why would the handsome man with the pretty girlfriend be interested in the less attractive woman? It was the kind of sexist jape that made me uncomfortable.

"I'm from Wales," Andrew replied inevitably. We knew that was coming but enjoyed the shared audience knowledge, while the Welsh accent guaranteed more laughs.

"Don't get funny with me, mate," said Hugo. "Are you, by any chance, Taffy, staring at, and thinking lewd thoughts about, my girlfriend?"

Andrew paused, then said "I'm from Wales." No laugh this time; we'd already enjoyed the repetition, it was time to move on. I was sure Richard, who had created the sketch, knew more about the rhythms of comedy than everyone else in the room, but even he couldn't guarantee which lines would work and which wouldn't. This comedy writing was harder than it looked.

"Alright, Taffy, come on – you, me, outside. Now!"

Andrew paused again. No please, not again. He smiled innocently.

"Okay," he said, the laugh this time a release for the audience who, like me, had been dreading the repeated phrase of geographical status.

Andrew and Hugo walked off. Richard smiled and nodded gently, which was our cue for applauding the end of the sketch.

"Right," he said, turning to the rest of us. "That sketch is okay but needs a better ending. Any ideas?"

Hugo looked at Fat Toby, Fat Toby looked at Debbie, she looked at me. I stood up and walked to the stage.

"Pretend to fight for a bit, okay?" I said to the men. Hugo looked down on me, as he did most people, with haughty disdain. But Andrew responded positively, and pushed Hugo away. A short dance of aggression continued, their moves bringing new laughs until I jumped up and reprised my Policeman Number Two role from an earlier sketch.

"'Ello, 'ello, 'ello," I said, aware that my own working-class accent was not exactly authentic. "What's all this, then?"

"He was lookin' at my bird," Hugo improvised, unusually.

"I don't need to know any more, young fella-me-lad," I said, borrowing inadvertently from my own comedy writing heroes Ray Galton and Alan Simpson. "You're coming down the station."

"But –"

"– Not content with portraying the working class as a race of thick alcoholics, you then make ancient jokes about the physical appearance of women."

Hugo's look of bafflement was so good I realised he wasn't acting it.

"And as for you, 'Taffy', your perpetuation of national stereotypes will win you few friends across the Severn Bridge. Come with me," and I frogmarched them off stage, basking in my triumph.

No one laughed. Either my ideas were too far ahead of their time or nobody found them funny. Or I was a terrible sketch performer. Probably all three.

Richard smiled. "Thanks, Barry," he said, and turned to the rest of the group. "Any more ideas?"

After the rehearsal, we gathered in the Mandela Bar and drank thirstily.

I chatted with Andrew, who was either really interested in what I had to say or was such a good actor that he knew how to pretend to appear interested. We talked about Cardiff and football. Every football fan I'd ever met had a personal story about why they hated Leeds United; his involved being chased outside Ninian Park by a gang of Neanderthal Leeds chaps hurling piss-filled Mackeson Stout bottles in their direction.

"I didn't quite get what you meant this afternoon," he said after a couple of drinks, "when you came on as the policeman."

"Well, Andrew, I love all the old stuff, you know – Two Ronnies, Morecambe and Wise, Frankie Howerd. But Benny Hill–"

"–He's so funny–"

"–Mhm, I think he's a great songwriter," I said, aware that this was not what most people loved Benny Hill for, "but some of his stuff about women is old fashioned."

"In what way?"

"They're either fit birds or battleaxes. Nothing in between."

"It's just a laugh though, innit? Like Richard says, we're laughing at him, not with him."

I could have continued but knew where this was going. Barry, you're a humourless, intellectual, man-hating women's libber who can't take a joke; you're the one with the problem.

I'd been struggling with this for years, unable to fully enjoy my comedy if I felt it was sexist. Maurice had tried and failed to make me love Are You Being Served? as much as he did.

It was all Sheila Rowbotham's fault. Sitcoms were where I bonded with Mum. We had no problem with the gentle sexual innuendo of Father, Dear Father or Wendy Craig's more graphic articulation of being a bored housewife in Butterflies, but I struggled to sit with her through the casual racism and dolly-bird stereotypes of Mind Your Language.

I bought a packet of salted peanuts to soak up the alcohol. When the barman pulled them off the poster at the bar, it revealed the hot-panted backside of an attractive woman, one pack at a time. I found myself once again dragged into conversation about the minutiae of joke philosophy, this time with Richard. He taught drama but knew a lot about comedy, and our shared love of Tommy Cooper had brought us close. We often communicated in Cooperisms – "Jug. Water. Water. Jug" and "not like that – like that" – which baffled the others and brought an exclusivity to our relationship.

"How are you finding the rehearsals?" he asked.

"Amazing, never done anything like this before," I said, realising that if I had drunk less, my response would have been more sober, in both senses of the word. "I mean, obviously, I spend hours rehearsing on my own."

He nodded, and said no more, like he was expecting me to continue. I liked Richard, admired his boldness about being gay, but that made it hard for me to articulate my misgivings about the tone of the show. How was it possible, I wondered, to lecture a gay man about sexual stereotypes? Instead, I asked, "How do you think the show is looking?"

"Okay. For this stage. I've done Edinburghs where we've rewritten the entire show the day before opening."

"How many years have you been going?"

"As a director? This is my sixth. And I went a few times as a student in the sixties."

"That must have been amazing."

"It was smaller. Less comedy. Too commercial now."

"I was there for a few days last summer. Couldn't believe how huge it was."

"Anyone who's anyone from the BBC goes," he said. "They're always looking for new comedy and drama."

"I don't think my kind of comedy is for TV."

"You don't do blue material, do you? They have their own circuit."

"I know," I said, "I'm from Leeds. I've played their clubs."

"Really?" he said, animated for the first time by my response. "I'm told they can be a tough crowd."

"Yes, but I didn't do that kind of thing. It's more, uh, punk comedy."

He grimaced at the word.

"Don't worry," I said. "There won't be any punks at our show. Not for the kind of comedy we do."

"What do you mean?"

"Traditional. I guess. The characters are a bit... out of date?"

"Nonsense," he said, shutting me down sharply. "They're people we see every day."

"I suppose so, but attitudes are changing," I said, wary of pushing too hard on this but, also, drunk. "Women's rights? Gay liberation?"

"The times they are changing," he laughed mirthlessly. Drunk as I was, I knew this was not the time to correct him: "'a': it's times they are 'a-changing' you ignoramus." "It's all fads. Women's lib. All nonsense. What do women know about comedy?"

I wanted to mention Carla Lane and Hattie Jacques, Barbara Windsor and Sylvia Sims, Lucille Ball and Mary Tyler Moore, but didn't think that would help.

"Punk rock?" he spat, like a Daily Express reader despairing at the nation's youth. "These crazes come and go, but the human condition, expressed in comedy – that never changes. If you want to see comedy at its most modern, read Shakespeare. Twelfth Night, Much Ado, Midsummer Night's Dream – it's all there."

I hadn't planned to stay on and get drunk but had been putting off going back to Celia. She had been hoping to stay with me in Edinburgh, but Richard had made it clear today that accommodation was strictly limited and no partners would be allowed. I thought about asking Harriet if Celia could stay there and dismissed the idea almost immediately, not wanting to dig too deeply to work out why.

In between the bouts of light-headedness and urge to sing Leeds United football chants on the bus home, I thought that if I was this concerned with men's attitudes to women, I should probably make a start by addressing this in my own relationship.

Celia was cross-legged on the floor when I came back to my room, already dressed for bed in the bright blue and yellow nightshirt that left her legs completely bare. My room was our room now. Celia still had her flat but stayed more often, and in this tiny space I barely used, her presence was more in evidence than mine. Tiny pots of moisturising cream, black pencils, sticks to line the eyes and accentuate the lashes, a stuffed peregrine falcon – something to do with a new routine she had been working on based loosely around Keats's Ode to a Nightingale – and a book called The House of Mirth, which I'd leafed through in a vain search for laughs.

She was happy to see me when I came. I struggled to position myself to hug her, and kissed her left cheek.

"Hello, my love," I whispered.

"You're drunk."

"That's right," I said, "drunk with love for my angel."

She stood and gently pushed me away in one move.

"And prawn cocktail-flavoured crisps, I'm picking up."

I belched involuntarily and she winced. Didn't blame her; I smelt the aftershock and winced too, almost retching.

"How was the rehearsal?"

"Okay," I said, coming in close to cuddle.

"Any news about accommodation? Barry?"

"Uh... no, not yet."

"Stop pawing me," she laughed, pushing me away again.

I turned away in a childish huff.

"Only trying to be affectionate."

She stroked my hair gently, filling me with love and lust, too drunk to distinguish the two.

"Let's get you into bed."

"Bed!"

"You need to sleep."

"Sleep with you!"

"Come on." She lifted me in one move, was stronger than I realised, and pointed me in the direction of the bathroom. I tried to bring her lips close to mine but this time she pushed me firmly back.

"Barry, I love you very much but there is no way I am having sex with you tonight."

I barely suppressed a raging fury fuelled by alcohol, and was scared by its power. I was confused by the word "love". Was it a throwaway confession, spoken solely to be contradicted by the refusal to have sex? It was said in the casual way people say things. I loved Heinz Spaghetti Hoops but didn't want to spend the rest of my life eating them; yes, that must have been the way she meant it, but it made me angry. And, thinking about Heinz Spaghetti Hoops meant that all that mattered was to get into the bathroom, kneel over the toilet, bend my head down and regurgitate what seemed like an endless stream of lager and prawn cocktail-flavoured vomit.

Later, I was at a Leeds United game, taking place inside a theatre. The crowd were roaring and pushing; I was a part of it, but also on stage, naked, masturbating. I came and there was a round of polite applause from the crowd, numbered cards held up by judges like in the Olympics. I could feel myself being shaken, aware that Celia was trying to wake me.

"Off to work now, see you later," she said, bustling out of the door as I was still half asleep. "Bloke rang last night while you were out; very keen to get in touch." She pecked me on the cheek, handed me a scrap of paper and left.

There was a name on the paper – "Chris" – and a phone number. Chris? Who's Chris? Kris! Calling me. I forgot about the pain in my head, grabbed some clothes and headed to the phone at the end of the corridor.

I dialled the number, recognising the 02 code as Birmingham. The phone seemed to ring forever. I was about to hang up when a low, slow but instantly recognisable voice arrived at the other end.

"Hullo?"

"Kris?"

"Hnh?"

"It's me. Barry."

"Barry? Oh yeah."

"You called? Last night?"

"It's six thirty in the morning."

"What? Oh, sorry. I didn't– I'll call you back."

"No, no it's fine, I'm going back to Devon today, stopping at Bristol for half an hour. Any chance of a catch up at the bus station this afternoon?"

"Sure," I said, ready to drop everything for Kris. "Aren't you rehearsing for Edinburgh?" I asked.

"Tell you later. Coach gets into Bristol three thirty. See you then."

"Bye."

I went back to bed, stopping only for a moment to once again position my head over the toilet bowl, releasing the last remnants of lager and prawn cocktail crisps from the night before.

CHAPTER 17

"Boom!" rang the drum
"Hey, you!" yelled the drunk
"Kill that drum or I'll kill you, punk."
Climbed up a hill
And crashed to the floor
Woke to the sound of knocking at the door.

"Hang on," I shouted through the pillow, and dragged myself to the door. Still dressed from the earlier phone call, I opened the door to Charlie, who looked at me as if he'd just seen my ghost.

"God! You okay?" he asked, with genuine concern.

"Yeah, bit of a session last night," I heard myself saying, like the kind of student I hated.

"Man, you look terrible," said Charlie. "Go splash your face."

In the bathroom, the smell of vomit was still clinging to the toilet seat, and I was in and out as fast as possible.

"What's going on?"

"Tell you in a minute," he said, and I trailed him groggily along the beige corridor, down the beige-walled staircase to the canteen, wondering if Celia – "my love" - was still there. He was marching fast, with rare determination.

"Where's Ingrid?" I asked, barely waking up as we queued for teas.

"Away for a few days. You know how she's matey with the guys who run SI?"

"Mm."

"You're not going to believe this, but all the left-wing groups have come together–"

"–you're right. It's not believable."

Charlie paid for our teas, picked them up and strode to a beige table.

"It's happened," he said.

"Even the Marxist-Leninists?"

"Well, the Marxists anyway. It's called Rock Against Racism."

"Catchy."

We sat down, a relief to stop moving. Charlie's urgency was causing me physical discomfort.

"Never seen you this bad."

"Thanks."

He stirred his tea slowly, getting ready to tell me his momentous news. He looked me in the eyes.

"Come on, what's the big deal?"

"They're looking for bands to do a launch gig at the poly."

"Great."

"Matt's band are on."

"They rock. And they're against racism. I hope."

"I told Ingrid to put Student Grunt on the bill."

"Wow! When is it?"

"A while yet, couple of weeks or so," he said.

"Do you think we'll be ready?"

"Come on, man. Ten-minute set. Five songs. We can play Bodies twice."

"I'll need an electric guitar. I'm broke."

"We'll get you one, no problem."

"What about Celia?"

"What about her? Oh, no, you haven't split up?"

"What? Why do you say that?"

"No reason. Why did you mention her?" My head was hurting and I was not enjoying this conversation. I needed a moment of silence. Or two. Actually, can you please stop talking, Charlie?

"She's working all the time. And she's got part one of her finals." And she told me she loved me and I'm not sure I'm ready to say it back. "When can we rehearse?"

I imagined Charlie and Ingrid, hanging out in her kitchen, Vesta ready meal rotating in the microwave, *Barry and Celia still together?* she asks. *I think so,* he says. *That one will never last,* she says, and they laugh gently in my little fiction; they're not judgemental but they can't help but feel smug.

"Celia doesn't need to rehearse. We'll do all the work and she can join us on the day."

My forehead throbbed like a bump on the head in Tom and Jerry. Charlie was fidgeting; even in my self-absorbed listlessness I could tell he was not in a great mood. I lit a cigarette, which further irritated him.

"She's so good. Come on, Barry, have faith."

"Everything okay?"

"Sorry, mate. Had a barney with Ingrid before she left."

"Oh, no."

"It's okay. She's spending a lot of time in London working on this project."

"That's great – isn't it?"

"For her, yeah. Means we're not seeing a lot of each other. And I don't want her to think I've been sitting on my arse all day while she's so busy."

"It's tough being a male feminist, Charlie."

"I do my bit," he said defensively. "You, however, are in a right state. What's going on man?"

"Okay. This Edinburgh business is pissing me off. They're all so bloody, I dunno, set in their ways. Not even sure I want to go."

"Barry, mate. Stop wasting your time with your la-de-da comedy pals. This is punk. It's now. It's the best buzz there is."

"You're right. Let's rehearse. Soon."

"Good man." Charlie jumped up. "Let's work out a time. Talk to Celia. I'll bring you that electric guitar soon."

He walked off, one more job completed on his packed "to do" list, back to his exciting routines, back to his relationship where the main problem was that he wasn't seeing his partner enough.

* * * * *

In a city renowned for its rolling hills, grand old buildings and striking maritime backdrop, Bristol's coach station was as pleasingly dull and functional as every coach station I'd ever visited. Trains conveyed the romance of exploration, cars the freedom of the open road, but for those with no money, the boring, motorway-bound coach was all we had.

I hung around inhaling diesel fumes, watching the dull procession of pallid teenagers and ancient grandmas alighting and boarding, alighting and boarding. The coach from Birmingham was "due", the board said, more in hope than expectation.

A man not much older than me, hovering, grey anorak with holes where the toggles used to be, caught my eye and smiled. He had dark, unwashed hair, his eyes too large for his face. I smiled back awkwardly.

"All right, my lover?" he said in a gentle Bristol accent. "Would you like to buy a watch?"

"No thanks."

"It's a good one."

"Sorry, mate," I shrugged. "Student."

I didn't know if he took it to mean "I'm broke" or "I have no need for the bourgeois constraints of timekeeping", but either way he walked off in search of another mug. The problem with trying to fob off stolen gear at a bus station is that almost everyone is as poor as you.

The Birmingham bus arrived, another poor timekeeper. More grandmas and pallid teens, but no sign of Kris – then there he was, grin recognisable from several yards, and we met with a comically male hug.

"Barry, great to see you."

"You too, Kris – looking well."

"We've only got a few minutes." He nodded towards a round, short man in tie and blazer, strolling away from the bus. "Driver's going for a quick piss then we're off."

"Okay."

"You know the Casablanca, bottom of the Royal Mile?"

"The porn cinema?"

Everyone who'd been to Edinburgh knew the Casablanca at the bottom of the Royal Mile.

"I've got a free slot there for the run of the Festival."

"That's good news, Kris."

"Would you like to do a show with me?"

This was the greatest moment in my life.

"Yes!" I responded instantly, knowing that everything else in my already packed-out creative life would have to fit around it. "I'd love to – but," not wishing to sound too needy, "I'm already doing two shows with the University Group. What time?"

"One thirty."

"Sounds fine."

"In the morning."

"Ah. Okay."

"That's why it's for free."

"Right. Aren't you doing any shows with Birmingham?"

"Nah, we fell out. They wouldn't let me do what I wanted."

I imagined Kris arguing with his own Richard and Hugo, articulating so much better than me things they wouldn't understand. I didn't doubt for a minute that he'd have been right.

"Haven't we missed the deadline for the Fringe programme?"

"Yeah, I checked," he said, business-like. Here was a man who knew what he wanted and how to get it. "We've missed the official deadline but they always produce a supplement. We've got two days to come up with a title and fifty words to describe the show."

"Bloody hell: how do we describe it?"

The driver came back and Kris turned back to the bus.

"I dunno, have a think. You've got my home number: call me tonight."

I nodded.

"Catch you later, Barry; it's gonna be great."

He walked off, then dashed back.

"One other thing. Can't stay with my drama company now. Can I spend a few nights at yours?"

"Er, let me check. I'll get back to you," I shouted, because he was already off and bounding up the steps of the bus. He turned and gave a big thumbs-up, pulling a face that made me laugh out loud. A roomful of punks, a mate at a bus station: Kris could win any audience.

He disappeared into the body of the coach and it disappeared round the corner, Devon bound. M32, M4, M5.

I walked from the station up the almost perpendicular St Michael's Hill, a small corner of Bristol in Edinburgh's image. In the next few weeks I had one rock gig, three comedy shows, a trip to Edinburgh to arrange, a month in the company of a troupe of students with whom I had nothing in common, a family difficulty I'd been avoiding for months; but none of this mattered because the funniest man I'd ever met wanted me to be a part of his world. Hours earlier, I'd been anxious, overwhelmed, broke. Was still. Nothing in those circumstances had changed – but I was no longer Barry Goldman, slumped over a toilet like a badly conceived metaphor. I was verified, established, funny-man Barry Goldman: long-haired, northern comic genius in a green-patterned tank top, thinking "This is what it must be like to be asked out by the most popular girl in the school".

How important was I in Kris's scheme of things? Had he been looking for a double-act partner for ages? A straight man? Or was I his last, desperate hope for somewhere to lodge in Edinburgh? He could stay with Harriet. I wouldn't have any trouble asking that. Celia doesn't need to know.

I reached the top of the hill and entered the university library, ugly and modern and totally at odds with its pseudo-Gothic surroundings. I needed to research an essay on Max Weber's Protestant work ethic but couldn't be bothered.

The phone call to Kris that night cost one pound eighty, and that was only the coins from my end. When my stash of ten-pence pieces ran out, Kris called me straight back from his parents' place, and we talked for ages about the kind of show we wanted to do. I say we, but mainly it was me listening, and laughing, as the ideas tumbled from Kris's mind and out of his mouth. They rarely followed from what we were talking about – just appeared, comedy conjured from nowhere.

At one point I had to stop him while I dashed back to my room to get a pen and notepad, and by the end of the call I had several sheets of foolscap crammed with sketches, characters and song and poem ideas. Kris was a star and this was my rock and comedy dreams rolled into one.

I didn't need Student Grunt.

I needed to tell Celia she couldn't stay with me in Edinburgh and chose the following day to break the news.

I prepared the speech in my head, repeated it to myself, edited, spoke aloud a couple of times, then kept it going round my mind, tweaking here or there to make it more conversational, spontaneous. "Celia, I've checked about the staying in Edinburgh... I've looked into every option for accommodation during the festival..."

I couldn't only parrot the words; they needed to sound sincere. I wanted everything to be right. Thought a nice meal would soften the blow.

"Aha, lamb curry!" were her first words as she came into the communal kitchen. "My favourite."

"You're in for a tasty surprise."

"Yes, I smelt it halfway down the corridor. Two exams today. It's been a long one," she said, hugging me from behind as I stirred the sauce. She brought her face close and kissed me on the lips. I smiled, awkwardly, sauce-speckled spatula in hand.

"Back on it, slave," she said, slapping my bum and fetching two plates from the cupboard. Connie, a plain, bespectacled geography second year from across the corridor, came in to make her own supper. I nodded to Celia towards our room, suggesting silently that we eat in there.

We sat together on the bed. I listened sympathetically to her dismay at the questions that came up in today's literature exam, accepting her animosity towards Hemingway and Steinbeck even though I'd never read either. Reaching the final mouthfuls of curried lamb, I gathered my thoughts to deliver The Speech.

"Barry..."

"Hmm?"

"I've been wanting to talk to you about something for a while. I'm not sure we can go on like this."

"Aha?"

"It's not fair on you Barry, not fair on both of us. I sometimes worry it feels like I'm using this place as a rent-free bolt hole."

"No, that's never bothered me-"

"Well it's bothered me, a lot, and yesterday I realised I spend too much time here" –she waved her arm, indicating the room – "is about my time spent in that canteen. I'm here because it's convenient."

"It's not a problem," I smiled, trying to hide my neediness and worried where this was heading.

"I've got a perfectly nice flat, in a nice part of town, away from student life, I've been neglecting the important things because I'm here so much."

"Are you saying... you don't want to be with me anymore?"

"No, no!" she said with genuine surprise. She moved the plates away – "Please don't get that impression" – cuddled close, then stared at me sympathetically, direct. For a moment I was a child, comforted and reassured, embraced in the arms of a woman who loved me.

"I want you to move in with me."

CHAPTER 18

I had no idea how long I'd been staring out of the window on the first floor at Celia's place, our place. Occasionally, someone opposite ran out of a front door, returning minutes later with a pint of milk or a sliced loaf, but most was Sunday afternoon silence and stillness – smart, stern Victorian houses, prim front gardens, well-groomed cars, only the leaves of the silver birches shimmered as they encountered the gentle rain.

It was great being a grown up. Moving in with Celia introduced me to a world I could never have imagined. There was a bedroom, with a bed that was big enough for two. A bathroom, exclusively ours, a kitchen for cooking and eating, and a living room for living. This is how adult couples live. I liked it. I felt guilty that there was still a couple of weeks' rent being paid on the student hall by my parents, but that had almost come to an end.

It was great being a grown up. The physical side of the relationship had improved as dramatically as the bed size. I was enjoying the proximity of Celia's beautiful naked body.

Trouble was, I wasn't the only one.

Before I'd gone to see a preview of Celia's Edinburgh show, she had warned me to keep an open mind. Infinity Theatre's creation, Das Kapital: The Musical, was a performance piece, Celia had told me, that sought to examine critically the contrast between ownership of capital and labour. Amusing songs like Machine Dream and What's The Kapital Of Russia? pulsated through the tiny theatre space at Bristol Arts Centre.

The highlight was Celia's solo performance – a sweet and moving ballad called This Body's All I Have. It began promisingly enough, an examination of female factory work as slave labour, but developed into a more unsubtle articulation of the parallels with prostitution. Modest Victorian petticoats and underclothes were removed with the sensuous delicacy and mesmerising stage presence that had drawn me to Celia in the first place, and by the end of the song it wasn't just the evil factory owner on stage gawping at my beautiful girlfriend, naked as the day she was born. An entire audience were appreciating the spectacle, comfortable in the knowledge that they were watching a damning indictment of capitalist power and not a live sex show in Soho.

I smiled enthusiastically in the bar after the show, full of praise for the cast and director, the challenging politics and amusing songs. Fortunately, everyone was too polite to ask me the one question I least wanted to answer. Eventually, Celia joined and broke the ice with a joke about us wondering if we recognised her with her clothes on, and we grinned our way through the time it took to finish our drinks – shorter than usual, in this case.

Walking to the bus stop, I still hadn't worked out which Feminist Barry I would be: the one who had no proprietorial entitlements over his girlfriend's body? Or the one who had just watched a bunch of leery men objectifying that figure? What would Sheila Rowbotham say?

We talked for a while on the bus about the music and the message but in the end it was me who brought up It.

"Your song, it was beautiful."

"Thanks."

"Best song in the show. How did you feel about... you know?"

"Naked."

"Yes. Well. Naked."

"You know me on stage, Barry. It's all or nothing."

"Or in that case, both."

She laughed. "Did it make you feel uncomfortable?"

The uncomfortable pause answered her question.

"No, of course not. I can see how it was pertinent to what you were singing about."

"Thanks," she said. "I appreciate that."

It felt like there was more to say, but we carried on home, arm in arm, until we got to the front door and Celia said: "Do you have a problem with it?"

"No, no, of course not," I heard myself saying. "It's your show. Your decision. Your body."

She held me close and kissed me. "You're a good man, Barry."

And that was it. We went through our late-night rituals, ending with us cuddling close in bed in our shared nakedness.

"You're not worried the audience will be a bunch of perverts?" I asked, surprised I was still thinking about it.

"No." She moved away, sat up.

"Okay."

"Are you worried, Barry? I thought you agreed it was my decision."

"I wanted to be sure you didn't feel... forced into doing it by Nicholas."

"You mean Neville. The director. It wasn't Neville's suggestion, Barry. It was mine. My body. My decision."

That really was the end of it.

* * * * *

"He won't come any quicker if you keep staring out the window," Celia said as she brought me a mug of tea and a Penguin.

"I'm not staring for Kris," I lied. "I'm still enjoying the novelty of having a window with a proper view."

"Does he know your new address?"

"Yes: he said he'd be on the two forty-five coach. Should have arrived more than an hour ago."

"Do you think he might have got lost?"

"I gave him directions. Bus or walk, it's not that far."

I understood this was a punishment for cockiness. The stern moral upbringing of childhood had turned weary old sayings into half-believed truths. "Don't brag", "What goes around comes around", "Pride comes before a fall."

Kris asking me to join him had seriously inflated my levels of self-importance. I was belligerent at Edinburgh rehearsals, certain I knew more about humour than any of them. Is Kris ever going to ask you to work with him, Hugo? I don't think so. But with the Festival approaching, self-doubt returned. I knew Kris had a lot to organise, and was having to commute between Birmingham and Devon, but it was getting harder to keep in touch.

What if Richard was right? Would Shakespeare's understanding of the human condition always be the only route to comedy? I already knew my world of non-sexist, non-racist, radical left-wing jesting was small and select. Would anyone outside our tiny circle care about my wishy-washy world view?

Kris's fall-out with his student group in Birmingham had been spectacular, he explained. He was having to organise everything for himself – travel, accommodation, publicity. There were plenty of good reasons for him to be missing my calls or failing to get back in touch, but as each day passed without hearing from him, I became convinced he had dumped me and was avoiding contact. Even when he finally called to say he'd be coming to Bristol, I wondered if this was part of an elaborate prank to string me along further. His failure to turn up now confirmed that.

"You sure you've got the right day?"

"Yes," I snapped.

We were both taken aback by the rage in my voice. I knew I should have apologised but was too angry. Angry at Celia for being there all the time, angry at Kris for not, angry with Hugo and Harriet and Maurice and my parents, and myself for being unable to contain my anger.

The doorbell rang, and I smiled.

"Sorry," I said, anger melting into a mixture of relief and contrition. I held her close, as if to emphasise the apology. What is the socially acceptable amount of time required for an apology hug with your partner when you're desperate to go off and do something else? I managed to hold for a full three seconds before she sensed my twitchiness.

"Answer it," she said.

I leapt down the stairs, bounced over the shoes and umbrellas straggled on the beige lino tiles and opened the door.

It was Charlie.

"Surprise!" he announced, beaming, electric guitar held high. "Let's rehearse."

"Wasn't expecting you."

"I know," he said, following me up the stairs, "but I picked this up and couldn't wait."

"Hey, Celia, it's Charlie!"

"Hi, Charlie," she called.

"Sorry to jump in unannounced," he said. "Any chance of joining us for a rehearsal... with an axe!" he emphasised.

"Okay," she said, but I could tell she didn't want to.

"Would you like a cup of tea?" I asked.

"Sure." He followed me into the kitchen, taking in the new

surroundings like he was deciding whether to move in. "Nice set-up you've got here, Barry. Proper grown up."

"Really? That's how I think of you two."

"Nah, me and Ingrid, we're free spirits."

"Yeah, peace, man. I'm not sure how long we'll be able to do this, I'm supposed to be rehearsing a new show, someone's coming over, could be any time."

"No problem, Barry, I didn't even know if you'd be in. Wrap your hands around this baby," he said in a deliberately ironic voice, handing me the guitar.

It was a Fenton, a make I had never heard of. The word was written in exactly the same lettering as Fender, at the end of the fretboard, so you could pretend you were holding a Fender Stratocaster, the Rolls-Royce of electric guitars, and not a cheap Taiwanese knock-off. I held it up to the light, strapped it over my left shoulder.

I'd never worn an electric guitar. It was surprisingly heavy. My acoustic was bigger, but most of its bulk was fresh air, an empty box encased by wood amplifying the sound. The electric required no box; it was simply a thin block of solid wood and plastic, fretboard tacked on.

The Fender Stratocaster was, according to most rock musicians, a beautiful example of precision engineering. The Fenton was not. I strummed a few chords, but they were barely audible.

"Where am I going to plug it in?"

"I'm picking up the amplifier tomorrow. You can stick it in your record player for now."

I squeezed past Celia, whose kit was taking up a lot of space in the living room, plugged the end of the jack into the hi-fi. It made a pop that gave me a slight shock. I strummed a few chords, and instantly understood the masculine potency of rock and roll.

This wasn't a musical instrument; it was a cross between a machine gun and a giant dildo. The right hand stroked gently up and down, pretty much at masturbation level. The left hand was at the end of the long, hard shaft of the fretboard, fingers producing musical notes by gently caressing the strings. The symbolism could not have been more sexually explicit. My left hand was finding the G spot, along with the C, D and F sharp minor spot. The experience was like a scene from one of Maurice's porn magazine stories, and in less than a minute I had regressed from sensitive feminist to horny rock God.

I threw my head back like Jimmy Page, hair falling back between shoulder blades, and attempted the two or three lead guitar solos I had earnestly learned to pluck on my old acoustic: Black Dog by Led Zeppelin, Layla by Derek and the Dominos, Dance on a Volcano by Genesis. I rarely admitted my closet love for those pseudo-classical, Christian-literary, semi-symphonic purveyors of pompous prog rockery; even Celia had been surprised to discover Nursery Cryme and Foxtrot hidden guiltily like a stash of Maurice's magazines behind my more prominently displayed Ian Dury and Talking Heads records.

Holding this giant penis substitute, I was the sexiest, hunkiest, funkiest guy at the party, whom all the women were craving the attention of. I was quite surprised that, instead of expressing the correct measure of awe, Celia and Charlie laughed. Whatever charismatic "x" factor Jimmy Page and Eric Clapton possessed that made the ladies swoon, I didn't own. Never mind, I thought: one more routine to add to Kris's comedy show, and I immediately forgave him for failing to show up. Nothing was funnier, it appeared, than a man thinking he could be something that he was not.

We argued into existence a set for the forthcoming big Rock Against Racism gig: Bodies by The Sex Pistols, New Rose by The Damned, Yorkshire Punk (the song that used to be known as

Yorkshire Reggae), Fascist Scum (one of Charlie's) and Bodies (again). We practised a few times, with and without Celia out of consideration for the neighbours. We may have been in the frontline of the angry, nihilistic movement that was terrifying decent society, but we were polite, middle-class nihilists. Our sound wasn't pretty, but it was getting tighter and I was becoming devoted to the sex pistol strapped around my neck. Celia and Charlie may have found my rock moves ironically amusing but I powered through Charlie's right-on anthem to left-wing values, convinced I'd unearthed a legitimate, non-sexist route to alpha-male sexuality.

CHAPTER 19

Boring boring boring,
Boring boring Gawd,
Boring boring boring,
Boring boring bored.
Boring boring gardens,
Boring boring weeds.
Boring boring Moortown,
Boring boring Leeds.

School weekends were always full of expectation: Saturday afternoons meant Leeds United, sport on TV, delicious anticipation of the football scores as they trickled through to the studio on the tickertape printer. I wasn't good at maths, yet could instantly calculate our position in the league the moment the score for a rival team came through.

But Saturday mornings, how they dragged. How slowly the morning synagogue service crept, as it was doing now, like time travel had been invented, and the rest of the world was zooming forward while we rose and sat, rose and sat, frozen in a world that seemed to have stopped developing in the nineteenth century, parroting meaningless thanks to an almighty and eternal God from 5,000 years ago. Rabbis robed in flowing white gowns sang and spoke in a language no one understood – "sang" is generous, as we wailed plaintively and tunelessly like sulking teenagers.

Home for a cousin's bar mitzvah, I was feeling the tedium more than usual today. Kris and I had made phone contact briefly and he apologised for not turning up, but with less than a fortnight to the start of the Festival, we were running out of time to work together. Charlie wanted one more rehearsal before the Rock Against Racism gig. Richard and Hugo were angry that I'd taken this weekend off. Half-written poems sat accusingly in my notebook, in need of love and nourishment but mostly time, which I didn't have.

Life with Celia was a little chilly, she had decided not to go to Edinburgh after all. "I thought about what you said Barry. About the pervy guys. The more I thought about it," she explained to me one night, "the more I thought: This is not a critique of capitalism. It's a bunch of horny, left-wing men critiquing my tits." I was sorry she wouldn't be in Edinburgh, a little relieved but mostly guilty about being the source of her decision. Still, one less accommodation headache. There were a million jobs but here I was, an atheist in a house of worship whose only religious request was "Please, God, let my people go."

We Jews had some cracking stories – Adam and Eve, Noah's Ark, Moses and the parting of the Red Sea, slaves, plagues, wars, sibling rivalry, sex, food, human sacrifice, burning bushes – but none featured today. It was all "Blessed is the Lord, may the Lord cherish you, I am an angry Lord, the Lord is holy, holy-holy-holy, blessed be thy name, oh Lord–" Enough already! Who are we, the Moonies? If I have to sit through this all morning, at least entertain me with more of that eye-for-an-eye, blood-and-guts malarkey.

"Is the Lord your Shepherd?" I whispered across to Dad.

"Shh," he scowled.

My father, not the Christian one who art in heaven but the bloke sitting next to me, was absorbed in the service, which surprised me. He was normally contemptuous about religion: even if God existed, Dad would say, I'd cross the street to avoid him.

Dad rarely talked about his active war service, but my sister and I had joined up the few stories he'd told to form a picture. Towards the end of the War he'd been involved in bomb disposal in northern Italy. One day, the officer ahead of him opened a booby-trapped door and was blown to pieces; another time, a soldier marching by his side stood on a landmine that blew off his leg. These random incidents had taught dad not to place faith in the wisdom of an unseen hand operating far above the sky. As for the idea that He was acting specifically on behalf of the Jewish people, World War Two had put us all right on that one.

The sun was light and gay outside, but inside was dark and gloomy. Odd rays of light sneaked through a corner of the stained-glass window behind us, but the building next door blocked out most of them. Years ago, this had been Moortown Movie Palace. The transformation from cinema to synagogue was complete but it could never quite shake off the fact that it had been built to keep light out. The men sat downstairs, while upstairs still resembled the upper circle and was occupied by the women. Centre stage was a large pair of velvet curtains, behind which stood a cupboard, the ark. At various points in the service, the curtains opened and closed, revealing the sacred scrolls used in the service but no exciting Pearl and Dean ads or main features.

You could argue, as Dad did during his contrary moments, that Judaism was a feminist religion.

"See how the women are upstairs," he'd say proudly, "looking down with disdain on the men."

"But we're only spectators," Judith laughed. "The service is run by and for men."

"And women aren't called to participate," I added.

"Anyway, Dad, feminism isn't about superiority but equality," Judith added.

His heart wasn't in the argument. He was only trying, like so many men of his generation, to make sense of this strange new world where women who worked in his factory were expecting to be paid the same money for the same job as men.

Judith was back today. She was upstairs, looking bored, like she didn't want to be there. Mum looked sad, like she didn't want to be looked at by everyone else in the community, judging her because she looked sad because her daughter Judith was there looking bored, like she didn't want to be there.

My cousin David's bar mitzvah was focused around the Ten Commandments. But this wasn't the famous part that everyone knew, His almightiness conveying easy-to-remember rules to Moses about lying, murder and adultery. This was from around thirty years later, when The People sought to amend the commandment about coveting your neighbour's wife, insisting that his ox and his ass should be added to the all-important list of non-covetables.

The Ten Commandments were not, I now understood, unchangeable decrees from God literally set in stone, but a bunch of man-made laws to guide people in their daily lives. This was a profound revelation: a story, actually told in the Bible, about how God is nothing more than a symbolic representation of the collective power of all humanity.

"When you hear the politicians in Parliament argue over minor issues," the Rabbi roared in his sermon, "they sound like little children, squabbling in the playground."

You're not wrong there, mate.

"But these are important matters and have far-reaching consequences."

I pictured a small gaggle of Jewish politicians and lawyers in the Egyptian desert, hungry and broke, yelling at each other about how Avram had seen Yitzhak eyeing up his tasty-looking ox in a funny way.

"You may not believe in God," he roared, and I swear he was looking directly at me, "this holy service may make no sense to you, but know that however busy you are, however much you think you have to do, it's important to stop every now and then, put yourself in a place far away from all that, and remember you're only here today because generations before you cared enough to devise laws that would survive long after they did. Barry."

After the service, Dad and I strolled into the small courtyard outside, my arm gently behind his back, looking like a normal father and son. He'd forgotten about our differences but was troubled and I felt protective towards him. It took a moment for my eyes to adjust to the bright sunshine. Someone walked towards me; with the sun above, it was difficult to tell who. He looked like a thinner, handsome version of Maurice but I still had no idea until he was close up and punching me hard, too hard, on my left bicep.

"Crikey, Maurice! Didn't recognise you. You've lost so much weight!"

"Thanks, you're still a scruffy schlock."

"Thanks. How's business?"

"Business is business," Maurice said, conveying the comedy voice and shoulder shrug amusing when between Jews, racist when not.

"Business studies," I corrected as Dad wandered dreamily towards Mum and Judith.

"It's going well, all thanks to you," he said.

"Why me? Have you renounced capitalism?"

"Not at all. I have embraced comedy."

"Is that a girl's name?"

"Ha ha, very droll. I've been putting on cabaret shows at the students' union."

"Ah, sorry for assuming it was always about sex for you. I'd forgotten it's sometimes about money."

I saw Mum and Judith gently bring Dad towards them. I wasn't the only one who had noticed him acting strangely.

"Are you suggesting I'm not committed to promoting the live comedic experience?"

"I think the phrase you used at my gig was 'wall-to-wall student totty'?"

"My social circle has widened."

"Your belly has shrunkened, though," I said, still unsettled by this familiar stranger. "Guess you'll be going to Edinburgh again, then?"

He looked blank.

"You're putting on cabaret gigs. Won't you want to catch up with the latest comedy?"

"I guess..."

"You've forgotten, haven't you? You only went last year because you thought you could get your end away."

He nodded in acknowledgment, no embarrassment. Fat or thin, Maurice remained reassuringly sexist.

"There's going to be some amazing, innovative stuff there," I added.

"You're not going, then?"

"With lines of that calibre, Maurice, I'm surprised you're not performing a one-man show yourself."

Mum was manoeuvring Dad from the crowd, keen to steer him from the polite company of her fellow synagogue goers.

The three of them set off home.

"I'm doing five different shows."

"Five!"

"Three will be rubbish," I said as we walked slowly, not bothering to catch up with the others. "Odd lines in plays and a sketch show. 'Shopkeeper'. 'Policeman'. 'Priest'."

"Father Goldman? I like it. Is Harriet going?"

"No idea. I'm calling her, anyway."

We reached the corner of his street, but he stood for a moment, almost like he was expecting me to do something. Maybe ask her if he could stay again? "Come on, Maurice, what else are you going to do all summer? Sit on your lazy, no-longer-fat arse and watch horse racing on the telly?"

"Okay. I'll think about it," he said, and turned away.

"Call you later," I said to his back.

I caught up with the others and hung back with Judith, out of earshot of Mum and Dad. Judith had always been a bit of a stranger to me, the age gap so pronounced when I was younger that we had almost nothing in common. I was starting to get to know her when she moved away.

I told her about the factory and the difficulties Dad was having.

"Do you think it's done for?" she asked.

"No idea. Had to cut back since January."

"You need to get a part-time job."

"I'm hoping to make some money in Edinburgh next month."

"How?"

"Doing a show." She turned to me, eyebrows raised. "I'm a performer now."

She snorted.

"What's that supposed to mean?" I asked. I knew Judith was sceptical about my poetry-reading.

"Whoever made money performing?"

"Elton John?"

"Don't rely on it, okay?"

She told me she had a new boyfriend, Craig.

"Ooh, what's he like? What does he do? Is he Jewish? Is he rich? Nice family?" I asked, mimicking the childlike excitement of our relatives whenever the prospect of new nephews and nieces arose.

"Yes, he's very rich. He's a drug dealer."

"As long as he's Jewish."

"He was an economics student. I'd known him vaguely at university."

"And is he?"

"Is he what?"

"Chosen? Snipped at birth?"

"What about me? Has that conversation finished already? You're worse than Aunty Eva. He goes out with me. Happens to be Jewish, yes."

"Are you bringing joy to your parents, Judith?"

"No, I am not pregnant, Barry. I'm running a women's book publishing collective. And, unlike you," she said as we arrived back home, "I'm making a living."

Standing at the doorstep, to our unpleasant surprise, was Grandma. Too poorly to miss the Barmitzvah service, well enough to join us for lunch.

"What time do you call this?"

"Lovely to see you, Grandma," I smiled convincingly.

"Hi, Grandma."

Mum and Dad, who had gone ahead of us, opened the door and let us in.

"You I don't recognise. Why don't you visit anymore?"

"I live and work in London, Grandma."

"Where's that? The moon? Three hours on the train last time I looked."

Grandma walked slowly from the hall entrance into the dining room. She stopped every few steps, Judith and I lagging behind like the servants she expected us to be. When she stopped, we stopped.

"Monty, what's happening with the business?" she asked sharply as she brushed past him and went to take her seat at the dining table. "I'm hearing bad things."

"It's shabbas; we don't talk business on shabbas."

Grandma laughed gaily – "That's a good excuse!" – but turned to us and pointedly ignored him. "During the week I can't ask him about business because he's too tired. And today I can't ask because it's your holy day of rest. I've heard them all now."

"Have you heard the one about the interfering mother-in-law, Rebecca?"

"Maybe Sunday you can fit me in," she said, ignoring Dad's hostility. "Don't tell me, maybe Sunday you convert to Christianity and you can't tell me then, either."

"Mum, stop fighting; it's shabbas", Mum said, hoping to distract us with a steaming vat of chicken soup.

"We're not fighting, Sybil; we're joking," Dad said.

"You might be," said Grandma. "I'm not laughing."

"Barry tells jokes now, don't you Barry?" said Dad, trying to lighten the mood but still sounding threatening. "You must know lots of mother-in-law jokes."

"I don't do mother-in-law jokes, Dad."

"Why not? Don't tell me: women's lib, is that it? Not you as well as her?" Judith gave me a pained look; she'd never seen him this aggressive.

"I don't have a mother-in-law. I wouldn't know what to say."

"You never see a horse in a pub but Tommy Cooper's got a great joke about that."

"I don't tell those kind of jokes."

"Monty, he's saying he doesn't tell jokes, you're saying he's a comedian: one of you must be a filthy ligna."

"Two kneidlach, Barry?" Mum asked, as she dished out the dumplings into the chicken soup.

"Yes, two please, Mum."

"Judith, do you know how long you'll be staying?"

"I have to go back later, Mum."

Mum continued to steer the conversation away from business, and comedy, or anything that involved Dad talking to Grandma.

I escaped as soon as I could and ran to Mum and Dad's bedroom, where I rang Harriet. She told me she'd already "come down" from Oxford, was working on the Mary Quant counter at Schofield's hating every minute, counting the days before going to Edinburgh. Of course she was going; she wasn't just going, she had the programme and told me the name of every show she had already marked to see, a mix of international theatre, bawdy comedy, contemporary dance and even a one-man show that BUTCH were taking, featuring one of Richard's drama department colleagues Mr Ponting as Dylan Thomas.

"I'm so excited you're going to be there."

"Me too," I said, "but I'm going to be working sixteen hours a day."

"That's a shame; it'd be nice to have someone to come with me to the shows."

And it would be lovely for me, I thought, aware I still had feelings for Harriet, who felt like a soulmate.

"I've got a friend who might need a place to stay for a few nights?"

"Sure, I'll ask Laurence. What sort of a friend, Barry?" she asked coyly.

"A performer. I'm doing a show with him."

"Another performer? Seen a lot of them this year."

"You've met someone, then?"

"Who are you? My mum? What do you care?"

"Curious," I said, winding the curly phone wire round my index finger. "Making conversation."

"Nosey. What about you?"

"Who are you? My mum?"

We carried on chatting, easily, relaxed. I told her a little more about Kris, fighting Nazis, Charlie and Ingrid and the band (but not the drummer); she told me about writing articles for her student magazine. I told her about Richard, and Shakespeare, she came up with a theory that our lives were like a Shakespearean comedy. I told her that Maurice seemed to have matured this year, but no, I wasn't trying to sell him to her as a prospective boyfriend. Why couldn't I talk like this with Celia?

Returning downstairs, I heard raised voices in the kitchen, Mum and Dad arguing, and I guessed correctly about me.

"He's got his own life, Monty; you can't force him back," I made out from Mum, who sounded furious.

"He's my son, it's a family business, I need him here now."

I thought of going in, then Mum said: "He's my son, too, and I'm not having him dragged into your family's problems."

Dad replied: "Trust you to take his side and gang up on me."

I decided there was no need for me ever to talk to my dad again.

CHAPTER 20

The last Student Grunt rehearsal went well. With the gig less than forty-eight hours away there was an urgency that brought us together. Charlie and Celia developed an understanding of each other's musical timing, which was vital for improving the band's sound, communicating in a way they never managed in the everyday run of manners and conversation.

I mentioned this to Celia as we were getting ready for bed and she laughed.

"I know," she said. "You find out a lot about someone when the two of you have to create something together."

"That's exactly what I'm learning with the theatre group," I said. "When I'm on stage with Camilla, it feels like she's enabling my performance. But with Hugo, I feel inhibited and can tell I'm never as good."

"Is that Hugo's fault or yours?"

"What do you mean?"

"You've had an attitude to this guy since the day you met him."

"He hated me!"

"And now he's having to work with you." She carried on removing her make-up in the bathroom mirror, occasionally looking at me in the reflection. "What if he's moved on? Only you're bringing negative energy to the stage and he's getting all wound up again?"

"Okay," I said, struggling to entertain the outrageous possibility that it wasn't Hugo but me who needed to change their approach.

I turned up for rehearsal next morning determined to be more understanding. The script was finished, our job to learn lines as quickly as possible – by the end of the week at the latest. But band rehearsals were taking all my time.

I'd already explained to Richard why I was running behind with the line learning, and thought it might help to tell Hugo.

"You have a band gig?" he asked, like a middle-aged professor being spoken to in a foreign language.

"Yeah, we're doing the Rock Against Racism show tomorrow at the poly."

"Rock against Racism," he repeated slowly, making it clear that at least two of the words were unfamiliar to him.

"After tomorrow it'll be over and I'll be fully committed to the shows."

"What made you think you had time to fit in another 'gig'? The Festival starts in less than a week."

"I tried to get out of it," I said.

"Obviously not very hard," he said, walking away, as though he had already wasted enough time in the dreaded proximity of the long-haired Jew.

The rehearsal carried on without incident, but when it came to my first batch of poems, Hugo tutted and sighed, rolling his eyes throughout, which made it hard to concentrate.

"When are you planning to be off the book?" Richard asked with barbed politeness.

"I use the book on stage for poems," I said. "I'll know all the sketch lines by Thursday."

"You can't have the book on stage!" said Hugo. "We'll look like amateurs."

"We are amateurs!" said Camilla.

"I always use a book," I said. "All poets do. It's like a prop."

"Looks more like a crutch to me," said Hugo, pleased at his little joke.

"You could have a lectern," said Richard.

"No thanks," I said. "I'm reading poetry, not giving a lecture."

"A lectern would be good," Hugo said to Richard, like I wasn't in the room. "Jenny!" he called to our lighting technician. "Can you pull up front spot three?"

Within seconds, a stunning yellow light illuminated the exact space where I was standing, shining straight into my eyes. I felt splodges of colour dance angrily in front of me.

"Don't look into the light, you idiot!" Richard shouted.

"I know!" I shouted back. "I wasn't expecting that!"

Hugo hauled a lectern across to me. This was a prop for a sixteenth-century drama and seemed like an absurdly over-the-top podium from which to deliver my slight rhyming jokes.

I placed my book on the lectern and, channelling the energy of Kris in Shakespeare doublet and hose, turned my performance into that of a ham actor delivering his lines in a manner suggesting that the words were less important than the person delivering them.

There were a few smiles and polite titters from the others – even Richard looked as if he was trying not to laugh. Only Hugo was failing to find this funny, turning red with anger. It took me another couple of moments to understand why the others were suppressing their laughter – unwittingly, I had been, down to the last syllable and overwrought inflection, mimicking Hugo the Serious Actor.

I hadn't meant to do this but it was too late to stop. Only now they read my doubting thoughts, and the performance fell apart. Kris would never have allowed his mind to wander like that. I tried another poem, one of my funniest, but the awkward atmosphere killed it, and each joke trailed into the dark, never to be recalled.

The others continued watching, a mix of pity and resignation. I had taken on the hated Hugo, and lost. His features remained impassively bleak. Richard looked straight at me, anger in his eyes.

"Sketch number 14," he boomed. "Martian Chip Shop." And, in a much quieter voice as he walked past me, "Lose the lectern."

That evening, Celia laughed as I told her about the incident with Hugo. "That'll teach me to offer you theatrical advice," she said.

"No, it was the right thing to do. I tried to be nice. He thought I was winding him up."

We'd been hoping to squeeze in one more Student Grunt rehearsal but Charlie didn't turn up until after eight. Ingrid had heard rumours the National Front were planning to attack the gig, and he'd been calling on friends, urging them to come in numbers the following night. He couldn't concentrate through the rehearsal; we sensed his anxiety and stopped quickly. I was relieved. I'd been feeling a new surge of affection for Celia and wanted to enjoy our time alone before Edinburgh.

I wanted to thank her for being there for me, for understanding when I brought home my daily Hugo miseries, putting in all that work with the band, keeping me sane as the madness engulfed. I wanted to say all that after Charlie had gone, but as soon as we'd cleared the living room and put the kettle on, the doorbell rang again. We looked at each other, nervous. All this talk of angry fascists disrupting our gig had made us paranoid.

I crept downstairs and, before opening the door, asked "Who is it?"

"It's me!"

I opened the door. Kris beamed.

"Slight change of plan," he said, stepping confidently in, dragging two heavy suitcases. "Have to go to Birmingham tomorrow." He explained that he'd managed to charm a couple of hours of student union office time to print the details for our show, and needed to talk to me about our leaflet.

Before we'd reached the top of the stairs he was detailing our itinerary, full of ideas and enthusiasm. Celia greeted him politely; this was the first time she'd met him and I was keen for her to understand why he was so special to me. But she was tired, had work early next morning, and left soon after we'd established that he and I needed to talk – and yes, of course he could stay the night.

I told him about the gig and, as we prepared his bed out of worn sofa cushions, I recounted my Hugo horror stories. He was a good listener, sympathetic, easy to be around. I told him I felt under-rehearsed for our show. He was reassuring. We only need a few short pieces together, he said; we have enough solo material to make up the bulk of the show.

We discussed ideas, laughed, improvised crazy conversations and wrote down the best of them. After about an hour we stopped, and discussed meeting and working once we were in Edinburgh.

"Let's meet outside the Fringe office, Saturday at two," he said.

"Can't promise," I said. "I'll be working with my company. Is there a phone number to call you at?"

"I'll be dossing on the Casablanca floor the first couple of nights. Maybe ring there?"

"Sure."

"Don't suppose I can grab some space at your company digs?" he asked.

"I've got a friend from Leeds who's planning to be there. Her brother's got a flat."

"Great! I'll be out most of the time. They'll barely know I'm there."

"They've got a broom cupboard. Literally. I stayed last year. If you don't mind sharing with cleaning fluids."

"Barry, mate: you're a star."

We talked more about publicity, leafletting, big plans and future dreams. I'd never known someone with so much creative energy and wit. Kris made me laugh harder than anyone I'd known until finally, barely able to keep my eyes open, I left him to sleep.

Next morning, Celia was already up and I could hear the business-like bustle and low muttering of the two of them, cups and bowls clinking, kettle boiling, suitcases clacking shut, Kris clearing away all traces of his presence from the night before. I hadn't slept well with the anticipation of the days and weeks ahead, brain fizzing with excitement – new lines for poems – and banality – must remember to give Kris Harriet's number. I shuffled groggily to the bathroom, heard Celia offering Kris a cup of tea, him politely accepting, thanking her warmly for letting him stay. I didn't hear the rest of the conversation but recognised Celia's laugh, the one from when she was most relaxed. Kris had won her over, naturally.

I joined them for breakfast, two slices of toast and a cup of tea, discussing in the slow murmur of wakefulness our plans for the day. Celia reminded me to pick up the van Charlie had hired to take our gear to the venue this afternoon, and Kris and I had a final talk about plans for Edinburgh.

"Gotta go," said Celia. She pecked me on the cheek and was out the door. "See you at the gig at five." As the front door closed, Kris looked at me and scrunched his lips, like Les Dawson as a dirty old man, then smiled and got up as well. Was he ironically mimicking the kind of sexist responses men gave when they saw an attractive woman? Or was he a secret sexist? I often asked these questions of myself. Either way, it made me laugh.

He cleared away his breakfast things, went to the bathroom, done before I'd finished my tea. A quick "See ya" as he walked past the kitchen then down the stairs with suitcases and gone, as efficiently as when he'd arrived. It was exhilarating and exhausting being in Kris's orbit. He filled my head with exciting dreams and possibilities. I realised I was still absolutely knackered and returned briefly to bed.

CHAPTER 21

The fantasy underpinning live rock and roll conceals a universe of mundane tedium in a thousand humdrum tasks. Even before arriving at the venue, our ten minutes of performing required equipment to be checked as present and working. The hire van had to be loaded as quickly as possible in the hope that thieves wouldn't spot the back-and-forth from the house, driven to the venue and parked in reasonable proximity to the stage door, and unloaded before traffic wardens had a moment to spot the yellow line parking.

"Left here... no, here," Charlie said sharply, shortly after I'd picked him up.

"There is no left," I said.

"Hang on," he said, turning the A to Z map 180 degrees.

"Sorry, right – turn right!"

I'd never driven a van before, never driven in Bristol, a city that had grown organically over centuries on hills with roads that wound and twisted, wide and narrow. I knew how to get there on foot but had paid no attention to the One Way and No Entry signs. Charlie was even more clueless with directions.

"There we are," he said triumphantly, as we drove down Park Street.

"This bit I know; it's the back entrance we need. Finding the lost city of Atlantis is easier."

Tiny roads meandered up and down behind Bristol Hippodrome, some blocked by fellow selfish parkers, one a dead end. Finally, we saw another van like ours and spotted Matt carrying a bass drum in a box almost as big as Matt himself. We pulled up behind them, saw the driver of Matt's van in animated conversation with a traffic warden, and decided that now would be a good moment to drop the gear as fast as we could. With the traffic warden preoccupied, we unloaded in record time.

I left Charlie with the gear and went in search of the next holy grail: an available parking space. Like King Arthur, I came to realise that such treasures might be unattainable, at least in this lifetime. I gave up and crawled to the multi-storey car park hewn into the hill where, a century earlier, Isambard Kingdom Brunel had pioneered the form. This had been the site of his Great Western Hotel, where you came to stay after taking the Great Western Railway from London, and Great Western horse-drawn cabs taxied you from the station, dropped you off at the top, then circled back down the Great Western Multi-Storey Horse Park Spiral towards the station.

The van was too tall, I discovered, when hearing the roof bang hard and loud against the height limit barrier. The cars behind had to reverse to allow me to escape. I wondered if this ever happened to Elton John. There was an empty parking meter nearby, I gave thanks to the glory of God and, after what seemed like a lifetime of manoeuvring, parked and got out.

Stuffing the meter with 10-pence pieces, I was aware of a small gathering of teenage boys in leather jackets peering at me. Friend or foe? Did the letters NF on their jackets stand for No Future or National Front? If I stared too hard, they might wonder why I was looking at them in a funny way.

I turned away. Too late: one stared back. I didn't recognise his face, but the spider web tattoo on his neck was familiar from our triumphant afternoon in Knowle. They'd seen my guitar case. This had stayed with me in the front of the van while the rest of the gear was unloaded. Did I look like a Rock musician, Against Racism? They looked like they might be For it.

Without glancing behind, I felt them following me. There were pedestrians nearby. I stayed calm but walked slightly faster, pretending to be one of those people who walks faster on a whim, without knowing who such people might be. And this wasn't me looking back, no. It was an ordinary, long-haired bloke flicking his hair and happening to glance behind; surely that wasn't eight of them now? Passed the Hatchet Inn, "Bristol's oldest pub", hatchet in my head, no thanks. I stopped. They stopped. In that instant, I saw looks of grim determination on their faces, closer and sharper than in all my years of following Leeds United, when most violence I'd seen had taken place at a comfortable distance. I'd never felt more Jewish.

There were fewer bodies. We were in a confusing garret of handsome Georgian streets, where each grand house was a solicitor's office and the daily work of managing the continued fruits of the slave trade took place. I recognised these narrow roads only as the ones I'd got lost in while driving a few minutes earlier. Everything was neat and in order, unlike my thoughts. I was lost in this English paradise of ordered wealth and civilisation. Hemmed in the tiny backstreets where the tightly packed terraces blocked out the light. I could have stepped in to McKinley Struthers, a law firm announcing its place in this world in the form of a shiny brass plate by the door, except that that fortress of refined wealth was designed to keep the likes of me and the punks out. Baskets of summer flowers hung outside the elegant houses, a riot of colour. (Please don't think of riots now, Barry.) Could almost hear the Dr Martens boots clumping behind.

Another dead end. Froze. Turned. Looked at them. Saw in my panic I'd missed the side of the poly. I walked into Unity Street (Unity is strength. For them though, not me). Faster now, back on to Park Street and the bustle and noise of city life. I crossed the road to safety. Slid behind the archway at the end of College Green council buildings and watched them emerge. About ten of them. They looked round, didn't see me, wandered back into town.

They didn't seem too bothered; following me had been a moment of sport, a small diversion ahead of tonight's big event, which was hardly reassuring. Waiting until certain they were gone, I ran to the back entrance, deciding not to tell Charlie, who was anxious enough today, but was surprised to see him still there, gear exactly where we'd left it.

"Where've you been?" he asked angrily.

"Why are you still here?"

"Been a mix up," he said. "We've been left off the bill."

"What?"

"No use getting angry about it, my lover," a middle-aged man called from the entrance.

"We're supposed to be sound-checking in fifteen minutes," I said, still not sure what sound-checking was.

The man sighed and shook his head. He was one of the local staff who looked after the numerous student drinking hovels round the city, dressed in the uniform of porters – white shirt, sober tie and grey suit – and speaking the uniform language of Bristolian jobsworth gatekeeper.

"Sorry, mate, I didn't write the list," – he held up the magical sheet of paper – "If it ain't got your name on, you ain't allowed in."

Aware of the danger around this gig, at this moment more aware than him, I understood this was not unreasonable. "Can I look, please?" Charlie asked in his politest, look-at-me-I'm-from-the-ruling-classes-you-can-trust-me voice. The porter smiled and shook his head sympathetically. This was one of the kinder ones.

A few select band crew, already ticked off the list, strode in and out around us. Occasionally, we heard the steady thump, thump, thump from inside of a single bass drum, felt it vibrate through our bodies.

"There's someone I know in there who can sort this," I said. "If he stays behind with the gear, can I go in? Promise I'll be straight back." He wavered. "I'll leave my coat," I said, relieved that people inside wouldn't see my distinctly un-rock-and-roll bottle-green anorak.

Wordlessly, the man sighed and nodded me in. I smiled back. "Thanks."

The room was vast, cavernous, bustling with men engaged earnestly in different jobs. For all its right-on taboo-bashing, punk had yet to impact on the all-male union of road crews. Ladies were deemed too ladylike for the drudgery of rock and roll, their rockin' role still considered ornamental.

Two blokes held a giant ladder while one at the top adjusted a spotlight to focus on the stage. Three more hunched over a giant console in the middle of the room that looked like Lieutenant Uhura's on the USS Enterprise. On stage, the drummer still rhythmically pounded his bass drum.

Others marched this way and that. One wore a pouch of tools around his vast belly, a tutu of screwdrivers. Most were overweight and over-hairy; I'd never seen so many beards in one room. They belonged to the immediate past, had been drawn to this world not by punk but by the post-hippy prog rock and West Coast pop that had filled football stadiums for years. I guessed they had all wanted to be rock stars, but lacked the charisma or talent. This was the crew of hardy foot soldiers the audience rarely saw, but without whom there was no gig. Not one looked like they were prepared to stop or be spoken to; this was their moment, the one time of day when you did as they told you.

I wandered aimlessly, ignored pointedly, until reaching the far corner of the stage I saw Matt and his band sprawling among their equipment, bored, like a family of teenagers at the airport, flight delayed by an hour.

"Matt!" I called, running over.

"Alright, man."

"Good to see you! We're on tonight as well."

He looked surprised. "Have you sound-checked?"

"Not yet." Must find out what sound-checking is.

"That can't be right, man: we're on first. First on, last to sound-check."

"Oh."

"You need to talk to Mouse."

"Who?"

"The social sec. The gig organiser. Him," he said, pointing behind me.

A tall, thin student strode towards us, clipboard in hand, anxiety coursing through every vein in his body. I could tell he wasn't happy to see me. This was going to be a serious conversation, but it would be hard not to laugh as I became aware from his pointy teeth and swept-back ears how he had earned his name.

"Hey, Mouse," said Matt. "These guys are supposed to be on the bill tonight."

"Student Grunt?" I said, newly embarrassed by our name.

"Student Grunt..." he said, making a show of reading his notes. "Sorry, mate, you're not on the list."

"It's okay: they can use our gear," said Matt.

"We're out of time," Mouse said. "Sound-check's running way behind."

"Kieran!" Matt shouted, and an imposing, spiky-haired punk who'd been sitting on a Vox amplifier rose and loomed over us, blocking out the light by his presence. "Student Grunt. Great band," Matt said, winking at me. "Is it alright if they use your drumkit?"

Kieran looked at skinny little Matt as though he'd been challenged to a fight by a fly. "Means we don't go on first," said Matt in a stage whisper. Kieran nodded.

"Sure," he said. "Lads?" he called to the rest of the band, "We're going on second!"

They cheered. A rock'n'roll lesson learned – no one ever wants to go on first.

Mouse shrugged. "Be quick," he called, already moving on to the next crisis.

We still had to bring our gear in. Charlie and I stored the drums in a corner at the back of the stage. Celia arrived and we introduced her to Kieran, who smiled awkwardly, unsure how to react to a girl using his drums.

Several microphones had been set on stage to pick up the instruments: one each for voices and amplifiers, but many more for the drum kit. That was why there'd been so much bass drum thumping earlier. Each part of the kit had to be listened to, each microphone adjusted.

"Drums, please!" yelled an anonymous beard from Lieutenant Uhura's console.

"Bass first?" Kieran shouted.

"The lot."

The lower you were down the running order, the less importance the road crew attached to you. Kieran had other ideas, and began playing the bass drum, a single, regular, thump, thump, thump.

"The whole kit! We haven't got time."

Kieran stopped, stood up slowly, stared straight ahead.

"Make time," he said, and sat down. Thump, thump, thump.

Admiring as I was of Kieran's deadpan authority, it meant that as soon as he finished, the beardy brigade switched off their machines and hurried to the exit for their pre-gig break.

"Sorry!" shouted a not-remotely-sorry voice from the distance. "You'll be fine with their gear." I had learned what a soundcheck was just in time to discover we weren't relevant enough to merit one.

Backstage, we picked up on the nervous energy buzzing around the gig. I had a scary anecdote to tell but now was not the time. Occasionally, we'd sneak a look into the hall, which was filling with punks dressed in regulation black leather and NF daubing. Nice Friend or Nasty Foe? Hard to tell.

The atmosphere improved in the dressing room but Charlie, Celia and I were not part of it. Nobody knew who we were but they knew our band had "student" in the name, which meant they weren't kindly disposed to us.

We struggled to make small talk, discussing instead the running order of songs for the fifteenth time. The torture was cut short when Ingrid arrived in a state of breathless excitement. She'd spent the whole day rallying numbers to ensure the gig went ahead without any trouble.

"How's it looking?" Charlie asked, urgently.

"Great!" she said. "There were probably twenty of them, if that!" The other bands stopped their chatting, and she gathered an instant audience. "We were watching from three lookouts. College Green. The Hippodrome. Top of Park Street. Mostly standing in twos and threes, so we weren't noticeable. Made them think there were more of them than us. Got them to follow our little group."

"How many of you were there?" asked a member of Matt's band.

"We had over a hundred ready to go."

Kieran let out a surprised whistle.

"They turned up by the Hippodrome," Ingrid added, and I wondered how soon this was after my gang of thugs had given up on me. "We gathered as an obvious Rock Against Racism group, about six of us, and ran into the side street, like we were running away from them." Everyone in the room was hanging on Ingrid's story. My story! "Had a dozen or so ready to meet them. They thought they could take us on. Only we had another twenty coming down the hill. Another twenty from Unity Street. You've never seen a bunch of Nazis disappear so fast!"

"Poor little things," said Matt.

I was relieved there'd be no trouble at the gig, devastated the moment had passed to tell my own scarier and heroic story. "I was this close," she said. "You could see the fear in their eyes. Not the psychos." What about spider web tattoo man? I screamed silently into the void. "Most of the kids there were probably just hoping to see the gig."

"Our Knowle fans," Matt chirped.

"They must have thought you were the steel band," said Charlie, and everyone laughed – a big laugh of relief like the ones in sitcoms that come after the serious moment near the end.

"We saw them run off and join another group, probably as many again," she continued. "Gordon hadn't wanted us to fight them; he knew our numbers were enough. If they'd stuck together, they probably would have made it to the venue."

"Sounds like they didn't have a plan," Charlie said.

"That'll be because they're thick twats," said Kieran, to more laughs.

The door crashed open. It was Mouse, looking marginally less anxious.

"Student Grunt. You're on now."

We jumped in shock. Celia quickly centred herself, settled her posture, smiled at me and walked out, a perfect role model of composure before a show, any show.

From the back of the stage we could see a few punks but mostly empty spaces. No wonder bands didn't like going on first. At this point of the gig, the main attraction was the cheap bar. Ian Dury's notorious anthem Sex & Drugs & Rock & Roll was blasting through the speakers: follow that, Student Grunt.

We waited for the cue from Mouse to go on. Dury faded, and a new song came up. Bodies, by The Sex Pistols. We looked at each other.

"Let's not open with this," Celia said, we nodded.

The music faded. The lights around the room went down. Mouse shooed us on with a dismissive hand gesture.

"Aren't you introducing us?" I asked.

"No time, get on now."

We walked on stage, fumbling in the darkness. On came the bright lights and the small audience cheered. Ironically, I thought? An air of mild curiosity filled the room. What would this band be like? Would the fascists reveal themselves? Was that a bloke with a spider web tattoo standing alone, arms folded, a couple of feet from me?

Charlie made it to the microphone – "We're Student Grunt" – and the crowd cheered, some laughed, relief. We plugged in, fed back, bled the ears of the crowd, turned the volume down, turned it up again, and began playing. A few kids ran to the front and danced in manic rhythm, politely. Anti-racist, here for the music, no gobbing. Our kind of crowd.

Fired by adrenaline and the suppressed nervous energy of the last few hours, we couldn't help but speed up. Celia always brought us back to the right tempo, her drums bashing us into line with expert authority. All my anxieties melted away – but it was over so quickly. We belted through our single performance of Bodies, ran off to cheers, talked about what we should do for an encore, but the lights came on and Bodies faded up again, weirdly, sounding slow and pedestrian compared to the breakneck version we'd finished moments ago. Mouse was there again to shoo us away as fast as he'd brought us on. In his mind, he'd done the band a massive favour letting us go on at all; he didn't want to have to think about us for a moment longer.

Backstage, sweaty and exhilarated, Celia and I hugged, oblivious to our questionable body odours. Performing in a band was a new excitement for me. Normally on stage my brain was the only instrument I was using, but this was a complete physical experience. I finally understood Celia, and what performing meant to her – couldn't wait to explain what those few minutes had shown me about our relationship.

After we'd packed away the gear, debriefed in the van home about carrying on with the group while celebrating our victory against fascism (sure, we hadn't fought in the Spanish Civil War but we'd done our bit), dropped off Ingrid and Charlie, arrived home and packed away our own gear, we sat down in the kitchen, exhausted, and Celia said, "Barry: we need to talk."

CHAPTER 22

The sun was shining. I'd never seen Edinburgh like this.

This time, I travelled alone on the bus from Bristol: a long, tedious journey up the M5, the long, long M6, through the north west of England up to Glasgow and then across to Edinburgh, avoiding Leeds and the father I was still not talking to. Miles and miles of mind-numbing motorway. Hours and hours to rewrite the conversation with Celia from a couple of days earlier. Except it wasn't a script, something I could change so she would see the error of her ways and give me another chance. That was it. Done.

"What do you mean?" I'd asked, hoping she wanted to talk about not being in the band anymore, knowing she didn't.

"You. And me. It's not working, is it?"

This was the directness I had understood that night for the first time and had fallen in love with.

"Why? Why do you say that?"

"You have your life, Barry," she said, picking at the label of the beer bottle she'd brought back from the gig. "I'm not part of it."

"We share a flat. We have the band."

"Why didn't you want me to come and meet your family last week?"

"It's a difficult time," I said. "Dad's acting strange. There's no way we could have spent any time together."

"Okay," she said. "Have you told them about me? Hmm? How do you think that makes me feel?"

"It's a journey for them. A slow one. I'm taking them there, gently."

She snorted, stood up, cleared away a few plates from earlier.

"I'm sorry, Celia."

"Yeah, well."

"I realise I should have talked to you about this. But it felt like, I don't know, family was something we didn't talk about. It's not like I know much about yours."

"Doesn't matter now."

"It does. I can see what a selfish... self-obsessed... idiot–"

"Yeah, you're probably right, though," she smiled, regretfully. "I find it hard to open up about my personal life, even to you."

"I'm here," I said, could hear the imploring in my voice. "Don't ever feel that way with me again."

"Barry. It's over. Forget it."

"Why? I can change."

"Ha!"

"Seriously."

"Have you spoken to Kris yet?"

"What?"

"Have you found him somewhere to stay?"

I finally found the courage to look her in the eyes, they looked watery.

"The person he's staying with. It's a girl I, a girl I used to..."

"Go out with?"

"Not exactly."

"Did you ask her if I could stay?"

"I was getting round to that. Then you said you weren't going."

"How bloody convenient was that?" she fumed. "Did you think, if I'd had somewhere to stay, it might have affected my decision about going to Edinburgh?"

I hadn't thought about that.

"Ah, Barry," she laughed, aware that I hadn't thought about that. "Never crossed your mind. You live with me, we share a bed. But it's not me you love."

I blushed, caught out."

"It's Kris."

"What?"

"You'll do anything for him."

"What are you talking about?"

My body language turned defensive. I wasn't gay; I was only physically attracted to women. If anything, was so obsessed with loving women I over-objectified them. But here was something else that hadn't crossed my mind, plain and clear to Celia. And she was right. I'd spent hours and days trying to work out my feelings towards her, but there was nothing complicated about my relationship with Kris. When he was with me, nothing else mattered. I would do anything for him. I loved him, unconditionally.

I discovered more from Celia that night. The first time she met me at the Molière audition, she knew she was attracted.

"Found out you were at Whittock," she said, turning away for a moment. "That's why I took the job there. Hoping to accidentally bump into you," she laughed. "That was how I knew about the band. Why I took up the drums."

"Mhm."

"I've done this before," she said, blushing. "Turned my search for love into a project. Saves me having to think about the messy, emotional stuff. I see it now."

"You looked so confident to me. Assured."

"I know. I'm an actor. A good one. Much better than you." We both laughed. The conversation brought us closer, I thought, gave me hope for us but only made her more

211

determined to finish. I was the one she had needed, to show her where she'd been going wrong, which made me proud and wretched in equal measure. Lying on the sofa cushions in her living room that night, where Kris had slept the night before, assured that it wasn't all my fault since our relationship was a result of her bad choice, didn't make me feel better – only more aware that for all my self-important grandstanding on the subject of women's emotions, I was, indeed, just like every other bloody man.

Next morning, I'd had to remove all traces of Celia from my life: take the hire van back, gather my meagre pile of belongings in the corner of her living room to pick up later, arrange to stay with Charlie for a couple of nights, channel all creative energies into the Edinburgh BUTCH shows, and pack for the four-week stay.

I fantasised that Celia would come home from work each night, stare at the corner of her room that was now a mini-shrine to Barry, and welcome me back, weeping, with open arms, as I returned from a triumphant Edinburgh Fringe, garlanded with trophies and adulation.

On the first night at Charlie's, a bloke stayed up late, explaining why Celia and Barry hadn't worked out. The bloke was me and the words were mine, but it sounded like a stranger.

Ingrid was sympathetic to begin with.

"Is it definitely over?" she asked.

"Oh, yes. No way back."

"I'm sorry," she said, sounding genuine.

"It's okay," I lied, fighting back tears of humiliation, and the urge to scream "She dumped me! She dumped me!"

"Do you think you moved in together too quickly?" Ingrid asked, glancing at Charlie's impassive face. He wasn't paying much attention.

"Why?" I asked, defensive.

"You can't always rush these things," she said. "Look at us!"

"We didn't rush," I answered petulantly, aware that we had rushed, wondering why I was picking an argument with close friends, defending a position I didn't believe. "Felt right at the time."

"Okay," Ingrid said, pulling back as I pushed her away. "What do you think, Charlie?" she said, trying to draw him in.

"What does it matter what I think?" he asked, a little harshly. "It's over."

"Do you have any words of comfort for your best friend?" Ingrid asked.

"Sure. Sorry, mate," he said, trying to sound sympathetic. "Shame about the band." Ingrid slapped him on the arm. "The gig was great; we had something going there," he said, more to her than me.

I was too wrapped up in my own self-pity to care, replaying those last conversations, apart from where I had kept her from my parents and denied her a room in a flat with a woman I'd barely hugged. Thinking how Celia had calmed me in those days leading up to the gig. She must have already decided to dump me, not giving away anything in those precious moments.

"You alright, Barry?" Charlie asked. "You're grimacing."

My face was clenched with embarrassment at how I'd behaved. There was more, things I'd never confess to Charlie and Ingrid, could barely admit to myself: the manipulative sobs, the guilt-tripping. Hated myself but couldn't stop it.

"Can't we give it another go?" I'd said to Celia again, some time after we'd established we were splitting up.

"Barry, this isn't working."

"I can't believe you're doing this," I'd said, lashing out, sounding like Grandma. Should have been enough to make me stop, but I couldn't let go; it was all I had. Celia wasn't fooled.

Apart from the Caledonian sunshine and extra luggage, the walk from Edinburgh bus station was the same one

I'd made with Maurice exactly a year earlier. Our BUTCH accommodation was in the same direction, but much further down Leith Walk. Out of the station, past the kinetic sculpture, another Oxford theatre company, new posters – only this year I was an official participant. I understood all the work that had gone into those posters, aware that students inside those church halls and rooms above pubs were working 20 hours a day to create a theatre out of nothing.

The glamour and magic hadn't disappeared; if anything, it was greater with the air of expectancy ahead of the Festival opening. This, for a month, would be my new home, where I would help make the magic happen. I needed to stop by at Harriet's to see if Kris had connected. He was my little secret; I was convinced the world would discover him and I'd be there, too. It was possible, for the brief moments of that journey to 397 Leith Walk, to dream and believe.

Harriet had said there'd be no problem with Kris staying at her brother's flat. Maurice was coming too, after all, and I looked forward to the three of us sharing comfortable time in our lovely Leeds tribe, oblivious to the intersection of culture and commerce around us.

Laurence was not happy to see me. His eyes were drawn to my luggage and guitar in plastic bin bag, before looking at me.

"Oh, it's okay: I'm not staying," I said. "On my way to my own flat. Popped by to say hello."

"Hello Barry."

"Is Harriet here?"

"She's at an exhibition."

"Kris?" I asked sheepishly, aware that the complete stranger he probably hadn't heard of two days ago was his new, instant flatmate.

"Kris, no, no, Kris isn't here," he said, irritated. "His suitcases, his sleeping bag, his eight-foot-high poster of Sid

James and Hattie Jacques, they're all here. Come in, come and have a look."

"It's okay, I'd better go. Here's my address and phone number for him... and Harriet. I'll be at the theatre most of the day."

"Sorry if I'm sounding a bit narked. I had no idea this fellow would be staying."

"My fault. I'm doing a show with him at the Casablanca."

"The porn cinema? Yes, he told me."

I apologised more and struggled down the stairs. In the short time I'd been indoors, the sun had disappeared, replaced by familiar sheets of Edinburgh rain. I had a map of where to stay and a Fringe brochure to assist, but Leith Walk was longer than I remembered from last year. Festival Edinburgh's invisible boundary was not far from Laurence's flat and, like Knowle in Bristol, once you made it a short way out of the centre, it was obvious that none of the middle-class trappings and benefits had reached this part of town.

The tenements were tall, imposing and as black as the clouds that hung over them. None had enjoyed the renovation and regeneration of those they resembled in the centre. There were no department stores or well-known brand shops: only greasy-spoon cafes, dark, unwelcoming pubs and open market stalls. The people looked different to those I knew in Leeds and Bristol; the young punks didn't look artistically skinny so much as malnourished and ill, while young, zombie mothers dulled by a steady intake of prescription Valium pushed prams around the streets.

My excitement at participating in the 1978 Edinburgh Fringe diminished with every step away from town, avoiding the stares of locals wondering why this scruffy weirdo had strayed among them.

Our accommodation looked like all the flats I'd ever seen in Edinburgh: big, imposing blocks with open entrances, long, stone staircases up three flights, the flat to be occupied invariably right at the top. A hastily handwritten sign had been pasted on the front of the door: "For the attention of Bristol University Students: THIS IS NOT WHERE BUTCH ARE STAYING, Go to St James's on the Mount. Apologies for the inconvenience." A helpful map underneath showed that our real accommodation was on a corner two streets away.

St James's on the Mount was a beautiful gothic pile, except it wasn't on a Mount and it was surrounded by miserable tenements.

I'd rarely been inside church grounds; for all I knew, there could have been a small and charming cluster of flats round the back. There wasn't. The church was small, dark and ramshackle, like something out of a Dracula film – all that was missing the rumble of thunder and a shock of lightning. I wondered how twenty students would fit in and whether we might have to move all our stuff outside every Sunday morning.

Another makeshift sign had appeared on the imposing wooden doors at the entrance. "Bristol University TCH:" it began, anxious to avoid the implications of a racy acronym in such holy surroundings. "Enter and turn left." Not as simple as it sounded, the door led straight down to a narrow spiral staircase – difficult enough for one person, unpassable for one man and his month of student belongings. At the bottom of the stairs, another solid wooden door greeted me. I had to push hard, but then it swept open and I was attacked by a gust of cold air that was like death. Even though it was August, winter had arrived early at St James's on the Mount.

The room was enormous, large enough to house 20 camp beds. It looked like a photograph of a military hospital in World War Two. Despite the cold, there were no windows: only a dim glow from a row of noisily humming strip lights, dangling precariously from the ceiling like angry electric hammocks.

I searched for a spare bed, most had already been taken. The biggest occupied group were in a cluster in the far corner nearest the toilet. All the edges had been nabbed. I found one in the middle and sat down, tired but not sleepy. We'd hardly be here for the next four weeks; sleep would be an extravagance, like regular meals and baths. But how envious I was of Maurice and Kris in Laurence's luxurious broom cupboard.

Everyone else was already working at the venue another mile or so up the road. We'd been ordered to head straight there as soon as we dropped our belongings. I tried to get off the bed and leave but couldn't, or wouldn't, move. Four weeks with a group of twenty strangers, working, eating, washing, sleeping in this dormitory. Except I'd be leaving them at one o'clock in the morning – "Sorry folks, popping out to do another show, be back before three." Another show! Was I mad? I didn't have a lot to do in the Bristol comedies but my presence was required every evening in the theatre –scenery had to be shifted and props placed – and, in the mornings and afternoons, leaflets dispensed.

Tired, hungry, miserable, broke, I began to cry. Alone, uninhibited, these were big, loud, wet sobs of self-pity, for no one else's benefit but my own. Others had described the feeling of exhaustion, emptiness and a life out of control that usually arrived around the start of the third week of working solidly at the Fringe. I had been here for less than an hour.

Scrunched in a ball of misery and angst, I hadn't noticed another person in the room. She glided across, sat on the edge of my bed, close. I made out her striking features, defined by straight, long blonde hair, formed into a smile. She turned away and laughed sadly. I hadn't known it was possible for laughter to sound sad until that moment.

"Welcome to the refuge of the road, Barry."

"Is this it, Joni?"

"Yes. This is it. There'll be moments. Hopefully enough to sustain you. But the rest is this. Years and years of it."

She moved towards me.

"Good luck, Barry," she whispered. I closed my eyes, opened them and she had gone.

"You okay, Barry?"

I jumped to attention in shock, not having noticed the very real Camilla. She jumped in mutual response.

"Sorry, didn't see you."

"No, I'm sorry: didn't mean to creep up on you like that."

"It's okay."

"What's up, Barry?"

Ahh, Camilla, I didn't know her well but what a relief, a release, to be alone with her, now.

"Tough week."

"Sorry, honey: everyone's stressed out. Always like this in the build-up."

"Right?"

"Wait until we're up and running. That's when the disappointment really kicks in."

I laughed. Camilla was funny, and wise. I hadn't told anyone from the company yet about my extra show and wondered if this would be the right moment.

"We all come here knowing we can't compete with the pros. Or the big universities with their subsidised comedy groups. But in this moment, before the Festival starts, we dare to dream this might be our year."

"Even Hugo?"

"Especially Hugo," she said, and I laughed again. "He's got what it takes to make it."

"You think he's talented?"

"Did I say talented, honey? Hugo has unshakeable self-belief."

"I need to find a way of getting on with Hugo. He took against me from the start."

"Stop mimicking him."

"That was so embarrassing. I didn't realise until I saw the look on his face."

"Work hard. Hugo likes hard work. Especially when he sees others doing it."

"Okay."

"Promise me, Barry. Promise me you'll give it your all, honey."

"Promise."

"Come on, let's go to the venue."

"Sure," I said, comforted by her kindness, certain I would confide in her later.

CHAPTER 23

"This," Richard had bellowed during one of our rehearsals in Bristol, "is our year. And this," he added with an actorly flourish, producing a photograph of a large, long, double-storey public building with a grand glass dome, "is our venue."

Standing outside the half-demolished bus station amid mounds of debris, until now I hadn't understood how ambitious his plans had been for the 1978 Edinburgh Festival Fringe.

The company's problems, Richard had told us one afternoon during rehearsals in Bristol, had always stemmed from having to share a hugely expensive space in the centre of town with other theatre groups. This year, he explained, we had a venue all to ourselves, one that had only come on the market for the first time this year: the former Exhibition Hall on Annandale Street, converted in the 1930s to the Edinburgh bus depot.

"A bus depot?" squealed Camilla.

"Is it close to the Royal Mile?" asked Hugo, not unreasonably.

"Not close," said Richard mysteriously, "but not far away, either." Not far from Laurence's flat, as it happened, five minutes down Leith Walk from the kinetic sculpture.

"It was where the conductors and drivers finished their day's work. The council have had to close it due to transport cuts. And the building already has a perfect name for us: Journey's End."

We laughed at the coincidence. What better way to herald the arrival of Edinburgh's newest Festival venue than to have it run by a single company and named after a famous play that was a regular Fringe hit?

Only when we arrived in Edinburgh did we realise the size of the undertaking. Like the popular joke of the time about people going on holiday to Spain only to find the hotel hadn't been built, serious demolition work meant that the two main theatre spaces we had been promised were now one enormous room. A huge pile of rubble in the middle implied that there had, in happier times, been a wall. Venue One was now twice as big as required, while a new Venue Two had to be fashioned out of one of the smaller rooms upstairs. The nicest thing you could say about Venue Two was that it was intimate. And in an additional mix up with the council, permission to sell alcohol had not yet been granted.

After days of weariness, raking over the past, lost in the present, paralysed by a lack of clarity about what was to come, finally I was presented with a simple problem – one barely constructed theatre – and an even simpler solution.

As Camilla had said, hard work. We knew what we had to do, and we did it. A bunch of students, almost two football teams' worth, we'd seen the old Hollywood movies where the kids said "Let's do the show right here!" and we cleared the mountain of rubble and rubbish to one far end in impressively quick time. Next, we had to shape this enormous space into a theatre. Churches and schools usually had at least one room with a raised stage and scaffolding for theatre lights; a former bus depot had no call for such frivolities and fripperies. Edinburgh bus drivers and clippies will have made their own entertainment, but not in this building.

I discovered a previously unknown talent for carpentry, bonding briefly with Hugo as together we fashioned a working stage out of plyboard and pallets. We even managed some laughs, testing our stage for sturdiness, deliberately over-acting our scenes by jumping on the boards while delivering our lines. Satisfied that we had made a rostrum to survive the next four weeks, we smiled. Awkwardly, I held out my hand to shake Hugo's. It was him who drew me closer for a hug, then he gently pushed me away, and said "You're funny."

"Thanks," I said, genuinely touched, and now he held out his hand, but as I brought mine to shake his he thumbed his nose and cocked a snook. Hugo was my new buddy.

We'd spent so long working on the stage that it was well after ten o'clock when our shift took a break. I ran to Laurence's, knowing it was late, and he would be pissed off, but had to ring the doorbell. Imagine my surprise, as his dirty magazines used to say, when the door was answered by Maurice.

"Oh, hi, Barry," he said, surprised in a way that suggested nothing seemed to surprise him anymore.

"It's all go here," I said, irritated that everyone I knew and liked in Edinburgh was staying in this nice, cosy flat, apart from me.

"You alright?"

"Yeah, sorry, knackered."

"What time do you call this?" he screeched in his comedy Monty Python voice.

"I know."

"You've missed Harriet; she went to bed five minutes ago." He moved in closer, lowered his voice. "Her brother's pissed off. They had a bit of a barney. 'Whaddya think this place is? A hotel?' You coming in?"

"No: gotta find Kris."

"Oh, yes, he's very annoyed with you."

I crumpled.

"Not really. He waited for a while; he's gone to your venue. Did you know it's a dirty movie cinema? I've offered to help him. In between watching the movies."

"Thanks. Catch up with you tomorrow, mate."

"Sure," he said. "Byee!" and went back in, casual and carefree.

I thought about going back briefly to our theatre building site, but it was after eleven and Kris was the priority. The pubs had closed and noisy locals were weaving up and down Leith Walk, to be dodged and avoided on the way to the Casablanca Cinema. Everybody knew where it was, though few admitted to having been.

Approaching the Royal Mile, the atmosphere and accents changed. The musically aggressive tones of inebriated locals were replaced by donkey-snort laughs of the Oxbridge students who, like me, had been working hard to get their venues ready in time. Further down the Royal Mile, the tourist trap of souvenir shops and tartan tat gave way to a darker, grimmer, unlit Edinburgh that felt like it hadn't changed since Robert Louis Stevenson had walked up and down in search of inspiration, as opposed to filthy movies. There were no tourists, no lights – only dark buildings, cobbled streets and a hint of hidden menace down every alleyway.

Men in long coats hurried past alone, hoping not to be seen, but we both knew where they had been or were going. What if I recognised someone? "It's okay," I would say, "I'm not here to watch naked women; I'm working on a pioneering new comedy show." I'd never been to one of these cinemas, and my righteous indignation at the misogyny and exploitation at the heart of this industry sat uncomfortably next to a genuine curiosity about what I might discover.

The Casablanca was a modest building, not allowed to announce its business too proudly thanks to council regulations, but there were four posters outside, advertising what was showing on each of the screens: Agent 69 In The Sign of Scorpio, Emanuelle, Emanuelle 2 and Confessions of a Window Cleaner. The first three showed innocuous photographs of attractive women – nothing more daring than you'd see in a glossy magazine or TV advert. The final poster was a cartoon of Robin Askwith, the star of the movie, cleaning a steamed-up window revealing an attractive lady stepping into the bath. I recognised the names of some of the actors – stars of my favourite sitcoms Dad's Army, Selwyn Froggitt, Till Death Us Do Part, and wondered how sexually arousing it would be to watch a film starring Alf Garnett's mouthy son-in-law, also known as Tony Booth, and his "silly old moo" wife, played by Dandy Nichols.

A bored, pretty young girl sat on a stool by the entrance, casually taking an inventory of her fingernails. Next to her stood a stern, tall doorman in smart suit, crisp white shirt and bow tie. He looked charming and solid, like he could entertain you with anecdotes while breaking both your legs.

"Can I help you, son?" he asked in a booming, friendly Edinburgh voice with more than a hint of Sean Connery.

"I'm doing a show here in a couple of days," I said.

"Aye, didn't think you looked like my regular clientele."

"Don't have a long enough coat," I said, and he smiled.

"You're welcome to come in and have a wee look around. Which is your show?"

"It's called Meep Meep."

"Ah, Barry!" he said and a big smile broke across his face. "Good to meet you; I'm Alistair. This is Heather. Kris is up the top somewhere. We're very excited to have you here; this is the first time I've tried anything like this."

"Looking forward to it."

"Aye, me too. Go on, have a look around."

The venue was smart, unlike most that I had been to in Edinburgh. It was, after all, a cinema – plush, dark carpet soft under my footsteps, subtle tasteful lighting, enough to guide you to your seat but not so much as to instantly recognise someone or be spotted yourself.

Continuing down a short corridor past Cinemas One and Three, two soundtracks bled through the walls and mingled like horny lovers – brash, brassy American funk from Cinema One, swirling prog-rock, classical-inspired keyboard from the other. But drowning out both was the unmistakeable primal moans of women enjoying euphoric sexual gratification. I wasn't an expert but, with my new-found, post-virgin knowledge, I wondered if this was a particularly common noise. Was it only dirty movie stars who found the act this ecstatically pleasurable?

Cinema Two was our venue. I gently parted aside its welcoming doors and entered the warm, dark space. A dozen or so men were here, dotted around in an almost perfectly mathematical equation of how much space one person could have to themselves, following the adventures of Emanuelle. A young couple smooched in the back row, challenging my simple preconceptions of typical clientele. "How can you betray the sisterhood?" I felt like saying, aware that this might have been met with baffled amusement, given my own presence.

The film was not sexy at all. Unless you're turned on by the glamorous locations of other people's holiday movies. The eponymous star was being politely chauffeured around various exotic tourist spots. They were, like her, very pretty, but nothing else was happening – exactly like other people's holiday movies. The music swelled dramatically, the camera zoomed intently close to her face, as if she was remembering a moment of intense sex, and once again the soft, ecstatic moans shuddered through. For all the sex on screen, the punters might as well have saved their three quid and stood in the corridor listening through the walls.

Inside the projection room at the back of the cinema, a stocky, bearded student slouched on a moth-eaten settee, reading The Female Eunuch. Every 11 minutes or so he had to stand up and switch the reels of the film, but in between times he took zero interest. He must have seen this film a thousand times. He looked up, diffidently; I mouthed "doing a show here" and he went back to his book. I wondered if we could use this room as part of the show, maybe even screen some short films, and imagined myself on that stage, blank screen as the backdrop. For the first time, Meep Meep felt like a real, solid thing.

Back in the maze of corridors, it was a puzzle to get back to the entrance. Three soundtracks were audible: funky jazz, soft-rock moaning and a rhythmic slamming that sounded like a door opening and shutting.

Walking away from Cinema Two, the rhythmic noise intensified. It seemed to be coming from the toilets, interspersed with a low, regular, animal grunting. In a moment, it was over.

While the soft, ecstatic recorded feminine moaning continued to mingle with the melodies in the background, Heather from the front desk emerged from the toilets, hair slightly dishevelled, adjusting her clothes. She smiled as she walked past, less embarrassed than I was, for sure. I stared for a moment, trying to work out what had happened. A toilet flushed, the door opened again, and I was greeted with a warm smile.

"Hey, Barry!"

"Hi, Alistair."

"Sorry pal," he said, adjusting his trousers, unfazed that I'd heard him having sex with Heather, "Kris left just after you arrived. We tried to find you..."

"Okay. Not to worry."

He smiled again, patted me on the shoulder and walked away.

I knew from the letters pages of Maurice's magazines that for sex between consenting strangers to happen, confident women had to come up to you at parties and demand it. I knew people got drunk at discos and had sex in toilets, but I couldn't make sense of someone having actual physical sex in a cinema built primarily for the purposes of masturbation.

I rushed back to Journey's End, but they'd all left, finished work for the night. Damn. My absence will have been noted. Another black mark.

I ran through the heavy rain back to the crypt, avoiding the weaving, angry drunks and stumbling teenagers, Meep Meep leaflets stuffed in my pockets. The church door was locked. I banged hard and eventually it creaked open. Richard, still dressed immaculate as always in blue-and-white striped shirt, greeted me like a long-lost friend.

"Hello, stranger!" he smiled sarcastically. "Wondered where you'd got to. Thought you might have been abducted by a UFO!"

Sleep was terrible that night: short, fitful, interrupted. The day had begun twenty hours earlier in Bristol, endless hours of dull, wet coach journey followed by hefty physical work (unusual for me), and walking up and down steep hills in the rain. I kept waking, aware only a few minutes had passed since each dozing off. It was almost a relief when my eyes blinked open to see morning, many of my nearby bed-mates already preparing for another long stretch of theatre building. The queue to the bathroom was six long and growing, allowing me to grab another ten minutes' precious sleep. The technical crew, anxious and keen, had already left. The rest of us creative thespian types, unfamiliar with early mornings, struggled with the prospect of the day ahead but the mood, like yesterday, remained grimly determined.

"Where were you last night?" Hugo asked aggressively.

"Some friends from home turned up," I said, contemplating my toothbrush, avoiding his gaze. "They're around the corner from the venue. Got them to agree to help us with leafletting," I said, making a mental note to ask Harriet and Maurice to help us with leafletting.

Our first show was only 36 hours away, but it looked like there was still several weeks' worth of work required to mould the building into shape. Ian, our technical director, who had done everything asked of him by Hugo and Richard in rehearsals with a shy and submissive demeanour, was now in charge. He knew exactly what was needed to make the theatre happen and barked in the same brutally impolite manner Richard had earlier adopted when addressing him.

I continued with light carpentry duties, but this was not my area of expertise. During our short lunch break, Ian, Hugo and Richard formed a huddle, and emerged with a small list of volunteers to be sent to leaflet the Royal Mile and hang posters in local shops. Half a dozen of us, including me, Andrew and Camilla, were sent on an ambitious leafletting crawl that would take us from the grand old National Gallery at the foot of the castle hill, up the steep steps to cross Cockburn Street, up the steeper steps to the Royal Mile, down steeper steps to the Grassmarket and across to the relatively step-free west end of Princes Street, home of the swanky Caledonian Hotel, where all the famous people stayed. Return to the National Gallery and repeat, rain or shine.

There was no shine, naturally, but plenty of rain, including the occasional torrential downpour which necessitated a short break, since the only people refusing to find shelter at that point were our fellow student leafletters.

Once the rain slowed, we developed a steady rhythm. Andrew and Camilla worked together, unwittingly charming the crowds with their comic incompatibility. I adopted a kind of low-key anti-sales approach that worked well for me.

"Come and see our shows! Only ten thousand tickets left!"

This initiated smiles; occasionally someone even looked at the leaflet in my presence.

"Ooh, Journey's End," a middle-aged, Home Counties lady with a champagne glass tinkling voice cooed to her earnest, bearded husband. "We love that."

"We're not actually doing the play; that's the name of our venue. It's a classic version of Lady Windermere's Fan."

Some of the student groups had put more thought into their outdoor marketing strategies. But then, they would have finished building their theatres or be performing in purpose-built venues, allowing entire crews to leaflet in armies of a dozen or more.

One troupe performing Arthur Miller's Crucible walked fully costumed in slow, determined rhythm along the cobblestones of the Royal Mile, indifferent to the fuming drivers who'd been foolish enough to imagine they could use this road during Festival time. Ignoring the angry car horns and raging drivers, the students performed portentous extracts from scenes depicting the courtroom drama of seventeenth-century witch trials. One man stood with them, a giant bass drum strapped to his body, beating a single note: rhythmic, haunting, mournful. It was terrible.

The actors were awful, costumes amateur, sincerity hilarious, but the spectacle filled me with melancholy. Maybe I was too tired to think straight, but this drama of what happens when poison enters a small community felt ominously topical. The world was awful, as it always feels, for sure, but the cold war between America and Russia was intensifying. Here, the system was breaking down: Margaret Thatcher's carefully chosen incendiary language of hostility was resonating across the country, there were fascists on the streets; these students were performing the final scene in the soon-to-be unfulfilled dreams of my generation.

What was my future? Or that of these hopeful young amateurs who, like me and hundreds of others, had dared to imagine this could be our moment of glory? What kind of world awaited? Would it survive? Three decades since the last war ended, six since the one before, were we due another world war where, instead of gas or planes, we needed to be on our guard against a single bomb that, when dropped on our cities, would be enough to destroy them completely?

I stared at the solemn thespians with their dark costumes, knitted brows and non-existent acting skills, accusing each other, as witches and heathens, in atrocious American accents, worried that if I stopped believing in their sincerity, the world could end, when, in a flash, the women ripped away their dark cloaks to reveal brightly coloured 1920s American moll costumes. The drummer continued his beat as the men disrobed to reveal sharp gangster suits, and the students clicked their fingers and danced in formation, singing Luck be a Lady from the musical Guys and Dolls with the same slapdash sincerity, oblivious to the ominous clouds and returning rainfall.

The American accents were not improved by singing, but the growing crowd were entranced as much by the effort as the execution. At odd moments, one or two of the guys and dolls broke ranks to hand out leaflets to the crowd. This was the Sussex University Drama Society – SUDS! – and they were not afraid to let us know they were performing these two shows at the Chaplaincy Centre, Venue 83, for the next three-and-a-half weeks.

I smiled politely at a young girl who handed me the leaflet, offering my own in exchange, which she looked at, delighted, as though I was the first person who'd thought to give her one.

"Bristol!" she exclaimed in an English accent, unsurprisingly, "I nearly went there! They have a great drama department! Are you a drama student?"

"No," I said awkwardly.

"We're all drama students! Come to our shows! I promise I'll make everyone here come to yours. Where are you?"

"Journey's End: it's a new venue, down Leith Walk."

"I love that play! Where's Leith Walk?"

"We're not doing the play, it's the name of the venue. We're doing Lady Windermere, you go down the end of Princes Street," I said, pointing, aware that the correct answer was "Too far off the main Festival area to attract a passing audience". She smiled and waved, no time to waste, more tourists to wow. "Come and see our show!" I called after her and continued dispensing more of our own contributions to the Edinburgh paper mountain.

Camilla came over and handed me a glossy, professional leaflet.

"Is this you?" she asked, pointing to a show advertised at 1.30 am: Meep Meep starring Kris Dean and Barry Goldman. Kris had been a busy boy at the Casablanca, in more ways than one.

"He's a friend. Had to pull out of his main show and needed someone to fill the gaps."

I smiled as charmingly as possible to counter her upset.

"What will you be doing?"

"I don't know yet."

"You're not performing anything that you'll be doing for our show?"

It hadn't occurred to me that this might be a problem. Suddenly, it did.

"Doubt it," I lied. "We'll be doing sketches together, nothing like the ones we're doing in our show," I said, feeling my confidence recede with every word. "It doesn't start until one thirty in the morning. I'm totally committed to BUTCH for the rest of the day."

"Honey," she said, not unsympathetically, "you'll be shattered. Maybe not today, or next week, or even the week after, but at some point in the run everyone in our group will hit a low, awful moment. You will, too – but you'll still have another show to perform."

"I'll be fine."

My only ally shook her head and wandered off.

Back at the theatre, where I'd been expecting a note from Kris, there was an envelope with my name on, but the handwriting was Harriet's. "Barry – ring your parents!! Harriet. X."

Before I could look for a phone box, Richard called me over. He took me to a small office on the first floor: a bland, anonymous room where all the bus station's filing cabinets had come to die. There was barely space for a small table in the corner. Hugo was already sitting cramped, arms folded, face set to maximum stern.

Had I done something wrong, performing in another show? Like not telling Celia about the flat, I must have known that, at some level, there was something wrong, otherwise I would have told them about it immediately. But was I breaking any specific rules?

The Casablanca brochure lay on the table, accusingly. I picked it up, confidently, which surprised Hugo. It surprised me as well; I had no idea what to say or do beyond "act bold."

"I'd like to apologise for not having told you about this. The truth is," I said, thinking fast, "everything happened too quickly."

They looked at me, not buying this.

"You'll see it's not in the official programme – didn't even know it was going to happen until last Friday." Four weeks last Friday, but hey. "Kris is a friend. He had to pull out of another show at the last minute and needed help." Is he a friend? I barely know him – only met him three or four times. Does he look like a desperate person who can't manage on his own? I'm far more excited to be working with him than you amateurs.

"Do you know what kind of entertainment they normally show at the Casablanca?" Hugo sniffed disapprovingly.

"Why didn't you tell us?" Richard pleaded.

"I was going to mention it, but to be honest," I lied, "it was so far at the back of my mind when there was so much else to do here. My thinking was to concentrate all energy towards our first show ready for opening day, then worry about the other show after that."

Even I was impressed by the image of this outstandingly loyal person. Maybe I wasn't such a bad actor.

"Remember I'd been in a band? I told you all about that and quit to concentrate on our shows." Careful, Barry, don't push it.

"We need everyone in this company to commit one hundred per cent," Hugo said, "and frankly, Barry, we're not seeing that."

"Can you promise us that commitment?" Richard asked.

"Of course!" I said, hoping they wouldn't notice Kris's leaflets crammed into my back pocket.

"Get to it, then," Hugo barked.

I ran downstairs and worked harder than I'd ever known: lifting stage and scenery parts to the main theatre, climbing ladders, pointing lights at the stage. Carried chairs upstairs and down, in and out of rooms, painted signs and arrows for directions, carted boxes of pizza back from the takeaway, hammered nails into wood and pulled them out again. It must have been after eleven when Hugo found me, sorting through a pile of stage props.

"Okay, Barry, Richard and I have discussed this."

"What's that?"

He hesitated, nervous in a way I'd not seen before. "You're going to have to drop the other show."

"But what about Kris?"

"We're sorry your friend is in such difficulty, but that's not our problem. We paid to get you here, and your accommodation; you're with us totally or you're out."

I was too tired and shocked to argue.

"Come on," he smiled. I'd never seen him smile, it was weirdly unnerving. "We're going back to the crypt."

I remembered on the way home that I had to ring my parents, but it was way too late to call now. I slept deeply, as we all did, and awoke confronted with the following choice: another 20-hour slog of a day, or the chance to quit and commit myself fully to Kris and our show.

It was no contest. I would quit.

How would they re-work the shows without me? Where would I stay? How would I pay for meals? Details. Energised and elated, I ran to find a phone box and dialled home, stuffing coins in as soon as the pips cried out. It was a surprise to hear Judith at the other end.

"Barry!" she said, "At last! What's happening? We've been trying to get hold of you for ages."

"What's the matter?"

"Dad's had a nervous breakdown."

"What?"

"Mum's at the hospital. You have to come home."

"But – I'm in Edinburgh."

"I was in London."

"But–"

"Barry. Come home. Now."

CHAPTER 24

Edinburgh bus station buzzed with excited young student performers over-laden with belongings, embarking on the biggest adventure of their lives, wondering if this might be their big break. The only difference between us was that they were arriving as the Festival began, and I was leaving, like a local resident with no interest in culture and a fancy flat to rent at an extortionate price.

It was another of those rare days of splendid Edinburgh sunshine, that seem to come at the exact time when you have to spend six hours in a stuffy old coach, travelling to Leeds.

I had conveyed the correct amount of sympathetic shock to Judith on the phone, while calculating how much time would be needed to stay in Leeds, and whether I could be back for opening night with Kris. The clothing business had collapsed in June – June! – but Dad had kept everything secret for weeks. It was only when Sheila Myers casually mentioned to Mum outside Hairport Lounge that she'd seen Monty in a greasy spoon café on Boar Lane during office hours that Mum confronted him.

"That was last Wednesday," Judith said. "He told her everything. The factory had been in deep trouble for months;

he knew at the start of the year it would be closing, he'd been laying off staff since Christmas–"

"–when I'd been working there."

The business owed thousands to other companies, and the factory was shut down. Dad had spent the last few weeks pretending to Mum he was going to work as normal - had driven in every day - but spent most of his time in meetings with accountants and auditors.

"I haven't spoken to him since last time we were there."

"Yes. He was acting strange then, wasn't he?"

"What do you want me to do?" I'd asked on the phone, before running out of coins.

"Once you're home? Take the pressure off Mum, go to the hospital, look after Dad."

"Got my first show tomorrow."

"Ha! You can forget that, mate."

"How long are you expecting me to stay?"

"A week? A month? How the hell should I know? There's Gran to look after. We have to sell the house."

"What?"

"Barry. Mum and Dad are broke. The old life is gone. We've got meetings with creditors and lawyers every day next week. You Mister Clever Social Sciences Student will have to grow up and get a job like the rest of us."

I looked behind through the back of the coach, watching Edinburgh recede. At least I'd been spared the dramatic "I quit!" conversation that would have killed off my university performing career. Although when I told them about having to miss opening night, I was surprised by the ferocity of Hugo's response.

"How bloody convenient," he yelled, turning Ribena purple.

"My dad had a nervous breakdown!"

"And...?"

"Hugo," Richard said firmly.

"Is he still alive? You have a poor sense of priorities, Barry."

"Shut up, Hugo. Sorry to hear that, Barry. We can cover for your absence in the plays."

"Not the revue, though," muttered Hugo.

Back I went, through the cute Scottish border towns that looked like jigsaw puzzles, a world of shortbread and castles and Kenneth McKellar singing in his kilt, backwards in space and time to the land of bow-tied northern club comedians I thought I'd escaped.

The sun was shining. The roads were clear. Whenever I was heading to Edinburgh by coach, it always rained and took forever. Today, the city couldn't get rid of me fast enough.

At least I wouldn't be working for the family business now.

I'd rushed to the station, no time to contact Kris – not that I could face him. I suspected he could also manage without me, and I didn't want to see his face when he heard the news, in case it betrayed a secret sense of relief. Instead, I left a hurriedly scribbled note at Harriet's flat. Checking my change, there was only enough money for a single to Leeds, no return. Have to borrow from someone to pay for that, I thought. As though I might need it.

There was no one to pick me up from Leeds bus station. I'd been a grown-up for a while, but this was the first time I'd arrived home without being greeted by Mum or Dad. Mummy, Daddy. Such childish words. I was the adult now.

Dad's factory was a short walk from the station, my urge to look despite the cumbersome luggage too strong to resist. This corner of central Leeds had been transformed by motorways and through roads, narrow streets bulldozed into grey, concrete thoroughfares. The factory wasn't far, but I kept getting lost. These new roads had been built to siphon traffic from the centre, which was far nicer as a result, but all that fast, smelly traffic had to go somewhere, and now I knew where.

It was like a scene from a gritty northern BBC Play For Today. Specifically, the one about clothing factories in Leeds, written by Colin Welland. The building was boarded up, a few windows smashed, the once grand sign "H Goldman and Sons – Quality Outfitters" faded and weather-beaten, damaged and askew like Dad. A more modern sign below announced the premises were being monitored constantly by Group Four Security Services. What would anyone want to nick from this grimy Edwardian hovel, full of ancient machinery that hadn't been maintained in years?

This had been Dad's life, his dad's before him. Grandad, whose parents had fled Lithuania, built this business that had played a small but useful role in the city's prosperity. Survived two World Wars but not three decades of peace. It had failed to keep up with this new world of speedily accessible trade routes. "Thank God your grandad never lived to see this day," I muttered in the voice of my dad. On balance, Grandad, who fought in both wars, would probably have settled for this. At least, as Hugo had delightfully pointed out earlier, nobody died.

The Bricklayers Arms was open, almost empty, a couple of old fellas looked up at this unusual sight, a kid with rucksack and suitcase, and electric guitar, long, greasy hair dampened further by the rain, sweating from the walk. I counted my coins, enough for a bus ticket home and nothing more, smiled guiltily at the barman, and walked back into town towards the number thirty-four bus stop.

At home, the cupboards were all open, wooden tea chests in every room, my entire childhood packed away. Judith was upstairs in her old bedroom, half-heartedly clearing her belongings. She looked up when I came in, the briefest of smiles.

Judith was some miles further down the escape road, comfortable with the life she had been building for herself while maintaining this link with the past. Last time I'd seen her, less than a month ago, I'd been so wrapped up in my own world I'd paid hardly any attention to her life. It was good to have her back, even if only for these passing moments.

"Found my old diaries. What an idiot when I was sixteen."

"Could have told you that, Judith."

"Listen to this: 'God I hate Mum.' Can you guess why?"

"She told you to tidy your room?"

"Stopped me from going out with Lester Berman."

"Molester Berman? Hope you thanked her. How's she doing?"

"Not bad. Had a right go at Grandma this morning."

"Good for her."

"Gran was subdued. Never seen that. Ever! Put Mum in a better mood."

"Apart from dealing with Dad."

"Well, yeah."

I told her about my short trip to the factory: the broken windows, the grimness. Apparently, Dad was desperate to see me. "He's very clear about it. One of the few things," she said.

"What's wrong? What is a nervous breakdown? Isn't it like people going a bit bonkers?"

"All I know is Mick Jagger had nineteen of them. Dad was muttering to himself."

"Isn't that the first sign of madness?"

"I honestly have no idea, Barry."

"Is he like Jack Nicholson in One Flew Over The Cuckoo's Nest? Or the Indian?"

"Enough already, Barry. They said his brain shut down."

I struggled to imagine what that meant. Hospital was where you went when the body broke down, not the head. Nobody talked about this stuff, Jack Nicholson and the terrifying Nurse Ratched all we had to go on.

"Does he seem normal?"

"Depends what you mean by normal. I think he recognised me. Didn't say much."

"Not sure I can handle this."

"You don't have a choice. Mum needs a break. Go see him now. Brotherton Wing."

"Can you lend me the bus fare?"

"I bet Elton John hasn't said that in a while."

The siphoning of traffic had done the trick; Leeds city centre was cleaner than I remembered. Our civic masters had transformed the grubby exteriors of the town hall, where I'd once seen Loudon Wainwright III supporting King Crimson, and restored it to its glorious Portland grey. The air was thick with pollution down by the factory but here, less than half a mile away, the trees blossomed in Civic Square. Opposite, the magisterial King George Centre proclaimed its mighty white presence to the shuffling shoppers, and to its left stood the graceful, art deco simplicity of Leeds General Infirmary.

Dad was in the ominously titled Psychiatric Ward on the third floor, filled with mostly older men. Many wouldn't be leaving any time soon, except in a wooden box. Mum was by his bedside, knitting a lengthy mauve scarf, cup of tea steaming on Dad's table. It could have been a tableau from home: Dad staring, zombie-like, at the TV screen, Mum by his side, also watching but not paying attention, knitting or ironing. All that was missing was the cigarette dangling from her mouth, defying gravity.

"Barry!" she jumped up from the chair, allowing the knitting to fall, and hugged me, close and long. She'd always cuddled and held me close but as puberty approached I'd felt awkward and embarrassed, and she learned to keep her distance. Years of unexpressed physical devotion poured into that wordless hug.

"Monty! Barry's here. Monty!" She prodded Dad's knees under the blanket. He looked up and smiled – not a big smile, but it was the first time I'd seen his face move.

"Barry!" he said. "How's things?" He seemed unsure who I was.

"How are you feeling, Dad?" I asked awkwardly, avoiding anything that might imply crazy, loopy loo, cuckoo, lost marbles, two sandwiches short of a picnic.

"Fine and dandy," he replied, sounding anything but fine and dandy. "Chipper," he continued in a sarcastic monotone, "full of beans."

"Tired," said Mum.

"I'm tired," he said, nodding towards the patient on his left.

"Sidney, loud nightmares," she whispered, almost silently, as though he might have the strength to be insulted if he knew we were talking about him.

"Moaning all night," Dad said, loud; Mum angrily shushed him.

"It's okay, Sybil, it's a hospital," he said, adding in a loud stage whisper, "where ill people come. Ill in the head."

"I'm off to get some fresh air; see you in a few minutes." Mum turned and almost crashed into a young black nurse wheeling a metal handcart, laden with pills and medicines, like the sweet trolley at a posh restaurant, from patient to patient.

Dad watched until he was sure Mum had gone and turned to me, intently.

"Barry," he said, ushering me to sit on the bed. He manoeuvred himself into a sitting position, looked again at the door, grabbed my arm.

"Glad you're here, son."

"Me too, Dad."

"The factory's closed, Barry."

"I know."

"Summer holidays."

"Mhm..."

"But it's in serious trouble—"

"—I know."

"When it re-opens, I need you to take over."

"But Dad—"

"–It's not easy. There's a lot to be done and I can't do it from here."

"I know, Dad. I'll be meeting the accountants soon."

"What's really important," he said, lowering his voice and drawing me in further, "Mum mustn't know. Or Judith. Not in front of the ladies, alright?"

"You think they don't know?"

"What? What are you saying?" he asked, and his face crumbled with anxiety like a child.

"I'm uh, sure they don't know. I'll spend next week getting to know everything about the business."

"That's good, that's good."

He stopped talking, caught his breath. The conversation had exhausted him, like he'd run a hundred-yard sprint. I stroked his arm gently, waited for his breathing to steady.

"Come on, tell me a joke. I'm in hospital, cheer me up!"

"I don't do jokes."

"You given up? Don't blame you, it's a tough business, show. You'll settle in at the factory sure enough."

"I read poems. Funny poems."

"Oh. Okay. Good to have a hobby, eh, Sybil?"

Mum had returned, relaxed after a crafty fag in the loo.

"Barry was telling me he's given up comedy."

"Not given up–"

"–No, back for a couple of weeks," Mum said, "to give you a hand with the business." Mum looked at me. And Dad looked at me. He smiled and winked.

"Off you go, then," he said. "Sure you've got plenty to be doing." Mum smiled and dismissed me with a wave.

Walking back to the bus station, I stopped to visit Virgin Records, housed in one of the city's distinguished pedestrian precincts. This shop had been my oasis when wondering if I'd ever get away from here. It had lost some allure now I was back.

In the early days, you sat on beanbags and listened to records of your choice on headphones, while willowy, long-haired assistants of either gender brought you free cups of tea. Then the Virgin label released Tubular Bells, which was a flabbergasting success, and Mike Oldfield became a teenage megastar. Something of the hippy ethos vanished from the shop – the tea and beanbags, specifically – but you were still allowed to listen before purchase.

I asked for the new album by Wire, which did not disappoint. Chairs Missing was another dazzling mix of melodic pop and ear-bleeding punk rage. Outdoor Miner was everything I wanted of a hit single – short, catchy, original, over so soon that I had to lift the needle and play it again, turning up the volume and humming along with the now familiar chorus. But this was Wire, never knowingly predictable, and the next song, I Am The Fly, was a howl of fury, loud and catchy but angry and dense, lyrics shouted rather than sung. I turned up the volume further to block out the pain, block out the world and, little did I realise at the time, help accelerate the onset of early deafness.

> *No no Wire,*
> *You are not the fly,*
> *The fly is me,*
> *My future I can see*
> *But every time I fly-er,*
> *Wire*
> *Towards my desire*
> *I whack against a slab of glass called "Leeds"*
> *And expire.*

Back home, with Judith and Mum at the hospital, I revisited Dramatic Scenes From Childhood. The stairs in the hall, where I'd clumsily spilled Dad's coffee over Judith's beautiful school art competition entry; breakfast table, scene of the infamous Battle of Bowie, when Mum and Dad refused to allow me to see the superstar in case the concert turned me gay. Everywhere, Arguments About Israel; not an inch of this house had avoided the sound of irate exchanges between me and Dad about the legitimacy of American-sponsored violence perpetrated by the Zionist state. And now look at the Zionist state of my dad. Israel wasn't the cause of our Middle Leeds war; it was simply the easiest excuse for me to argue my way to a new life.

I lay on the bed in my packed-up bedroom, stared at the ceiling for ages, no Joni or Yoko for company.

Later, I was cooking my familiar Leeds signature dish of fish fingers, peas and mash when the phone rang. It was Harriet. Such joy!

"Barry? Is everything okay?"

"Sure."

"How's your dad?

"Okay, I think... How's Edinburgh?" I asked, not wanting to know.

"Busy." Me too, making fish fingers.

"Laurence still fed up?"

"He's fine. The others are never here. Maurice is helping Kris set up his show." Our show. Celia was right: I loved Kris and the thought of him two-timing me with Maurice was unbearable. And I was responsible for bringing them together.

"Is Kris okay?"

"Yes. He said not to worry; he totally understands."

We talked more, easily, about the madness of the flat, Harriet entertaining as always, excited to be writing about the Fringe for her student magazine. I was almost able to forget my anguish until she said: "I'll be here for another week. When are you coming back?" and I answered, without thinking, "I'm not coming back."

"What?"

"Tell Kris I won't be able to join him. By the time we're sorted here, Kris will have a show; it'll make no sense to fit me in."

I could barely believe the words coming from my mouth. I'd been prepared to put up with a hell of a lot – four weeks sleeping in a crypt with 20 strangers whom I'd be performing with in crappy shows – if it meant spending a month with Kris. But I was seventeen again, and Maurice had taken my loved one away again, and in that moment my Edinburgh dream was over.

"Gotta go now," I said, not adding "Coronation Street's about to start."

"I'll call you again," she said.

"Sure, if I can squeeze you in."

I went upstairs to my parents' bedroom, ignoring the familiar knick-knacks, the Goblin Teasmade by Mum's bedside, framed photographs of smiling family members on the dressing table, and opened Dad's wardrobe. I picked out a sober, smart, dark-navy suit, light-blue shirt, and a silver-and-black-striped tie. I tried on the suit jacket, a good fit; we were almost the same size and build.

When Judith came home, I gave her a pair of scissors and asked her to cut my hair.

"I haven't done this in a while. Want me to cut off the loose ends?"

"No, I want it short. Cut it all off."

"You sure?"

"Yes."

That night, I looked at Barry Goldman in the mirror – short-haired, clean-shaven, suit and tie, prepared for tomorrow's meeting with Goodwin Brackup Chartered Accountants and Surveyors. Barry Goldman the comedy poet was nowhere to be seen, and I wondered if he would ever be back.

CHAPTER 25

A DAY IN THE LIFE
OF AN EDINBURGH FRINGE GOER
By Harriet Fink

Call me Ishmael. I won't answer, though, because I'm trapped in a whale and I can't hear you. Also, that's not my name.

I'm not a participant here, – I'm a mere spectator – but oh, the roads I travel, the hills I climb (and, like Sisyphus, the same ones I descend), the torrential rainstorms I dodge in and out of to bring you this report, to convey, like Leopold Bloom in Ulysses, a single epic day. Only I'm not in Joyce's Dublin but his Celtic capital cousin Edinburgh, to experience life at the Fringe.

I am not Ishmael, or Leopold Bloom, or James Joyce. I am Harriet and this is Edinburgh, the city they call the Athens of the north – but with its ancient castle and violent hills, greystone tenements and steep, cobbled roads, and with the Festival in full flow, I wonder that had Socrates made the Royal Mile his home, had he performed his great comic philosophies to these crowds, would he not have returned to his Athenian birthplace and declared it the Edinburgh of the south?

If the Edinburgh International Festival is a cultural banquet of exquisite dishes from around the world, delicate and expensive, the Fringe is an all-you-can-eat buffet that is starting to imagine itself at the head of the table. All the world's a stage, as the great Bard said, and he could have been talking about Edinburgh in August. Every step takes you into a new scene, every corner turned brings you to a colourful troupe of dancing students; walk past them and behold, a panoramic vista like something out of a Kubrick film – and all this witnessed on a simple, single journey from your front door to the first live show of the day.

The Fringe day barely begins or ends – you can probably find a show for any hour –but I've plumped for the reasonably civilised start of eleven o'clock in the morning. A strange time to be witnessing Woyzeck by Georg Büchner, you may think, but there is something weirdly reassuring about seeing so much stage blood, guts and death before lunchtime, intensely realised by our very own Oxford Actors Society. One wonders how they will summon enough energy to be back in time for their evening adaptation of Witchfinder General, of "witch": more later.

I too must conserve my energy – a mere spectator, as I say, and yet, like Bloom, I am expecting to have attempted eighteen heroic feats before the day is out. My next task is easy enough; I only have to cross the foyer of this converted church hall (like so many theatres here), carved into the rock on the Royal Mile below the castle, to enter a different universe, populated by tiny children whose trendy parents have been forced to bring them along, to witness the magic and mayhem from Oxford Children's Theatre show, Babes In The 'Rood.

If you're wondering how I can fit two shows before lunch, Fringe performances are much shorter than their bloated cousins at the International Festival. You may witness, if your budget allows, a three-hour rendition of Swan Lake by the Bolshoi Ballet at the sumptuous Kings Theatre on Leven Street. Fringe theatre allows no such luxury; most come in under an hour, which in Woyzeck works out at a death every four-and-a-half minutes.

I could, if churlishly inclined, profess disappointment with Babes In The 'Rood, aware of the Oz-like machinery behind every trick purported to be the work of magick powers. I am, however, the wrong demographick for this show, and the dozens of small children screaming with glee at the stage greet the return of each disappearing spotted handkerchief as Portuguese villagers hailed the miracle of Our Lady of Fatima.

With four Herculean tasks behind me (I count leaving the house and arriving at the theatre on time as two), lunch beckons, but I have so many shows to see. Because this is the Fringe and there is, literally, something for everyone, I head down the steps – there are almost as many steps in Edinburgh as there are Fringe shows – to the Grassmarket, which, I surmise, used to run markets and be covered in grass. Neither of these traditions still holds but the name remains, and the ancient buildings and cobbled streets remind us of a past not yet obliterated.

Here on Teviot Place an innovative new theatre company of Oxford students, Dreaminspires, have taken the idea of lunchtime theatre to its literal conclusion. Cooking Up A Storm is an hilarious drama set in the kitchen of a student flat and tells the story of first conflict, then romance between Gavin, the earnest vegetarian, and Sophia, an Italian beauty who is not all she seems. Each character prepares their favourite dish and at the end the entire audience are invited to choose from the results of this culinary conflict: bolognaise or nut loaf. The food was as delicious as the performances: a show you can really sink your teeth into.

Anyone who has experienced a busy morning followed by a hearty lunch (I chose Italian) may well be aware of the natural urge to snooze lightly, to prepare for the long day ahead. I decided my time would be better served – and, indeed, that I could be kept forcefully awake – by the astounding feats of surrealist theatre company Crystal Theatre of the Saint. Ideas Are Animals by Paul Bassett Davies and promoted by Oxford Revue Company is the most extraordinary piece of theatre I have ever seen. If I told you it was about two men (played by Paul, and John Schofield) who spend their lives trying to get the better of each other, that barely begins to do justice to the twists and turns of this inspired and hilarious drama. At times, it's an almost cinematic experience, with four standard strip lights used to astonishing effect to box the actors in, or create incredible spaces and shapes suggestive of worlds to be discovered. This show will stay with me for a long time.

Edinburgh venues are within close walking distance of each other. Don't be fooled, though, by the straight lines on the map of the Fringe guide. It may look like the Fringe office is only 50 yards from Cowgate, but it's not until you're standing on the Royal Mile, trying to work out which sheer cliff to walk down, that you realise that a wrong turning can make this a 15-minute journey.

At this moment, my fellow Oxford fellows and college colleagues, I must confess that I have, briefly, been unfaithful. My plan was to review only those shows emanating from our beautiful adopted hometown, to record those like us, still immersed in our studies but who found the time between seminars and essays to create dramatic works of art. However, the lure of A & R at the Traverse by Pete Atkin was too much to avoid. Atkin is not a student; he graduated many years ago from the home of our boat-race rivals. His name may be unfamiliar, although you will probably have heard of his more noted collaborator, the hysterical TV newspaper critic Clive James. When he's not watching the little box for our entertainment, James is creating comic poetry; Atkin, a gifted musician, sets these to song, with mostly little more than a single guitar and his voice. Atkin is not a dazzling player, but the combination of these and James's poetry produces a beautiful whole.

Together, they have recorded six albums, all played to death on my sturdy Dansette, and I was not going to pass up this opportunity of discovering if Atkin's playwriting skills matched his abundant musical abilities. I was not disappointed. The play itself is an all-too-brief but biting satire of the music industry, literally in that the management side of the record business, the artists and repertoire department (the A & R of the title), bite chunks out of the souls (and incomes) of those they are charged with protecting. The play is punctuated by Atkin's own songs (of course it is) and, to my delight, a brief appearance (mentioned in the programme) of the man himself (too many brackets).

If the Fringe is about undergraduates in search of an artistic voice – a few may find this the first step in their professional journey, but many will return to their colleges having learned that the bohemian life is too perilous for them – it's also about professionals who have found theirs and are searching for ways to stretch themselves. For artists like Atkin, the creative journey incorporates the continuing search for new avenues.

But these thoughts occur later, right now there's no time to analyse what I've just seen: I've barely ten minutes to get from the Traverse to St Andrew's Church, and to traverse this journey is normally a brisk 15-minute walk. Difficult at the best of times, now to be achieved during Edinburgh rush hour. For those whose pleasure it is to spend their lives in this beautiful city, life goes on. Vans gotta drive, buses gotta bus, commuters gotta get home from the daily grind. Add the familiar Edinburgh rain, sheets and sheets, the drops so hard and fast they hurt. But arrival is achieved, another epic task ticked off on Ulysses's imposing checklist.

I've come to see Universally Challenged, a new comic revue by the Experimental Theatre Company, a semi-professional outfit with its origins in Queen's College that straddles the worlds of undergraduate and professional comedy. These five talented gentlemen are the next generation of Monty Python – funny, posh, surreal, physically odd, and destined for a rich and varied future in the world of light entertainment.

And now, my friends, another confession. It's 6.15 pm, I have seen six shows today, and fear if I continue at this pace I will doze off and snore loudly at a particularly sensitive moment in a mid-evening drama. But if I stop now, I may never continue.

I decide to take a break. My flat is close, as is the venue of the next show; a shower, fresh clothes and a light snack should be sustenance enough to see me through the remainder of the day. I'm expecting to witness the RC Sherriff epic war drama Journey's End, one of my main texts next term. Disappointingly, I discover this is not the play but the name of the venue. I am clearly not alone in this deception, a giant hand-written poster explaining as much is the first sign to greet you. I decide to stay as the company's production of Lady Windermere's Fan is about to begin.

It's hard to go wrong with Wilde's almost perfect comedy, but Bristol University Theatre and Comedy Horde somehow pull it off. All the elegance and mannered idiocy is steamrollered by a performance of such gurning and hamming as to be almost unwatchable.

Back to the Oxford Actors Society, after what feels like a lifetime of Wilde abandon (wish I had). Witchfinder General is a little-known film that has become popular among students,

I would like to say for its radical exploration of absolute belief and organised religion against the backdrop of the English Civil War, but suspect more because of its graphic portrayal of sex and violence, and the beauty of its lead actors.

This is a bold adaptation, a visually stunning work that doesn't so much follow the film as turn it into a piece of demanding physical theatre – gruesome, gripping and, in a development that could not have been envisaged when it was made in 1968, an attempt to draw parallels with the demonisation of witches and the current attacks on the women's liberation movement.

During this play, my emotions become confused. A slight quip has me shrieking with laughter; a small, tender moment sends me into a deep sadness. I leave the production feeling dizzy, disoriented and despairing. I am three-quarters through my odyssey, at that place in Aristotle's three-act drama where all is lost. I walk out of the theatre emotionally spent, intimidated by the crowds and the noise: guns, cannons and electronically boosted bagpipes. Yards away, the castle is hosting the Royal Edinburgh Military Tattoo, a world as far away as it's possible to be from my own lowly, poor-but-happy artistic milieu that challenges everything that theirs stands for: violence, nostalgia for colonial power, military might. I wonder if my generation stand at the edge of a world that we are about to leave, ready to leap into a new one – a leap of faith. It could be over a cliff, like the sheer edge confronting me at the foundations of Edinburgh Castle. And then I wonder if this is how every new generation feels before they step into their uncertain futures. What the hell is happening to me?

I am suffering cultural overload, a familiar experience for seasoned Fringe fans. Hours of theatrical spectacle designed to push my emotions to their limits have made me incapable of rational thought, and for a short period I take leave of my critical faculties. I think I might be driven insane by this when across the road I spot my old friend from home. He's staying in my flat, but our tastes differ and our cultural paths rarely cross. We are friends, nothing more, not close, but in my current state he is Hermes here to rescue Persephone from the Hades pit of despair, to save me from myself. I am supposed to be seeing another show now, but M suggests we find a quiet pub and suddenly, in this city of a thousand shows, of spectacular spectacles and extraordinary personal feats, nothing seems more inviting than a poorly lit alehouse, a crappy old juke box playing Metal Guru by T Rex and a pint of Heavy.

We catch up with each other's epic journeys. M likes music, mostly, and comedy, but also hanging out in pubs. His tales of tourists encountered and students excited are as entertaining as many of the shows I have paid money to sit through. This is all new for both of us, yet M has grounded me. Our lives are heading in different directions, but we are from the same place. He is my anchor.

Refreshed, re-energised and, let's be honest, rat-faced, we begin act three of today's story. I agree to accompany M to Clouds in West Tollcross, one of the few Edinburgh venues open all year. I must confess that punk rock has largely passed me by, yet it feels as though the energy that powers it is part of what I'm beginning to see more of at this Festival.

Wire are, on the surface, every prejudice about punk I expect to be confirmed. Four young men dressed in black: brash, angry, too loud for this small sweaty venue, sneery and threatening, not unlike their audience, a world away from the tourists and local families I've seen at every other show today. However as their set continues it becomes more melodic, the tunes catchier, jingle-janglier; these songs wouldn't be out of place on Top of the Pops, yet they remain true to their Wire-ness. I can't imagine Elton John singing a song about Morse code, but I can imagine Noel Edmonds, flanked by a bevy of simpering teenagers, introducing them to the TV cameras.

The day itself has ended (it's now past midnight), but M and I have discovered our second wind, and we clamber back up yet more steps behind Edinburgh Waverley: yes, the city has named its railway station after a novel by one of its most famous sons, like if King's Cross had been called Copperfield Station, and off to the Tempting Tattie, a baked potato emporium that has long been providing cheap sustenance for generations of impoverished Oxford students. I spot a crowd of familiar-looking second years from my college. This coincidence feels incredibly exciting and I realise I am still in a state of heightened emotions.

There is one last show to visit: another flatmate, who M is helping with props and lights, is performing at one thirty in the morning! It's in a cinema that is for most of the rest of the day exhibiting films of, ahem, a questionable pedigree. Let's just say that the men in raincoats who are the audience for these films are not after compelling characterisation or thrilling plot and leave it at that.

I'd like to tell you that the five of us in the audience who laughed incessantly at Kris Dean's one-man show Meep Meep, a bizarre comic conglomeration of Samuel Beckett and Wile E. Coyote, believed we had seen the future of comedy, but it was two o'clock in the morning and this was the tenth show I had seen in the space of fifteen hours, and I no longer trusted my instincts.

Instead, M, Kris and I wandered gently back into the night, home by three, exhilarated, energised and utterly exhausted. Next day, I rose from a deep slumber and, rejuvenated by the deepest of dreamless sleeps it is possible to imagine, wondered if I might be prepared to set forth again, to create my next volume of Ulysses.

Reader, I took the day off.
Harriet Fink, 2nd year English Lit, Somerville College.

CHAPTER 26

My first night back in Bristol was spent behind the bar at The Clifton, where the landlord grudgingly hired me despite repeating frequently that this was a "locals" pub. This idyllic corner of Bristol, with its sweeping crescents and spectacular panoramas, was occupied by the wealthiest and most preening of the student species, but they were not welcome in the Clifton pub. As bad luck would have it, that evening by complete coincidence a troupe of wealthy and preening drama undergraduates, who had been performing Japanese Noh theatre in the late September dusk of Goldney Gardens, arrived in full oriental gear and colonised a substantial corner, nursing half pints which they conspired to make last the entire evening.

Unsurprisingly, that was also my last night at The Clifton. I was more suited to working in the Nelson Mandela bar at the union, and finally got to learn who Nelson Mandela was.

The pay was not great, but this was one of the few industries not currently striking for more. The news was dominated by increasing industrial disruption. Working conditions had been declining for years due to lack of investment - but you wouldn't have known that reading the papers or watching TV, where a daily tale was peddled of angry, red-faced working-class men holding the country to ransom with their ever more outrageous demands for higher pay, which we were assured they would only spend on booze and fags.

It was cheap foreign imports from South-east Asia that had killed off H Goldman and driven his Son to despair. I had spent the previous two months in Leeds clearing up the mess, trying to bring order to the chaos of Dad's business. Despite having studied economics the previous year, nothing learned in the lecture hall proved of any use. I probably hadn't been paying attention, but beyond the fact that all economics is about demand and supply, and there was no demand for Dad's supplies, what mattered most was a lot of furious people were owed a lot of money but there wasn't enough to pay them back.

Judith dealt with the house sale and Mum looked after Dad, although, to complicate matters, Grandma had fallen at home, and was two floors above Dad at the hospital. In more uncharitable moments, Mum wondered whether this was a cry for attention from her mother. There was so much to do that we never got a moment to step back and speculate on how the hell we'd got to this situation, and that suited The Family That Never Talks About Its Problems perfectly.

Having decided not to go back to Edinburgh, new habits became routine. Every day spent wearing a suit and tie and meeting with accountants and auditors, another sliver of my soul was crushed. A daily procession of bald, besuited men took it in turns to read documents and sigh judgmentally at the selfish behaviour and failure of my father. Dad's oldest friend Harry Shulman turned particularly nasty, taking the failure as a personal slight. Perhaps if Dad had broken his leg or been in a car crash they would have been more sympathetic, but if men go funny in the head that's a crime.

Sympathy was worse. A couple of times I had to connect with Elkan Fink, Harriet's dad and a senior accountant at

Goodwin Brackup. I'd met him before and liked him best of all my friends' parents. Elkan knew of and was genuinely interested in my creative life. It was he who proudly showed me Harriet's article for the student magazine. I complimented her to him, told him what a great piece of work it was, though every sentence, every word, stabbed me – a painful reminder of what I'd left behind. It was like I'd organised a party and everyone arrived, but as soon as I left they had a great time without me. Handing the article back to Elkan the next day, I couldn't wait to discuss how to correct the incremental discrepancies in Dad's balance sheet - anything to suppress the joy and unpredictability of words with the steady, reliable, unemotional stream of numbers.

Dad's nervous breakdown was not the terminal illness we had all, in our ignorance, feared it might be. I was worried, aged 14, when I discovered that not every 14-year-old sat in their bedroom writing poetry contemplating the misery of the universe and the inevitability of death. What little I knew of madness was that it happened mainly to people who wrote poetry about the misery of the universe and the inevitability of death. Additional information came from Colditz, the hit TV prisoner-of-war programme. In one notorious episode, a prisoner feigns madness to facilitate his escape, but by the end has worked so hard to foil the Germans that he has genuinely gone mad. Millions watched this show; at school we talked of little else for days after. Madness, we'd learned, was something that could happen to anyone, simply by pretending.

While an unlikely route to insanity, it was at least progress from the normal mad TV character, a shock-white-haired scientist who said he'd discovered a cure for all the world's ills, being dragged to the nearest loony bin screaming "You're all mad! I'm the only sane one!" In Leeds, our experience of madness was limited to observing the mentally handicapped

and silent who worked in a dark, imposing Victorian
monstrosity on the corner of Scott Hall Road and Potternewton
Lane, scary-looking men with empty eyes and scars on their
forehead, who caught the same buses as us but whose space we
studiously avoided. We had no desire to find out more – and if
anyone in the local community had a mentally ill relative they
kept pretty quiet about it.

Dad's condition, we were told, was not unusual. Apparently,
it was not uncommon for men to act oddly as they approached
middle age – even those whose lives appeared relatively stress
free. Dad's old schoolfriend, Harry Levy, bought a sports car.
Hymie Baker the dentist, who served with Dad in the army in
Italy, left his wife, Sadie, and moved in with his dental hygiene
assistant, Linda – half his age. Maurice joked that he was using
his tongue to check her molars.

The cure for Dad was rest and calm, and he was getting
plenty of that. He no longer imagined there'd be a business to
go back to, but occasionally panicked when I relayed horror
stories of auditors and accountants. One day in hospital he got
quite cross with me over some tiny accounting discrepancy but
quickly apologised.

"Barry?"

"Yes?"

"I've messed up."

"It's okay, Dad."

"I've messed your life."

"No, you haven't," I said, though the thought had crossed
my mind.

"Forgive me, Barry."

"It's alright, Dad–"

"It's not alright!" he said, trying not to cry.

"We've spoken to the doctor; you're going to be fine. We'll
be fine."

"Barry, I'm so sorry," he said, and hugged me so close I could feel the tears dripping onto my shoulder. We must have been like this for five minutes before he let go.

Charlie and Ingrid had also enjoyed an eventful August. The success of our Rock Against Racism gig had brought Ingrid to the attention of Head Office. Her calmness in a crisis was deemed an asset for Socialist International high command.

Rock Against Racism was a huge success over the summer – massive open-air gigs in London and Manchester attracted thousands of fans, but no trouble. The fascists stayed away – or, as seemed more likely, the punk fans who'd been attracted by the excitement of gang membership had given up on fascism and stuck with the music that had attracted them in the first place.

There had been a rare show of unity between the many warring micro-factions of the far left, and out of this stunning victory emerged a new organisation, the Anti-Nazi League. Who could argue with a name like that? Nazis, of course, and a few disgruntled groups on the left, suspicious of Socialist International allowing the bourgeois lackeys of the Labour Party to lend their support. But here was an organisation guaranteed to win popularity across universities and polytechnics as the new year began. Great name, great aim and, crucially, great badges.

I was staying in the spare room at Charlie's flat: a damp, windowless basement that in better days would have been the servant quarters for the grand, imperial houses above, in the bold and sweeping Royal York Crescent with its panoramic views of the River Avon and Mendip Hills.

I didn't see Charlie much; when he wasn't staying with Ingrid he was rehearsing with his new band, The Left Overs. Charlie and Ingrid were still in separate flats, even though they were the most solid couple I had ever known. Why had they not officially moved in together? I was too busy to find out. No bands or demos for me right now. They dropped by the Mandela Bar to see me one night – to invite me to a meeting, unsurprisingly, while cracking jokes about how the short haircut had sapped my political strength – but I didn't learn any more about their personal lives.

The bar filled quickly. It was still Freshers' Week and I had to give up on our conversation to serve under-priced alcohol to over-privileged students. It was no fun being the grown-up in the room. I recognised a few from last year, but it was mostly new kids, fresh-faced, excited and scared, some of the boys hiding their insecurities by shouting and laughing louder than the rest.

Within an hour, most of the excited young adult children had disappeared into meeting rooms, hoping that their shared love of photography, ballroom dancing or Nicaraguan politics would connect them with strangers from completely different parts of Guildford.

I was a big second-year now, one foot in the real world, learning about proper work. I discovered that, when bar work isn't busy, so rushed-off-your-feet-you-don't-notice-the-time-fly busy, it's knackering and boring. Also, other students who worked here did so because they loved drinking.

Sheryl was a second-year and, unusually for an engineering student, female. She worked hard – serving, clearing, washing glasses, emptying ashtrays – but she always had a pint of Somerset scrumpy on the go. She was a fast and thorough worker, every few minutes punctuated her chores with a calm, measured, steady gulp of festering apple. This was a potent local brew, popular with Minehead skinheads in search of mindless town-centre excitement on Saturday nights, but Sheryl was calm and sober even after three pints.

Unlike the other engineering students I knew, Sheryl was outgoing and conversational, with a manner that immediately put you at ease. Even when we were busy, every customer was treated to a smile and brief chat. She was average size for her height, which surprised me, considering the mountain of yeast and sugar she was tipping down her throat every night.

"Guess I'm one of those people with a high metabolism," she offered when I hadn't realised I'd been watching her finish that third pint.

"You consume impressive quantities."

"For a girl, you were going to say, weren't you?"

"That would have been sexist–"

She raised an eyebrow.

"–but if I hadn't, that could also have been misconstrued. What if I'd said 'Crikey, Sheryl, you drink more than anyone I've ever known, male or female' – which isn't true, by the way – which would have been worse."

She laughed and her hair, a neat bob, jumped as her head fell back. I had missed these easy, flirtatious conversations around people my age.

Shortly before last orders, Camilla came by. In the many dull, empty hours I'd spent in Leeds that summer, on buses or staring at the ceiling in my bedroom, I had fixated obsessively on Kris and his show, desperate to know how it had gone but too insecure to contact him and find out. I'd speculated unhealthily about Maurice and Harriet, that the article told me so much more than I wanted to know about their blossoming relationship. I thought about Celia, usually with a shudder of embarrassment, but had completely forgotten about Bristol University Theatre and Comedy Horde. There was no space for it.

I was genuinely pleased to see Camilla, but it didn't look like the feeling was mutual.

"Hey Camilla, how was Edinburgh?"

"Okay thanks. You got a few minutes?"

No 'hun' tonight. "Sure, I'll be done soon: can you wait?"

"It's okay," Sheryl called, "I can finish here; you go."

"Thanks," I said, and we walked down to the foyer.

"Everything okay?" I asked, but she didn't respond. "Do you want to go for a drink? There's a late bar over the square."

Camilla stopped before the main entrance and turned to me.

"Barry, we had a meeting tonight of the committee."

"And?"

"We decided to expel you from BUTCH."

"Ah. Okay."

"You are banned from working with the group. Permanently."

"Right."

"Is that all you can say?"

I shrugged. This wasn't that surprising. "What else is there? I messed up. I should have told you about the other show. Then my dad nearly died," I added, over-dramatically. "I had to go back to my family."

She turned away – annoyingly, I thought.

"Do you think I should have stayed in Edinburgh, Camilla? Do you think I should have said 'Sorry, Dad, I've got a more important job to do, stand in the pissing rain telling people it's not a play, it's the name of the venue? Why don't you come instead and watch us make a pig's ear of The Importance of Being Earnest?'"

She didn't answer straight away. I wondered if I'd gone too far but didn't care.

"Do you know how hard we worked to get you into the group?" she asked quietly. She turned back to face me, had been crying and hadn't wanted me to see. "Have you any idea how close Richard was to kicking you out?"

"Richard?"

"Hugo and I could tell your comedy gave our show something different."

"Hugo? He had an odd way of showing it."

"You never gave him a chance! He fought and fought to get you in, all so he could stand there and watch you humiliate him for cheap laughs."

"He was rude to me from the start!"

A small crowd of first years were loitering, pretending they were still chatting, but craning their necks to see what was going on.

"I thought you were a good judge of character. He's rude to everyone. He's not the most socially skilled but he's a kind soul, and he's one hundred per cent devoted to the group."

"But I–"

"You, having sneaked in above our quota-"

"-You're telling me this now?"

"-repay him by taking the one thing we picked you for," she said, emphasising these words as if I needed reminding of my shortfall in every other area, "the one thing, and swan off at one o'clock in the morning to do it somewhere else."

I thought about responding but had nothing to say.

"You took one look at all the hard work we were doing and decided it would be more fun to hang out with your mates than put in the graft required to make our shows work. You're a selfish, lazy, disloyal prick!"

"Camilla!" I said, wondering if the gathering crowds were seeing their friendly barman in a new and negative light.

"And cruel. You can't even remember the correct Oscar Wilde play! It was Lady Windermere's Fan!"

She walked out, followed by the small, hovering crowd, who allowed themselves a closer view of me, to see what a monster looked like. For the first time that year, an audience had watched two members of BUTCH give a compelling, five-star performance.

CHAPTER 27

"Fantastic innit, pal?" he said in the thickest Leeds accent I'd heard in a while. "Haven't seen a day like this in months, certainly not since the summer, eh? Come far?"

"From Bristol."

"Oo arr, country yokel, what brings you up north?"

"I'm from Leeds."

"No you're not, pal; that's not what we call a Leeds accent."

In Bristol, I was known as the flat-capped whippet owner. Heard in a taxi heading out of Leeds City station, I was labelled foreigner by my Pakistani driver. Nothing was so strong in Leeds as the north-south divide.

"I'm here for a family funeral."

"Ahh. Ah, right," he said, registering for the first time my reason for asking to be driven to a cemetery. "Picked a nice day for it, pal."

It was unseasonably beautiful. The sun was already high in the November Leeds sky, but even the clear light, warmth and small, golden shadows cast across the trees in the distance couldn't disguise the bleakness of Gildersome Jewish graveyard. With the constant thrum of motorway on one side and a long, uninterrupted line of complex electricity pylons on another, there was never a picturesque view to be had from this bleak field in the dingiest, poorest suburb of south-west Leeds.

I'd come straight from Bristol. We Jews like to bury the corpses of our loved ones, remove all physical traces of the dead from the living, as quickly as possible so we can get on with our rending of garments and begin mourning in earnest.

There was no time to go home and comfort Mum and confront the new circumstances; it was pick up the first train from Bristol Temple Meads and head straight to the cemetery or miss the funeral completely. Whichever rabbi made up these rules in the wilderness hadn't expected relatives to have moved half a country away.

In grudging acknowledgment of the solemnity of the occasion, my driver shut up. I stared out the window, aware of our proximity to Leeds United but disorientated by the new motorways that had sprung up like low-budget Formula One racetracks: Monaco, Rio, Hunslet.

"Someone close?" he asked after a brief silence.

"Yes," I said, "My gran."

"Been ill long?"

"My whole life."

He laughed.

"Happen," he said. "Buried the mother-in-law last week."

"Sorry," I said.

"Yeah, I know. She wasn't even dead yet." He smiled and winked.

I smiled politely, not in the mood to pick a fight over sexist mother-in-law jokes with my potential comrade-in-arms in the fight against racism.

There were no other mourners when we arrived. A few old blokes in muddy, grey overalls lolled about, an older pair stood by the chapel, mumbling quietly, smoking. People work here, I understood, a banal observation that still shocked me. The idea that, every day, men spent their working lives among the dead and their families. What stories could they tell? What secrets might we learn spending so much time in the proximity of raw, unsullied grief? This struck me as the kind of question a not-very-good poet might ask, convincing me further that my future lay elsewhere.

Ambling around the gravestones provided a short glimpse into the largely uneventful history of Leeds Jewry. There were a few familiar surnames, grandparents and great-grandparents of friends: here's Hymie Sacks, the tailor whose family business was one of the few surviving in the city, still proudly producing jodhpurs for the British Olympic riding team; Max Saffer, an older boy from my school who had died on his seventeenth birthday. He passed his driving test that day, celebrated by taking his parents' Hillman Imp for a spin, smashed into a wall on Gledhow Valley Road. I remember his gang that following week, wandering the school corridors sullenly, unable to cope with the kind of loss you don't expect at that age.

A few mourners arrived, aging relatives and friends of the family, including Gran's cousin, Betty, whose physical resemblance to Grandma shocked me, and I blushed at the shameful realisation that I had barely been giving her any thought. Grandma, as hinted to the cab driver, was a hypochondriac; she manipulated mum and made her feel guilty about not spending enough time with her. Then she fell, and Judith and I joked about how well she must have practised to make it look convincing. There were no broken bones and she rested for a few days, seemed okay until a sudden drop in blood pressure showed that she had been bleeding internally. While Dad was recovering well downstairs in the same hospital, Gran was rushed to intensive care and died within twenty-four hours. She was still alive yesterday.

More relatives appeared, cars creeping slowly through the gates as if in respect for the dead. Half-remembered family and friends of my parents emerged from cars, squinting awkwardly in the late autumn sunshine. A familiar rust-orange Volvo estate cruised in; it was Maurice's parents and I was surprised at my delight when Maurice exited from the back, wearing the kind of sheepskin coat favoured by football managers and commentators.

"Alright, mate," he said, coming to hug me, then pulling away to shake my hand. "I wish you long life," he added, the traditional Jewish response to the close relative of someone who has died.

"Do you do that for grandparents?"

"Don't ask me, pal, I'm not the chief rabbi. What does it even mean?"

"No idea. Thanks for coming, Maurice."

"Yeah, at least she's spared having to watch United the rest of the season."

I pushed him away in mock outrage as a long, black car pulled in and reversed funereally towards the doors of the chapel. The mourners turned to watch as the graveside workers gently eased the casket onto the trolley. Not just me who's mesmerised by the proximity of death, then. Everyone staring at the box was imagining Grandma inside, with us yesterday but not today, looking the same as we'd always known her only no longer alive, about to be buried in the ground. We pictured ourselves in there, worried obsessively, like Ray Milland in The Premature Burial, that we might one day accidentally be buried alive. Perhaps that was only me.

Another dark, sombre vehicle appeared with Mum, Judith and Grandma's sister, Pearl. The car Dad and I should have been in. What a tragic sight. All those weeks feeling sorry for myself, measuring Dad's illness and Grandma's demands only in relation to the difficulties they caused me, but it was Mum who suffered most while showing it least. The two people closest to her in life – one changed forever, the other gone.

I hugged Mum close, mumbled "Wish you long life", and worked out when she didn't say it back that you don't wish it to the deceased's grandchildren: they're not close enough. I never understood the phrase; it hadn't come from the religion. You're saying to someone who has lost their closest relative: "I hope you don't die just yet." Maybe it was invented to offer more emphasis than "Sorry for your loss". In the end, it was the hug that meant most. Holding her close, I cried for her grief, and my own, for all the injustices in the world, the pain and sorrow of those who mourn. Because funerals aren't about the dead, are they? They're about the living, and how to cope with drastic new circumstances. I cried selfishly for my singleness, the end of my writing and performing career, knowing I'd need to be there more for Mum and Dad, and at the meaningless-ness of it all. Was this all that Grandma amounted to? A family, a miserable, unfulfilled life, and a death: what was the point?

The tears were quickly wiped away and the cries stayed silent. We were Jewish but also English, and a funeral is not the place or time to be indulging in such public displays of raw emotion.

Rabbi Labofski's service was short and dignified. He had known Grandma, spoke warmly about her family life and charitable work. Had probably made a speech similar to this a dozen times, but it came from the heart and was what we needed. Judith, calm, together Judith, my big sister who always seemed like an adult, stood motionless, tears streaming down her face.

We followed the coffin to the graveside, silent as death. Murmured conversations filled the background; I wanted everyone to shut up. This was the first funeral I'd been to, too young to go to Grandpa's, and no other death of a relative had been deemed close enough to merit my presence.

Grandma's coffin was lowered into the ground. What was I expecting? Angels to fly in from behind the brilliant sun, the lid to open and Grandma transported to a heavenly paradise? Of course not, but it was still shocking. The hollow pit, two spades standing in a mound of earth close by, like we'd turned up to a building site during the labourers' lunch break.

What I hadn't been expecting at all was this: after mourners' prayers, the rabbi nodded to Mum and Pearl, and each of them picked up one of those spades, shovelled up a heap of fresh ground and heaved it back over the coffin. *What?*

Was this a Jew thing? Or a Leeds thing? Less than a day after Mum dies, her children are the first to cover her coffin with soil? There's no coming back now, Gran: you're six feet under and the ones ensuring you stay there were closest to you in life. I was still gaping at the spectacle when they handed the shovels to me and Judith. We were actively participating in burying Grandma. It seemed an astonishing ritual from another era, but as I stabbed hard into the pile of earth, lifted the spade and dropped the soil on the casket, I felt a connection with Grandma and everyone who had come before her, and with all the creatures that still lived, above and below the ground, and everything that lived on the planet. And I thought, even if I become the greatest poet the world has ever known, I'm still going to end up down here, with the rest of them. Which weirdly cheered me up.

The whole ceremony, from hearse to ground, was over in less than an hour. Everyone was invited to ours for cream cheese and smoked salmon bagels. Mum had somehow found the time to make a spread for the family. Maurice came over and hugged me again.

"Sorry, mate, exam this afternoon; can't come back to yours."

"Exams? What's the matter, Maurice? Where did your parents go wrong?"

"Poetry's all well and good, Wordsworth, but some of us gotta learn how to pay the bills."

"You have a good time in Edinburgh?"

"Yeah," he said, giving nothing away.

"Come on, I read Harriet's article. 'My hero.' That was a result."

"Me and Harriet?" He laughed, shook his head.

"I don't believe you."

"Naah, me and Harriet are just good friends. Always have been."

"Since you 'failed to get your end away' last year."

"Thanks for reminding me Barry."

Surrounded by death, mourning and grief, the crisp, cold sunshine and a heightened sense of my own mortality, I was still able to feel a surge of excitement that there was the faintest of hope that the beautiful, talented comedy critic might find a place in her heart for the former-poet-turned-barman.

"You spoken to Kris since Edinburgh?"

"Haven't had a chance," I said, to make it sound like I'd been too busy, and not too scared to find out more. Despite everything, I still fantasised that Kris would turn up from nowhere, like he'd done before, to re-establish our comedic relationship and drag me away from this new tedious life. "I'm staying for a couple of days: maybe catch up?"

"I'll try and come to your house for prayers."

Judith called and I joined her and Mum in the funeral car. We didn't talk much on the way home, though there was much to say. In a moment of dark humour, Mum asked if we could stop at the hospital and drop some things off for Dad, but the driver suggested it might not be wise to pull up outside Leeds General Infirmary in a car of this type.

Another shock was when we stopped in a small, suburban cul-de-sac a couple of miles from home, and I realised that this was now where we lived. Since I'd last been to Leeds, Judith had sold the house, installed Mum, and helped her unpack. I knew this – Mum had visited me in Bristol on her own a couple of weeks earlier and told me about the new place – but it was like visiting a stranger's house.

Judith, head porter at the Goldman Hotel, showed me to my room. This house was about half the size of the old one and my new bedroom contained the furniture of two. There was almost nowhere to put my body, apart from the bed. An old wardrobe from the upstairs landing took up too much of one wall side and could only be opened halfway. I peered inside and recognised old clothes no longer worn, board games no longer played, records long given up on. The Barry I'd left behind had been carefully transported here, and all he did was take up space.

Downstairs was smaller: what would Dad make of the shrunken kitchen, with its formica-topped bar and matching stools? He, too, was yet to see the new house. The living room furniture was familiar but too large for a room this size, like a fat man squeezed into a small armchair. The mirrors were covered with bedsheets, another tradition of death in a Jewish house of mourning, all the better to reflect inwardly on the person we lost rather than care about such frivolities as our outward appearance. You're not expected to leave the house for a week – and, anyway everyone expects you to look like shit.

We'd barely been back before the guests arrived, and the next hour was spent in a conversational loop: "Yes, Bristol, second year that's right, I know, time flies, yes, he's much better now, thanks for asking, coming home next week, I know, amazing they were both in the same hospital at the same time, you're right, Mum was rushed off her feet, yes, up and down the hospital stairs, like Florence Nightingale, yes, Grandma, too, lovely lady, that's right, ill quite a lot over the years, especially since her husband died. Dad? Nobody knows, we think it was stress related, you're right, yes, it was a shock, but the whole clothing industry in Leeds has been suffering from cheap imports, not really, the garment unions aren't traditionally militant, more to do with cheap imports, yes, Izzy Lieberman's coat factory in Harehills, I heard, it won't be the last to go, I guess, no, she wasn't Jewish but the sex was great, didn't tell anyone in the family, no, sacked before I'd done a show, yes I've given up performing, my life is effectively over, I'm a barman now..."

People came, stayed for an appropriate amount of time and left until it was the three of us, alone in the kitchen, coming to terms with the new world and learning how to sit on barstools.

"I like this kitchen," I said.

"Yes, it's fine, said Mum, "for midgets."

"Did you hear about Izzy Lieberman?" Judith asked.

"I know," Mum said.

"Won't be the last," I said, falling in like Judith with the rhythms of the Leeds Jewish conversation she and I had left behind, completing the shortened version of the story we'd all heard ten times today.

"Does Dad know much about this place?" I asked.

"Yes, he's quite excited," said Jewish Leeds Judith, brightly. "I took some photos, then Mum showed them to him after they'd been developed."

"Mmm," said Mum, not playing along with our charade.

"Is he going to be okay?" I asked.

"Are *you* going to be okay, Mum?" Judith asked, like an admonition.

"Yes, we'll be fine," she said, even as the tears began.

She recovered slowly, thought about taking a cigarette, decided against.

"What a year," she said, between sniffles. "First the business, then Dad, now Mum."

I leaned over, gently stroked her arm.

"And Celia," she said.

I stopped stroking her arm, looked up, smiled weakly, started again.

"How did you know that?"

"You know Lucy Featherman? Chicky Featherman's daughter? She's at Bristol; she mentioned it."

"Yeah, that's over now."

"Okay," said Mum, trying to sound supportive but clearly delighted.

Sitting up in the TV room, chatting with the healthier patients, joking and laughing about the funeral he'd managed to avoid attending, Dad was completely different from my last visit. He was sad for Mum, but what else might he have been thinking when the woman who had spent her later years bullying him and manipulating his wife was no longer around to make their lives a misery?

A large, jolly, Irish nurse berating the smokers – "Well, if you're planning to get lung cancer you're in the right place for it, duckies" – cleaned around them, while others watched darts on the telly, gripped by the unlikely drama.

Despite his end-of-term mood, Dad was concerned about Mum.

"You and Judith looking after her?" he said.

"Sure."

"Wish I could help, but it's going to be a while before I'm much use."

"Come on, Dad–"

"–Barry, let's not pretend. The last few months have been a write-off. I'm feeling much better but there's a long way to go, and I don't want to be a burden–"

"–You won't be–"

"–I will, and I'll need you and Judith to spend more time with her."

"Sure."

All those years I'd been desperate to leave but, like the pilot in Colditz who had feigned madness to escape, I paid the price by entering a whole new prison.

"You not going to be a rock star, then?"

"What?"

"Given up wanting to be a comedian?"

"Suppose so."

"Shame."

"You think?"

"If you could get on the telly like Bernard Manning or Ken Dodd, you could earn a fortune."

"I'm not that kind of comic, Dad."

"Or Ron. Bet he's raking it in."

"Ron?"

"You remember Ron. Lazy sod. Trouble-maker. Loudmouth at the factory."

"Oh, Ron! What do you mean?"

He nodded towards the TV, which was showing the Darts World Championship. A large man in a tight, bright tee shirt, cigarette in mouth, was throwing arrows at a board.

"Eighty-three," a voice boomed as the man removed his darts and walked away.

"Ron," the booming voice fell to a stage whisper, "you require ninety-two."

The camera zoomed in close to three darts on the pub table. I didn't need to see him; I recognised the arrows before he picked them up. The man who had referred to me as the ruptured duck walked to the board with stout determination, exactly as I remembered from the Bricklayers' Arms, ready to throw those gold-plated missiles. Dart one, double sixteen, perfectly placed, before I had time to calculate, thwack, dart number two, bang into the twenty, then the final dart – thump! Double top! Forty scored, a roar from the crowd in the pub on TV, a cheer in the hospital. Not from Dad, though; he sat with his arms folded. Me neither, as I thought, everyone's a star now – even unemployed Ron from the cutting room. Everyone apart from me.

"Lazy sod."

* * * * *

"I'll have to go back to London for a couple of days. How long can you stay?" Judith asked when we were alone that evening in the kitchen.

"A week at the most."

"And when can you come back?"

"Don't know, can't stay away too long, I'll get behind in my lectures. And lose my job."

"From a pub? You can work up here if you have to. Money's not the main priority."

"It is for me," I said, sounding like a grown-up.

"I'll help you," she said, leafing carefully through the pages of her 1978 Letts Diary.

"The best help you can give me," I said, settling into this new, male adult voice I was starting to enjoy, "would be to come here more often. I can do the student holidays."

"What about me and Craig? Doesn't our life enter into it?"

"What about my studies?"

"It won't be long. And you don't have to worry any more about your secret girlfriend."

"I was going to tell–"

"Course you were!" she laughed. "Waiting for the right moment."

How did she know I was going to say that?

"Oh, yes, Barry, I've been out with that guy a few times. 'Sure, I'll leave her. Gotta pick my moment.'"

"I wasn't cheating on her!"

"It's the same thing. Just a bit sadder when it's Mum and Dad. Either way, it's the behaviour of a selfish prick."

I picked aimlessly at a small cluster of old rice caked to the formica top, nothing to say.

"You need to be here, Barry."

"You're better with Mum, organising the house and–"

"–You mean like Mum and Grandma? Little lady stays at home? I can't believe I'm hearing this. You told me you were a women's libber."

"Of course I am, but that doesn't mean I have to give up my life, does it?"

"What do you think women do, all the time? What do you think Mum might have done with her time, if she hadn't taken full responsibility for her own Mum? And now Dad. This is her life now. A lifetime of looking after Dad."

I sat in silence, staring across the kitchen bar at Judith. I wondered what Yoko and Joni would have to say about this. Surely they'd agree with me?

"Doubt it," came a sneer from that corner. It wasn't Joni or Yoko, but an older lady, Mum's age, in a dark-green blouse and grey pleated skirt. I stared.

"Don't recognise me, eh, Barry? Only your fancy lady pop stars. It's me, Sheila. Sheila Rowbotham. Happen Joni can afford to pay someone to do the ironing. Can't see Yoko scrubbing John's shirt collars. Always had you down as a fair-weather supporter, Barry. Women's rights when it suits you. Typical bloody men! You really are all the bloody same!"

"Have you any idea what Mum wants to do?" Judith asked.

"What do you mean?"

"Ha!" Sheila shouted and vanished. Judith stood up, turned away from me, stared out the kitchen window.

"Help Dad get better?"

Judith carried on staring ahead, flicking the fringe away from her eyes.

"She'll have more time now," I said. "Won't be so hassled looking after Grandma."

"A sales rep." She turned again, looked at me, laughed. "You've no idea, have you? Mum always wanted to be a sales rep. Travelling round Yorkshire. Visiting shops. Getting them to buy stuff."

"What stuff?"

"I don't know. Clothes? Toys? Cosmetics?"

"Like the Avon Lady?"

Everyone knew the Avon Lady. She was part of a massive TV advertising campaign – "Bing bong! Avon calling" – where ordinary people answered the door to smartly dressed ladies selling make-up from the Avon cosmetics company.

"No, Barry. It doesn't matter exactly what it is. She wants to do something that isn't being a housewife or caring for the family. But she's had to give up on that."

"What do you care? You used to fight with her all the time about wanting to get away and do your own thing."

"Exactly!" She slammed her hands angrily on the bar top. "We can't afford to give in anymore. If women want to work, we have to fight for the right!"

"What am I supposed to do, then?"

"Your share!"

I folded my arms. Not quite ready yet to admit I was wrong.

"Stop being part of the problem, Barry. Take responsibility. You and me. We have to do what we can to look after them, and

I'm prepared to do fifty per cent. Which means you have to do the other fifty."

She sat down, picked up her book. I tried to think of an argument against what she said that wouldn't end with "I don't have to do more than I'm doing because I'm a man!"

The phone rang, and it took us a moment to work out where. Unlike the old dial model that sat comfortably on the table, this new machine had push buttons and was mounted on the wall like a work of art. Judith picked up the receiver.

"Hello?... Who's speaking, please?... Aha... Yes, he is. Hang on a moment."

She handed the receiver to me.

"Chris?" she said.

"Oh." I took the phone. "Hi, Kris."

"Hey, Barry. How you doing, mate?"

"Okay, uh, my gran just died."

"Yeah, sorry to hear that."

"Yeah, well. Good to hear you, man."

"You too, Barry."

"How did Edinburgh go?"

"Yeah, uh, it was pretty disastrous, really."

"Really?"

"Money-wise, yeah. Hardly any audience."

"Sorry to hear that. I read Harriet's review."

"Ha! Yes. That was, that was quite something." I'd never heard Kris sound this awkward.

"Did Maurice tell you I was here?" I asked.

"Yeah, that was one thing that came out of the show."

"What?"

"Maurice."

"What about Maurice?"

"Didn't he tell you? He's promised to help put on a show next year."

"Like a promoter? Or a manager?"

"I guess."

"Crikey."

"He helped me through the Festival."

"Yeah, sorry I wasn't much use on that score."

"That's okay."

If ever there was a moment to push that Kris and I might do a show together again, this was it. I could feel that moment slipping away.

"I was, ah—"

"—Will you be in Leeds over Christmas?" he asked, which seemed like a weird question. Maybe he did want to do a show with me.

"Not sure. Having to work a lot in Bristol, but I could be."

"I might be coming up."

"Planning to spend some time with Maurice?"

"Well, I guess. Harriet mainly."

"Harriet?"

"Flippin' 'eck, Maurice doesn't tell you anything, does he?"

"Tell me about it."

"Ha!"

"Maurice never tells me anything about anything. Ever."

"During the Festival, you know, I... I started seeing Harriet."

Course you did. You! Not Maurice. You were staying with her. I set the two of you up.

"Mhm."

"Sorry, mate: thought you knew. Maurice told me you and her—"

"—Nah, that was never a thing, just good friends."

"Right. Okay," he said, sounding relieved. I imagined the conversation they must have had on the phone earlier. Maurice will have said something like "Barry, remember him? You were about to do a show with him (and frankly, bud, you dodged a bullet there), give him a call. He's at home in Leeds, his gran just died", and Kris will have accepted his duty.

"I have to go," I said. "Maybe see you if you're in Leeds."

"Yeah, would be good to catch up."

"Sure," I said. "Bye."

I put the receiver back in its new wall position and laughed.

Celia had made me see how love of Kris had damaged my relationship with her. But it wasn't just Kris, was it? It was Harriet. I never told her about the flat because I was holding out for the chance of being there myself. I'd never stopped hoping that Harriet and I might be something – even though we'd not even been on a date.

I spent much of last Christmas with Harriet and Maurice as a chance to escape from dad. Not this time though. This time round I'd be foregoing the Christian holidays. Harriet would be home soon but I couldn't imagine seeing her. It would be too painful to be near her as long as we both loved the same man.

CHAPTER 28

January 1979. Secretaries, legal officers and administrative staff tidied their desks, anticipating the end of their first day back at Senate House after the Christmas holidays. Outside, in the dark of deep winter, a small gang of students led by Charlie and Ingrid snuck by lamplight into the building, occupied Churchill Meeting Room on the first floor, and barricaded themselves in.

By the following morning, a giant banner had been unfurled across the whole of the front of Senate House:

SACK THE VICE-CHANCELLOR, NOT GORDON!
MUCKLE WON'T BUCKLE!

How on earth had my gentle, unassuming sociology lecturer become the first celebrity student cause of 1979?

Like millions across the country, staff at Bristol University had complained angrily about what they saw as a meagre pay offer from the government.

Gordon being Gordon had led his fellow academics out of the lecture halls and onto the streets – not enough to cause disruption, but shortly before Christmas he was suspended by the University. Ingrid and Charlie took up his case and began a legal challenge, insisting Gordon be reinstated.

No one took much notice to begin with, but Gordon reframed the issue, turning it into a debate about how the vice-chancellor's office were using government finance to favour their pet projects. Instead of publishing their reasonably uncontroversial finances in full, the VC opted for angry self-justification, fuelling suspicion and mistrust where there had been none. Gordon remained suspended and the story mushroomed.

I was too busy working to stay involved in student politics, and had no idea about the occupation until lectures next morning, when everyone was talking about nothing else. I ran straight to Senate House. The entrance was blocked by half a dozen policemen, unsure of their role in this outbreak of student misbehaviour. Like us, they'd seen nightly footage on TV of strikes and marches, of their colleagues across the country getting stuck in with batons and shields. This was more complicated. The students were already inside; it would take a big, clumsy operation to remove them.

A BBC local news cameraman and journalist were watching the event; nearby, a group of university staff were talking quietly, urgently. I recognised one as the vice-chancellor's press officer and moved closer to eavesdrop. Someone was calling for the nuclear option: "storm the barricades", throw out the leftie irritants. Another urged caution, nodding to the presence of televisual scrutiny.

I was admiring the effort that had gone into the giant banner when suddenly my arm was grabbed from behind. It was Matt. I started to speak but he put his finger to his lips. He led me from the front of the building round the side, all the time looking around, urging me to stay quiet. We reached a black metal door, he knocked rhythmically, four beats then two, but there was no response.

He looked at his watch, following the second hand until another minute passed and knocked again, four beats plus two. Again, no response.

I had no idea what was happening. Matt was holding a large Gateway supermarket carrier bag packed with shopping. This next minute seemed to take forever. That's a nice watch, Matt, I thought, distracted.

He knocked again, and the door opened outwards, silently. Third time lucky.

"Ingrid!" I said without thinking, shushed instantly by both of them. They took me quietly up the back stairs and through a door into the anonymous first-floor lobby. All the offices were locked but the meeting room was open and we were greeted by a dozen or so of the most familiar teenage revolutionaries. Matt held the shopping bag high and a great cheer erupted. Provisions! From behind enemy lines!

"Barry!" Charlie shouted, hugging me in comradely solidarity. He had that familiar studenty whiff of a bloke who has been up all night and is still in the clothes he'd been wearing since the day before, but without the aroma of hash or alcohol. This was no party: it was strictly business.

"Brilliant!" I said. "How did you do it?"

"Been planning for weeks."

"Wondered what you'd been up to."

"We thought about telling you but knew you'd be working."

"Yeah, I'm a scab."

"We'd done a recce on the building, worked out where the fire escape led. Ingrid was here for a meeting yesterday."

She joined us, passing a jam sandwich hastily assembled from Matt's shopping bag ingredients to Charlie, and took up the story.

"It was our monthly student welfare meeting with the staff. I popped out 'to the loo'" she said in air quotes, "opened the fire escape – and here we are."

"Me and Matt came in at the front and distracted them while Seb led a bunch round the side. They all came in the same way as you."

"How can I help?" I asked, excited by the buzz of political activity around me. It lacked the rock-and-roll atmosphere of the anti-racist punk gigs, but also the fear and threat of chain-wielding neo-Nazi skinheads.

"Publicity!" said Ingrid, handing me a small, plastic film container. "This is all the photos we took when we occupied. The film needs developing."

"But don't take it to Boots!" said Charlie.

"He's not an idiot!" Ingrid said, a little harshly, I thought, but they both looked tired and were understandably irritable. And my first thought had been to go to Boots. She scribbled an address on a scrap of paper. "This is Carina from Photo Soc. She's expecting them; she'll develop them as soon as you drop them off."

"Anything else I can do?"

"You around this evening?"

"Sorry, working," I said, aware that this would sound better than 'my mum's coming to stay and I'm hoping she'll help with my laundry.'

Carina lived in a flat in nearby Cotham, an idyllic academic enclave whose timeless Englishness reminded me that, even among my lefty, punky, arty middle-class friends, I was still the outsider. This feeling was heightened every time Mum turned up, as she had today, an old-fashioned Northern Jewish intrusion into my south-western English world.

Mum was booked into a small bed-and-breakfast in Hotwells, around the corner from Charlie's. She was here for a change of scenery, she and Dad both agreed that she needed the respite from him. I'd given up on the damp and moved to a bedsit in Ashley Down, comfortable enough but far from student life – not that I was participating beyond those studies. It was the kind of anonymous suburban dwelling I'd spent years escaping from. Two mornings a week I delivered bread across the city from a local bakery. Daylight arrived as this first part of my working day was coming to an end. I was earning enough to send money home, which was handy because Dad was too proud to sign on. I thought Mum would force him but she understood, and probably shared the burning shame he felt, at no longer providing an income for the family. He was also keen not to have to stand in the same queue as the people whose wages he had once paid.

"How are your studies coming on?" Mum asked, deeply inhaling from her cigarette, as we carried on staring out the window of her room, hypnotised by the quiet, steady passage of sand-bearing container ships from Avonmouth Docks down to the floating harbour, a few hundred yards below us, where they unloaded their cargo and returned slowly up the river, back again within an hour.

"About as fast as these boats," I said. "But steady."

Mum and I were developing a new relationship. She'd arrive from Leeds full of small talk about Dad and his irritating habits, the mountains of paperwork around Grandma's death, the minutiae and slights of local life. Eventually those topics would be exhausted as she acclimatised to the world around her. She was shocked at the start by how much walking I did.

"Even when you go to work?"

"It's only five minutes on foot to the bakery in the morning, twenty to the bar at night."

"So many hills!"

"One day I'll take you and Dad to Edinburgh."

"No, thanks. You know Mimi and Leslie Heron, Nigel Heron's parents?"

"Yes, went to Scotland for a holiday two years ago, Isle of

Mull, and it was cold and rained–"

"–Every day!"

"Yes, every day. You said. I know, it rains a lot in Scotland. You should still go to the Festival, though; you'd enjoy it," I said, leafing casually through the David Lipsey economics textbook I'd brought with me, even though I barely understood a word.

"When things are back to normal," she said, enjoying the luxury of being able to take the cigarette out of her mouth when she smoked. There was no drudgery for her at the hotel. "Grandma had some money I didn't know about, and we can sell her flat as soon as I've sorted her belongings."

"Is it strange not having her around?"

She didn't answer at first, took another drag and exhaled slowly.

"I go to the flat, and each time I'm determined to clear it out, so we can sell it. And I'll make a cup of tea. Sit down. Have a cigarette. Then I'll notice something, like a mark on the kitchen top. And I have to clean it."

"Mum!"

"I know. It's silly, isn't it?"

"Don't you have enough cleaning and scrubbing at home?"

"Ha! Don't I. Your father never lifts a finger."

"You should make him," I said, partly to my imaginary friend Sheila Rowbotham. "It's not good for him, lounging around the house feeling sorry for himself."

"That's what I say!"

"And how does he respond?"

"He smiles and agrees! Then he'll say something like 'Trouble is, Syb, you're so much better at all that than I am,' and he goes back to doing the Telegraph crossword."

"What's stopping you from clearing Grandma's?"

"I don't know. Maybe I can't bring myself to get rid of her stuff."

I could see her welling up. She hated being seen as weak.

"Sorry," she said, pulling herself together almost immediately. Or, more likely, suppressing the grief, storing it for later when she would be alone.

Together, my parents built a home and a life in the city where they were born, in a way that their parents and grandparents before them hadn't been able. How painful it must have been to see the next generation, the first to grow up without the threat of war or extermination, Nazis and fascists, flee from their homes – not in fear of their lives but because they were too bored to stay.

"Can I ask you a favour, Barry?"

"Sure."

"Next time you're in Leeds, stay for a few days longer. Help me clear out Grandma's flat."

Next morning, I picked up the photographs from Carina. She was a pale, freckled girl who reminded me of Joni. I wondered if her complexion was due to hours spent in the dull, red light of the photography developing room in her basement. I was fascinated by this curious, half-lit world that photographers inhabited, dark rooms surrounded by plastic trays full of pungent chemicals that transformed reels of film into black-and-white pictures.

Each photo told a small part of the story of the great Bristol University Student Occupation of January 1979. Here's Charlie and a few others entering the building, a young receptionist looking on in bemusement, boredom almost; another shows the gang outside the meeting room, big smiles, all victory and hope. Here's Ingrid, holding papers and giving instructions, there's Charlie to one side. At first sight I think, as always, what a fabulous, glamorous, perfect couple, but something jars. Nothing serious, but he's there but not there, engaged with the activity but not with Ingrid.

Maybe it's a moment the camera captured, and seconds later they'd be Team Ingrid and Charlie again. But it articulated an uneasiness I had glimpsed the day before, without realising. Ingrid looked different, bigger? Bloody hell, was she pregnant?

CHAPTER 29

The first thing I noticed was the smell: the familiar, musty odour of Grandma that no amount of Mum's scouring could remove. I'd expected her to have taken it with her last November, but the aroma was so powerful it had permeated the furniture, an earthly reminder of her presence. No wonder Mum struggled every time she came here.

I half-expected to see Grandma propped up in bed, backed against a cluster of pillows, pale and miserable. Instead, I was shocked by the intense sunlight blazing through the bedroom windows. All those years with the curtains closed, the room in permanent darkness like she'd been rehearsing for the only future she could be certain would arrive.

It was early spring, when colour and life return to the trees and thoughts turn to summer holidays, sunny beaches, Edinburgh. I thought about it only in terms of the fact that I wouldn't be going.

The Bristol occupation commenced in a glorious burst of idealistic winter activism but staggered across the seasons. Snows cleared, frosts diminished, blossoms blossomed, still the occupation continued. The clandestine fire exit stratagem had been halted when the inadvertent setting off of fire alarms became so frequent it was annoying the occupying students almost as much as the Senate House staff, who had gone back to work within days. More, in fact, since the wailing sirens were a welcome interruption to the tedious chores of university administration.

The socialist vanguard were allowed to use the front entrance, the occupation inconvenience so minor to the university that they let it continue, figuring correctly that many students would give up on grounds of boredom. I continued visiting, daily at first but less as the term continued. This lack of commitment didn't go unnoticed by Charlie. Someone had discovered the vice-chancellor's home address, and there'd been talk of sending a personal letter – tied to a brick, Charlie had suggested, to Ingrid's horror, but he insisted it was a joke. I stopped thinking she was pregnant, but there was still something wrong between them. The occupation had soured their relationship and I missed the old couple.

A date had been set for Gordon's hearing and he was allowed to visit us in the lecture hall once ahead of his tribunal. It was the last week of spring term and was greeted like a rock star with whoops, cheers and stamping of feet.

That address was typical Gordon, textbook Muckle: funny, self-effacing, not afraid to challenge our prejudices but more powerful as a result. He took us on a short but entertaining tour of the recent stand-off between government and workers, illustrated the difficulties facing any ruling party in a liberal democracy. If anything, he'd said, it's harder for those of us brought up to be mistrustful of power to know what to do when we have it.

"We are the radicals, the free thinkers, enemies of the state," he boomed. "We're more comfortable in opposition. In

STAND UP, BARRY GOLDMAN

power, we're protected by the forces we usually oppose. The point arrives when we think we need it. That's how power gets things done. Who doesn't want power? The ability to change things as we please?" Gordon continued, sounding almost like Dad explaining why you can never trust the unions. "We expect our leaders to change that overnight, which is why it's easier and more exciting to call for revolution than to actively change how government operates. Which, as you know from many of my previous lectures, is boring."

We laughed but he became serious. "My own case began with no control over the process but I had time to put it to those in authority who disagreed with me. If I win, that'll prove it's possible for individuals to challenge the status quo and change it."

It was an impressive argument, backed by the recent agreement between unions and government that resolved the strikes and made workers better off. April 1979 was a great time to be a public sector worker.

I caught up with Charlie on the way out of the lecture theatre building, expecting him to be more enthused.

"I spent seven weeks at that occupation," he said, as we climbed Pro Cathedral Lane like weekend mountaineers towards the students' union.

"Amazing," I said. "Sorry for being such a part-time supporter."

"I was looking at all the other students thinking, tossers. All cheering Gordon, hardly any lifted a finger to help when we needed it."

"Maybe they didn't know how."

"Maybe they could have used their initiative. It's not difficult. It's obvious who the baddies are."

"To us, sure. What if some of them were angry they weren't getting taught?"

Charlie stopped.

"Bloody hell, Barry, not you as well?"

"What?"

"You're all so bloody reasonable. Excusing the bastards. Ingrid's been like this."

"It's not excusing them. It's seeing it from their point of view. Like Gordon said."

He snorted.

"We won't change them if we don't know what motivates them."

"They're a bunch of useless, right-wing bastards," he half-smiled. "You right-wing bastard. Gotta nip home, catch you later," and he left me to walk alone to the Mandela Bar for my lunchtime shift. On the way in I passed a large, handwritten poster pinned to the door of Meeting Room One that said "Feeling funny? Audition NOW for BUTCH at the 1979 Edinburgh Fringe!" and I thought: "Bloody students."

That had been less than a week earlier. Grandma's flat in Leeds was on a different planet. Strange to think she had once done what I was about to – years ago she would have removed the many traces and memories of Grandpa. I imagined grief could be triggered by a half-remembered shirt. Opening her wardrobe, I removed the dresses in clumps and divided them into three piles – jumble, keep, or bin. This was not my specialist area of knowledge. Would Mum want to wear a dead woman's dress? Some looked grand but hideously old fashioned, like what the Queen would wear. Others might be nice enough for Judith. I trusted my instincts and pushed through.

Shoes were harder to decide. Grandma had accumulated a fair collection; a few worn pairs and the odd single were easy to throw away, others a mystery to my untrained male eyes. I settled on one giant shoe mountain for the church jumble sifters to sort themselves.

Thinking I'd cleared them all away, under a pile of neatly folded shirts I found a single shoebox in the bottom corner, untouched for years. Which pair had been kept in the dark for so long? Wedding shoes? Grandma's favourite pair? I took it out and removed the lid, careful not to disturb the thick layer of dust on top.

Inside were a bunch of old papers and a ration book, faded photographs, letters, yellowing newspaper articles – and a silver brooch in the shape of a World War Two Spitfire plane.

There was nothing remarkable among the papers. The articles were local stories, how most armaments for the West Yorkshire (Prince of Wales's Own) Regiment were being made at the Barnbow munitions factory in east Leeds, a couple of technical pieces about innovations in rifle engineering.

I knew a small amount of local war history. Leeds had escaped the bombing relatively unharmed compared to Bristol. Life had continued without the kind of upheavals experienced in mainland Europe. Mum was a kid and Grandad, who had fought in Mesopotamia in the First World War (how he loved saying that name), was in his forties and too old to be called up at the start. He'd spent the early part of the War at Leeds Town Hall, administering call-up papers for army, navy and air force servicemen.

What I didn't know, until reading these papers, was that Grandma was a working girl in the early years of the war. Her job was at the munitions factory.

Many women had been hired to replace the men who had joined the army. Not Grandma. She was already working - in research and development.

Grandma, miserable Grandma who had spent her last decades – my whole life and longer – in a slothful semi-existence, had been, in her day, a ballistics and munitions expert.

Blimey, Becky: you kept that one quiet.

Among the documents was a typewritten letter offering her the job, directions written in pencil on the back, sketches, detailed representations of casings and the guns they were to be used for. There were further drawings, the illustrations became more complex, pictures of planes and gun coverings on the wings.

Underneath these fading papers was a dark-blue notebook with a hard cover. More drawings, notes about developing less bulky weaponry for gunners. Occasional sentences appeared among the pictures.

October 3 1940 – visit to Air Transport Auxiliary Catterick. Damaged Spitfire flown up from Lowestoft. Wing gun casements poorly designed.

October 28 – discussions with Air Chief Marshal Christopher Noxley Forris. Very important man!

January 8 – allowed to bring the children to ATA. Squeezed them in to the Spitfire! Lovely day out for them.

The number of drawings decreased and, while there were more written entries, they gave away very little about Grandma's true feelings. Over the course of her visits to Catterick, she discovered that women were being trained to fly Spitfires across the country. A damaged Spitfire would limp back to a coastal RAF station, then be flown for repairs or munitions overhaul to stations like Catterick and returned to battle.

Grandma, whose life I thought had amounted to nothing, was not only a self-taught munitions and ballistics expert but a thrill-seeker in search of Spitfire flying action. By early 1941, she was taking time out from Barnbow (and the kids) to fly the newly repaired planes across the country.

February 10 1941 – my first solo test flight! There's only room for one body in a Spitfire, so all the training could not have prepared me for this. Once I had her in the air it was remarkably straightforward.

March 12 1941 – Solly left for north Africa. They're signing up the older men now. I am sure he won't be sent out to battle, but it is still frightening. Pearl will have to spend more time looking after the children.

July 7 1941 – Solly's 42nd birthday. He sends regular letters but nothing much of interest allowed. And I'm not allowed to write to him about my work. He would be proud if he knew.

The entries through the summer were mainly technical notes about handling a Spitfire. Neat. Clear. Determined. Who was this stranger?

16 September 1941 - my pilot qualification. Excited but not able to tell anyone. Not even Pearl or the children. I can expect to be called away at any time, to Catterick or the new airfield at Elvington. We pick up the planes and fly them to Southampton. I can be away and back in less than two days so the children barely notice. At work I must act as if munition design is my main job. Because all the other workers in my office are men, I can pretend that I go off at odd times because I have a woman's condition that means I have to go to hospital. So far it has worked. Everyone too polite to ask.

4 November 1941 – back from first round trip. Lucky on the way down, skies clear, in complete control of my crate. How it must feel for the pilots taking these machines across the English Channel! Wondering if this time they'll be the ones left behind. Terrible journey back, thunderstorms and lightning. At one point it felt like I had been struck, I swear the plane was knocked off course by the ferocity of the storm, had to circle three times before landing. Audrey from ATA v. impressed with my handling.

7 February 1942 – had to stay two nights in Southampton. Plane picked up nasty engine trouble on way back from a recce. Billeted in the men's quarters. Everyone frightfully this and terribly that but a few proper gentlemen. (Then something crossed out by Grandma)

16 April 1942 – Solly home on leave for three days. Children v. excited.

By now, the entries were becoming shorter and less frequent.

13 August 1942 (Just the date. Grandma didn't write anything else here.)

24 October 1942 – Hearing about fighting in Egypt. El Alamein, close to where Solly is stationed. Doubt if he is in the front line but very worrying. Children not told.

6 January 1943 (left blank)

17 April 1943 Pearl complaining about my hours. Is hard for me to be away from the children but she says she is finding it harder to discipline them. She tells me they are showing signs of naughtiness, answering back and making a mess. They are always so well behaved when I am around.

19 September 1943 – Final flight with ATA from RAF Acaster Malbis. Girls all marvellous. Presented me with gift of a charming brooch. Looking after the children priority.

16 April 1944 – Solly home! For good.

* * * * *

It was the start of the summer term, our first day back and we'd been hoping for a larger gathering outside Senate House for Gordon's tribunal. In the end, there were fewer than a dozen stalwarts of Socialist International plus a couple of Gordon's teaching colleagues. Grey sky, steady drizzle, tense mood, Charlie and Ingrid not talking to each other.

After about twenty minutes Gordon appeared, huge grin telegraphing the result. He hugged each of us in turn, explaining what had happened between comradely squeezes.

"It was set up like a court room," he said. "The university put their case that I was an insurgent troublemaker, all the usual lefty stuff, nothing they didn't already know."

"You kept quiet about the petrol bombing then, mate?" Matt asked to big laughs.

"My advocate read the testimonies from senior vice-chancellors from across the country, and a signed letter," he said, emphasising the last two words, "from the head of Avon and Somerset Constabulary." We oohed in suitably pantomime fashion. "I kept thinking, who is this fine, upstanding fellow they're talking about? Sounds like a right creep."

"Gordon Muckle, friend of the filth!" Ingrid said. We cheered and laughed again.

"Comrades," he said, changing the tone, pausing to make sure he had our full attention, "Pub!"

I made my usual work excuses and walked off to the students' union, surprised when Charlie tagged along.

"Not joining Gordon and the gang?"

"Nah, got some essays to sort," he said, which didn't sound like Charlie, who had never to my knowledge turned down a lunchtime Socialist pint in the cause of academia.

"You and Ingrid sticking around for the summer?"

Charlie turned away.

"We're not going out anymore."

"What?"

"Yeah, well."

"What happened?"

"I don't want to talk about it," he said, speeding up slightly as we crossed the road. I caught up and waited until he did want to talk about it, which was three seconds.

Ingrid *had* got pregnant, and it had been at that time when I thought she looked different. She didn't want the baby, had an abortion. Mhm, I thought, remembering the slogan from the pro-choice march we'd recently been on: "Not the church! Not the state! Women must decide their fate!" Charlie remembered it, too.

"I know," he said, off my look. "It was her choice."

"Did you want it?"

"No!"

"So why...?"

He took a while to answer.

"It was so... I don't know, matter of fact."

"You don't think Ingrid was just a woman exercising her right to choose?"

"Yes! No... I..."

"The revolution is for other people, comrade," I said.

He stared at me with a fierce anger I'd never seen before.

"Well, thank you, mate," he spat out, and left. I was about

to go in when he turned back. "Oh yeah, did I tell you it wasn't mine?" And this time he walked off for good.

Camilla, Hugo and a small group of performers were in the bar, I nodded the briefest head tip and comforted myself knowing that they were preparing for another summer of inevitable Scottish disappointment, one more gang of privileged, tiresome Oxbridge rejects set to be humiliated and bankrupted again by the toff university comedy elite. I remembered the months of dreams, dashed and crushed in moments, now a spectator of the lives of everyone around me, and wondered if I'd ever see Charlie again.

In the quieter moments at the bar I played a little game. Imagine, I said to myself, if Camilla or Hugo came over now, full of contrition, and said: "Barry, we're weeks from going to Edinburgh and there's a magic ingredient missing from our programme at the moment, and we realise it's you." What would I say? Honestly?

I would say "Sorry, guys, you had your chance with me and you blew it." No, I wouldn't; that would happen in a film. How about "Are you kidding? I wouldn't appear in your poxy amateur hour student show if you paid me!" Sitcom. "Sorry, guys, thanks for asking, but I haven't written anything in a year and I can't afford to give a month of my life free to the Edinburgh Fringe. I need the cash." Yes, that was the one. The boring truth.

"Hi, Camilla: what can I get you?" I smiled as she came to the bar.

"Three halves of Woodpecker, please."

"Coming right up."

While I was pulling the drinks, she tiptoed on her tiny feet, leaned closer to the bar, looked around, then said: "Have you, er, made any plans for this summer?"

CHAPTER 30

"I'll strive unceasingly to fulfil the trust and confidence that the British people have placed in me," the lady said on the news as I watched, alone in my Ashley Down bedsit, in horrified silence.

"And I would just like to remember some words of St Francis of Assisi, which I think are really just particularly apt at the moment," she continued. "Where there is discord, may we bring harmony. Where there is error, may we bring truth. Where there is doubt, may we bring faith. And where there is despair, may we bring hope.'"

I'd bought the local paper for the first time ever that day, shocked by its massive headline, "BRITAIN AND BRISTOL GO BLUE". There was a picture of Michael Colvin, my new MP, a Tory who won with a seven per cent swing from Labour. He was shaking hands with a number of supporters wearing blue rosettes and big smiles. One man in that small gathering was wearing a large camel coat with a big collar but peeping through at the base of his neck, unmistakeably, the top part of a tattoo of a spider web.

CHAPTER 31

Margaret Thatcher, Prime Minister. How did it happen? None of us knew anyone who voted Tory, apart from our parents, and certainly not in Bristol. The vice-chancellor, perhaps. Even the Bristol University Conservative Society students were walking round the union looking sheepish.

Nobody admitted voting for them. "I didn't vote Tory" became the must-have badge of the moment. Rock Against Racism, the Anti-Nazi League, strikes, pay rises, victories against the bosses: it was as though the last year had been a dream and we were waking up to the reality.

Students still drank cheap beer at the Mandela Bar, Bristolians still bought bread from the bakery and I was making enough to see my way through another year at university.

I found out the duller truth about BUTCH, why Camilla had asked if I might be available for another Edinburgh summer. They had secured the rights to an obscure play by JRR Tolkien called The Homecoming of Beorhtnoth, Beorhthelm's Son, but permission had been removed at the last minute and there was a thirty-minute lunchtime show gap to fill. Sadly, I was not to be the stopgap of their hopes.

Back in Leeds, Dad was pleased with the election result, if slightly concerned at the idea that a job as important as prime minister could be entrusted to a woman. But, as Mum pointed out, his mother-in-law had flown Spitfires during World War Two. Mum and Pearl were still coming to terms with Grandma's secret life and had been trying to piece together that period of their lives.

"She took us to the factory once, I remember that," Mum said over Saturday lunch when I'd returned for the summer break.

"Really?" I said.

"Must have been about ten? What I remember best was the rabbits."

"What?" Dad said.

"The factory was boring. But it was surrounded by fields. Women and older kids wandering up and down. We had no idea what they were doing. Then a rabbit jumped through the hedge and a bunch of people pounced on it! The one who managed to grab it put it in a sack!"

We gasped, horrified.

"Of course," Dad said, "rabbit meat's quite tasty, like chicken."

"You ate rabbits!"

"There wasn't a lot else," said Pearl.

"Were we so badly behaved, Aunty Pearl?" Mum asked.

"Not really. You were sad. You missed your mother."

Pearl went quiet, withdrew. Today there was enough chicken for everybody – Mum's roast was delicious – but she wasn't hungry.

"What do you think those gaps in the diary meant, Aunty Pearl?" I asked, to silence. "You know, where Grandma wrote the date but nothing else?"

"I don't know," she said sharply.

Dad caught my eye.

"What do you think, Barry?" he said, winking.

"What do you mean, Monty?" Mum said.

"Well, come on, love, it was the war. The men were away from home. Solly was gone for years. She was young. Pretty for the time, eh, Pearl? Passing her days away from home with a number of handsome young gentlemen with handlebar moustaches..."

"I don't know what you're talking about, Monty," said Pearl.

"Oh, come off it. Remember: I was posted in Italy at the end of the war. The local men were all away."

"Monty. What are you saying?" asked Mum.

Dad coughed nervously.

"I'm not saying anything, love," although he'd already said more than enough to arouse a whole set of suspicions about his own war stories. "Just... you always said your mother never seemed as happy as when you were kids."

"True," Mum agreed. "She became a right old battleaxe, didn't she? Hey, Auntie P?"

If there was anything more to add, it wouldn't be coming from Pearl, staring sullenly at the untouched food on her plate.

Later, I met Maurice at the Friesian Cow. Barely pausing for breath, he provided every detail from between 1943 and 1945 of every so-called mensch in the community who had served abroad and shtupped every foreign beauty who had given the liberating hero from Leeds a loving welcome. We were meeting Harriet; she hadn't arrived yet and when I got to the pub I'd almost not recognised him. As well as losing weight, Maurice had changed his image. He wore a suit and tie: less businessman, more ska fan.

"Looking good, skinny fella," I said.

"Thanks, mate," he said. "You still look like a shlimazl."

"I'm a working man now, Maurice: you should try it."

"Hey! Me, too, mate. It's a tough world out there."

"Remind me what it is you're doing: coal mining? Carrying out bombing raids on the European mainland? Oh no, putting on comedy gigs, that's it. Exploiting innocent young performers so you can afford to dress like a rock star."

"What do you think of the look?"

"I'd say 'boring provincial Jew auditioning for The Special AKA'. At least you've had the decency not to bring shame on the community by wearing a pork-pie hat."

"Thanks. I'm wise to what's happening now, Barry. I know what's cooking on the comedy scene."

"What's cooking? Ooh, sounds eaty, Maurice. Tell me, what's cooking?"

"I went to London."

"Did you see the Queen?"

"No, I went to a new comedy club." Despite assuring myself that that dream was over, those words still hurt. "In Soho. Upstairs from a striptease club."

"Tough choice for you, Maurice."

"It's comedy from start to finish. None of your scruffy folk singers with their fingers in their ears. And all the performers aren't ninety years old."

"Sounds exciting."

"Listen mate, I've asked Harriet to join us."

"Mhm."

"You're okay with that?"

"Of course. Why wouldn't I be?"

"Sure."

"You staying with her this summer?"

"Dunno. But it should be a great year for comedy Barry. This Thatcher business has really got them going."

"What do you mean?"

"The jokes. So funny!"

"I bet. You probably voted for her."

He shuffled awkwardly.

"I was joking, Maurice! Did you vote for her?"

"You can't ask me that! Did nobody tell you it's a secret ballot?"

"You voted for her! Bloody hell, Maurice."

"Doesn't matter who I voted for. Tell you what, though: she's good for comedy. You should make a comeback."

"Ha! Sure, me and Frank Sinatra."

"Hi, guys. What you having?"

Harriet remained reassuringly immune to the changing fashions. And who cared? No one else carried off a Marks and Spencer beige top and pleated grey skirt with Harriet's style.

"My comedy days are over, Maurice. Same again, please," I said, pointing to my beer.

"You've changed," she said, surprising me.

"In what way?"

"I don't know. You look older."

Maurice laughed. "Well, you haven't changed, Harriet. Blunt as ever."

She had changed, though. Not physically, but she was more mature and purposeful. There was a world out there, moving on without me.

"Are she and Kris still...?" I asked Maurice as she left for the bar.

"Didn't work out." He shook his head. "For the best. Don't talk about it, okay?"

"Fine," I said, not quite understanding. I knew Maurice was helping Kris again this year; we were both working hard to avoid the topic.

"Guess who's working in Edinburgh this summer?" she asked as she sat down.

"Scottish bar staff?" I asked.

"You going to be there?" Maurice asked, and she smiled.

"Do you mean working working or hanging out in a theatre twenty hours a day working?"

"Both. I'm being paid by a London magazine to write reviews."

"Excellent!" I heard myself say and mean.

"They saw your piece, then?" asked Maurice.

"So you'll be up there with the knight in shining rude-boy outfit?" I said, pointing at Maurice, who smiled modestly. She nodded.

"That's fantastic news! I'm sure you'll both have a smashing time."

"You not coming this year, Barry?" she asked.

"Afraid not. The world I introduced you to is no longer one I'm part of."

"I think you'll find my free flat helped somewhat."

"Now you mention that," said Maurice.

"Of course," she said. "Laurence is going to Israel this summer so there's an extra room. Does Kris need to stay?"

"At the flat?" Maurice asked, eyebrow rising involuntarily.

"It's okay. It's fine."

Maurice looked at her. I did, too. Trying to work out if she was over whatever had happened last summer or forcing herself to believe it.

"We'll hardly see each other. I'll be working the whole time... For God's sake, Maurice, I'm not a pathetic little girl, I'm over it. We're both adults. I've got a job to do, and so have you and so has he." That settled it. I admired her determination and self-belief; it reminded me of Kris, the opposite of me. "Shame you weren't able to work with Kris again, Barry."

I looked at her, wondering if she'd misunderstood what had happened last summer.

"I couldn't come back. Had to sort out my Dad."

"I meant this year."

"Well, I've got nothing new since then. Working man now."

"After your gran died, I saw Kris. He was wanting to do a new show with you for this summer. Said you never got back to him."

"He never got in touch!"

"Oh. Okay."

"Maybe he was saying it to be nice to me. Did you know anything about this, Maurice?"

"It wasn't anything definite," he said. "Far as I knew, by the time they were putting the programme together he was determined to do a one-man show."

When I got back to my unfamiliar home, drunker than normal after a rare night spent on the other side of the bar, Dad was still up, working at the kitchen table. Businesslike, despite the outfit of green striped pyjamas. His briefcase of Very Important Documents, which I was used to seeing at the bottom of the bookshelf gathering dust, now lay open, papers surrounding it in small, neat piles. Quiet piano music was coming from the record player, which was unusual because Dad almost never listened to music, apart from Fiddler on the Roof, whose success had made him happier than almost anything else in his life.

"Barry," he smiled and looked up. "Been checking through the accounts from last year."

"Any problems?"

"No, no, not at all. You did well."

"Thanks."

"All the debts had to be cleared. And you cleared them."

"Yes. You should have started this financial year with a clean slate."

"Yes, yes, all good," he said, looking at the figures. He was wearing his thick-framed spectacles that made him look like Ronnie Barker. "You were quite generous, I see."

"I didn't want you and Mum to have any debt hanging over you."

"No, no, you're right. And I bet that bastard Harry Shulman threatened fire and brimstone if you didn't get the money back to our creditors."

"Not a nice man."

"Not a nice man," he repeated. "Personally, I would have carried some of this over, maybe spread the load over five years—"

"—Dad, I had no idea at the start. As far as I knew, the only money you had was the spare cash I was sending to Mum each week. This was before the house sale. I saw how it could have been possible to pay less up front, but..."

"What?"

I couldn't answer straight away, hadn't allowed myself to admit the truth until this moment.

"I was scared." I waited for Dad to respond, but he was expecting more. "Had no idea when you'd get better... if you'd get better. None of us did. It's not like you'd broken a leg; none of us had a clue what to do with you."

Dad lowered his head and studied the paperwork – either looking at the figures in more detail or hiding his tears.

"I had no idea how to deal with money."

"Ha! I can see that," he laughed. "You did well, Barry."

"Thanks. Would you like a cup of tea?"

"No thanks."

"What's this music?"

"Chopin. The Nocturnes."

"It's lovely."

"Finally started listening to music. Funny what illness does to you, isn't it? I start listening to music, you become a businessman."

"I did not become a businessman, Dad."

"And I don't think you ever will." We both laughed. "And I mean that as a compliment. I should never have tried to make you a part of the family business."

"I shouldn't have fought you so hard. Family is family." We sat for a few moments in a silence that felt less awkward the longer it continued.

"Kind of lucky you failed, though," I said.

"I should never have discouraged you from doing your comedy thing."

"Yeah, well, at least I tried it."

"You can again."

"I don't have time. It's either studying or work."

Dad put the papers down, took off his glasses, rubbed his eyes.

"Barry, you're okay. I'm picking up bits and bobs of work. Got some consultancy. Not everything about my work ended in failure. Please. Do your comedy."

"Thanks, Dad. I appreciate that. But it's too late for me to go to Edinburgh."

"I thought that wasn't until next month?"

"I don't have a show."

"Well, bloody well write one! It's only July. What are you waiting for?"

I had seven tedious coach journey hours to Bristol to mull over Dad's suggestion. The M62, with its breathtaking views across the Pennines, was always inspiring, not least because in the past I had always felt my mood lighten as soon as the coach had left behind my familiar Leeds landmarks. Today, though, the clouds were low and the view was limited. All I could think of was how circumstances had thwarted my plans at every opportunity. I didn't think there'd be much call for a show entitled An Afternoon Of Comic Failure And Whingeing Self-Pity. I was too far removed from that world; there was no way back.

When we got back in the coach after stopping for a loo break at Keele Services, there was a problem with the engine. The driver informed us that they'd have to send a replacement coach from Stoke, which would arrive, all being well, within a couple of hours.

What did I care? There's nothing to look forward to in Bristol, I moped. You're just like Grandma; she may have died but you have inherited her can't-do attitude. Don't do anything about it, Barry. Like grandma, like grandson: one short, exciting adventure in your life terminated by circumstances outside your control.

Keep those dreams locked away while others who started in the same place as you shoot ahead into the crazy, exhilarating world. Stay angry and bitter about the deal life has given you: a nice, comfortable, middle-class life punctured by a few months of having to experience what being poor is like for everyone else most of the time, you pathetic, pampered, miserable middle-class loser.

The new coach arrived – same as the old coach, only smellier.

This was never a quick journey at the best of times. Today, the traffic was appalling. The fates were punishing me for heading in the wrong direction.

We crawled towards Birmingham and I fell into a series of sporadic half-sleeps lasting minutes, sometimes seconds. Across the carriageway, I felt the coaches soar past, every one with an "Edinburgh" sign on the front. One of them was so close on the other side of the carriageway I could see the faces of the occupants. It slowed down to a crawl as it went by and there, clear as daylight, was Kris, smiling hello, waving goodbye, then the coach grew wings and flew away.

CHAPTER 32

Tourists panicked, scuttled in search of shelter, huddled under arches, cramped together along steep, dark-covered alleyways.

A ridiculous troupe of skimpily dressed students ignored the furious rain and complete lack of audience, and continued singing and dancing their hearts out, refusing to heed parental warnings of yore to wrap up warm or not feel the benefit.

The torrent was so efficiently hard that raindrops had seeped through my clothes and rucksack, every leaflet mashed into a general pulp.

Miserable, soaked, nervous, scared, bored, worried, single, overwhelmed, on the verge of tears. Scruffy, trapped, friendless, utterly alone, my first show less than 24 hours away, script barely finished, hideously unprepared.

It was great to be back.

Clouds parted, the cold Scottish sun peeped through, and we remembered why we always forgave Edinburgh, whatever it threw at us. The sodden leaflets became a useful conversation starter with Glaswegian teenagers and council workers queuing for Fringe tickets in their lunch break.

The last few weeks had been frantic since I'd stopped working behind the bar and sought to get a show and a life in shape for the 1979 Edinburgh Fringe. There had been few distractions: Charlie and Ingrid together again, apparently on my doing, had moved to London to work for the Anti-Nazi League.

Ingrid had written to me shortly after that last meeting with Charlie – "I've no idea what you said but it made him come back" – and explained what had gone wrong. Charlie had spent the winter months pursuing the rock-and-roll lifestyle with his band, "which I thought were complete rubbish, not nearly as good as Student Grunt!", she wrote. But when the occupation started, he had to quit.

"I wish you could have been there, Barry; you're good at keeping him grounded! Playing in a group diminished his maturity by many years; he blamed me for trashing his dreams and pushed me away." She understood why it had been hard for me to be more politically involved but that meant she had no one to turn to. "I needed a shoulder to cry on," she wrote, "and it turned out that that shoulder belonged to Gordon!!"

Bloody hell. Gordon. Another confident, competent man who knew how to get off with women. I tried imagining what a little Ingrid-Gordon child might have looked like, quickly banished the image and carried on reading. "Not sure how it happened, I guess we were all wrapped up in the excitement of the occupation, but one thing led to another and, well, I'll leave the rest to your imagination! It was what we both needed at the time."

Gordon! His quiet determination and solid morality made him a better human being than most of us. But that beard! Those glasses! You could see how Sheila Rowbotham had her work cut out with me.

Gordon and Ingrid were no longer a thing. I'd seen Charlie briefly again after they got back together, and found out the extent of my role in their reconciliation. "Yeah, man, I was indignant. In a rage. But then I remembered what you had been like when Celia dumped you and I thought 'no way am I gonna be *that* guy'." Cheers, mate.

Away from the ardour of politics, I was back in Edinburgh among the passionate souls of showbiz. Hugo was nicer to me now, since it looked like I was doing the company a huge favour. This year's BUTCH effort was greatly slimmed down from last, lessons learned after the Journey's End debacle. Accommodation was the top floors of the venue we were performing at: a small student house on Niddry Street, one of those cobbled roads that plummeted off the Royal Mile like a sheer mountain face.

I wasn't in any BUTCH shows apart from my own but had promised to leaflet for them. In a couple of hours spent on the Royal Mile I saw the world go by: tourists, workers, kilted Scotsmen, skinny punks and desperate alcoholics, television stars and air hostesses, newspaper sellers and mums with their kids, and then, striding towards me, with a smile that instantly reminded me of the tenderest, most intimate physical moments of my life, Celia.

We hugged for a moment, stepped back and viewed each other like exhibits at an art show.

"Suits you," she said. "The haircut. New image?"

"Yes, boring working-man chic. You're looking well."

"Thanks..."

"How's the drumming?"

"Great, I'm in three bands now. Thanks to you."

"Sorry."

"You're welcome." There was a moment of awkwardness: had we run out of conversation already? "It's good to see you, Celia. What are you doing here?"

"Nothing special. Only a show that's twenty-four hours long."

"When do you sleep?"

"We do three shows a week. First one's tomorrow."

"Sounds incredible. What's it about?"

She handed me a leaflet.

"Everything."

The show was called Bloody Hippies.

"How does a show about hippies – bloody hippies – get to be twenty-four hours long?"

"It's about hippies from the beginning of time."

"Okay. I guess those cavemen look a bit like Neil Young."

"It starts with Epimenides, the almost mythical Greek figure, and tells the story of hippies who changed the world. Jesus. Buddha. Richard Branson."

I laughed. It was easy being round Celia again. We sat on the steps of a grand old building, like two grand old friends.

"I play a follower of Bhagwan Rajneesh in modern Los Angeles. A slave girl in ancient Egypt. And France."

"Busy slave girl."

"No, the country. I play 'France'. It's a comedy, you know."

"Guess that means you get to show off your knowledge of Lecoq."

"Very amusing. I play the drums a lot, too. What about you?"

"My show's barely twenty-four minutes. And it's filling a gap left by JRR Tolkien. Didn't even make it into the programme."

"Oh, dear... Still, you're here now, Barry. How's things? What's your year been like?"

"Ah." I could have elaborated, too much detail about the family she was excluded from knowing, too many apologies about what might have been. "Nothing special. The usual. How about you?"

"Yeah, okay," she said, sounding like it had been special and unusual but not wanting to rub it in. She didn't need to tell me, though; the improvement in her life since dumping me was plain to see.

"Sorry about, you know," I said, not knowing why I'd chosen to reopen that festering wound. She took my leaflet-free hand in hers and smiled.

"Shut up. Gotta go. Here," she said, standing up and handing me a ticket, "come tomorrow night. It's the opening show; we could use a crowd."

"I'd tell you to come to mine, but you'll either be sleeping or performing."

"You don't have to see ours in one go – maybe catch the first few hours or so."

"The opening scene? Sure."

I spent the rest of the day working on my show, time creeping slowly during the technical run, speeding in the dress rehearsal. All the student group came. Camilla said she enjoyed it; "Nice," she said. "Sweet, not what I'd have expected from a bloke." Even Hugo laughed a couple of times, in the right places.

Sleep was fractious and interrupted, dreams featuring incomprehensible exam papers and walking naked up the Royal Mile hoping no one had noticed, with only leaflets for concealment. The morning flew by, a mix of daze and adrenalin, and, before I knew it, my first performance was about to begin.

The show went okay, I thought, for a first gig – a bit rusty, first time in front of a crowd for more than a year. The Bristol gang came again to make the room look full. There were a couple of reviewers and half a dozen or so actual paying customers, one or two I recognised from the show queues whom I'd persuaded the day before.

With that momentous first show out of the way, I was ready for my first reward.

Edinburgh had changed my life, opened my eyes to a world of future possibilities. Of all the experiences and new sensations, though, nothing had affected me as strongly as my discovery, on that first visit two years earlier, of the Scotch Pie.

These delicacies, never seen in England, were famous locally for their peppery meat taste and solid build that meant you could eat them on the move without losing a crumb. But what made them stand out was the hot, greasy fat that oozed from that first, special bite. Delicious and disgusting in equal measure, these pies were the essence of what it meant to be performing at the Fringe: brief moments of gratification encountered through a deeply unhealthy lifestyle. Only one destination mattered at the end of my gig and it was the bakery next door.

The greasy aftertaste lingered long into my afternoon of helping at the box office and backstage with the opening performances of the other Bristol shows. When that shift was completed, I went to find Bloody Hippies, intrigued by the idea that it was possible to engage with an audience for a whole day. Even within my short half-hour of a show, there'd been an energy dip about eighteen minutes in, requiring extra effort to win the audience back.

Celia's venue was further than expected – down the Royal Mile, past the Casablanca, unapologetically concentrating on pornography this year – "We tried art once and we won't be doing that again in a hurry, thank you very much" – past Holyrood Palace, round the side of the giant slab of Arthur's Seat looming behind, away from the cosy limits of Festival Land until, climbing steeply once more, I reached a dilapidated red-brick building, the disused cinema that had been taken over by Celia's company and, like last year's bus station of despair, converted into a theatre venue.

A small audience of around twenty had gathered outside, waiting for the doors to open. Conversations began: familiar Edinburgh chats, strangers bonding over shows already seen, recommendations for those to come. I'd noticed a young couple yards away having what appeared to be an argument. Others had, too. We were all too polite to mention it, but as the voices grew louder and the moment the show should start had passed, there was nervous looking at watches, hope that we would soon be allowed into the theatre, preferring artificial drama you pay to watch to the real-life one unfolding nearby.

The great wooden doors creaked open and a kindly man in toga and sandals invited us to join him on an extraordinary journey. He welcomed us like a guide, joking about the length of the tour ahead.

"Excuse me one moment," he interrupted himself, walking towards the bickering couple. "Shut up!" he roared. "We're trying to do a show: you're ruining it for us all," and led us indoors.

The bickering couple followed, sullen, arguing more; she said he was holding her back, he told her she had responsibilities within the relationship.

The man in the toga put his finger to his lips and they stopped talking.

"If women are expected to do the same work as men, we must teach them the same things," he said and, amazingly, I recognised this quotation, which was either Plato or Socrates. Not everything in the political philosophy section of my studies had vanished the second it entered my brain.

We understood that the show had begun while we were still outside, our unease part of the opening, and now, not just an audience watching a play, we were the crowd gathering to witness the trial of Socrates. All of us were aware in that moment how quickly a crowd of strangers could bond to ignore the tiniest threat to their well-being. The barrier between actors and spectators had broken down, like the first time I'd seen Kris. Infinity Theatre's Das Kapital was a superficial challenge to our perceptions using the cheap gimmick of titillation. This was the real deal. Celia had found her people.

I knew a little about the trial of Socrates and was thrilled to be a participant. It was astonishing how, with the simplest of stage sets and props, we had been drawn into this world, and over several hours that flew by we travelled across time and the world, Egyptian slaves on a building site, wealthy wine tasters in modern California's Napa Valley, moneylenders banished from a temple by Jesus.

In between scenes, we strangers talked about what had happened, revealing more of ourselves than could have been imagined. Within an hour, they all knew about my show, that I used to go out with the bongo player in the Egyptian pyramid scene, that she had been right to dump me. The show spoke to each of us in different ways. One man, a doctor, said it had made him understand for the first time how to see his work through the eyes of his patients; a couple who had been mostly quiet discussed how their inability to have children had made them lose touch with each other.

More joined the crowd, others left because they had to go back to their families and friends but determined to return and see the rest of the show. I had planned to stay until 10 pm but finally dragged myself away just before midnight, exhausted, overwhelmed and inspired by the spectacle.

That show taught me how the artifice of acting offered new ways of seeing ourselves, and beyond. Trying to make sense of the world by laughing at it and making others laugh with me: this was what I wanted to do for the rest of my life.

CHAPTER 33

The Scotsman
Barry Goldman – Mother-in-Law Jokes
Venue 62, Bristol University Comedy
12.45 pm (1.15 pm)

*

The Edinburgh Fringe is a vast cornucopia of entertainment and drama, thousands of heroic endeavours by mostly young people determined to stretch themselves and help us see the world through different eyes. One morning you may witness the beginning of an amazing Hollywood career, in the afternoon you could catch the end of a student dream.

Yet in all my years of reviewing, I doubt if I have ever come across a show as earth-shatteringly appalling as this ill-conceived student so-called comedy. Barry Goldman is a poet, he claims. He is many things – scruffy, shambolic, rambling, nervous, uncharismatic, unfunny – but poet is a stretch. Don't expect good jokes – or, indeed, any jokes – about one of our favourite comedy staples. This show could win a Fringe award, but only for Most Misleading Title.

It's the story of Barry's gran, seen through the eyes of her son-in-law. The premise is she flew Spitfire planes in World War 2. (Sure, and my wee Auntie Morag pulled the trigger in Hitler's bunker.) And then she became sad and miserable because her husband came home from fighting the war, and she wasn't allowed to fly Spitfires anymore.

There are a few funny moments. Barry's gran provides a rich source of gags with her eccentric behaviour, and his dad is a suitable substitute for Les Dawson, who could teach Barry a thing or two about comedy writing and performing. But this is a show that should have been hijacked before take-off, taken to a deserted airfield and blown to pieces. I was tempted to give it no rating at all but, at a mere 30 minutes, it earned one star for brevity.

Anthony Troon

The low murmurings audible from the kitchen stopped as soon as I opened the door. Camilla and Richard were at the breakfast table while Jessica (Titania, Lady at Bus Stop, Cabaret Singer) was making toast. A look of panic darted between them; Richard subtly reached to cover the newspaper he'd been reading.

"It's okay, I've seen it. Early edition comes out around midnight."

"I am so sorry," Richard said. Camilla came and hugged me, had no words but I appreciated the sympathy.

"I loved your show," said Jessica, proving, as I'd already suspected, that she was not a great actor.

"Don't worry. I'm okay."

"Kenneth Tynan once likened Gielgud to a totem pole," said Richard, well-intended but not helpful.

"Today's newspaper, tomorrow's chip wrapping," Camilla said, and the horror struck that twenty-four hours from now the Edinburgh fish suppers would be offering punters a second chance to mock the shambling, scruffy, unfunny poet with the audacity to imagine he could come to their city and perform a show.

Walking back from Bloody Hippies, buzzing with excitement, ideas exploding faster than I could make sense of them, I'd been surprised to see the next day's newspaper, a glimpse into the future, for sale outside the Scotsman newspaper offices opposite Waverley station. A few students were queuing; like me, they quickly discarded the main body of sober broadsheet and pulled out the fabled Review Section. A great Scotsman review this early in the Festival was first prize in the lottery. I skimmed through the pages – few reviews so far – and there it was.

The opening sentence was promising, luring me in exactly as the journalist had hoped, and it took me a few more lines to ascertain its true nature. I still didn't quite believe it when I got to the end and read again, as if that might improve it. Bafflement gave way to devastation. I wanted to cry. I wanted to kick the vendor's stand down and steal all the papers and burn them. In a valiant act of self-hatred, I read the review one more time, committing phrases to memory, imagining audiences shouting them at me.

In my dreams that night I was heckled mockingly by an audience including Mum, Dad, Celia, Anthony Troon's Auntie Morag, Mr McCunn the bullying geography teacher, and Maurice and Kris together, looking at each other conspiratorially and laughing at something to do with me that I'd never know.

The compassionate sighs of my Bristol colleagues only made things worse, reminding me that in four hours I would have to go on stage and repeat the entire ill-conceived student so-called comedy again. I'd arranged to meet Harriet and Maurice for breakfast at the café up the hill, and wondered how many of the strangers I passed might have seen the review. All of them? Would they make the connection? Would they point and laugh? Should I cancel the show? Go back to Leeds? Was bar work the only vocation I was suited to?

The large plate-glass windows of Tha Wee Brekkie were steamed up with cold breath and hot tea but I spotted Kris in a second. My heart jumped. Meeting Celia rekindled an old friendship, but this love had never died. Maurice was by his side, reading the papers. As soon as they saw me, I spotted the "Do you think he's seen it?" look between them.

"I've seen it," I said, and much to my surprise and theirs, they laughed. Was my anger funny?

"Oh, man, I'm sorry," said Kris, "Happens, mate."

"Thing is, Barry," said Maurice, "You've got it all to do again now."

"Cheers, mate. Any more helpful advice? 'Call the Samaritans'?"

"I mean, you'll have forgotten about it by the end. Trying to be sympathetic."

"Sorry," I said in my least sorry voice. Kris handed me a leaflet for his new show: glossy, great pictures and reviews, all paid for by Maurice.

"You'd better get out there, Kris: I'll join you in ten."

"We're coming to see you today," said Kris, getting up. "Catch you after the show."

Maurice made like he was studying his own important papers, trying to avoid eye contact. "Harriet's coming, too. Says sorry not to be here: she's reviewing a show."

"Reviewers. Hnh." I took Kris's vacated chair. "How come everyone's seen this Scotsman piece?"

"It's a stand-out. A work of art."

"Better than my show: that what you're saying?"

"Admit it, mate: it was funny."

"Hmm. Your show going well, then?"

"I think so. Trouble is, Kris works best with a partner."

He stopped suddenly, like he'd said something out of turn.

"You know, last time we met, Harriet said something about him wanting to work with me?" I asked.

Maurice shuffled in his chair as the waitress brought over a feast of egg and chips. I asked for the same and a cup of tea, and watched him eating.

"What?" he asked in a voice that reminded me of the fat bully who'd harangued me on the bus that day I first spoke to Harriet.

"In the pub. You made up some story that he had decided not to work with me."

He carried on eating.

"Didn't you?"

Finally, slowly, he put down his knife and fork.

"It was a joint decision."

"You persuaded him."

"Barry, you're a funny guy, you've got some great ideas. But you're not a double-act partner. You're Barry. Same on stage as off. You're not an actor."

"And when did you become Mr Comedy Expert?"

"I've watched a lot in the last year, mate. There's a few like you. But there's no one like Kris. He needs someone to bounce off, but it's not you."

I tried to answer, but no words came. I stood up, slapped the table so hard people looked, and stormed out of the café dramatically. Maurice was right. I wasn't an actor, there was no way I could have faked that rage – nor the embarrassment of storming out then having to step back in and call over to the waitress at the counter to cancel my egg and chips and cup of tea, please, thank you.

There was nothing to do but walk, walk away, fast and furious, avoiding people I knew or strangers in case they had read that review. Downhill and up again, stomping out of Edinburgh with such rage-powered determination I thought I could carry on all the way to Leeds, eventually slowing down and turning left, without thinking, towards Arthur's Seat.

Two years earlier, I had stared in awe at the magnificent slab of rock and promised myself that one day I would climb it. One afternoon I'd made it as far as Rankeillor Street, having worked out the way to the top was somewhere between the police station and Southside Youth Club (Venue 82, according to the Fringe programme). I'd given up after a few minutes, not yet attuned to the local weather and slipping around the sudden, sodden downpour in my summer sandals. Today, in sturdy shoes and bright-red anorak, I could reach the top.

Within minutes I was climbing, placing a distance between myself and that review. A gang of hardy ramblers were already at the top, taking photographs, lounging on hillocks, admiring the view. They didn't look far away. A couple of pathways rose gently up and round, but others ahead of me were taking a more direct route through the gorse and damp heather, and I followed. The more the city shrank behind me, the greater was the prominence of Edinburgh Castle. Rage had powered me this far; now I had to concentrate on every step.

I lost sight of the other walkers but continued up and, catching my breath, thought I'd reached the top. It was an illusion. Just when you think you've reached the peak, another craggy hill looms in front. I stopped for a moment to appreciate the instant metaphor and wiped the tears from my eyes, no longer caused by self-pity but contact with the cold North Sea wind.

The path to the top from here was clear but steep. I followed a middle-aged couple clambering gingerly up the rocks. Trailing them wasn't easy; at one point, the man slipped and dislodged a few stones that careered towards me – not too close but particles of dust went into my eyes and for a moment I couldn't see. Treading carefully around where the stones had been dislodged, I gripped, stepped up the jutting-out lumps and hauled myself to the top.

I'd done it. Reached the top of Arthur's Seat. Achieved a thing in Edinburgh.

My poetic mind searched for the kind of words worthy of Wordsworth but the best I could manage was "Wow." First thing I noticed looking north was the Forth Road Bridge, that same view I'd seen for the first time from the bus two years ago. Scotland looked big then; from here, it looked enormous, miles of unknown countryside. Turning in a slow circle to the right and looking east, I could make out the area of Laurence's flat, Journey's End, last year's student accommodation, then across and round, nothing but fields, round, round, past Craigmillar, back across the fields and hills south of Edinburgh, then north, where legend told that this was Sean Connery's milk round, when he dreamed of getting away from this place I dreamed of arriving at, finally, to the incredible city itself.

Up here, there was no way of knowing a festival was happening. You couldn't see any tourists reading The Scotsman, clumps of students handing out leaflets, jugglers, acrobats, fire-eaters, opera singers, Kris. Buildings and monuments that loomed as I trudged up and down those streets in search of an audience were like Lego. Nothing about the Edinburgh Fringe could match the grandness of the city itself. I was a tourist, admiring the view, enjoying my health and the newly revived well-being of my dad. I had no idea what lay ahead – but then who did? And ten, twenty, forty years from now, who would remember Anthony Troon's review? What would that mean to the world? Nothing, that's what.

A light, misty drizzle fell gently like a cover placed carefully over the view by a stern Scottish Presbyterian minister. That's enough enjoyment for now, son; go back to your work.

I descended slowly back to town, back to the real world of made-up stories.

The mist turned into fog, and after a few minutes I lost sight of the track, and everyone else going down. Every direction was steep, too steep to walk down and too risky to clamber. I stood transfixed, wet, cold, unsure what to do, turned to face the sheer cliff behind, inched delicately along the rock, hoping this might take me to a place of relative safety. The ground beneath my left foot crumbled, sending small stones hurtling down at speed.

I clung as tight as was possible to the unreliable scree, frozen, unable to move forward, but it was too dangerous to go back.

What if I fall now, I thought, break my neck? Die? What relevance would Anthony Troon's review have on the shape of my future? Oh, no! What if people thought I'd thrown myself off Arthur's Seat as the last, desperate act of a sensitive poet, life torn apart by one lousy review? I laughed at the thought that poor Anthony would be blamed personally for my death. It was so funny, I could feel myself holding on for grim life, trying not to lose balance because my body was shaking so much. And I worried that I might literally die laughing. I imagined Anthony being door-stepped by actual journalists, hassled to explain his actions and what drove him to write such a disgusting deconstruction of my personality, and all the critics at the Festival, as a mark of respect to the performers, would for one day only give five star reviews.

Inching forward, I could feel the occasional rock jagging out of the face, and was able to hold and walk slowly, still clinging to the cliffside as though my life depended on it, which it did. Even as I felt my fingers losing their grip. I took deep breaths, one step each time I breathed out, inching to what I hoped would be a place of safety.

In the distance, I saw a couple of hardy walkers, treading carefully. I kept them in sight, aware that as a matter of life and death I needed to avoid looking at my feet. Keep looking ahead, not down. More bloody metaphors. The path evened out and sloped gently down to Holyrood Park.

My show would begin in 40 minutes. I was alive. That was all that mattered. Nothing could upset me: tourists blocking the pavements as they walked past with The Scotsman review, students thrusting leaflets into my hands.

I arrived back at the theatre in the cheeriest of moods, even looked on kindly at the lengthy queue near my venue, already forming for a successful show nearby. Today I would be taking a perverse pleasure in telling Grandma's story, and would be nice to myself because I was about to perform a show I'd written at the Edinburgh Fringe. Even if Anthony Troon was right, there was no shame in trying and failing.

Approaching the entrance of our theatre, I saw the long queue was for a show in our venue. Trying to work out what else was on at the same time as me, I was still baffled, and it wasn't until I'd strolled past them and into the venue, I finally understood.

This was the queue for my show.

Maurice was correct: it was a stand-out review. I gave it five stars. Cheers, Anthony.

I recognised some faces – a couple I'd spoken to in the Fringe Office queue the day before, two or three members of the audience for Bloody Hippies, but most were carrying copies of that review. They had read it, and something about this one-star horror had intrigued them. Were they all there to mock me? If so, they were still prepared to pay for the privilege. Maybe their grans had flown Spitfires. Hugo stepped out from the theatre, beaming madly – "Our first sell-out show of the run!"

He called to a group at the back that there were no tickets left for today, but if they wanted to come another time they should buy their tickets now, and they gathered eagerly around him.

*****

I wouldn't say my mother-in-law was fat
That joke is not where I'm at.
I wouldn't say my mother-in-law was thin
Wouldn't know where to begin.
I wouldn't say my mother-in-law was mean
That would be obscene.
I wouldn't say any of this for sure
Because
I do not have a mother-in-law.

The show went well, especially after I incorporated some of Anthony Troon's lines. The audience laughed in all the right places, and it was amazing to think that they had all come to see me, and there were so many of them. I couldn't see Kris or Maurice, fantasised that they would have been turned away from today's sell-out. I spotted Harriet in the corner, delighted that she had made the effort. She was surreptitiously making notes but seemed to be enjoying the show. I was so glad she was there.

She came up at the end and gave me a big hug.

"That was great," she said. "The gardening correspondent of The Scotsman knows nothing."

"Thanks," I said, smiling at the crowd as they left, "but he did bring me an audience."

"I know. You'll get a much nicer review from me."

"Isn't that nepotism?"

"Barry, you know I've always loved your work."

"Listen, I know you're busy: you got five minutes for a chat and a tat?"

"Barry, it will be my pleasure to buy you lunch," she said, and we strolled arm in arm to the Tempting Tattie, making small talk about shows we'd already seen. Harriet was off to see Bloody Hippies next time it was on and I insisted on joining her. It was strange and yet easy to have so much in common with someone from the world I'd been trying to leave – had needed to escape, for sure, but couldn't have done it without Grandma's story. Home had its uses.

"Bloody Maurice."

"What made that come out?" she asked, as we arrived at Edinburgh's most celebrated jacket potato emporium.

"Oh, I dunno. You were right about Kris. He'd wanted to work with me this year but Maurice stopped him."

"He's a clever man, that Maurice."

"What? You taking his side as well?"

"What are you talking about?"

"Ah, I'm sorry."

"Barry, you and Kris..."

"What?"

"You're both funny, but what you do is different. That show just now, it's great. Nothing like what Kris would do."

"But he's so funny! And he wanted to work with me."

"Yes, but aren't you glad you came this year with your own show?"

"But Maurice–"

"–Maurice knows. He could see you and Kris wouldn't work. Same as me and Kris: he saw that, too."

"Don't tell me Maurice made you split up with Kris!"

She stopped walking, turned towards me, and laughed.

"Oh, bless you, Barry! What an idea!"

I followed her into the shop, wondering what either of us might say next.

"Tuna and mayo, please. What would you like, Barry?"

Okay. Would have preferred something more profound, but it could have been worse.

"Cheese, please. And baked beans."

"Barry, I enjoyed your show. And I like what you do. But do you think one bad review would change how I think of you?"

"How do you think of me?"

"You're like, coming home. Familiar."

"Everyday. Mundane."

She laughed again.

"Kris was exciting to be with. You and I both felt that didn't we?"

"Mhm?"

"But he's going somewhere already. We can join him for the ride, or we can choose our own path. And I've always thought you and I might take that path together."

"I never realised."

"Took me a while to work it out. Maurice knew. It must have been obvious from that first gig you did in Leeds."

"When it comes to relationships, Harriet, nothing is obvious to me."

"Yes, I can see that."

"I wanted to be with you. But had no idea how to show it. Always needed others to act first."

"I know," she laughed, reached her head over and kissed me gently on the lips. The kiss smelt of Birds instant coffee and I could tell we were being watched with curiosity by the sallow-faced teen dolloping bright-orange beans into my baked potato. But it was the most satisfying kiss of my life so far.

"Are you trying to tell me something?" I asked, as she gave the boy behind the counter a Clydesdale Bank fiver, that most lavishly illustrated of notes, while I picked up two plastic forks and a pair of napkins, she took her change and two steaming potatoes, and we walked out of the Tempting Tattie into the welcoming grey skies of Edinburgh, together, a new double act.

ACKNOWLEDGMENTS

Thank you to everyone for buying and reading this book. Please leave a review online, especially if you enjoyed it. I mean if you didn't then by all means tell the world. In the world of self-publishing, success is to some degree reliant on the kindness of strangers and Amazon reviews.

If you want to keep in touch, find out more about what I plan to write next, watch out for news and chapters from forthcoming books, please join my mailing list, which you can find on my website https://davidjcohencoms.com/

AND MORE THANKS...

So many people helped along the way, apologies if I've missed anyone.

When I was still assuming that this task was beyond me I was greatly encouraged by a number of friends who had moved from the world of stand-up and comedy writing to find success between the covers – notably Lissa Evans, John O'Farrell and Jonathan Meres. If there was one book that made me imagine the task was possible it was The Rotters' Club, so thank you Jonathan Coe for writing that.

Thanks to Fiona Thompson, Rebecca Abrey and Colin Swash for offering sound advice at the early draft stage (Colin suggested what turned out to be in my opinion the best joke in the book), Tim Dawson and John Dowie for reading when the book was complete but still in need of serious overhaul, to Wendy Brandmark and the immensely helpful City Lit readers' group, and a special thanks to Emer Bruce and Pete Sinclair for going several miles beyond the call of duty and friendship with tons of advice and great ideas every step of the way, especially for titles.

Al Murray made sure there were no embarrassing gaffes in my description of drumming, and Kev Acott did the same with mental health in the 1970s. Ta chaps.

A big thumbs up and cheers to my beta readers Howard Gardiner, Susan Graham, Carol Parradine, Phil Smith, Richard Stephen, Peter Warren, Gareth Wilson, Howard Martin, Mícheál O'Fearraigh, AD Cook, Tizz Raj, Natalie Elvin, Philip Briscoe, Eileen Wilson, Helen Ward, Sid, Ray Prowse, Sarah Wright, Victoria Taylor Roberts, Kim Brooke, Ian Hamilton, Deb Roberts and Kirsten Gorman.

The world of self-publishing is an incredible place and it's possible to lose your way down any one of a million rabbit holes. Luckily we are blessed with three extraordinary individuals who spend huge amounts of time telling us what to do when they could be writing themselves – Orna Ross, Joanna Penn and David Gaughran. I couldn't have produced this book without their remarkable online guidance and generosity.

Stand-up comedy's first self-publishing superstar Caimh McDonnell pointed me in the direction of Reedsy, an organisation for new authors, and editor Scott Pack, whose brilliant notes six months before publication fundamentally changed the book. The fabulous Vivienne Riddoch untangled my garbled syntax in the final edit and taught me how to use commas. Finally Reedsy sent me to Rafael Andres, whose cover design was masterful. Which was further boosted thanks to the delightful quotes from Jo Brand, Jack Dee, Linda Grant and David Quantick.

Family and friends have been exceptionally supportive during my months of self-imposed writing lockdown that ended shortly before covid began. Too many to mention all but special thanks to Caro and John H, Philip, Janna, Jill, Graham, Fiona, John P, Martin Bostock, James Cary, Paul Bassett Davies, and my lovely agent Kate Haldane. And to Lynn and Geoffrey, the finest in-laws a man could hope for, Reuven and Ruth and families, the many supportive Bindmans and Cohens and above all Miriam and the kids for, well, everything.

This is a work of fiction, even though like me the main character grew up in 1970s Leeds, attended the Edinburgh Fringe from 1977 to 1979, went to Bristol University, occasionally worked for his dad (whose business collapsed in 1978), wrote silly poems and sometimes visited a synagogue. All characters are fictitious except for certain Prime Ministers and rock stars. A small number of real names have been used in acknowledgment of the enormous influence those people had on my life at the time, but only they will know.

Printed in Great Britain
by Amazon